Princess of the Enclave

Jordan St. James

House of Q LLC
Knoxville

Princess of the Enclave

Text Copyright © 2025 Jordan Quintana

Published in the United States by House of Q, LLC, Knoxville, TN

ISBN (Paperback) 9798285088660

HouseofQLLC.com

For Gustavo

Author's Note

The events in this story take place immediately following those told in *The Silversaar Legacy*.

When Things Are Set Right
Book 1

On Your Hands
Book 2

Freely Given
Book 3

Map of the Realm

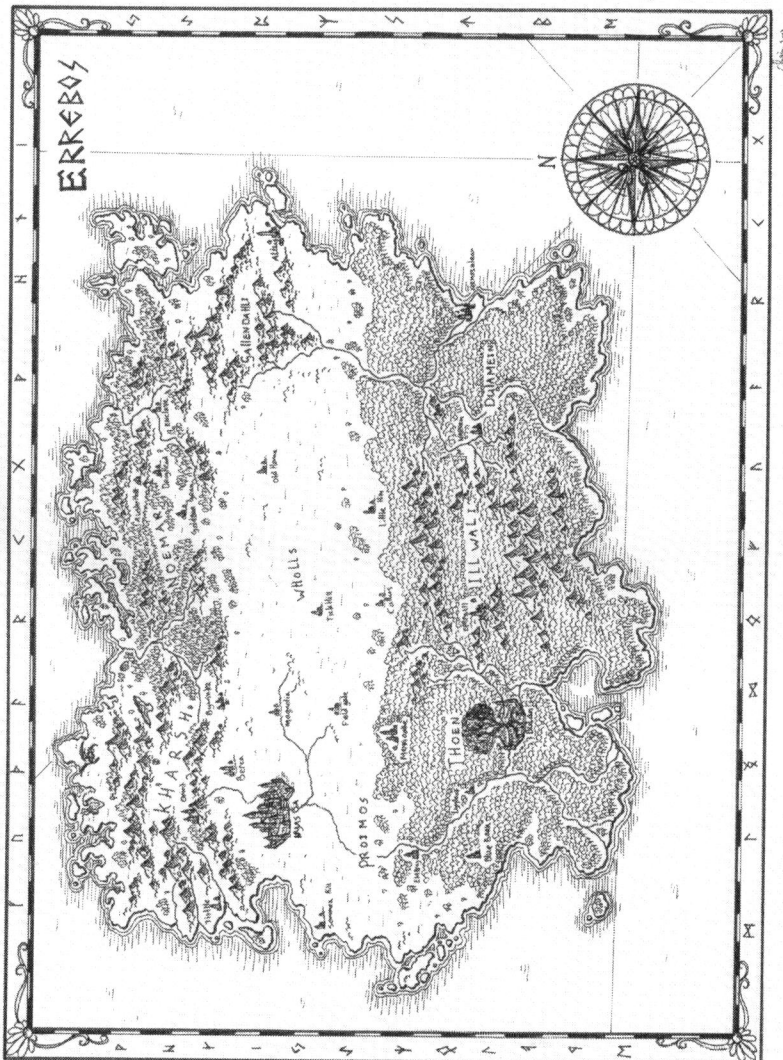

1

Pounding on the door snapped Kal awake with a jolt. He propped up on an elbow and strained his senses to gather his bearings. Purple murk filtered through a high, open window covering everything in the faintest glow. Outside was the early morn commotion of the grand City of Hollis. The clatter of wagon wheels over cobblestone. The bark of delivery men at work before sun-up. The squawk and brays of the domestic menagerie.

Kal's eyes landed on the lady's handkerchief amongst the clothes strewn over the floor. Why she hadn't stayed until morning was beyond him.

More muted thumping against the door.

Kal threw back the tangle of covers. Resisting the temptation to growl choice words through the hardwood, he swung his legs over the side of the bed and scanned for a shirt. What could anyone want this early? He was a craftsman. An artist. There was no one, short of the governor himself, who ought to demand his attention prior to sunrise. Even then.

"Kalomir."

Kal's agitation faded by hair's breadth at the sound of the familiar voice, low and worried on the other side of the door.

"Kal, open the door."

Something hardened in Kal's gut. He located his discarded tunic. Tugging it over his head, he hobbled forward in the dark and barked his shin on the chest beside the door. He swore under his breath.

He unlatched the lock and pulled the door in. "Yakov, what are–?"

"Quiet." Yakov glanced over his shoulder. He tugged his hood to further shadow his face and swept inside like a phantom. Wrenching the door from Kal's hand, he shut it softly. "You don't have much time."

"What are you about?" Kal said. "And do you got any idea what hour it is? For all you know, I mightn't be alone."

"I knew you were alone. It doesn't matter. You need to leave."

"Slow down. Leave?"

"Hollis. Gallendahi. The East, altogether." Yakov picked his way around the room, searching in the low light. Frantic, nervous, quick. "Gather your things, and don your outer clothes. Where's your rucksack?" He stopped to visually sweep the floor. He curled his lip, momentarily distracted by the mess of Kal's space. "Gods, you live like an animal."

"I can't leave. I'm due at the palace in a few hours."

"If you go there, you're a dead man – assuming Isak waits for you to come in."

New concern crept over Kal. He knew the nobleman's reputation as a hard man. He'd been happy with the quality of Kal's work until now. "Why?"

"Your lady friend from last night – do you know who she is?"

This caught him off guard. "Her name's Zena. She's a vintner, come to see about the wine cellar at the palace. They just finished it –"

"Wrong."

"What do you mean, *wrong?*"

"Her name isn't Zena, it's Yvane. She's Isak's wife."

"Impossible. The noble family isn't due to move in until the palace is done." Granted, Isak was frequently around, but that was because he was particular and didn't trust his specifications to be carried out to his liking unless he kept a close eye on the progress.

Yakov shook his head fervently. "She's here on a visit. Didn't you hear me tell you Jessika was going to be in town this week?"

It took Kal a moment to place the name because he'd never met her, only heard mention. "Jessika, your sister? The one who works for Isak's family?"

"That's the one."

"I thought she was coming to visit you."

"No, you fool. Jessika's one of her ladies in waiting. Lady Yvane has been searching for an opportunity to get back at Isak for his many affairs for months. According to Jessika, she was hungry for the prettiest, most talented person she could find. Her words, not mine. Apparently..." Yakov gave an irritated sweep of the hand. "You caught her eye."

Kal brought a hand to the hair atop his head. The time with her returned to him in a rush. They'd shared a coy glance and a few pleasant words at the palace. He never expected to see her again. He was pleasantly surprised when she appeared at *The Green Helm* – which leant to the idea that she was, in fact, a vintner. The tavern was a popular evening destination for merchants, artisans, and managers participating in the construction of the new palace. Kal knew, because he was there almost every night.

The hollow, slightly-used feeling which nudged his insides when she left now roused to life in earnest. "It's not true."

"Kal, it is. She lied to you and got you to take her to bed. Her degree of interest never struck you as odd?"

Kal said nothing.

Yakov noticed a canvas bag sagging against the chair and snatched it up. "She intends to go to her husband to fling it in his face. Which means Isak's going to send everyone at his disposal to find you."

"How do you know all this?"

"My sister. Haven't you been listening? Lady Yvane disappeared last night, and Jessika showed up at *The Green Helm* looking for her."

"When?"

"An hour after you two vanished. Apparently Yvane left instructions for Jessika to meet her there – to wait for her while she enacted her revenge scheme. Given the absence of the Lady, Jessika concluded she'd ensnared her hapless victim. *I hope he enjoys his night – unlikely he'll live to see another.* Again, her words, not mine. A while later, Lady Yvane – your Zena – arrived to gather Jessika, saying, *The deed is done.*"

"Oh gods." Kal staggered back a step. He felt like he was standing outside himself, watching his life slip through his fingers like sand. His well-paying job, his comfortable apartment, any moral standing he thought he possessed. Gone. "I'm a dead man."

"Death, my friend, is preferable to what Isak will do if he catches you." Yakov thrust the canvas bag against Kal's chest. "Gather your things now, and run."

"Half my tools are at the palace."

"You're not getting them back."

✧

Ten minutes later, they took the back exit into a shadowy alley behind the building. Yakov produced a small sack from beneath his cloak. "Here. Some food and little money. Stay off the road. Get as far away from here as you can."

"You've saved me, friend." Kal tucked the bundle away. "Thank your sister."

"She doesn't need encouraging. She's a gossip," Yakov said. "No one can know we had this conversation. No one can know I was here. If it gets back to Isak that I warned you..."

The heavy risk Yakov was undertaking settled over Kal. He gave a tight nod, clapped Yakov in a rough hug, and disappeared into the shadows.

2

One Year Earlier

A baby's cry filled the one-room house, and a wide grin bloomed across Wynne's face. "You did it, Hannah!"

Catreeny passed the infant to Wynne's waiting hands as Hannah craned her neck for a better look at her child. Wisps of hair curled away from her face, and she wore the same anxious-hopeful expression Wynne had seen before.

"A boy," Wynne said.

"A big boy, too, considering he's a month early," Catreeny said, like she didn't really believe it.

If Hannah felt any shame, she was too exhausted to show it. Too relieved it was over. Too eager to meet her son. Wynne laid the newborn in her waiting arms, and Hannah cradled him close, unable to pull her eyes from his sweet face. Bone-deep satisfaction washed over Wynne as mother and baby shared their first moments, face to face.

Catreeny's frank voice interrupted the peace. "Now. Let's pray the afterbirth comes out in one piece, or it's about to get unpleasant."

"What?" Hannah's worried eyes snapped to the head midwife, then Wynne.

"It's going to be alright," Wynne said in her most reassuring voice. "Remember, we talked about what to expect."

Even so, Wynne lifted a silent prayer. Catreeny had explained that pregnancies were risky. Complications arose and tragedies struck. Childbearing required bravery. Wynne hadn't witnessed the death of a mother or child in the course of her training. She hoped she never would.

The gods were apparently attentive that evening. As Catreeny cleaned up, Wynne brought a cup of water to Hannah.

"Look at that head of hair," Wynne said affectionately as the baby snuggled in Hannah's arms, stomach full and drowsy.

Hannah beamed and freed a hand to take the cup. "Blonde, like Willem."

"At least he don't got a walleye like his father," Catreeny added as she wrapped the rest of her belongings and tucked them into her bag. "Not yet, anyhow. The lucky boy."

The room chilled as Hannah stared daggers at Catreeny. Wynne held back a grimace. During childbirth, emotions ran high, and Catreeny's behavior was often less-than-sensitive. While she left a wake of offenses, she also saved a lot of lives. Her skill was second to none.

Catreeny either didn't notice the look, or didn't care. Wynne guessed, the latter.

"It's late," Wynne said. "Catreeny, I can finish the clean-up if you want to head home."

"I'll come 'round mid-morn to check on you and the babe," Catreeny said to Hannah as she moved toward the door. "Try not to bleed to death in the meantime."

"I hate her, Wynne," Hannah said the moment the door shut. "I wish it was just you."

She wasn't the first mother to express the sentiment. Or the second. Problem was, the Enclave was a small village. Until Wynne finished her training, it was Catreeny or no one.

"By the time you have your next, I'll be midwifing on my own," Wynne said. "Catreeny won't have to be here."

Hannah dropped her eyes. "Assuming Willem comes back."

"He'll come back." It was a promise Wynne couldn't make. They both knew it. It was what they told each other about the men who'd ridden off to confront the evil reigning from the throne on the other side of the continent.

They'll be back. Be strong for your little ones. It had been two months since they left. No one knew when they'd return.

Or if they would.

At sixteen, Wynne was barely an adult by Baldomar standards. She didn't have a husband to miss or little ones to raise alone. Her brother Omri left with the bulk of Baldomar fighters, like Hannah's husband Willem, Tess' husband Skeggis, and his younger brother Peder.

Like Harek Jaeger.

Hannah bobbed her head and blinked back the water collecting in her eyes. Wynne placed a hand on her shoulder and turned her attention to her son. "Enjoy this. A new life has entered the world. You did great."

✧

Most of the village was still asleep when Wynne plodded home. She was expected to perform the day shift scouting. She considered whether to attempt an hour of shut-eye before her watch began at sunup, then decided against it.

She slipped inside on quiet feet and shut the door gently. The house was still at rest, except for Wynne's mother, Susi. She was in the habit of rising early. Especially when troubled.

Wynne passed through the greatroom with its long plank table and a crackling hearth and entered the kitchen where candles contributed a flickering warmth to the space. Susi stood with her back to the doorway, kneading. Lumps of dough rested along the counter running the length of the room. Unless there was an event Wynne hadn't heard about, this was another testament to her mother's emotional state.

She's probably worried about Omri.

"Hello, Mum."

Susi whirled around and placed a hand on her chest. "Heavens, Wynne! You gave me a fright. I didn't hear you come in."

Wynne pecked her on the cheek.

"How'd the birth go?"

"Hannah did great. Baby boy."

Susi's face warmed into a smile. "I want to pop by later and bring her some food. You'll come?"

"I can't. I need to wash up before my watch."

"That's right. Scouting at dawn." Susi's eyes jumped around the kitchen, making a quick inventory of their pantry. "You should eat before you leave. I'll put together a bundle."

Individual bedrooms were a luxury by Enclave standards, but Wynne had never known anything different. The Thar house was one of the biggest, best constructed homes in the village. Wynne was grateful for the space.

In the privacy of her own bedroom, she tossed her filthy smock into a bucket with salt, and scrubbed herself clean using the cold water from her washbasin. The shock of cold sent an awakening chill through her body, which she needed.

There was no telling whether the day would bring the typical autumn frost of Noemar or if the strange warmth would persist. It was as if the gods saw fit to prolong the summer this year. Still, that didn't make it warm. Noemar was the northernmost province in Errebos. Brisk year-round.

She tugged on wool leggings and thick canvas trousers, and layered her sweaters. Doubling over, she swept her sandy hair into a knot atop her head, then checked herself in the handheld mirror on her table, straightening the small hammered gold disks which dangled from her ears.

She didn't look like the rest of the Thar family. For a Baldomar, she was short and light – the perfect build for a scout. She'd been told she bore a resemblance to her biological mother, Inorra. Wynne never knew her.

She collected her cross-body satchel, the hatchet she'd lovingly named Splitter, and her hunting horn. On her way out the door, she kissed her fingertips and touched the smooth wooden pendant which dangled from a cord on her wall. It once belonged to Inorra, too.

She found Susi halfway through packing a bundle. A plate on the counter held a roll and two hard boiled eggs. The sight of the piping cup of tea nearly made Wynne weak in the knees.

"Thank you, Mum," Wynne said, standing to eat.

Susi popped to her toes and retrieved the crock holding the family's store of brick, a hard fatty mixture of nuts, seeds, and cranberries shaped into squares. "How's the scouting been for you?"

"Better."

"I'm proud of you for sticking with it. I know you considered quitting a while back."

The raid a year earlier had shaken everyone. With the men's more-recent departure stretching the watch thin, Wynne couldn't quit in good conscience, even if she wanted to. She reasoned that midwifery wouldn't be enough to keep her busy all the time, so it was worth continuing work which offered regular pay.

"Do you feel safe?" Susi asked.

Wynne considered as she picked the eggshell. The risk hadn't changed, but Wynne's confidence in her skills had. "I feel prepared."

Susi seemed to accept the answer. She added a square of brick to the sack, along with an apple. "I need to know your times for the next few days."

Wynne bit into the egg and grasped at her memories through the fogginess of fatigue. Rakel kept them on rotating watches to keep things fair. If one person suffered with an undesirable watch, they all did. "Dawn to mid-afternoon today. Noon to dusk tomorrow. Overnight the day after that."

"Is there a day later this week when you'll be available around dinner-time?"

Something in Susi's tone caught Wynne's attention. Her chewing slowed. "Why?"

"Your father and I want to invite Garriden for dinner."

"By dinner, you mean...?"

"Yes."

Susi kept her tone deceptively light. A dinner invite, such as the one she was suggesting, was anything but. It was a way for a head of household – usually the father – to size up a potential husband for his daughter.

Baldomar reached adulthood at sixteen, which meant that Wynne had been considered an adult for a few months. Most Baldomar women married within a year or two of this. Usually to a slightly older man who'd demonstrated the ability to provide for a family.

Wynne knew other cultures pushed back the mark of adulthood. The elves, who were longer-lived, became adults at thirty. She'd heard people of Proimos were considered adults at nineteen. Prolonged adolescence always struck Wynne as strange. What was the point? To enjoy youth as independently and frivolously as possible? That wasn't her people's way. The Baldomar had suffered war and continuous genocide for over three-hundred years. In their society, strong families were paramount.

"Garriden?" Wynne said slowly, not bothering to hide her distaste.

"Yes, the minister."

Wynne responded with a flat, "No."

"He's religious and well-respected in the community. He has a wonderful sense of humor."

"He's blind."

"That's not the most important thing."

"True. It's more important that *I'm not*."

Susi cast her a tired look.

"Funny how his lack of sight hasn't stopped him from being able to find food. Or deliver it to his mouth," Wynne said. "He's as good as a snuffle-pig."

"Be kind, Wynne."

"He's about as round as one, too."

Susi pressed her lips together and released a controlled sigh. "We want the best for you."

"*Garriden?*"

"He may not be a strapping young Baldomar. He's still a good man."

"He's twice my age."

"The younger men are gone. We don't know when they'll be back. Or who will be back." It was quiet for a beat as Susi frowned into the bundle of food. She tied it closed. "You're a good, marriageable age. You must consider your options. If not Garriden, then your other options."

Wynne tried to ignore the uneasy twist behind her ribs. As far as she was concerned, there weren't any. She was an elder's daughter. She shouldn't have to settle.

She drained the rest of her tea and drew a deep breath, taking care not to sound ungrateful. At least her parents wanted her opinion on these matters. It was more than some folks got.

"I love you, Mum. We can talk about this another time. I need to relieve Maeve."

✧

Wynne's concerns fell away from her as she entered the section of forest which stood between the Enclave and its western border. Ordinarily, the early shift was her favorite. Despite her exhaustion, today was no exception. She relished the birdsong and the rising sun filtering through the prickly branches. The faint scent of pine carried on the crisp, mountain air. Clouds of hot breath furled before her. She kept her footfalls swift and silent, and broadened her skills of observation to focus on the forest around her.

Maeve was forbidden to leave her post until Wynne arrived at the lookout tower. The scouts usually accomplished this by attempting to get as close as possible, unnoticed. It was difficult to achieve. It'd become something of a game.

Wynne craned her neck upward, whistled the greeting, and waited. A moment later, Maeve's brown head and shoulders peeked out the window overhead.

"I saw ye before ye whistled. Nice try."

"Rats."

"Come up."

The heavy rope ladder unfurled from an opening in the floor, forty feet overhead. The height didn't bother Wynne, and she climbed into the enclosed platform without trouble. "Quiet night, I presume?"

"Aye, except this." Maeve gestured for Wynne to follow her to one of the windows. She passed her a looking glass. In the distance, thin trails of smoke indicated several campfires and the presence of a small caravan.

"More refugees?" Wynne asked.

"Based on where they're coming in, I'd say so."

"Any idea how many?"

"Hard to say at this distance. Could be twenty. Could be fifty."

Twenty, the Enclave could handle.

Fifty would be a problem.

Several new dwellings, including two boarding houses, had been erected in recent months to accommodate the influx of newcomers fleeing surrounding war-torn areas. Even so, there simply wasn't enough room in town to house everyone. Many of the newcomers were downtrodden, hungry, and poor. Some expressed an interest in remaining at the Enclave permanently. Of these, few had taken measures to lay down roots. Others expressed the desire to return to their own lands once the chaos unfolding in the wider world settled. It was yet to be seen.

"Ye want me to wait?" Maeve asked. Wynne heard the unspoken, *In case they're a problem.*

"No, you should get some sleep. If it's anything like the last group, it'll be mostly women and children."

"Well, be careful. In case they send a scout of their own ahead."

"If they do, I'll find him."

"I know ye will."

"You mind letting my pops know we've got newcomers headed this way?"

Though he was one of the village elders, Elric Thar was a carpenter by trade and involved in planning the construction of new buildings. With this many newcomers, it was better to avoid springing the news on him by way of four-dozen weary travelers outside their door.

"Will do." Maeve scooped up her bag and made her way to the hole in the floor. "Rakel knows. She prolly told him already."

Before Wynne left the lookout for the standard patrol of the perimeter, she leaned against the window frame and watched the wisps of smoke. Her thoughts wandered back over the last several hours.

It was hard to pin down the unsettling flutter at the back of her mind. She wasn't sure she understood it herself.

Of course she wanted a family of her own. A loving husband. Children. Fulfilling work. Who didn't? It was a deep-seated longing she'd harbored for years. Learning midwifery seemed like the most natural outgrowth of this. She loved babies. She loved mothers.

As rewarding as the work had been, it did little to fill Wynne with the desire to bear children of her own.

You had to be brave.

Wynne didn't feel brave. Not about that.

She pulled herself from the window. It was easy enough to push this out of her mind. She was incredibly busy. Happily busy. Starting a family felt like a distant dream. Meanwhile, her parents wanted the best for her, and they'd never force her to marry someone she disliked. She'd consider children once she married the right man. At the moment, it helped that no one in the Enclave met that description.

As she climbed down the ladder, a dissatisfied pang lodged within. She wondered what Harek Jaeger was doing right now.

3

"I saw Hannah and the new babe," Tess said. She cradled her own baby in one arm while dragging a chair across the rough-hewn floor toward the fireplace. "She said Catreeny was a real treat."

Wynne lifted her chair and followed. Tess knew Wynne didn't like speaking ill of Catreeny. She shrugged. "She can be honey-like."

Tess laughed, flashing the gap in her smile. "Once you get past all the bees."

She plopped into her chair and started to nurse her son.

"Wot is she playin' at with her sass? Good gods. Hannah and Willem ain't the first to welcome a child eight months after the weddin'."

Wynne stared into fire. She said nothing. She had no interest in speculating. Sometimes babies came early. Tess' son arrived several months before he should've. For a spell, they feared he'd be too small and too weak to survive. If not for a blessing from Kalane, the dragoness who lived in the mountain nearby, he probably would've died.

"I'm kickin' for glee for Skeggis to meet Asmund," Tess said.

"Meet him?" Wynne turned to look at her. "He was there for the birth."

"I mean, take him off my hands. Gimme a break. I'm tired." Tess patted the baby gently. "Skeggis only got two days with him before he rode out. He don't know him at all."

Wynne conceded with a nod.

"Also, *there for the birth* is rich."

Wynne remembered. Skeggis passed out and wound up with a concussion after several bouts of nervous vomiting. "I gotta say, I didn't see that coming."

"Makes two of us." Tess sighed and looked somber for a moment. "I miss him."

Wynne hummed. Tess' widowed mother-in-law, Brinja, had been helping when she could. She was otherwise managing her newborn and a tiny farmstead almost entirely alone.

"How're you handlin'?" Tess said. "It strange not having your brothers around?"

"A bit. Josef, not really. In all the time I've known him, he's been away more than he's been here." He was her only living connection to her family before the Thars, but they weren't close. "It's more strange with Omri gone, not cracking jokes or involved in everything my pops does. I think my father feels his absence more than he lets on."

"How's ol' Barky?" Tess asked, meaning Rakel. As a former scout, Tess shared an appreciation for the challenges which accompanied dealing with the head of scouting and border patrol.

"She's been talking to Nialls and my pops about starting a watch in town."

"A watch?"

"To keep an eye on things. Maintain order."

"It hasn't got that bad, has it?"

Wynne held her hand level and rocked it side to side. "Mainly the newcomers. Fighting. Theft. Folks not keeping their pigs under control. The biggest pain is the tavern."

The tavern was a new fixture in the village. It attracted a nightly crowd of mostly non-Baldomar who had nothing better to do with their evenings than drink and carouse.

Tess sucked her teeth. "Say wot you will about the tavern, it's made things more lively 'round here."

"We have a dragon queen as our closest neighbor. We're not short on lively."

"Fair. But you know wot else it's brought that we're short on?"

"Money?"

Tess squinted at Wynne. "Men."

"I suppose."

Tess freed a hand to point vaguely to indicate the village. "There's more than there's been in a long time."

"The handful I've seen leave much to be desired."

"Damaris hitched one."

"I'm sure Bruce is a fine man, and I'm happy for your sister. I'm only saying, the non-Baldomar aren't like us."

"They're not all unproductive, drunk pervs."

Wynne said nothing.

"Look. We can't afford to be overly choosy when it comes to marryin'. Our people woulda died out a long time ago. 'Specially true now. You might not like the fruit, but you better eat it while it's ripe. That's how it is."

"So abandon standards, or die alone?"

"No. I mean, a good man is a good man. Baldomar or not."

Wynne gave her a knowing look. "All this is easy for you to say. You got the one you wanted."

Tess relaxed against the back of the chair with a satisfied smile. "I did. Don't act like you got no options, though."

"Who?" Wynne said, though she sensed where this was going.

"Harek."

Heat came to Wynne's face. "What about him?" she said too quickly.

"You tell me. Do we like him today?"

Wynne pressed her mouth into a line as she tried to sort out the rumination of her own heart. "I don't know."

Tess snorted. "Sounds 'bout right. Let's hear it."

Wynne rolled her eyes and forced out a breath. "He's my friend."

Tess rolled her free hand. *Go on.*

"He's cute and kind. It's not enough."

"Well, you went and noticed him, and now he's smitten."

"I know," Wynne said with a groan. "It was sweet for a while, but he never acted on it. He's too meek."

"He went to war." Tess flashed a palm, making her bracelets clack together. "Not defendin' him. Only sayin'. That's bold."

"He did the very thing which he – and every capable Baldomar man – ought to have done," Wynne said. "It's a good thing. It doesn't make him marriage-worthy. For Silversaar's sake, what has he done to prepare himself for a family?"

"Some men take longer to get there."

"Skeggis jumped at the opportunity to build a life with you as soon as he knew you were interested," Wynne said. "I can't help but feel we're unequally yoked."

"Wot do eggs got to do with anything?"

"Nothing. I mean *yoke*, like what you attach to oxen. You've heard my pops talk about the oxen and the field of life."

"Ah, yes. Elric's oxen. The most romantic of marriage symbols."

"I don't mean to disparage Harek. He's a wonderful friend, and I care about him –"

"–but he's beneath you."

Wynne hesitated. That characterization cut close and put her on her heels. "No."

"Come on. He's a too-shy butcher's boy who still lives with his parents," Tess said. "You're Wynne Thar. Daughter to an elder. Sister to the Erlander."

"*The Erlander*? Is that what we call Josef now?"

"Gotta ring to it."

Wynne chuckled. "What's gotten into you?"

"No sleep. This whole mornin's been tits and crap. I won't remember half of this conversation."

Wynne laughed harder, then sighed. "I miss scouting together."

"Good times. Wot was I sayin'?"

"Harek."

"Aye. How you're better than him. Continue."

Wynne winced. "I don't think I'm better than him."

Tess made a doubtful hum.

"Alright. Maybe I am," Wynne said, peeved and feeling like she needed to justify herself. "I can't marry just anyone. I won't. If I'm going to attach myself to someone for life, I want a man who acts like a man. Harek wouldn't make a good husband. Not for me. Not as he is."

4

The warriors of the Enclave returned with the sound of a horn and banners raised high. Jubilant cheers filled the village. Families hurried to receive their heroes. Nearly a hundred fighting men had gone.

The returning group appeared smaller.

Wynne waded through the crush of people in search of the familiar faces of her brothers and Aeryn Haranae, her would-be sister-in-law. She noticed Willem and cast her gaze over her shoulder for Hannah hovering nervously at the fringe of the crowd, clutching her newborn as she anxiously scanned the swarm. Wynne called to her and pointed with a wild, sweeping gesture. She beamed as Hannah's face lit up.

The joyful bellow of Leland Jaeger pulled Wynne's focus from Hannah's reunion. With his wooden leg, he struggled in the muddy, sodden earth but had braved the fields with his wife Micha and their three youngest children in search of Harek. People slid out of the way, and Harek appeared astride his chestnut gelding, Judge. He looked less the overgrown boy Wynne remembered, and more a man. He sat tall with his sword and shield at his side. He broke into an easy smile at the sight of his family. He directed his horse forward, followed by the largest dog Wynne had ever seen.

A wardog.

When did he get one of those?

Dismounting, Harek shook the hair from his eyes, rumpled the dog's ears, and noticed Wynne. His smile took a brighter quality and something within her chest lilted. She waved. Half a beat later, he was lost amidst his parents and sisters.

Later.

"Skeggis!" Tess' cry came from Wynne's left. Hugging Asmund to her chest with one arm, Tess stood on her toes and waved a hand overhead.

Like most Baldomar males, Skeggis was a mountain of a man, fair-haired, and loud. The crowd parted as he urged his horse forward. When he was near enough, he leapt from its back, closed the distance in two strides, and enveloped Tess in a hug.

Brinja appeared behind Tess and welcomed her eldest son with a tight embrace. Her whole face smiled. Without hearing the words exchanged, Wynne felt herself pulled in by the tides of emotions, sharing their joy.

Skeggis placed his hand on his mother's cheek and kissed her forehead. When he pulled back, his expression was grave. The tides turned to a crushing wave as Brinja's face paled, and she threw herself into Skeggis' chest. As Brinja wept, Wynne's mind swam.

Oh, no. Peder...

A heavy chill ran the length of Wynne's body. The need to find her own family pressed upon her with new urgency.

She threaded her way through the masses, passing dozens of familiar faces. Taige Goodhill. Tess' eldest brother, Roran. Sender Fife, the portly, middle-aged healer.

No Josef.

No Omri.

The fear creeping into the edges of Wynne's heart sharpened.

Elric's voice drew her attention to the right. She elbowed her way around several individuals and noticed Jairus first. Her little brother's shaggy brown cap was situated a head above everyone else. Folks shifted to reveal Jai sitting upon Elric's shoulders, Susi beaming, and Omri beside his horse. He seemed to have grown too. He was filthy and grinning, as though he found the whole thing amusing.

Wynne darted forward and staggered him with a fierce hug.

✧

Omri brought with him a bounty of news about the outcome of the war, the dragons, and those who hadn't returned.

"Josef has a mechanical arm?" Wynne asked, hardly believing her ears.

"Never seen anything like it, Wynne." Omri brought a heaping forkful of Susi's best cooking to his mouth. "Oh! He and Aeryn got hitched."

Wynne dropped her utensil in her dish and threw her hands in the air. "Why didn't you start with that?"

"Kalane presided."

"Was it a lovely ceremony?" Susi asked.

"I wasn't there. I heard about it after. Small ordeal."

Wynne resumed her meal and smiled to herself. Josef and Aeryn were alive and well. Hearing they'd finally become husband and wife caused a swell of good feelings to bubble inside her. She'd always wanted a sister. Now she had a sister-in-law. *Close enough.*

"Word is they're gonna start an academy for rune-bearers," Omri said.

"What's that? It sounds fancy," Wynne asked.

Omri held up a finger and swallowed. "It's like what they did here, but more official. With the Empire dissolved, all these regions and cities are responsible for their own protection now. Josef and Aeryn plan to continue passing on the runes. They believe everyone should be able to defend themselves."

Elric drummed his thumb on the table as he considered.

"They're gonna be careful about who they work with," Omri continued, directing the comment toward Susi. "If they learn that people are misusing the runes, Aeryn can remove them."

"Remove them?"

"She's done it before, apparently. She became some sorta dragon-slaying war hero among the elves. They love her."

"They're not starting the academy in the South?"

"No. Goldbur Gren."

Elric's bushy eyebrows climbed up his forehead. "As in, our ally city which Malachai burned to the ground?"

"It's being rebuilt," Omri said. "Terms for the end of the war included the old Empire doling out funds to rebuild what Malachai destroyed. Efforts have already begun. Those taking part are to be paid good money."

Wynne's spirits sagged. "They're not staying here?"

Omri shook his head. "The world's changing. Josef and Aeryn wanna use what they've been given to shape it for the better. In fact, quite a few of our people wanna hand in it. Some say Goldbur Gren might even grow into a nation of Baldomar one day."

"Others are leaving the Enclave?" Susi asked.

"About fifteen or twenty from the warband. Some wanna work, then come home after earning some money. Others plan to uproot and establish themselves in the Gren permanently."

"Any idea when they're goin'?" Elric asked.

"Soon. Before the snow starts."

The conversation lulled and Wynne's thoughts swirled over the news. These were good, exciting changes. Still, she felt the loss of Aeryn and Josef with a selfish press of melancholy.

Omri wiped his mouth with a napkin. His spine straightened. "I've something to say." He waited a beat for everyone's full attention. "I'm gonna start building a house."

Elric rumbled in his chest, proud. Susi's eyes creased. "That's wonderful, Omri."

"There's more." Omri took a breath, like he was working up courage. "I'm gonna receive a dinner invitation in the near future. I'm gonna accept the offer. Once my house is finished, I'm getting married."

Susi and Elric exchanged a silent conversation with a glance. Wynne wondered whether this was Omri announcing a general aspiration, or if there was someone specific.

"Who is it?" Elric said.

Omri cleared his throat. "Lara."

The happy smiles of Susi and Elric faltered.

"Waylas and Pia's daughter?" Susi asked, as if secretly hoping there was another Lara she didn't know about.

Omri nodded once.

A dinner invitation from Waylas shocked no one. At eighteen, his eldest daughter, Lara, was Omri's age. Not beyond the typical window for marriage, though nearing the upper edge. This wasn't due to a flaw of hers. She was kind, beautiful, and industrious. It was her parents.

It was well known that Waylas and Pia harbored aspirations for their girls to marry up in society. This left Lara with few options in an otherwise dwindling pool of prospects. They'd even attempted a dinner with Josef a year ago, which had been an uncomfortable experience for all.

As Wynne studied Omri, she realized with a thrill that this was more than a prediction. A tightlipped little smile affixed itself to her mouth.

Elric rested his fork and spoke carefully. "Son, have you given this thought?"

"I have."

"How much thought?"

"Enough. At the end of the dinner, when Waylas asks if I'd accept Lara's hand in marriage, I'm saying yes."

"You've never been to this kind of dinner before. You're not obligated to accept the first offer of marriage you receive."

"There are many other young ladies you might consider," Susi added. "After the raid last year and the war, we have so few eligible young men in the village, there's no rush."

Wynne glanced dispassionately in Susi's direction as their conversation about Garriden came to mind.

"Once you're married, you have to make it work – whoever you choose,"

Elric said. "It's like the oxen. You don't want to find yourself yoked with a woman who'll make you miserable."

Susi placed her hand over her husband's and nodded heartily. "Yes. It's important to pick a good woman from a good family."

"Lara is a good woman," Omri said, resolute.

Susi extended a palm. "She's a lovely girl. However, marrying Lara gives you Waylas and Pia for in-laws."

"I'm aware."

"Have you thought about what that might be like?"

"I'm not concerned."

Susi's eyes darted briefly to Elric. "I think they'll make your life unpleasant."

"They're a pain in the backside," Elric said flatly.

"They're not that bad," Omri said.

"Son, we've known them longer than you," Susi said. "You're an elder's son. That carries respect. A certain...standing, within our clan. I'm concerned Lara's family considers you a means to an end. I wouldn't put it past them to encourage a marriage simply to improve their station, or gain influence in the community."

"Lara isn't like that."

"I agree, she seems like a sweet young lady. The fact is, her parents *are* like that. You don't know how they'll influence her."

Omri clenched his jaw and took a controlled breath.

Susi realized she'd struck a nerve, and her eyebrows pitched in the center. "We only want you to be wise."

"Consider yourself forewarned," Elric said. "We're not forbidding you from marrying Lara, if that's what you really want –"

"Good, because I love her," Omri said.

Wynne covered the lower half of her face with a hand. Her eyes jumped between her parents and Omri. *I knew it!*

Omri continued with steady confidence. "I know her parents are ambitious. Pia is catty. Waylas acts too big for his britches. I also know they raised a wonderful woman. You're gonna have to get used to them in the family."

Quiet fell.

Wynne waited for her parents' response, suspending the same spoonful of mash since Omri broached the topic.

"Can I have another roll?" Jai asked, breaking the quiet. With a little shush, Wynne distractedly grabbed two from the bread basket and plopped them in front him.

"How long has this been going on?" Elric asked. "You and Lara."

"It started three months before the warband left."

"You never let on," Susi said.

"We agreed to keep it quiet. I wasn't quite ready. She knows what her parents are like," Omri said. "After what happened last year with Josef, she wanted to avoid public embarrassment if it didn't work out."

"Waylas and Pia don't know about your feelings for one another yet?"

"No. We've been thinking about how to let Waylas think inviting me to dinner was his idea."

Another silent exchange between Elric and Susi.

"Is there anything else we should know?" Elric asked.

Wynne heard the unspoken question. As long as Lara wasn't pregnant, there was still hope that Elric might not have to welcome Waylas to the family. As soon as a child was involved, they were as good as married even without a ceremony.

"There is," Omri said gravely.

Thinly veiled dread passed over Elric and Susi.

Omri let them squirm for only a moment more, then flashed a grin. "This meal is delicious."

5

The Baldomar took every opportunity to come together and celebrate. Three days after the homecoming, they packed the meeting hall to capacity. Tables and benches had been moved outdoors to make space inside for the dancing to come later. The overflow of villagers spilled into the grassy area out front as people gathered to hear the elders' address and honor the fallen. Then the festivities began.

Children played in the yard alongside the meeting hall and their shrieks joined the hubbub of jovial conversations all around. Food tents and colorful pavilions boasted an assortment of pies, beer, turkey legs, venison sausage, and salt potatoes. The smell of smoked meat and apple cider carried on the air. The milder weather, accommodations, and good cheer reminded Wynne of the harvest festival, which usually happened shortly after her birth-day. It was skipped this year.

She came dressed in her best. She'd woven her tresses into a complicated series of knots ending at the crown and let the rest hang loose where it fell below her shoulders. Her dress matched the blue in her eyes while the yellow flowers stitched along the neckline accentuated the gold in her hair.

She was most excited for the opportunity to enjoy the music and dancing later, and she didn't want a huge meal to weigh her down. Still, she knew her parents would want her to eat with them first. *A concession.* As she filled her plate in one of the food tents, she kept an eye open for Harek. His family was usually involved in coordinating the food for big events. She didn't see him. No surprise there.

The Thars' table provided a keen view of several open-air tents and the doors of the meeting hall. Wynne kept an ear attentive to the conversation while remaining observant to the activity taking place beyond their pavilion.

As folks finished their first helping of food, they moved around to mingle and visit with their relatives and neighbors. Catreeny and her husband Ben Hodd eventually joined the Thars' table. Everywhere the eye turned, Wynne noticed groups of warbanders together. It was as if a brotherhood had formed amongst them, with war forging friendships which didn't exist before and strengthening the bonds which did.

Catreeny noticed too.

"The true heroes of the Baldomar are the childbearing women." With the sweep of her finger, she gestured to the horde of warbanders congregating near the beer tent, including her eldest, Grigory. "All those heroes? We did that."

Susi laughed and clinked her mug against Catreeny's. A few other women nearby responded with, "Hear, hear!"

Wynne caught the sound of drum, fiddle, and tin whistle in the distance. Unable to resist the pull – lively music made everything more fun – she finished her food as quickly as she could without drawing her mother's ire. Anticipation bounced around inside her as she made her way through the grounds toward the open doors of the meeting hall. She paused in the entryway to assess the room.

Musicians played on the platform at the head of the hall. Fires blazed in the hearths situated along the sides. The space was less than a third full. Seven pairs of dancers moved over the open floor in the center while others milled around the edges, talking, watching, and enjoying the music.

Someone tapped her shoulder, and she turned to meet Omri's smiling face. "Wanna dance, sis?"

For an answer, Wynne hooked her arm in his. They skipped onto the floor. More pairings filtered into the hall before the song came to an end. When it did, people clapped for the musicians and cheered for more.

Suddenly distracted, Omri straightened his posture, and a change came over him. "I'm gonna let you go, sis. My lady is here."

Wynne followed his eyes to the far side of the hall. Lara wore a pink dress and with an elaborate braid over her shoulder. Her face warmed when she saw Omri.

A surge of giddy excitement ran through Wynne. She gave him a nudge. "Go."

Wynne stepped aside for a rest and watched her brother approach Lara.

She needed a new dance partner. She could count on Catreeny to start a giant circle at some point during the festivities, but Catreeny was occupied.

Nearby, a knot of young ladies also watched Omri and Lara. Among them, Simone and Tawna looked like they smelled something sour. Though once her friends, Wynne's circle didn't overlap with theirs much anymore. She always suspected Simone disliked her, which influenced the others. It bothered Wynne more when she was younger.

"Wynne..." Simone sidled up beside her. She shook her sheet of vivid red hair away from her shoulders. Her long sloping nose was a little pink from the sun. "Is there something between Lara and Omri?"

Omri leaned closer to Lara and spoke something into her ear. Lara laughed. They shared a tender look which made Wynne melt a little.

His plans weren't Wynne's to share. Not yet, anyway. Still, Wynne didn't like the look in Simone's eye, and she couldn't help herself. "It seems to me they can't stand each other."

Simone's expression turned ugly at the sarcasm. Wynne rolled her eyes and peeled away, prowling the edge of the room, just to be rid of her. Scanning the hall again, she spotted Harek in the open doorway.

He wore a clean black shirt and his furry vest, which was one of his nicer garments. His searching eyes took in the activity and brightened when they found her, like they had the other day.

The flutters returned. Wynne popped to her toes and waved.

He ran his fingers through his overgrown curls, pushing them away from his forehead as he wove through the crowd toward her. He stood tall, if a little stiff, and moved with purpose.

Wynne smoothed the end of her hair over her shoulder. As he neared, she threw her reservations to the wind and swooped in for an embrace. He wrapped his arms around her, strong and gentle. They'd never hugged before. Not like this.

"Would you like to dance?" he asked, reminding her how much she liked his voice. It was deep and resonant.

She pulled back and gave him a playful arch of her brow. "I didn't know you danced."

He responded in kind. "Of course I do."

Wynne hummed. "Usually you're outside with the food."

"I had other things on my mind today." He extended a hand.

She placed her palm gently in his. "That so?"

His grin took an impish quality. He gripped her hand and yanked her toward the dance floor. Wynne yelped with delight. He twirled her before leading her to the center.

So it went for hours. They galloped and twirled around the hall, laughing like kids, enjoying the music and one another's company. One dance blended into the next. The crowd shifted around them, at times forcing them to share the floor with a multitude, or thinning to give them space. They occasionally stopped for a drink or food, only to return to the hall for more dancing.

At one point, the sisters Hleni and Bera, took the platform and started to sing. Cheers rose. In the second verse, they were joined by Elion, Aeryn's brother, who added the male harmony. Together, they belted out a rousing tune which everyone knew, and energized the crowd.

With the rest of the room, Wynne and Harek added their voices to the refrain every third line, punching the air. It was tricky to manage while continuing to dance. More than once, they misjudged the next step only to knock elbows or step on each other's toes. By the end of it, they were out of breath, hanging onto each other, laughing.

The song came to an end with raucous applause.

Sweat pricked along Wynne's hairline. She fanned her face and blew out an exaggerated breath. "I need a break."

They staggered toward the doors. A handful of passing warbanders greeted them on their way out. Harek paused briefly to knock knuckles and slap them on the back. Normally, he disliked the press of the crowd. During lively gatherings, he was usually in the yard behind the meeting hall, helping Leland man the spit, checking the smoker, or keeping busy where he didn't have to brush shoulders with too many people. Seeing him at ease, enjoying the camaraderie, made a smile come to her eyes. It had been happening all night.

The sun was sinking behind the western trees. The cool breeze felt lovely. Several bonfires contributed light to the ongoing festivities outdoors. Food, drink, and fellowship flowed everywhere the eye fell.

They meandered between pavilions, going nowhere in particular. Shoulder to shoulder, so close their arms brushed. Harek pushed the hair away from his damp forehead, relaxed. "This has been a great day."

Wynne hummed in the affirmative. "Even better than the last Harvest Festival."

Harek hoisted an eyebrow. He knew the Harvest Festival was her favorite. "You don't say?"

"Well, yeah. You've been dancing with me."

His smile deepened. His gaze lingered for a moment.

"I'm going to get another drink," he said as they drew up alongside the beer tent.

"Another?"

"You want one?"

"No, thank you."

"I'll be right back."

"I'll be here."

Wynne idled, brushed her temples with the back of her hand, and sighed. She spotted Waylas and Pia at a table in a pavilion across the way. They were huddled in an urgent conversation. Waylas got up and left in a hurry. A few moments later, Susi appeared. She touched the end of Pia's table, and Pia's demeanor changed instantly. She sat up straighter, pasted a smile to her face, and with a sweep of the hand invited Susi to sit.

It wasn't unusual for Susi to make the rounds at these sort of events, or in general. She was an elder's wife, which carried certain expectations. Even so, she genuinely cared about others. In light of Omri's pronouncement, Wynne recognized Susi was making an effort.

Harek returned, a third of his pint gone already. He rested a hand on her shoulder.

A gust of cool air sent a shiver over her skin.

"Cold?" he asked.

"Actually, I feel like my clothes are sticking to me," she said. "I'm so sweaty, I could go for a dip in the river."

He assumed a playful grin. Stepping closer, his hand traveled to her waist. "Is that an invitation?"

Wynne threw her head back and laughed. She moved nearer to his side.

"Did I hear, *river*?" The booming voice of Skeggis came from closeby. They broadened their little circle to include him and Tess. Skeggis clapped his hands and rubbed them together. "Who're we throwing into the Bekker?"

With a gap-toothed grin and a wild look in her eye, Tess hooked her arm in his. "You can throw me in."

Skeggis gave his wife a suggestive glance. He turned back to Wynne and Harek and jerked his thumb to indicate Tess. "Gotta be careful with that one. Somehow every time she ends up in the Bekker, all her clothes come off."

Wynne's eyebrows shot up her forehead. She shared an awkward glance with Harek. They chuckled for a lack of a better response.

Tess simply shrugged. She grabbed Skeggis by the hand and pulled him away. "Your mum's got the baby. Let's go."

The parting remark hung in the air for a beat before Wynne and Harek doubled over laughing.

"Sounds like the river's gonna be full tonight," he said.

Wynne braced a hand on the stitch in her side, and touched his arm. "Oh, I've missed you," she said as she caught her breath.

Harek's laughter died down.

"I've missed you, too," he said. A little quieter. A little more serious. His eyes went unfocused on an indistinct point in the grass. He went still for the length of a breath. "I've been thinking."

He met her face. Red splotches had settled on his cheeks. The smell of beer rolled off his breath. He reached out, gently holding the side of her head with one hand. He kissed her cheek.

He pulled back, and Wynne felt herself flush. A pleasant albeit confused tangle of nerves began to bounce in her chest. He'd never done that before.

"I think we should get married," he said.

"...What?"

"Will you be my wife?"

The pleasant buzz inside of Wynne ground to a halt. She stared at him for a moment. "Oh, Harek..." Her shoulders dipped. "You know we can't."

His spike of confidence faltered. "Why?"

"You're not ready," she said, keeping her voice both gentle and direct. She thought that much was obvious, but apparently it wasn't. "How do you intend to support a family? Where would we live?"

"We can figure that out later."

Pained, Wynne pressed her lips together and tilted her head. *No, that needs to happen first.*

She took a breath and her face softened. She knew she was wounding him, and hated it. Still, it had to be said. "No, Harek."

He furrowed his brow. For a beat, he said nothing. He threw back the rest of his drink and wiped his lip on his sleeve. "Okay."

He walked away as the festivities continued around her.

6

A cool drizzle seeped from the sky. Wynne's watch couldn't end soon enough. She went directly to Tess and Skeggis' house without consideration of changing her wet, muddy clothes.

Asmund rested in the baby basket beside the table while Tess attended the cast-iron pot on the hearth. Wynne made happy faces at him as she warmed her fingers on a mug of tea, half-listening as Tess recounted the list of repairs Skeggis was doing for his mother.

Tess wiped her hands on the side of her tunic and plopped into the chair opposite Wynne.

"Something happened at the celebration last night," Wynne said.

Tess' face brightened. "Tell me."

"Harek kissed me."

"He did?" she cried. Asmund made a fussy noise.

"On the cheek."

Tess deflated a little. "Oh. I guess that's sweet."

"There's more."

"More?" she asked, once again intrigued.

Wynne cringed inwardly. "He asked me to marry him."

"He did wot?" Tess shook her head and blew out a breath. "Wot'd you say?"

Wynne turned up her palms. "What was I supposed to say? He was drunk.

He was riding the mirth of celebration. Do you think he ever talked to my father?"

Tess dragged her cup toward herself, took a sip, and pulled her lips away from her teeth as she swallowed. "Ain't likely."

"Correct."

Tess hummed in disapproval. Asmund continued to fuss. She rested her mug and lifted him from the basket. Laying him on her shoulder, she patted his back. "You talk to him since?"

"I haven't seen him. He left when I told him no. I've been scouting all morning and came right here." The interaction replayed in her mind with a pang. She knew she'd wounded him. She sympathized to an extent. "I feel embarrassed for him. Still, this shows I'm right."

"'Bout wot?"

"What we talked about last week. This was not the behavior of a mature man ready to lead a family."

"You're right. It was the behavior of a smitten, drunken fool. That's not how it's done, if that's wot he really wants."

"Exactly."

The baby released a tiny burp, and Tess eased him into the crook of her arm. "You think he'll still wanna marry you once he sobers up?"

Wynne shrugged. "He said he's been thinking. For all I know, it was the potvalor talking," she said with an edge of contempt. She felt affronted that he would propose to her, drunk. Was it too much to hope that he'd say what he meant, sober-minded?

"I'll put it to you 'nother way. Do you want him to marry you?"

Wynne dropped into quiet thought as her heart twisted. "I do."

"I thought as much. So wot are you gonna do about it?"

"You thought as much?"

"I saw the way you looked at him. And danced with him." Tess tilted her head and fixed Wynne with a knowing smirk.

"We were having fun."

"Oh that's good. You can keep havin' fun together when you're married."

"He lives with his parents."

Tess gave her a tired look. "He just needs the proper motivation. A good woman can do that for a man."

"Sounds like putting the cart before the horse."

"He's not perfect, but don't be dainty. If you don't hitch your cart to that horse, someone else will."

Wynne scowled at a gouge on the tabletop.

"Do you think you're too good for him?" Tess asked.

"Of course not."

"He's just not good enough to be a husband?"

Wynne hesitated for the length of a breath. "He's not."

Tess rolled her eyes.

"Can we please talk about something else?"

Asmund made a sleepy noise, pursed his lips, and snuggled closer to Tess. Wynne smirked despite herself. "How's it been with Skeggis back?"

"We broke the bed."

"Oh, gods, Tess." Wynne used a hand to shield her eyes. Her cheeks burned. "I meant with the baby and being a family again."

"I don't think I can put words to it." Tess' eyes creased into a smile. "Havin' a man in the house...it's a good thing."

"How are you all coping with the news about Peder?"

"It don't feel real. For Skeggis, it's like livin' it all over again. 'Specially seeing his Mum. Now she's got nobody, but us."

Wynne's eyebrows pitched in sympathy. She took another sip of tea.

"We're prolly up and goin' to Goldbur Gren."

Wynne looked up, shocked. "What?"

"Not now, obviously." Tess shifted her arm to indicate Asmund. "We'll prolly miss the good-pay opportunity. We gotta convince Brinja to join us."

"But you're leaving?"

"Eventually." Tess shrugged. "I can't blame him wantin' to go. Wantin' a fresh start. You know Aeryn and Josef Erlander are settlin' there when all's done.

Startin' some academy. Skeggis wants to help them."

That didn't surprise Wynne. She felt blindsided by the pronouncement nonetheless. She contended with a heavy tug of loss. "First Josef and Aeryn. Now you and Skeggis. Who am I gonna have left?"

"You could have Harek."

Wynne shot her a look. *Not funny.*

"Wot?"

7

In the lane outside the boarding house, Wynne surveyed the dwindling baskets of apples, bread, and hunks of dried meat in the cart. She made a mental count, praying there'd be enough. There were still a few folks to serve before she and the others moved to the south side of the village.

Conflict in the wider world had resulted in an influx of newcomers among the needy families of the Enclave already struggling to survive with the fresh loss of a father or husband. For Wynne, the weekly outing was an opportunity to interact with her people and bring tangible help. A little food and some fresh socks wasn't much, but it was something.

Her gaze traveled again toward the boarding house and landed on the approaching woman, who'd only been at the Enclave for a week. "Hiya, Nollie."

The young widow waved a bandaged hand as she swished through the grass in the company of her young children. Her family was one of ten bunking here.

Wynne made it a point to remember as many names as possible, a practice reinforced by her parents. *It's important to be known,* Susi said. *It reminds us that we serve people, not faceless, hungry mouths. It keeps us accountable to one another.*

Remembering names was trickier with the children. There were so many of them.

Wynne adjusted the sling over her shoulder which she'd crammed full of freshly knitted socks. She crouched, bringing herself level with the kids. The little boy clung to his mother's skirt. Opposite him, a girl a year or two older, clutched a rag doll, browned and grubby with love. "I'm Wynne Thar. Remind me of your names?"

The girl moved closer to her mother's side. "Hollyn."

Wynne turned to the boy. He looked about Jai's age.

"Dieter," he said.

"Hollyn and Dieter," Wynne said, committing the names to memory. She pointed to the girl's ragged doll. "Who's this?"

The little girl adjusted her doll so Wynne could better see it. "Posy."

"That's a good name."

"I made the apron."

"You did? Your stitches are straighter than mine."

A little smile crawled onto the girl's face. Her eyes jumped to Nollie, who smoothed her hair.

"What are those?" Dieter pointed to the marks on Wynne's knuckles.

Wynne turned her hand over. "These are called runes. I was born with them."

"You can use magic?"

Wynne knew her people's history. The Baldomar were heroes of old, favored by the dragon king, Silversaar. From what she understood, there were few Baldomar left in the wider world. Until recently, the Enclave had been a small, isolated village. It was still surprising to hear how their reputation preceded them, especially from the mouth of a five-year-old.

"I can," she said. "I'm not going to do any tricks now. Though I'll show you something we Baldomar do, and you can do it too."

The kids perked up.

"This is how we greet one another." Wynne balled her hand. "Can you make a fist like this?"

They did.

Wynne gently bumped each little fist in turn, and Posy the doll for good measure. "Knuckle up."

Beaming, Dieter stared at his fist, as if some of the magic stuck to him.

Wynne passed each child a fresh pair of socks. "You, and your mother-in-law too?" she asked Nollie.

"Yes, the four of us."

Wynne dug two more pairs out of her sling. "Dieter, Hollyn, I'm going to give your mum the food, so be good helpers and hold these for her."

Drawing from the supplies in the cart, Wynne loaded a loaf of barley bread, four apples, and a hunk of dried meat into Nollie's empty, tattered basket.

"Thank you," Nollie said, adjusting her handhold to support the basket's heft. She winced and drew a sharp breath, favoring her bandaged hand.

Wynne indicated the discolored wrap. "What happened?"

"I cut myself...."

With as much time as she spent outdoors, Wynne was adept at assessing and treating minor wounds. "Do you mind if I take a look?"

Nollie offered her hand. Wynne carefully removed the dirty bandage and tried not to make a face. The gash spanned the width of the palm. The surrounding skin was red and inflamed. Greenish fluid seeped from a partial crust along the cut.

Infection.

"I know someone who can help with this," Wynne said. A ripple of stress passed over Nollie. Wynne patted the air. "It won't cost you, and it won't hurt. I'll be back."

She trotted up the path, where a bend offered a better lay of the land. Catreeny, Ben, and Elric were heading back to the cart after delivering food and blankets to another family at the second boarding house. The thwack of hammers and indistinct voices of laboring men carried from the direction of the third, partly-finished boarding house up the road. In the other direction, Wynne spotted Susi doting on a baby. Villagers flowed around them, about their business.

Where's Sender?

Jai appeared at Wynne's side and tugged on the hem of her tunic. He angled his round face upward and pointed to the runes scrawled down his left index finger. "What do they say again?"

Each Baldomar was born with a set of three runes on each finger. Individual symbols held their own meanings and minor magical effects. When combined, each set of three yielded more powerful magic, called the allur. Runes varied from person to person, so the allur took many forms, much of which was discovered through trial and informed guesswork. The first step was understanding the symbols themselves.

Wynne wrinkled her nose and tried to recall. Reading runes was like learning another alphabet, knowledge which had been lost to her people until recently. Her thoughts jumped to the piece of parchment tacked inside the kitchen cupboard, listing each family member's runes and the associated meaning.

"That one's *bear,*" she said, pointing to the dominant rune on the largest of his little knuckles. "I can't remember the rest. Ask Mum." She nodded to Susi, who now traveled toward them.

"Mumma!" Jai darted up the lane. Wynne followed. "Mumma, what do my runes say?" He held up his finger.

Susi grabbed his hand and frowned to bring them into focus. "Bear, shape, nature."

Jai concentrated. "Bear, shape, nature..."

"I don't want you testing magic right now. Where's your coat?"

"I'm hot."

"Where is it?"

Jai pointed toward the cart, where he'd tossed it haphazardly onto the bench and missed. It lay in a crumpled heap near the donkey's rear leg.

"You need to wear a coat. It's autumn and it's chilly," Susi said.

"I'm not cold."

Susi placed her hands on her hips. Never a good sign. "Put it on, and you can run around and play until we go to the south side. Or don't, and sit quietly on the bench until we finish."

Jai sagged and trudged to the cart for his coat, as though he'd been issued a terrible punishment. Wynne sympathized to an extent. For a late-autumn day, it was mild.

Catreeny and Ben drew up, snickering. Susi shook her head as Jai shrugged into the buckskin and left the front flapping open. "Always a negotiation, with that one. I don't know where he gets it."

"We're Baldomar. Stubbornness is in the blood," Catreeny said.

"He's been working hard to memorize the bear-set," Wynne said.

Susi chuckled. "And none of the others."

"Do you know where Sender is?"

"He brought a basket to Arlo and Fay fifteen minutes ago."

"If I know that man, he'll still be there, chatting-away," Ben said.

Caring for aged parents was a point of honor, but Arlo and Fay were childless, which meant the responsibility fell to the community. In their old age, they needed considerable help. Wynne wove down one windy lane, then another, and found the elderly couple beneath the overhang of their stout cabin, talking with Sender.

Sender was an easily identifiable man with thinning mouse brown hair, an expanding waist, and a hunch. Though nearing forty, his round, friendly face and patchy beard gave him a younger appearance.

The white tufts of hair around the sides of Arlo's sun-spotted head were also visible at a distance. A native Heartlander, he had a smaller frame than most Northerners. Fay was bundled to the nose in a sweater, scarf, and fur-lined coat.

"It was nosing in my flowers," she said, as animated as ever. "So I says, *Arlo! The pigs are back!* He hurried for the crossbow. Well. That pig musta known his time was nigh. He scuttled out of there right-quick."

"That's fortunate for him," Sender said. "And your flowers."

Fay hummed. "You know what I think?"

"What do you think?"

"I think Arlo put the fear into him."

"He'd put the fear into me, too." Sender gave Arlo a friendly pat on the shoulder. "I've seen you with that crossbow, my friend."

Fay brightened as Wynne approached. "Wynne, dear!"

Wynne waved and noticed the overflowing basket of bread, fruit, and dried meat nestled inside the open doorway. Sender's delivery. "How are you, Fay?"

"Oh, good. I was telling Sender here, how those pigs been getting into my garden," Fay said. "I heard one bit a child last week."

"I saw Omri this morning," Arlo said to Wynne. "He came by to look at the plot of land behind our property. Said he's going to the council for permission to build."

Uninhabited land in and around the village was considered communal. Once a person built on it, and especially if it had been with the same family for years, it was considered private property. To avoid disputes and make it official, a person needed permission from the elders if they wished to establish a house or a place of business on unclaimed land.

"We all know what happens after that. You fill it with family," Fay said in a sing-song way, blue eyes twinkling. "The boy must be getting ready. He seemed motivated."

"I'm not surprised. Responsible young man, that one," Arlo said. "Older than his years. Diligent, like his parents. He'll be a good neighbor to have."

Fay winked at Wynne. "Tell me, who does he have in mind? Surely, you must know."

Wynne laughed and scratched at the knot of hair on the back of her head. "Well..."

"You can tell us. We won't gab it 'round the village."

Wynne didn't believe her. She liked the older couple, but Fay was a notorious gossip.

She scrambled for a response. "I – he hasn't been to a dinner yet." Which was true. That wasn't until this evening. Wynne turned toward Sender before Fay pried for more. "Can you help with a healing matter over at one of the boarding houses?"

"Certainly," Sender said.

Fay placed a gentle hand on Wynne's arm. "I'm sure you know more than that, dear."

"You'll need to show me which one," Sender said, continuing to address Wynne. "All these new buildings look the same to me."

Wynne glanced between Fay and Sender, looking apologetic. "I'm sorry, Fay."

"Duty calls, my friends," Sender said with finality. He and Wynne bid the elderly couple farewell and made their way toward the main road.

"You really don't know which is which?" Wynne asked when they were out of earshot.

"Of course I do. I was there every other day when they were building it." Sender jerked thumb over his shoulder. "I was trying to spare you from more questions you can't answer."

"Many thanks." She offered her fist and he bumped it with his own.

"What's the situation?"

"Infected cut."

Sender hummed acknowledgement. It was sometimes hard to believe he and Rakel were related. She was all sharp angles and brutal efficiency. Fit, ambitious, and prone to saying no. Sender was friendly to everyone. Humble, kind, and willing to be of service. The time away with the warband seemed to have affected him. He was the same Sender, but he carried himself differently. He was at ease and decisive. It was a good change. It made Wynne like him more.

They found Nollie lingering outside the boarding house, arms wrapped around her middle as she watched the children run around the grass. They shrieked and darted, shouting new rules in an ever-evolving game of chase.

"Nollie, this is my friend, Sender Fife," Wynne said as they drew up.

"I'm told you have an injury which needs attention." Sender gestured to the dirty bandage on her hand. "Is that it?"

"Yes." Nollie hesitated, then offered her palm.

Sender carefully unwrapped the cloth. "Let's see what we have here. Hm. That looks painful."

Wynne had always known Sender to be gracious with his patients. The wound had clearly been poorly cared for. Catreeny probably would've broached

Nollie with a harsh word like, *If it needs amputation, it's your own fault.*

"Do you mind if I clear this up and close the wound?"

"What are you going to do?" Nollie asked, a note of caution in her voice.

"I'm going to use the allur – magic. It doesn't hurt."

Nollie hesitated again. "Alright."

Sender laid his hand carefully atop the palm and spoke. "*Fyrir therr hondum.*" The inky runes across his knuckles glowed fire-orange. When he lifted his hand, the cut was gone. The skin was soft and smooth.

"Oh my gods," Nollie said. Sender shared a grin with Wynne. Nollie released a little laugh and worked her palm. "It feels much better. Thank you."

"In the future, if you get a cut, it's important to keep it clean and change the bandage often. Wynne, do you have extra bandages?"

"In the cart."

"Grab her a few? Nollie, if anything else like this happens, or someone comes down with a bad cough or fever, come see me. I can't fix everything, but I'd be glad to help how I can."

Nollie flicked a droplet of water from the corner of her eye. "Thank you."

Wynne felt a friendly, affectionate pull for Sender as she retrieved the spare bandages. Moments like these kept her going. She noticed her parents up the lane, arm in arm as they took the path toward Zak and Fiona's house. Food and one of Wynne's candles rested in the basket hooked around Susi' free arm. Elric carried his bag of tools. It warmed Wynne's heart to see her parents doing good to their neighbors who desperately needed it.

Side by side. As it should be.

That. That's what I want.

She imagined, not for the first time, a future continuing this service alongside a family of her own. As always, the husband in her mental picture lacked form. He didn't feel like a real person. At least, not one that she knew. With disdain, she returned her focus to the task. She wondered – also not for the first time – if she knew any unattached man who'd engage in this work with her. Sender didn't count. She couldn't name one. Not even Harek.

8

At the sound of the latch, Harek glanced over his shoulder. Skeggis was visible above the fence. The big man swung a meaty arm over the top to unlock the gate. The dogs who'd been resting nearby snorted themselves awake. With a deep bay, Luka popped to all fours. Yamma roused her old bones with more effort.

"Easy," Harek said.

The brown eyes of both beasts darted to Harek, awaiting further instruction. He gestured for them to lie. Luka tucked his back legs beneath him and lowered, paw by paw. Old Yamma flopped sideways with less grace.

Harek jerked his chin toward Skeggis in greeting and tossed the bucket of pig guts into the feeding trough for the other hogs. He and Skeggis were an unlikely pairing of friends. Up until recently, Harek didn't like him. Riding out with the warband shifted their dynamic from acquaintances to brothers. Skeggis was good-hearted, dense, and frequently obnoxious. In battle, with magic at hand, they were a force to be reckoned.

Skeggis sauntered into the workyard. "Behold. He lives."

Harek gave him a wry look. "What brings you by?"

"You. No one's seen hide nor hair from you the last three days. Where've you been?"

Harek made a noncommittal grunt. He gestured toward the Jaegers' outbuilding where the butchering took place. "Here. Working. Recovering."

"Still hung-over? The feast was days ago. Surely, you can hold your drink better than that."

Harek said nothing. That wasn't what he meant. He wiped his hands on his filthy apron. "How's your mum?"

Skeggis eased his considerable bulk onto a rain barrel situated at the corner of the structure. "She's doing her best."

Harek nodded. He lost two siblings in his life, a baby sister when he was ten and his elder brother Eoin in the raid last year. Skeggis' younger brother, Peder, perished in the battle of Nyassa weeks earlier. The ordeal had sobered him.

"Tess told me what happened," Skeggis said.

Humiliation washed over Harek afresh. He frowned at an indistinct patch of dirt near the trough and released a slow breath. Wynne's words – her rejection – cut the knees from beneath him.

It wasn't even the *no* which bothered him most. It was the assertion that he wasn't *man-enough*. It was the look on her face which said more than anything. *I'm being gentle with you, but you should know this already.*

His whole life, he'd been known as Leland's quiet kid. Omri's quiet friend. One among many and easy to overlook. Wynne noticed him. She treated him like he mattered, quickly moving beyond the pretty girl who was nice to him, to one of his closest friends. They held a deep affection for one another, he thought. After surviving the battle in Nyassa, he concluded that he didn't want to live the rest of his life without her. For the first time, he felt like he had a spine-enough to do something about it.

He botched it.

"I made a fool of myself."

Skeggis shrugged. "We're men. We do that. Question is, what are you gonna do now?"

"I've been trying to figure that out." The options ruminating in the back of his mind lurched and shifted to the forefront, demanding attention with an urgency difficult to ignore.

"What have you come up with?"

"I figured an apology is in order."

Skeggis snapped his fingers and pointed loosely. "That's good. Start with that."

That was the simplest part.

"Drunk or not, I'm surprised she said no," Skeggis said.

"Me too."

"Did she say why?"

"I'm not husband material."

Skeggis dropped into quiet thought. He gave Harek a side eye.

"What?" Harek said.

"You're not gonna like it."

"Spit it out."

"She's right." Harek's defenses kicked in as Skeggis proceeded to count on his fingers. "You work for your pop making next to nothin'. You live at home with your parents–"

"I could build a house of my own if I wanted to."

"You haven't yet. And look at you. You look like an overgrown kid."

"Hey."

"You haven't bulked up yet. No shame, brother." Skeggis gestured down the front of himself. "Next to all this, you're gonna look lackin'."

"Anything else?" Harek said, now sorry that he asked.

"You've liked her for ages. You ever told her so?"

"She knows. Besides, why does it matter how long I've liked her?"

"Women like that sort of thing, and you have to be direct about it." Skeggis made a chopping motion in the air to emphasize the point. "Baldomar women like a man who's direct. Even the bossy ones."

"When did you become an expert on women?" Harek said, annoyed.

"Which of us is married?"

Harek threw up his hands in mock surrender.

"I'm just saying, I feel like I *get* women now."

"I seem to recall it took you a while to figure out Tess liked you."

"And you saw how quickly I acted as soon as I found out. That's romance, my friend."

Harek said nothing. Another way they were different.

"Look. I know you're embarrassed," Skeggis said. "Feeling lousy. Worthless. Depressed. Wondering if you'll die alone –"

"Alright, alright."

"I've come to bring you hope."

"Could've fooled me."

"Wynne didn't say she'd never marry you. She said you're not ready yet." Skeggis pointed at Harek and leveled a knowing look at him. "There's your hope."

He wasn't wrong.

"Her qualms are all things you can do something about," Skeggis said. "You want a wife, then act in a way that'll attract a good woman. Wynne, or someone else."

"There is no one else."

"Fine. Wynne, then. So what are you gonna do?"

The blurred outlines of Harek's plans sharpened. Harek glanced at Luka. His wardog had been a gift from an ally general for his valor in the Battle of Nyassa. In the short time since, Harek had grown to love him. Harek's rune-given ability to speak with animals aided the loyalty and understanding between them.

Luka wasn't just a dog in the same way Judge wasn't just a horse. He represented what Harek was capable of achieving. Of who he was capable of being.

His thoughts drifted to his time away and the war he helped win. To the glory he earned out in the wider world, and the comparative lack of it here.

He loved his home and his family. He loved Wynne. But he lived in a shadow.

"I know what to do."

9

From the treetop lookout, Wynne leaned against the window frame. The rising sun gave the sky a purple cast which shed a pinkish hue over the land. She drew a deep breath. The crisp morning air was a welcome shock to her lungs. The forest was peacefully quiet apart from the birds.

Scouts were told in training to be constantly vigilant. Experienced scouts could pay half as much attention and still have a sense for when something wasn't right. Wynne was in the latter group most days. The peace of the morning gave way to her wandering mind.

She'd managed to talk her parents out of hosting a dinner with Garriden, the blind minister. She wasn't going to be able to squirm out of these dinners forever. They had an argument to make. Wynne was the right age. This is how her people handled these matters. They wanted her to enjoy a family of her own.

With all the returning heroes, the midwives would be incredibly busy nine months from now. She only hoped it would keep her busy enough until the right suitor presented himself. Certainly, she'd feel less panicky about the whole ordeal with the right person.

Her thoughts drifted toward Harek and a complicated set of emotions unfurled within her. She was still bothered by his drunken proposal. She'd made up her mind not to seek him out. What would she say anyway? This was made easier by the irritating fact that he seemed intent to avoid her.

Inwardly, she lamented how this was proof he wasn't right for her. His behavior stood as yet another example of a perfectly good opportunity gone to pot, which seemed to be the defining characteristic of their dynamic.

Her conscience twisted miserably at the allegation, and she walked it back.

She was brought back to the day on the bridge, two weeks before her coming of age. One week before the warband left. No one knew how long they'd be gone or whether they'd return, and Wynne felt like she was straddling a knife's edge. She, like everyone else, wrestled with the press of grief and uncertainty.

In her heart of hearts, she hoped the impending departure would finally inspire Harek to find the boldness she wanted from him. They wouldn't be the only ones. Everywhere she turned, declarations of love abounded. There'd been two hasty marriages that month already. As he walked her home, the hopes which had been toying with her heart for months danced around the edge of her mind.

She didn't remember why they'd been teasing each other. It was the same comfortable play which characterized so many of their interactions. He'd push. She'd take the invitation and push back. At one point he gave her an exaggerated up-down and remarked, "That's an awful lot of lip from you."

"What are you going to do about it?" She took a step toward him and lifted her chin. A playful dare as much as an invitation.

Harek watched her for a beat, reading her mood. Without warning, he swept her off her feet and threw her over his shoulder.

Wynne yelped. "What are you doing?"

"Teaching you a lesson."

"What has gotten into you? Put me down."

Harek marched toward the footbridge spanning the Bekker.

"Where are we going?"

"Swimming. Well, you are."

"You better not."

"Look at that. The water is nice and clear."

"*Harek –*"

"Wynne."

"Don't you even think about it."

"Hmm – hey!" He squirmed as she dug her fingers into his ribs. "I wouldn't do anything to make me drop you."

Wynne growled and balled her hands.

"Now say you're sorry."

"This is very undignified."

"Is that a, *no?*"

Wynne assumed a lofty air. "I will not debase myself –"

"Alright, then."

She felt the shift of his muscles as he broadened his stance and braced to hurl her over the edge of the bridge. "Harek! Don't you dare – I am the daughter of an elder –"

"You're adopted."

Wynne shrieked as she sailed through the air. A surge of cold and wet enveloped her body and closed over her head. He leapt in after her. The splash hit her in the face.

And just like that, the opportunity closed as things swung in the direction they always did – play. Not much else.

She liked those times. It made her feel like he truly enjoyed her. They made her enjoy him in a way which longed for more.

The snap of a branch drew her out of her thoughts. She pricked her ears, identifying the rustle of feet through the forest detritus far below.

"Wynne?"

The pleasant deep voice surprised her. She crossed to the other window in a hurry and thrust her head out. At the base of the lookout tower, Harek craned his neck for a glimpse into the branches. He was accompanied by his wardog.

"What are you doing here?" she asked. "It's early."

"I know. I need to talk to you. Can you come down?"

Wynne's heart thrummed against the tension. *What does that mean?*

She hesitated a moment too long, and Harek's expression slid into a mix of disappointment and frustration.

"I'll be right down," she added quickly, to make up for her delay.

Back inside, Wynne gave herself a moment's pause before dropping the rope ladder. A dormant longing stirred inside her as she recalled their time together at the homecoming feast. The hours dancing and laughing. His hand on her waist. The way he smiled.

How the evening ended.

She smoothed the wisps of hair away from her face, rubbed the front of her teeth with the edge of her sleeve, and straightened her overclothes. She tossed the ladder through the hole.

She reached the bottom and angled herself toward him, one hand on the rope. She kept her expression impassive. His hair stuck out from beneath his knitted cap, nearly reaching the collar of his heavy hide jacket. His beard was combed and trimmed and his clothes cleaned. He looked nervous.

The wardog stood at ease by his side, occasionally glancing up at him for direction. It looked like a timber wolf with flop ears, only thicker, with droopy lips and wrinkles. More like a bear than a dog. Wynne knew Harek wasn't the only man in town to be gifted one – Skeggis had one too – and Wynne heard there was an interesting story behind it. If it was any other time, she'd ask. But it wasn't, so she didn't.

"Hi," she said, keeping her tone light and open. She wasn't about to fake normalcy between them, but she didn't want to punish him.

"I wanted to apologize," he said, looking her square in the face. "I regret my actions the other day. I was drunk. Too forward. I realize asking you to marry me like that..." He cleared his throat and dropped his eyes briefly, as if gathering his thoughts, or his nerves. "You deserve better."

It disarmed her.

The tension in Wynne's shoulders and forehead eased. "I forgive you."

"I do want to marry you."

A riot of feelings erupted inside Wynne, and it was difficult to keep a smile from her eyes. "I –"

Harek held up a palm. "Don't say anything. I've been thinking about what you said." He plowed ahead as if he couldn't afford to lose focus on the things he needed to get out. "You're right. There are matters I need to take care of first. I'm gonna do that. There's no chance of your pops approving of me as is. Right now, you could throw a rock and hit any number of men better suited than me." There was no self-pity in his voice. No baiting for reassurance. "So, I'm planning to leave for Goldbur Gren."

Wynne's perfect happiness died. "Wait –what?"

"There's a group of twenty or so, heading out in a few days. I'm going with them."

Reeling, Wynne tightened her grip on the rope ladder to reorient herself physically as much as mentally. "You're leaving?"

"Not forever."

"You're not going to winter here?"

Harek shook his head. "They need help now. The pay is good, and the opportunity won't last forever. I'm going to work hard and earn some money so I can set things in order for us."

At a loss for words, Wynne contended with a pang of grief far greater than she expected. Stories from Omri about the dangers of the world blew across the back of her mind. Some part of her wondered if she'd ever see him again.

Weak in the limbs, and before she could talk herself out of it, she closed the distance between them. She leaned into him and he held her tightly. She shut her eyes. "I'm going to miss you."

"I'll come back to you. I promise."

Dearest Wynne,

I am writing from Goldbur Gren. Or what remains of the Gren. I recall stories of it from my father. As a boy, the idea of stone buildings and even roads was enough to excite my curiosity. It's strange to see it now. It's a pile of rubble. In a way, my hopes and expectations feel equally shattered.

However, work has begun to clear the way for the future Gren. I'm astonished at the progress. This week, we intend to start construction of a preliminary defensive wall. Our people are wielding magic with such ingenuity and skill. At the battle of Nyassa, I felt proud of the destructive power we brought to bear. Now, I find myself filled with a far greater pride for what we can create. Wynne, I truly believe Goldbur Gren will someday be finer than Nyassa!

The efforts to make it a basic, functioning city will take many months. You wouldn't guess it by the amount of optimism. You'd think we'd have it built in a fortnight. I think this is in large part because we are well-supplied and our leadership is working to keep morale high. Josef and Aeryn are nearly unrecognizable. You would be proud.

Right now, I'm working with the majority of the laborers in clean-up. Each day is long, and the work is strenuous. Josef joked that I am a natural at breaking and moving stone. He sometimes refers to me as Stonebreaker, his old moniker.

Unfortunately, it's not without incidents. Yesterday a partially collapsed building shifted unexpectedly and crushed a man's leg. I am taking great care, and accidents of that nature are rare. Eventually, the clean-up will come to an end, and I've been looking into other opportunities.

I've been assigned the task of cook by my bunk mates. They're convinced I use magic when I prepare the meat. I'm convinced they simply haven't enjoyed a properly cooked piece of meat until recently.

I've found camaraderie with many new people. Cain, a human from a city in central Noemar, is an adept archer and flute player. He's also a wit, but I won't have him knowing I think so.

Finnion is a Baldomar. He's our age and grew up as a slave in a noble house which served Malachai. The lord of house bought him as a child with the intent of using him for his magical abilities. Of course, he couldn't understand his runes. He won't say much more on the topic, but I'm convinced they heaped abuses on him for his failure to produce magic. He has frequent nightmares and talks in his sleep. I've made it a point to help him in every way I'm able. He's reluctant to learn his runes and use magic which draws the ire of others. Still, he works tirelessly and has been a good companion in all other ways.

I intend to write as often as I am able, and I hope my letters continue to find you well. If it pleases you, I would be glad to receive letters in return. I think of you fondly and often.

Yours,

Harek

10

Present

Afternoon sun peeked through the sweeping pine boughs. Wynne dreamily trod along the worn forest foottrails as beams of light fell on her face. Usually, the Enclave was blanketed in snow by now. Instead, leaves carpeted the forest floor in shades of scarlet, brown, and gold. Another mild autumn.

In the year since Harek left, he'd written a stack of letters which she'd read and reread a dozen times. In quiet moments like these, she found herself thinking about him and what the next letter might bring.

A tell-tale snuffling instantly brought her reverie to an end. Her senses sharpened.

She moved silently, searching for the boar nearby. She spotted it in the distance, scrounging in the undergrowth. Heart pounding, she pressed herself against the nearest tree and remained motionless while she observed. The tusks indicated an adult male, yet by any other measure, he was a runt. Perhaps his physical impairment carried over to his intelligence. Roaming the forest alone was a sure way to get himself killed by a dozen different predators.

Including Wynne.

He continued to root in the soft earth, ignoring her.

She waited and listened for any sign of the herd. When she allowed herself to settle upon the conclusion that he was alone, she felt herself shift from a survival-mindset, to *hunter*.

The Enclave prohibited hunting alone, particularly if the prey was boar.

Unilaterally aggressive, their size, strength, and fearless demeanor made boars dangerous.

The opportunity was too good to resist.

Careful to avoid sudden movements, Wynne's hand traveled to Splitter hanging from her belt.

"Fyrir therr hondum."

She whispered the allur and felt the familiar warm tingle of the runes beneath her gloves. She was adept with her throwing axe without magic. With it, she never missed. That's what she needed. A quick kill, with no room for error.

She cocked her arm, planted one foot forward, and sent Splitter cutting through the air. She felt her connection to the axe end when it struck its target, and the boar fell without a squeal.

She returned the axe to her belt and crouched beside her kill. She gave it a pat. "You're going to feed many people. Now, how am I going to get you home?"

Ahead, the ferns shivered. Wynne stopped breathing as the enormous snout, flashy tusks, and bristly head of a much larger male emerged. Her eyes grew wide as she felt herself shift to *survival* once again.

The boar screamed and lurched toward her.

Wynne shot to her feet. She tore back the way she came. Without uttering the allur, she felt her magic flowing. She found herself deftly dodging and weaving through every obstacle, simultaneously picking a path which would hinder her pursuer. This wasn't a race she could win flat out.

She also couldn't keep it up forever. She needed a sturdy, low-hanging branch to swing onto. Or a boulder upon which she could make a stand. Or enough distance to give her the time to turn and strike out with an axe throw.

Right now, it took everything she had just to keep from being gored. She could feel the beast's hot breath on her heels, closing in.

Her magical senses warned her before her mind could comprehend that a man had stepped into her path from behind a wide tree. She crashed into him, and they became a tangle of arms and legs.

The boar drew to an abrupt stop, apparently startled by this. Wynne looked up as the beast observed in confusion. Her eye contact might've been enough to jar its senses back to the chase. It charged. With efficiency of movement, she grasped her axe, cried the allur, and hurled Splitter.

And it was over.

Wynne sprawled onto her back, chest rising and falling as she caught her breath. With legs still splayed across the man's, she turned to appraise her unintended casualty.

Stunned, he looked back at her with chestnut colored eyes. She rolled off him and stood as gracefully as she could. She noted his rugged traveling clothes, the oversized pack, and the dirty boots. *Traveler or refugee.* She guessed he was close to thirty. Despite her initial assessment, she found her normal scout's suspicion overridden. *He's handsome.*

The man pushed himself upright while she brushed and straightened her clothing in vain.

"Good gods," he said as he took in the scene before him. He had the accent of a Northerner, but his cropped hair was uncommonly dark for a man of Noemar. His beard was a shade darker than that, thick and even. His bright eyes met hers and a smile rested naturally on his lips. "You saved my life."

That was an exaggeration. Still, he struck Wynne as good-natured, so she responded with a smile and extended a hand. "I also ran you over. It was the least I could do."

On his feet, he rivaled Baldomar men. He was tall and strong.

"That was the best part," he said as he dusted his trousers. He flashed another grin, revealing a row of straight, clean teeth. "The throw was good, too. I'm Kalomir."

"Wynne."

"Is there anything I can do to repay you, Wynne?"

Wynne recognized a hint of suggestion in his tone.

She decided to take advantage. "You could help me haul the boar back to town."

"There's a town nearby?"

She pointed in the general direction. "We call it the Enclave. It was once the sole refuge of the Baldomar." She allowed a hint of playfulness to enter her voice. "Do I look like a forest-dwelling wild-woman?"

He motioned with his hand to all of her. "I mean..."

Wynne feigned shock. "Now you're definitely helping me carry these back."

"*These?*" He laughed. "I think you took a hit to the head."

"I killed another one back the way I came."

Kalomir's face fell as he looked down on the large boar.

"Don't worry. The other is smaller," she said. "Follow me."

Kalomir's relief was apparent when they reached the first boar. "Is this why the big one was out for blood? You killed its child?"

"It's not a child."

Kalomir responded with a look of disbelief.

Wynne considered. "...I guess it could have been."

He nodded.

She suppressed a laugh at his expression. "Less talk. More help."

Kalomir bent to grab the hind legs, but she stopped him.

"Wait. We can do this the easy way or the hard way."

"There's an easy way?"

"Depends. Do you have any line?"

"I do."

"Then, yes. There is. May I use it?"

Kalomir produced a sufficient length of rope from his pack.

"I'll cut a sturdy branch," she said, removing Splitter from her belt again. "We'll tie the boars up and carry them between us. I'll check the wood if you'll take the rope and haul this guy back to the other."

When Wynne returned, dragging a freshly hewn branch, she went to work. She laid the pole beside the pigs. As she tied one then the other by the ankles, she caught Kalomir's eyes on her, subtly enjoying the view.

"What are you looking at?" she asked, keeping her tone neutral.

"I was just admiring your knot-tying."

Wynne smirked and rolled her eyes as she tightened the next knot. "Where are you from?"

"A small village outside of Austerholt."

"That's a long journey on foot."

"It is? I thought I was getting close."

Standing, they each grabbed one end of the pole and positioned it on a shoulder with effort.

"I suppose it is, in a sense," she said, wincing as she adjusted her end into a more comfortable position. They started walking. "You don't know where you are?"

"I'm in the wood just outside the Enclave. Once the sole refuge of the Baldomar."

"Oh, aren't you clever? What were you doing so far from home?"

"Work. I ran into some trouble and decided to return."

"That's more vague than an explanation. Are you a criminal?"

"I couldn't bear to frighten you with the truth."

"Criminals don't scare me."

"Is that so?"

"Of course not. I'm a Baldomar."

"Oh, gods. I'm so sorry," he said, suddenly embarrassed. "I had no idea you were a child."

Wynne stopped walking and looked at him over her shoulder. "A child? I'm a woman, thank you."

"But I thought the Baldomar were all giants. You're...not." At this, his genuine tone faltered and he smirked.

Her eyebrows climbed. *Short jokes?*

Wynne let her end of the branch drop suddenly a few inches.

"Gods –" He lurched to recover.

Wynne snickered.

The weight of the boars was nearly unbearable for Wynne. She and

Kalomir fell into a contented quiet for a long while. He broke the silence after twenty minutes of steady walking. "How close did you say the town is?"

"We're not going to the town."

"Where are we going?"

"There's a farmer with land abutting the wood. We're going there. Then we're going to town."

"Why?"

"Because I can't carry these gods-forsaken things all the way in. We're getting a cart." Wynne shook her head. "I killed these mongrels and right now I feel like I've lost."

"Good thing I came along when I did."

✧

They waded through the high grasses onto Lugh's land, following the sound of his voice. The middle-aged farmer stood in the yard at the back of the house, complaining to Rakel about the pigs which had wandered into his garden to root around.

Rakel frowned at their approach. She was a tall, imposing woman with ice-blue eyes made more striking by heavy kohl. To her right, Peig the cow stood in the open doorway of Lugh's barn, eyes half-lidded, chewing cud. A hodge-podge of handmade barding covered her bulk, with ribbons pinned to the shoulder like she was a decorated general.

Kalomir's voice came from behind. "Is that cow wearing leather armor?"

"You noticed. A word of caution, don't mention it." Wynne allowed her voice to carry, as she greeted the spirited farmer. "Lugh! I need a favor."

He cast a curious appraisal at the pigs dangling between her and Kalomir. "Look at that! Rakel, you're ahead of this. I'm glad you got your best on the job."

Rakel said nothing.

"What kind of favor?"

"I need to borrow a wheelbarrow."

"A'ight." Lugh left them without further question to retrieve one from his toolshed.

Rakel jerked her chin at Kalomir. "Who are you?"

"I'm Kalomir."

"Kalomir what?"

"Kalomir, son of Kiren. From Austerholt."

Rakel made a noise halfway between a hum and a grunt. "What are you doing here?"

As Kalomir reiterated the vague version of what he told Wynne, Lugh returned with the wheelbarrow. Half-listening, he dropped the legs in the grass and helped guide the boars into it. The weight on Wynne's upper body lessened. Her whole body seemed to sigh.

Lugh waggled his hand to indicate his land. "Don't suppose any of your kids been runnin' around here?" he said, almost accusatory.

"No, sir. No children," Kalomir said.

"I assume you need a place to stay," Rakel said.

"Yes. Is there an inn?"

"No. You'll want to see Elric about lodging and food." She turned to Wynne who was in the middle of untying the rope. "Can you take him?"

"I need to get this to the Jaegers first."

Rakel's eyes jumped beyond Wynne to the dirt road leading into the village. She spotted Omri with his bag of tools, talking with Skeggis outside of Brinja's house. Wynne recalled the long list of repairs Tess mentioned, and she guessed Skeggis had enlisted Omri's help for the bigger ones. Which was smart. Omri had learned a lot from Elric and was handy.

Rakel placed her finger to her lips and emitted a shrill whistle, drawing every eye in the vicinity. She waved Omri over with a single flick of her hand. "You can go," she said to Wynne.

Wynne turned to Kalomir and passed the coiled rope back to him "Omri'll get you situated. He's a good one to talk to if you have any other questions. Where to work, where to buy and sell."

"Alright."

"I'll probably see you around. Good luck. Many thanks, Lugh. I'll bring it back."

Wynne hiked up the wheelbarrow with a little grunt. Maintaining control was more difficult than expected, but she managed to avoid embarrassing herself. As she crossed Omri's path, he slowed, spared a questioning look at the wheelbarrow full of pigs, and decided not to ask.

"Who's that with Barky?" he said, dropping his voice.

Wynne glanced over her shoulder and caught Kalomir's eye. He offered her a smile, and she returned it. "A newcomer."

11

Wynne eased the wheelbarrow down the bumpy dirt road. Kal watched her go. He wished she hadn't. He recognized his level of interest might've had something to do with her being the first woman to smile at him in weeks. It was quite a smile.

Really, it could've been any number of things. The way her hair rested over her shoulder. The steel blue eyes. Her petite frame. Though her clothing obscured her shape, the layers didn't hide everything. She was gorgeous. Funny. She carried herself with a refined strength, spirited energy, and ladylike composure he'd never quite encountered. He liked how she pushed back at him. As if their interaction was a game she was willing to play.

This couldn't be the last time they talked.

He never got the icy woman's name. With a few blunt words, she passed him off to a young man named Omri, then returned her attention to the farmer and his issue with trespassing hogs. Kal guessed Omri was around ten years his junior. He was shorter than Kal but wider, with a thick head of ruddy brown hair and the build of a man who'd have a barrel chest given a few years. He carried himself with friendly competence and seemed willing to regard Kal as an equal, which put him at ease.

Kal nodded up the lane in Wynne's direction. "Who is that?"

Omri glanced. "That's Wynne. She didn't tell you her name?"

"She did. I'm just wondering about her. I want to talk to her."

Granted, that wasn't all Kal wanted to do, but Omri was a stranger and Kal was new here. Until he got used to the local customs and familiar with who was attached to whom, he thought it best to behave himself. Or, at least keep his speech clean.

"To thank her," he added. "Do you know where I can find her?"

"She lives at the Thars' house."

"Alright." That meant nothing to Kal, but it was a small village. It shouldn't be that difficult to find. Kal watched her disappear up the lane. "Is she attached?"

He couldn't read Omri's expression. "She's not."

"Good to know."

12

Wynne rooted through the coneflower patch at the edge of the front yard. A hen strutted nearby with an assortment of soft clucks, like she was annoyed that Wynne discovered her spot.

"I don't know what you have against the nest box, you odd bird," Wynne said as she fished four sandy-brown eggs from amongst the stiff, leathery leaves.

More clucks.

Wynne added the eggs to her basket, stood, and brushed her hands clean. She'd been up since dawn, and after two hours of morning chores, collecting eggs signaled the last of it.

She heard her name and glanced up the dirt road running before the house. All smiles, Kalomir sidestepped a passerby. He held his shoulders back and waved. At a glance, it was evident that he'd had a decent night's rest. He wore the same bark-brown trousers as the day before, and a dark red sweater with elbow patches. Wynne liked the color red. It looked good on him.

"Look who it is," she said.

"Good morning," he said as he drew up to the property. He braced a hand on the post-and-rail fence and hopped it. It made Wynne second-guess her estimate of his age. Hopping fences, while bold and amusing, was behavior she'd expect from a younger man, not one nearing thirty.

"You look like you're in a good mood. Spend a comfortable night?"

He placed a hand on his chest. "Like heaven. A little crowded, but dry and warm."

"Glad to hear it."

Something on the ground near Wynne's feet caught his eye and distracted him. "Why is that hen giving you a dark look?"

"She's mad I found her secret egg-laying place."

"What is it with you and animals?"

"I don't know what you're talking about. Animals love me." The hen pecked at her boot. Wynne shooed her gently with her toe. "Cut it out."

Kalomar shook his head, wearing a little smirk.

Wynne pointed at him, not really offended. "Not a word."

He mimed locking his lips and tossed an imaginary key over his shoulder.

"What brings you by?" she asked.

"I was looking for you. I spoke with Elric yesterday. You know, the elder? Big, bald man with the bushy beard?"

He doesn't realize he's talking about my father. Why hadn't Omri mentioned the connection?

The most-likely answer only took only a beat to work out and had less to do with Wynne and more to do with Omri. His sense of humor had a mischievous bend to it, and he could find humor in everything. Growing up under the attentive eyes of Susi and Elric, he got away with very little. He relished the opportunity for a little fun when he could. *Probably enjoying the anonymity.*

"He said there's plenty of work available while the weather holds," Kalomir continued. "I'll be at the lumberyard all day."

"I'm glad you found some work so fast." She found it endearing that he felt the need to come by and tell her how he was settling. Then again, she'd been the first person he met here. There was a friendly connection. "How long do you think you'll be staying? The winter?"

"At least."

"I suppose that means I'll be seeing more of you."

He flashed a charming grin. "I hope so. You should call me Kal."

"Kal?"

"Short for Kalomir. Don't tell me you forgot my name between yesterday afternoon and now."

"How could I forget? It was a memorable afternoon."

"I'll say. It's not every day a beautiful woman winds up on top of me in the woods."

"Not every day? Only some of the days?"

Kal hesitated. "Never, actually. You'd be the first."

Wynne laughed a little and his smile broadened.

What are you doing?

The chiding thought blew across her mind. That answer was simple enough, too. Kal might've been a stranger, but he was friendly and easily one of the better-looking men in the village. Despite her reservations, part of her enjoyed his attention. Normally, she never received interest in this manner. This was, in part, the result of her own choices – she kept clear of the tavern and avoided brazen fellows. Primarily, it was her parents. From what she'd gathered, almost no one wanted to be the first to test Elric by demonstrating an outright interest in his only daughter.

"I noticed there's a tavern not far from here," Kal said. "Would you care to join me later? Let me buy you a drink to thank you for your help yesterday."

At the word *tavern*, Wynne contended with a tug against her good mood, and it made her uncomfortable with herself. She had no right to be disappointed. What did she expect? He was a newcomer, not a Baldomar. It wasn't like Kal was a consideration, the vagabond. The remark brought her back to earth. She patted the air. "You don't need to do that."

"I want to." He touched her on the arm.

Wynne wasn't sure how to respond.

The invitation might've been a gesture of interest. It was also Kal's way to test the waters. To see who and what he could get, and she knew it. Since she wasn't about to get drunk and fool around with him, she reckoned he'd move on. Quickly. Though it was hard to categorically dismiss him, she'd seen and heard enough to know how it went.

"Kal, I appreciate it, but I'm working late tonight."

"How late?"

"Midnight." She realized, as the word left her mouth, telling a relative stranger when she was getting home might not be wise.

A riffle of surprise passed over him. "What can you possibly be doing so late?"

"I'm a scout."

"Ah. Now that makes more sense than *killer of pig children.*"

She smirked despite herself.

"If not tonight, what about tomorrow?"

"Another late shift."

"When are you available, then?"

Wynne took a breath. She had to hand it to him. He was persistent. "I'm not going to the tavern with you."

His grin faltered.

She rested a hand on his arm. "If it makes you feel any better, I'm not going to the tavern with anyone. I don't like the tavern."

"What do you like?" he asked, hope rekindled. He sounded genuinely interested, and she almost felt bad for turning him down.

A sudden crash erupted inside the house. The front door banged open and a furry brown blur darted into the yard. A bear cub.

Kal and Wynne each took an uneasy step back. The cub hesitated when it noticed them. It stood on its back legs, placed front paws on its hips, and urinated in their direction.

Kal's face bent in confusion. "That bear just came out of...?"

"Oh, no, you don't!" Susi's voice carried from within the home. The bear returned to all fours and beat a hasty retreat. Its path curved away from Wynne and Kal as it loped toward the far side of the yard.

Susi burst through the door. She was drenched down the front and long, frizzy strands escaped the knot pinned atop her head. She had a focused, albeit wild, look in her eye as she glanced right, then left. Spotting the bear, she hiked up her skirts and pursued. "Jairus, get back here!"

The cub's pace increased precipitously.

Wynne suddenly realized the significance of the runeset Jai had been working to memorize. She tried not to laugh and failed. "I need to help with this."

She dashed around the other side of the house to intercept her little brother, leaving Kal startled and confused in the yard.

13

Kal disliked the lumberyard. There were limited tools, and most of his own were useless here. The work was strenuous and dull. Chop that. Move this here. Stack those there.

As soon as they learned he was a skilled fine carpenter, they set him the task of cutting roof shingles. Hundred of them. It required a certain precision to make a consistent size with as little waste as possible. It was dissatisfying and repetitive. Still, it beat hauling logs or working the two-man saw to cut boles down to size.

The lumberyard was situated on the northwest side of the village, near the place where Kal and Wynne entered from the woods the other day. He hadn't seen her since the previous morning, but she floated around the edges of his mind whenever it wasn't occupied. Which, given the menial nature of his work, was often.

He visited the tavern the night before and would again later. The ale was decent. The food, edible. A man had to eat, and he hadn't yet figured out what else there was to do around here. During his visit, he noticed the establishment didn't attract the most ladylike of women. The atmosphere was great if he was interested in low hanging fruit. If Wynne refused to go there, that said something about her. About what kind of woman she was.

Difficult to reach.

Difficult, but not impossible. Kal didn't mind the challenge.

The lumberyard also sat near the grounds where knots of Baldomar went to practice their magic. Over the racket of tools and the conversational cussing of men at work, he sometimes heard the clang of swords while Baldomar men sparred one another in the distance, or the gallop of hooves as people trained with their horses, or cries of the phrase they used to initiate their magic. He glimpsed the occasional burst of flame or flash of light. It kept the day semi-interesting.

He tossed another shingle into the growing pile nearby and noticed Omri speaking with the foreman, Visseny. They knocked knuckles – another interesting custom – as their conversation came to an end. Before departing, Omri spotted Kal.

Kal lifted an arm in a wave.

Omri sauntered over and observed the stacks Kal accomplished in the last two hours. "Shingles, eh?"

"Hundreds of them," Kal said. "What brings you by, friend?" It wasn't work. He remembered Omri mentioning that he was rather handy and trying to build his business. Whatever that meant.

"Placing an order. Building material for my own house."

Kal pointed at the pile with his straight edge. "So I should blame you for all this?"

Omri raised a palm in mock surrender. "Look, every Baldomar man worth his salt buys or builds his own house. Especially if he wants a wife." He considered for a beat. "Usually."

"I thought you had a house."

"It's not mine. I'm only keeping it inhabited while the owner's away."

"A wife, eh? You got someone in mind?"

"Her name's Lara," Omri said, brightening.

Kal had seen that look before. He'd worn that look before. "Good for you, friend."

The mention of women turned Kal's mind involuntarily to Wynne. As if Omri sensed this, he asked, "Did you talk to Wynne?"

"I went by the house where she's staying. I asked her to the tavern."

"How'd that go?" Omri slipped his hands in his pockets.

Kal searched for the right words. "Hard to say."

"She turned you down?"

"She did."

Omri hummed. "She's not really a tavern-going kind of gal."

"She mentioned. What kind of gal is she, then? Do you know her well?"

"Probably better than most." Omri caught the look on Kal's face and added, "Not like that."

"Oh. Okay. That's good."

"What do you want to know?"

"What does she like?"

"She likes babies."

"Babies?" That made him a little nervous, though he supposed it was a good quality.

"She's training to become a midwife."

"She told me she's a scout."

"She's that too."

"Huh."

"She's one of a kind."

"You don't have to tell me," Kal said, hastening the next time their paths crossed. "What do people do around here for fun?"

"We like celebrations. Hospitality. We practice our magic. We work...."

Kal winced. "For fun?"

Omri shrugged. Excited by a new thought, he snapped his fingers and pointed at Kal. "The Ice Throw."

"What's that?"

"Every year on the first heavy snowfall, we hold a friendly, village-wide competition. People take to the street, pack the snow into hunks, and huck it at each other until there's one person standing. It's the best day of the year."

Kal cracked a grin. "That does sound fun."

"You said you're from Austerholt? I heard the winter's brutal further north."

"It is. Which is why I'm planning to winter here. Assuming it ever shows up."

"How's your aim?"

"Decent."

"Then we need to talk about teaming up. We might even unseat Nialls this year."

"Who's Nialls?"

"Another elder. From even further north than Austerholt." Omri pivoted. He shielded his eyes and cast his gaze toward the training grounds. "You see that man with the white hair and face tattoos?"

Kal couldn't see tattoos at their distance. Still, he knew who Omri meant. Yesterday, Nialls made a brief, unsettling appearance in the tavern. He didn't sit. Didn't order a drink. He simply surveyed the room as though searching for a potential trouble-maker, spared a few words with barkeep, then left. Though he seemed to have a good camaraderie with the other Baldomar men, he made the icy woman feel like a warm summer day.

"That's Nialls?"

"He's the reigning Ice Throw champion."

"There's a champion?"

"Of course there's a champion. You get the seat of honor at the feast afterward. There's dancing. Music. Beer. It's a good time."

That sounded like a good opportunity, when the time came. His mind drifted back toward his interaction with Wynne the day before.

"When I went by yesterday, there was a bear," Kal said without preamble.

Omri's eyebrows jumped. "A bear?"

"I was speaking with Wynne when it ran out of the house, peed at us, and fled."

"Ah, yes. I've seen that bear."

"You have?"

"It's her brother."

"You're joking."

"Nope."

Kal gave him a wry look. "Yeah, alright."

✧

Noon approached. Kal considered whether to stay at the lumberyard to eat with the other men, or wander toward the training ground. The activity had continued and sparked further curiosity.

He wondered what Wynne's runes did. Especially after talking with Omri, he couldn't get her out of his head. Maybe there was a magic-related reason behind it.

Visseny plopped another section of bole for Kal to cut. "Last one before we break."

"Alright." *Thank the gods.* Before the foreman sauntered away, Kal stopped him. "Question."

Visseny's feet slowed. His perpetual scowl shifted. "Ask."

"Your runes. They're magic."

"Yeah..."

"You have to use the words to make it work?"

"More to it than that. You don't, if you're practiced enough."

"What can they do?"

"Mine, or in general?"

"Either. Both."

Visseny cast a palm to the air. "All kindsa things. We got people who control fire. Snow. Alter their weapons. One lady could shoot a bow and arrow and it turned into a lightning bolt."

"You're kidding."

"Nope. Real useful fighting dragons," Visseny said. "Not all runes are combat related, though. We got craftsmen who work metal like nothing you've ever seen. Folks who can multiply the food they prepare, or the wool they spin. Some people speak other languages without ever having learned them." Visseny snorted. "One guy I know is ridiculously lucky. Got the runes for *luck* on four different fingers."

"Sounds useful in a game of cards."

Visseny chuckled. "Took about five seconds for him to figure that out. That man shoulda been dead many times over, the number of scrapes he's been in. Always seems to come out unscathed."

"Is there a rune for...making someone like you?" It sounded stupid when Kal said it out loud. This was reflected back to him in Visseny's expression. "You know, for making an impression. Are there ones which make it so you're attracted to someone? You can't stop thinking about them?"

As he spoke, Kal realized that his attempt to clarify only made it worse. He couldn't seem to stop himself from blathering.

Visseny gave Kal a funny look. "What are you talking about?"

With a flush of embarrassment, Kal dropped his eyes to his block and tools. "Nevermind."

Dearest Wynne,

Horses.

That was my response to you when you asked me what I'd do for work, if I could do anything. I remember the day two years ago as clearly as I remember what I ate for breakfast this morning. You'd found me working in the yard and instantly read the heaviness weighing on me. You leaned on the fence, face open and full of spunk. "What's the matter?"

I hesitated, wondering whether to burden you with complaints about my lot. In response, you hopped onto the fence, swung your legs over, and sat prim. "Tell me your woes. I'm all ears."

It brought a much needed smile. You knew I only needed a nudge.

"It's my brother's gelding," I confessed. Eoin had perished in the raid two months prior. His home and the stable was burnt and damaged beyond repair, but several animals survived, including Judge. My family lacked the space for more than the shire horse, so they'd been paying Ned Goodhill to stable him. "My father wants to give Judge to Taige."

"I thought your family was keeping him?"

I shook my head no. "Horses need a lot of care. My folks don't have the time, and paying Ned costs more than they're willing to spend. I don't think he should go to Taige."

"Who should he go to?"

"Me," I said emphatically. "Judge is not just a horse. Eoin worked hard for him. I learned to ride on him. He should stay in the family."

"Have you told this to your father?"

"No. I've been mulling it over. With what I'm making, I could afford him. I could assume all responsibility. Then he's not a burden to my folks."

"Harek, these are worthwhile points to make."

I made a noncommittal noise. At that moment, Yamma appeared in the open doorway. The old girl noticed us at the fence and bounded forward in her long-limbed, furry half-sprint. She braced both paws on the fence to bring her face close enough to lick yours. With a word, I brought her back to her senses, and she returned to all fours and slunk toward my side.

"Thank you for saving my new sweater," you said. It was the dark red one with the black edge, and it looked nice on you. "You're good with animals."

"Animals are easier than people," I said, giving Yamma a scratch behind the ears.

You laughed at this. "Well, sure. They can never tell you when you're wrong."

"Oh, they disagree aplenty. Trust me. Granted, it's never anything too substantial." Yamma huffed and flopped at my feet. "I hear you're working with Catreeny now."

"She's agreed to start training me in midwifery." You wrinkled your nose. "Do you think it's strange?"

"Why would I think it's strange?"

"It's filthy work."

"I do filthy work. At least you're helping to bring about a miracle. Someone has to do it. I think you'll do a fine job."

Your smile reached your eyes.

"Does this mean no more scouting for you?"

You shrugged. "After what happened, my folks have reservations. So do I. I also don't want to leave the scouts shorthanded. They've gone through the trouble to train me."

"Have you considered a dog to go out in the woods with you?"

"No, unless you're volunteering to train it."

"I wasn't, but –"

You perked up with a little gasp. "You could do that! Train wardogs, or horses."

"Don't know if I got the chops for that."

"I believe in you." You gave me a nudge and a playful smile.

"It's funny you bring up animal training. Before Josef and Aeryn left, he suggested I try working with horses, because of my runes."

"Have you?"

"A bit."

"How do you like it?"

"I'd do it all day, if I could."

"You should definitely do that. You'd be good at it," you said with conviction. "I don't have the patience. I like animals, but I think I'm better with people."

"See, I feel the opposite."

"That's not true, though. People listen when you got something to say."

"I appreciate that."

"You know what that means? It means talkin' to Leland about the gelding."

You will be pleased to know that I've found side work caring for the horses in the Gren. It's a far cry from the work we spoke of at my father's fence those years ago, but it's something. My foremost responsibilities continue to revolve around the labor necessary to shape the Gren into an inhabitable city.

At present, this involves working with stone to lay main roads. I've been given charge over a group of twenty. Besides laboring alongside them, I ensure they have necessary materials and plans, communicate with leadership, and do my best to keep morale high. I feel like I'm learning the finer points of leading as I go, which has been humbling and exhausting. Still, I've got a good crew (including Cain and Finnion, who were the first to follow me into this project). It helps that we've been extremely productive, and the pay is better than the clean-up work.

I remind myself often that my efforts sow stability for our people's future, and every day brings me closer to seeing your face again. Perhaps our great grandchildren will trod these very roads someday.

Yours,

Harek

14

"Are Pia and the girls joining today?" Wynne asked as she helped herself to a second cup of tea during breakfast. As much as she enjoyed the weekly rounds, two days of back-to-back late shifts left her body wishing it was still snuggled under her covers. Tea and physical activity usually did the trick.

"They'll be busy." Susi finished cutting Jai's slab of ham for him. "The Gren has requested two-hundred sweaters for the winter."

Wynne's thoughts jumped to the letter from Harek which came with the courier yesterday. "Two hundred sweaters?"

"Fellas need to keep warm," Susi said with a little smile. "Pia is organizing the sweater initiative."

"Pia's handling that?" It sounded like the type of duty Susi tackled. Wynne wondered whether Pia elbowed her way into the job because it made her important, or if Susi delegated the responsibility to keep Pia out of her hair.

Susi hummed in the affirmative and wouldn't quite meet Wynne's eyes. "It's a good use of her time and skillset. It puts people to work, and gives many women the opportunity to earn some money."

Wynne brought her cup of tea to her lips. "How are your efforts with her going?"

Susi said nothing for a moment. "They're going. Do you think Leland's finished smoking the boars you caught?"

Wynne nodded as she swallowed a too-big gulp. "I thought I'd take the cart to pick them up after breakfast. That way we have time to divvy it before we go out."

"Perfect."

"I'll join you, Wynne," Elric said. "Wouldn't mind stopping in to see ol' Leland on my way to Visseny's."

Wynne enjoyed the time with her father. Ordinarily, Omri liked to be involved in everything, but the dynamic had shifted since he left the house, and she gladly filled the void when suitable. "What's at Visseny's?"

"I got to see who he can spare at the lumberyard." Elric crammed half a roll into his mouth, chewed and swallowed. "Construction on the last boarding house is gettin' real close. We need it done. We could be havin' an Ice Throw next week. I also want to talk to Leland about how he's handlin' the new pig rule."

Wynne tried not to giggle. "What's the new pig rule?"

Elric opened his mouth to respond when a harsh voice outside gave him pause. The table fell quiet. Wynne, Jai, Elric, and Susi listened to see whether Lugh would continue on his way, or had caught the ear of a passerby before making it to their front door.

They heard the indistinct voices of two other men, followed by more irate jabber.

"A little early for visitors," Susi remarked.

"It's Lugh," Elric said.

"Nevermind."

Elric took a breath, as if mentally girding himself before he stepped into elders' duties for the day. He shoved the rest of his breakfast into his mouth and washed it down with his remaining tea. He pushed his bulk from the table. "Wynne, you coming?"

"Yes, Pops." Wynne threw back her cup and burned the roof of her mouth. Wincing, she swallowed, then collected the empty wooden troughs in a stack.

Susi took them from her. "Jai will get the rest. Go get ready."

The animated conversation outside continued as Wynne and Elric laced their boots and threw on their coats.

"Don't know how long this'll take," Elric said, casting an apologetic glance at Wynne. "There's a chance you might need to hitch Pearl and take her to Leland without me."

"Maybe it won't take long," Wynne said.

"It's Lugh." Elric kissed Susi goodbye. He wrapped an arm around Jai's shoulders and pulled him into his side. "Be a good helper for your mother today."

The lane outside the Thar house was a popular destination for conversation. Lugh had stopped to chat with Ned Goodhill and a younger man named Corbin Unger, who worked on the Goodhill's farm when he wasn't tending his own. Corbin was a plain-looking man, with light brown hair cut close to the scalp. His short beard grew thickest across his lip. All in all, he wasn't bad-looking as long as he kept his mouth shut. His teeth, while clean, were crooked and too big for his mouth. Wynne had never heard anything negative about him.

"G'morning, men," Elric said as he marched down the footpath.

"Morning," Ned said, and Corbin echoed the greeting.

Lugh's scowl broke when he noticed Wynne at her father's shoulder. His sour demeanor vanished instantly. "The great pig-slayer!"

"Now there's a title a girl could lean into," Wynne said with a chuckle. Elric cringed.

Lugh rapped Corbin on the arm with the back of his hand. "You didn't see it," he said, addressing Ned and Elric as well. "Few days ago, some newcomer's pig wandered onto my property. Granya caught it nosin' in the garden, uprootin' the beets. She went out to shoo it away and it tried to *bite* her. Got her skirts instead. Tore a hole in 'em."

"Is your wife hurt?" Corbin asked.

"No, but it's more mendin' and food lost. The nasty blighter fled before either of us could do somethin'." Lugh's face tightened and he rumbled in his throat. "I was in the midst of tellin' Rakel, whence comes this young lady..." He gestured toward Wynne with an approving wink. "...with two wild pigs suspended from a pole."

Ned's eyebrows jumped. "Two?"

"Two," Lugh said with emphasis. "It was like Elsey and Angus' weddin' all-over again. You remember the boar she caught with Aeryn?"

"How could anyone forget?" Corbin flashed a grin which made it easy to avoid any unwanted flutters.

"Our huntsmen better rise to the challenge." Lugh jerked a thumb at Wynne. "This one's been giving them the what-for."

Wynne blushed at the words of praise. "You're kind, Lugh."

Ned shifted his weight. "How'd you get two wild boars on a pole by yourself?"

"She was with the newcomer from Austerholt." Lugh snapped his fingers. "What's his name?"

"Kal," Wynne said at the same moment Elric replied, "Kalomir."

Elric gave her the briefest, curious glance.

"Regarding the newcomers." Lugh's tone grew serious again. He sighed and shook his head. "It's not good, Elric. Not good."

"What troubles you, Lugh?" Elric asked.

"They been lettin' their pigs roam. They bite. They raid our gardens and our coops." Lugh grew increasingly worked up as he rattled off his list of grievances. "We can't afford that! We got enough problems with the wild ones doin' that."

"The pigs have been a problem," Elric said. "We put the rule in place. Folks'll either learn to keep them contained, or they'll be paying for the meat."

"Their rotten kids are even worse," Lugh continued. "You know they were comin' on my land, mockin' my cow?"

"Not Peig?" Wynne said in disbelief.

"They're merciless."

"For shame."

Elric hummed. He shot Wynne a glance. *You're encouraging this?*

Wynne suppressed a tightlipped little smile. She caught Corbin's eye and noticed he was struggling to do the same.

"It's a good thing Peig's a hearty ol' lass," Elric said. "She's got the fortitude."

Lugh nodded, marginally comforted. "It just ain't right, Elric. Winter's comin'. They're eatin' us out of hearth and home."

Ned dropped his voice. "You talking about the pigs, or the newcomers?"

Lugh cast him a wry glance. "I meant the pigs, but now you mention it...."

"Ah, don't be stingy, Lugh. I remember when you were new to this village."

"It's not the same. You know it. I know it. They're not like us. What if they stay?"

"Too soon to say whether they will or won't," Elric said. "Can't blame 'em wanting to stay. Enclave is a good place."

"Probably better than what they're leaving, many of them," Corbin said.

"There's my point," Lugh said. "Why would they leave if they got it made here? At our expense? Spring comes, then what?"

Elric raised a palm. "It's a meal once a week out of our excess, for only the neediest among them. We've all needed help at times."

Lugh grumbled to himself.

"They're payin' their own way for everythin' else," Elric said. "If they really want to be successful here, they're gonna have to learn."

"But what if they keep coming? How much can this village take? It's gettin' crowded...."

Elric cast Wynne a subtle glance which she understood to mean, *You best go. I'm gonna be a while.*

Once Lugh got going, it was better to let him finish. He didn't really want an answer. He only wanted to gripe. When he paused for a breath, Wynne bid the group farewell and peeled away.

She hitched the cart to the family's donkey, Pearl. When she finished, she scratched the old girl behind her soft gray ears, then led her into the yard, toward the front where the conversation amongst the men continued. She met her mother by the door.

Susi pressed a gold and silver coin from the community fund into Wynne's palm. "This should do for Leland's trouble."

Her eyes jumped over Wynne's shoulder, toward the men in the lane. Corbin noticed the pair of them looking and straightened up a little. Susi dropped her voice. "Pray for your father. He's been having a lot of these conversations lately."

"About the pigs or the newcomers?"

"Both. And how we're to sustain if things continue the way they're going." Susi took a breath and pushed the wisps of hair away from her forehead.

"Are people really that upset?" Wynne knew the tavern was a nuisance. Most folks she spent time with harbored more compassion than resentment toward the plight of the newcomers, even if they disapproved of their leisure time or how they managed their animals. It surprised her to hear that Lugh's general resentments were more prevalent than she realized.

"It depends who you ask," Susi said. "Folks are restless. It's been a trying two years. They want to feel good about the future, and it's difficult to plan when you've got the promise of change. No one's quite sure how it'll play out."

"What do you think?"

"I think we do well to remember that many of us were in a worse state when we came here," Susi said. "And your father's right. They're gonna have to learn to be productive if they want to be successful here."

✧

Wynne remembered the first time she went to the Jaegers' at Harek's invitation. She'd hurried through her chores that morning. After freshening up, she rooted around the kitchen for a clove to chew when Omri sauntered into the room.

He gave her a funny look. "Did you change clothes?"

"Yes."

"Where are you going?"

She avoided meeting his face. "The Jaeger house."

"Why?"

Wynne resisted the impulse for snark. *None of your business, Nosy.* "Yamma had puppies."

"Are Mum and Pops getting a dog?"

"No."

"Then why are you going?"

"Harek asked if I wanted to see them," she said, forcing her voice to remain lighter than she felt. The featherweight hum in her belly now felt more like she had a fish out of water flopping around inside her. "I couldn't go yesterday, so I said I'd come by today after the morning chores."

"He didn't ask me."

Wynne turned up her palms. "Do you know where Mum keeps the cloves?"

"We're out."

"Rats."

He eyed her for a moment and new mischief entered his smirk. "Oh. I think I see what's going on here."

Wynne dropped her eyes as heat rushed to her cheeks. She returned items to the cupboard in a hurry. "What's that supposed to mean?"

His tone took a loaded quality. "The reason why you got through the chores so quickly."

"I didn't –"

Omri mimed milking the goat, pitching hay into the donkey's stall, and collecting eggs in an imaginary basket at rapid speeds. When he was finished with his comical imitation, he braced one hand on the edge of the counter, one on his hip, and his eyebrows jumped in an unspoken, *Well?*

"You're hilarious."

"You're not answering the question."

"There was no question."

"Yes, there was. Did you hurry through your chores because you're eager to see Harek?"

Wynne said nothing.

Which delighted Omri. "You got sweet feelings for ol' Jaeger boy!"

She pointed a finger at him. "Don't make it awkward."

"I would never," he said with feigned innocence. "Frankly, I don't think either of you need my help there."

Visiting the Jaeger house didn't feel the same with Harek gone. The property took up a corner plot near the center of the village. The main dwelling, a sturdy log cabin, was one of the larger homes in town. It was perpetually packed to capacity with Harek's immediate family, both grandmothers, and their dog, Yamma. Several outbuildings occupied the Jaegers' land, including a barn and yards for animals, a slaughterhouse, a smokehouse, and a toolshed.

As Wynne drew up to the corner, she heard Leland's belly laugh from the structure he used to conduct business. She couldn't help but smile. She'd known him her whole life and liked him. He had a self-deprecating sense of humor which put folks at ease. Like Wynne, he genuinely enjoyed talking with people. She wondered who'd come to call.

She knocked on the doorframe to announce herself as she entered. Leland waved hello and continued to listen to Kal, who stood at the counter finishing his thought.

Kal glanced over his shoulder and his face lit up. "Look who it is."

Wynne returned the smile and tried not to overthink the squirmy feeling in her chest. She recalled greeting him this way last time she saw him. Returning the remark was a show of continued friendliness. She liked that. Still, it made them seem more familiar than they were, in front of Harek's father, no less.

"Wynne, you've met Kal?" Leland asked, none too perturbed.

"We've run into each other," she said.

Kal's grin broadened.

"He's makin' me a new leg," Leland said.

Wynne cocked her head. "A new leg?"

"You want to see what the dog did to the old one?" Leland clopped around the counter which separated him from customers. He presented the leg, which was wooden from the knee down. The once smooth wood was splintered and frayed with teeth marks.

"Yamma did that?" Wynne asked, shocked.

"Chewed it to bits."

"Naughty."

"She's not been right this past year," Leland said. "Acting up. First, she was jealous of the wardog. And ever since Harek left, she hovers near the door, like she's waitin' for him to come home. Micha says she's missin' him."

Wynne hummed in sympathy.

"You hear there's another group headed out in a week or so?"

"To Goldbur Gren?" That was news to Wynne.

"Aye. A dozen more men."

"Goldbur Gren, the burnt city?" Kal asked. "I thought it was a pile of rubble."

"It was, but they've been workin' on it for a year. From what my son says, they're makin' great progress. It's our closest city. Be awful nice if it ain't aspirin' to wipe us off the map!"

"I'll say."

"They say the world is changin'. Crazy to think, for the first time, it's a real possibility we ain't consigned to this village because we're dead anywhere else. Anyhow, new leg for me." Leland knocked on the counter. "Kal, show her."

Wynne's eyes fell to the assortment of intricately carved goods arrayed across the counter, including a wooden serving spoon with ivy and fruit carved into the handle, a door-knocker in the shape of a dragon, and a small plaque depicting a scene of waves, fish, reeds, and a leggy water bird.

Wynne pointed. "Kal, you made these?"

"I did."

"May I see?"

He gestured for her to go ahead.

She picked up a small box, which was carved all over with flowers in bloom. She turned it over and ran her finger over the ridges. Elric liked woodworking, though it was more of a pastime to make toys for children. Kal's craftsmanship made his projects look amateurish by comparison. "This is beautiful. You're very talented."

"I like this one," Leland said, indicating the dragon.

"Your people are friends with a dragon who lives nearby?" Kal asked.

"Aye. Queen Kalane."

"I was informed she's rather protective over her mountain."

"Who filled you in?" Wynne asked with a nudge of concern.

"You remember Omri?"

That was good. Omri was usually thorough. Still, Wynne needed to make sure. "He warned you never to set foot on it?"

"In no uncertain terms." Kal turned his attention to Leland. "This gives me an idea."

"Surprise me," Leland said.

"I hope I don't disappoint."

Leland clapped and rubbed his hands together. "Wynne, I assume you're here for the pork."

"Yes, sir."

"I hope you brought somethin' better than a wheelbarrow this time."

"There is a proper cart out front."

Leland disappeared into the back room and Kal loaded the samples of his work into a leather bag slung across his body. "The boar and its child?"

She gave him a look.

"Would you like a hand?"

15

"No lumber yard today?" Wynne asked as Kal accompanied her up the lane.

"Later. It's market day. A man's gotta eat. You wouldn't want me to starve?"

"Of course not," she said in kind. "I'm excited to see the finished piece for Leland. Where did you learn your craft?"

"Through a lot of practice," he said. "In Austerholt, there's snow on the ground five months out of the year. Not much to do except sit inside, drink, and whittle. You laugh, but I'm not exaggerating. Carving is a popular artform further north."

"I didn't know that."

"Also, when I was ten, my mother sent me to live in the city. I learned a good deal about the finer parts of carpentry from the folks I stayed with."

"You're a carpenter by trade?" she said with new interest.

"I am a master of my craft."

Wynne wasn't sure whether this was Kal bragging or admitting a special recognition he'd attained. She felt too silly to ask. The Enclave didn't have demarcations of skill beyond describing whether someone was *in training* or knew enough to do their job properly.

"Your mum sent you to the city – by yourself?"

He dipped his chin.

"Is that typical?"

He shrugged. "Not unusual. Especially for folks in the outer settlements. More opportunity for work or learning skills in the city. With me out of the house, it was one less mouth to feed."

"Do you have a lot of brothers and sisters?"

"No. It was only me and my mum. My father left when I was two. She died when I was thirteen."

Wynne contended with a pull of grief on his behalf. "You've been on your own since thirteen?"

"The folks I was living with were kind enough to let me stay. They were good people. I finished my apprenticeship and followed the work." Kal dug his hands into his pockets and gazed down the path ahead.

Wynne gave the donkey's lead a gentle tug and steered Pearl around a turn. They walked together in quiet for a few paces as Wynne considered his story. He struck Wynne as a good deal more worldly and experienced than she previously assumed. She wasn't sure how she felt about that.

Kal broke the quiet. "I got to ask. The bear?"

Pulled out of her thoughts, Wynne's mouth twitched in the corner. "That was my little brother."

Kal angled his head in disbelief. "Your brother is a bear?"

"My brother is a six-year-old Baldomar boy who just figured out how to use his runes to turn into a bear. What you saw was him trying to escape a bath."

"I'm speechless."

"Prepare yourself. If you're here any length of time, you'll see some strange things," she said. "Although, Jai's little trick? That one takes the prize for me."

"What about you?"

"What about me?"

"Your rune magic. What can you do?"

"I'm a good throw with an axe."

He hummed. "Surely that's not all."

Wynne hesitated. "I am...extremely aware of my surroundings."

"What does that mean?"

She bit her lip, suddenly sheepish.

"What?"

"Don't laugh."

"Now I'm really curious. I promise I won't."

Wynne mustered her dignity and pressed ahead. "If I'm using magic, I could close my eyes, and make it through the woods without tripping, walking into a tree, or getting lost."

Kal fought back a smirk, and failed.

She gently pushed his arm. "You said you wouldn't laugh!"

"I'm not laughing. I'm only curious when that would be useful."

She thought for a moment. "Say I was kidnapped, blindfolded, and dropped in the forest. I could make it home."

"Is that a common problem around here?"

"Well, no. But if it was..."

Kal chuckled. Wynne turned a little pink and laughed too.

"I like your laugh," he said.

She felt her face grow warmer. "Thank you."

They crunched over the gritty road, walking shoulder to shoulder without speaking for a moment. Wynne chanced a glance at him. He was wearing a light brown shirt with an open collar. There was no food in his beard. He looked like he'd had a wash recently. She found herself admiring his dark hair.

He noticed.

She saw it in his posture and the way he opened his shoulders. The adjustment in his gait brought him a few inches closer to her side.

"I realized I never got an answer to my question," he said.

"What question?"

"What do you like?"

"You want to know what I'm interested in?" She thought for a moment, then waved a hand gracefully toward the cart, watching to measure his response. "This. Taking care of my people."

Kal regarded the heaps of smoked boar in the cart. "You must really love your people."

"I do. We try to do this once a week," she said. "I like helping and work which brings me around others."

"Scouting seems like an odd choice, then. Solitary work."

"I like being outside, too. We live in the most beautiful place, with the forest, river, and mountains. Also, scouting wasn't always solitary. We used to have partners." She tilted her head as she considered. "Although, that wasn't always great."

"Why's that?"

"Scouts are a rough crew." It sounded more gracious than *They're tolerable, but mean.*

"Correct me if I'm wrong. It doesn't seem like the best fit for you, then." He flashed a palm. "Formiddle threat to wild boars, though you may be."

Wynne was smiling as she shook her head.

"You're not like anyone I've ever met."

"Is that so?" That sounded nice, and she wanted him to keep going.

He shrugged. "I could be wrong. Perhaps you've some deep, dark secret or terrible flaw, but I haven't seen it yet. So, in my mind, you're perfectly lovely."

Wynne hoisted an eyebrow. "Kal, are you flirting with me?"

He returned the look. "Should I be?"

Her grin intensified despite her best efforts. She stopped the cart. Meeting his eyes, she took a deliberate step toward him and laid a hand on his chest. "If I wanted you to, you would know."

Kal placed a hand over hers.

In an instant, Wynne fully realized the close proximity she'd created. She hadn't thought about it before. At once, her every sense seemed crisper. She felt the rise and fall of his chest under her palm and the weight of his hand over hers.

The playful interest in his expression intensified. A little thrill shot through her.

Do I want him too?

She held his gaze for a beat, soaking in the rich brown of his eyes, and her focus darted briefly to his lips. He leaned forward.

Startled and instantly yanked out of the moment, Wynne's flutters of enjoyment rolled over and died. She stepped back before he closed the distance and pulled her hand free. "I need to go."

She dropped her eyes and searched for the donkey's rope lead, red in the face and embarrassed. By him, or with herself, she didn't know.

I wonder what Harek would say if he saw this. A new pang of guilt stabbed into her.

She grabbed for the rope and fumbled it. A wave of heat bloomed to life inside her as she made a second attempt. She gave it a gentle tug and trundled away without another glance at Kal.

16

Wynne spent the rest of the day in dread of crossing Kal's path. What would say? What was she supposed to say? Almost immediately, her heart confronted her with the notion that their near-kiss was, in part, her own doing. To an extent, she'd encouraged his interest.

Encouraged, and enjoyed it.

It made her feel like a wretch, but was probably the only aspect of the exchange which kept her from feeling totally repulsed. Truth was, there was a moment. They both felt it.

Granted, she hadn't expected him to swoop in and ruin it with his forwardness. Who tries to kiss a relative stranger in the street? How sensitive were men to mild encouragement, anyway? Was this a unique Kal quality, or men in general? She was going to have to be more careful to avoid unintentionally raising hopes.

The outing to distribute food provided a meager distraction. She kept to herself, too flustered, embarrassed, and guilty to confess to anyone. After an early supper, she tried to get a block of rest before her watch began at midnight.

Sleep didn't come easy. Her conscience tormented her, and she half-expected Kal to come by the house after his work to apologize. For longer than she cared to admit, she kept an ear pricked for a knock on the door before exhaustion finally claimed her.

✧

Susi shook Wynne's shoulder an hour before her watch. The warm flicker of candlelight danced over the dark room. Wynne rubbed the sleep from her eyes. "Did anyone come to the house while I was sleeping?"

"Omri came by for a late supper," Susi said.

No surprise there. "No one else?"

"No. Were you expecting someone?"

"No," Wynne said with an unexpected tug of disappointment. She gave her head a little shake and forced a smile. "I don't know what I was thinking."

Overnights were awful. Traversing the woods in the dark gave Wynne a cold, crawly feeling and made her feel like an animal. Hunter or prey, she wasn't sure. As much as she loved the forest, she recognized she was a social creature. Darkness, solitude, and the lack of adequate sleep too-often put her in a bad frame of mind if she wasn't careful.

Between this, and the day she'd experienced, she was ripe for misery. She knew it.

After the initial patrol of her stretch of woods, she climbed up high and safe in the lookout tower. There she planned to remain until it was time to make another pass before her watch ended at sunup. With a lack of anything to occupy herself, she brooded.

She tried to assuage her sense of guilt. She wasn't pledged to Harek. She hadn't done anything overtly romantic. It wasn't as if Kal was a real consideration.

Try as she might, she couldn't shake it.

So he didn't come by. Maybe Kal was embarrassed. It was hard to imagine him with a sense of shame, but it was possible. The alternative was that her reaction had deterred his further interest. She wasn't sure how to feel about that. Or how she should feel about it.

I've known him for four days. I won't let him kiss me in the street, so now I'm yesterday's news? This thought lodged against her heart with a painful prod and a spark of anger. *Fine.*

Better to know it now. Let him find someone else. What was she even thinking, feeling any kind of way about this? She was a Thar, and he was a vagrant. A chancer, if ever she saw one.

Sure, he was likable. Charming. Talented. Direct, for better or worse. He was quite the contrast to Harek. Harek was wholesome. Genuine. Humble. Safe.

She wasn't sure Kal was any of those things.

Maybe she just liked the idea of him.

Maybe she was disappointed because she wanted him to be better than he was.

✧

The forest was lighted by the muted gray-green of dawn when Rakel's shrill whistle pierced the quiet. Wynne threw her head and shoulders out the window and located Rakel on the forest floor, hands on her hips. Normally no one associated Rakel with a breath of fresh air, but this morning, she was a welcome sight for more than one reason.

I can leave!

And, *Another person!*

Wynne's exhausted grin took on an over-eager quality. "You're early."

"Always a risk," Rakel said. "You see me coming?"

"Yes, ma'am."

Rakel sucked her teeth. She prided herself on going undetected until she wanted to be seen. Wynne's little victory would put her in a bad mood. Wynne felt a little bad for the other scouts who'd deal with her later.

Then again, she'd been more even-tempered lately. Wynne had noticed a correlation between the attitude improvement and last year's announcement that Josef and Aeryn were settling in the Gren, instead of returning to the Enclave. It was no secret Rakel disliked them.

By the time they were on level, Rakel didn't seem half as bothered as Wynne had known her to be when spotted early. This, and the mere presence of another woman, made Wynne fight back the desire to hug her.

Which – more than anything yet – confirmed to Wynne that her mental clarity had been compromised.

In the early morning hours, the windy roads of the Enclave were vacant. Which was just as well. Wynne wanted to avoid conversation. She needed to clear her head, or get some rest, or both.

She decided she required the ear of a friend to untangle her knots. A confession was called for, but it was too early to visit Tess. Though she longed for adequate sleep, she reasoned that if she kept moving, she could wait a few more hours. She busied herself with a good wash, a fresh change of clothes, and a braid. She devoured breakfast while standing and paced, drinking her tea.

"Heavens, Wynne. Settle," Susi said. "What's got you in a tizzy?"

"I'm not in a tizzy. There's no tizzy."

Susi cocked an eyebrow, unconvinced.

"I need to see Tess this morning. I'll get sleepy if I stop moving."

"Ah." Susi used a fire-poker to shift a log in the hearth.

"Where's Pops?"

"He was called upon by Omri when you were in the other room."

"Awfully early. What for?"

"He needs advice on some matter about the new house."

"I thought he was still stockpiling material. He hasn't started building, has he?"

Susi shook her head. She moved to the tableside and started folding a basket of laundry. "Apparently Waylas has been sticking his foot in with all manner of opinions about where, precisely, he should lay a foundation, and dig a well, and a cellar, and plow a garden, and raise the barn…"

"I didn't think Omri planned to finish all of that before he and Lara married."

"He doesn't, and he needn't. A place for them to sleep and eat is more than sufficient." Susi shook out a napkin with a snap. Her eyes went unfocused as she folded it into a neat rectangle. She sighed. "Oh, Omri. It had to be Lara."

"I like Lara."

"I do too. I know he wants to provide the best for her, but I worry. I'm a mother, I can't help it." Susi pushed out a cleansing breath. "He'll figure it out."

A fat bear cub waddled into the room, as if he did this every day.

From the tableside, Susi glanced dispassionately in the bear's direction. "Jairus Thar, go back into your room and put some clothes on. Right now. You can't collect eggs with bear paws, and you'll scare the hens half to death."

The bear that was Jai made the heaviest, most woebegone sigh, as if all the cares of Noemar had been laid across his shoulders. He hung his head, made a slow turn, and plodded back toward the narrow hall leading to the bedrooms.

"Today, Jairus."

Jai made a noise halfway between a snarl and a grunt.

Susi's mouth grew dangerously small and her eyebrows shot up her forehead. She abandoned the tableside and marched after him.

Sensing discipline closing in, Jai found the motivation to move. He disappeared into the hall quicker than a shot.

Wynne decided she'd waited long enough. She drained the last of her tea and called across the house, "I'm visiting Tess. Be back in a bit."

She pulled the door open to find Kal approaching the front gate. He drew to a complete stop when he saw her. The air bottled in her lungs for a startling moment.

"Hi," he said with much less bravado than she'd come to expect. Though alert, he looked about as tired as she felt. Almost like he hadn't slept. Though he hid it well, an anxious energy buzzed about him. It made her wonder whether it was due to their interaction the day before. Perhaps it was too presumptuous to assume.

"Do you have a moment?" he asked.

Wynne bobbed her head. He let himself into the main gate. No jumping this time.

She traveled the footpath from the house toward him. The least she could do was meet him halfway, or closer to the road, in case the conversation was audible from inside.

Kal stood straight-backed, but his swagger was gone. His expression was open and humble, and he maintained steady eye contact as he spoke. "I made an utter fool of myself yesterday. I saw an invitation where there wasn't one. I made you uncomfortable. That was not my intention. I'm truly sorry."

The angst brewing inside Wynne for the last twenty four hours relented.

"I appreciate that." She hesitated and drew on the reserves of her humility. "To be fair, I see how I contributed to the...situation. I'm sorry, too."

Kal nodded.

There was a quiet lull. He ran a hand through his hair. It was less of a preening gesture, and more of a self-conscious one.

"I was enjoying our conversation," she added.

"I like talking with you."

"I like talking with you, too."

He offered her a small, tentative smile, which she returned. "Please don't take this the wrong way. But I meant it when I said I think you're lovely."

A pleasant bloom slowly built within Wynne, softening her edges. "Thank you."

"I should go. They pulled me from the lumberyard to help finish a boarding house."

Wynne recalled Elric mentioning this the day before. The boarding houses weren't too far from Tess' home. A bold thought entered her mind. "I'm going that way. Would you like to walk with me?"

The corner of his mouth hiked up in a genuine smile.

Dearest Wynne,

I remember the day when the first refugees came. It was shortly after you'd urged me to state my case about keeping my brother's gelding. I'd come by astride Judge in triumph to ask you along on a ride. You heartily accepted, though you seemed uneasy. When I asked you why, you confided, "Horses make me nervous."

I was shocked. "You don't like them?"

"I don't trust them," you said. "But I trust you." You pressed close to my back and held tightly before we got started.

I'm grateful you couldn't see my face. Your words made me feel like a king. I confess, I may've directed Judge to trot just fast enough to keep you sitting close. In hindsight, I'm struck with the suspicion that you knew and approved, given how you never told me to slow down.

We saw the motley caravan in the distance led in by Rakel, Roran, and Oleksy – two wagons, animals, and people on foot with stressed, dirty faces. Fifteen souls in all, and a third of them children.

"More Baldomar?" I asked.

"It's too many to be Baldomar," you said.

"Might be."

"Do you see a Keeper among them?"

"They're all dead except one."

"Exactly. Those aren't Baldomar. However they learned about this place, they had no trouble finding it."

With a glance over my shoulder, we shared the sudden realization that Kalane's wards were either ineffective or no longer in place. When was she planning to tell us this? It worried me. You patrolled those woods. After the raid, it took you tremendous courage to get back out there.

If I recall correctly, most of those fifteen were still at the Enclave when I left, having established themselves and sought work.

We've had a handful of families from the wider world come to the Gren also. Time and again, I see how difficult it is to uproot with next-to-nothing, save immediate family and a few hogs, then plant someplace new. I admire your compassion for them and the hospitality that moves within the hearts of our people. Still, the flood of newcomers which followed the first fifteen to our doorstep has brought mixed results. Good or bad, it promises to utterly shift the dynamic of the Enclave. Please keep me informed. I pray often for your safety amongst these strangers. Do me a favor, and stay away from the tavern.

What this city will look like when all's accomplished is a frequent topic of conversation. If you were to listen to my compatriots, each man would have a castle and rolling estate. I've never seen a castle, except for in Nyassa. Plans exist to build at least one. From what I hear, they can be dank and cold, which makes me think living in one would never suit you. You love the sunlight and fresh air too much. Still, all this has me curious what you would like in a future home?

Yours,

Harek

17

Sometimes Wynne believed that misfortune favored her people. Favored, and even then, misfortune picked favorites. Her brother, Josef, for one. His life was the story of one trial after another. He'd experienced more than most people could bear. He overcame it. He was a leader. A hero.

An exception.

Six years ago, Zak and Fiona married. They had their hopes and little farmstead with room to grow. They had plans. Wynne remembered the day of the accident, four months after the wedding. One slip off a ladder, and Zak was paralyzed from the waist down.

It was Wynne's earliest memory of truly recognizing the outpouring of generosity from the community as the young couple waded through the trial which changed the course of their lives. Elric and Tawna's father Cedric, a wheelwright, coordinated to make a chair so Zak could get around. Other men built a ramp and a long low porch, so he wasn't confined to the house. The support of the little family now fell almost entirely on Fiona. Susi and other women of the village came alongside her to help her form a plan.

As the months and years progressed, hope that Zak would improve slipped away. The couple mourned, each in their own right. Wynne was struck by Fiona's dogged loyalty. Her love for Zak remained fierce. She was one of the most industrious, faithful women at the Enclave.

Today, Wynne would have the honor of assisting in the birth of their first child.

The baby they never thought they'd have.

Standing in her doorway, Fiona cringed. She held the side of her rounded belly, breathing through another wave of discomfort. It passed, and she freed a hand to wave goodbye. The birthing pains had just begun, and progress was slow, which gave Wynne and Catreeny time to finish the weekly distribution before returning.

Despite Wynne's excitement for Fiona and Zak, she contended with a generous measure of trepidation. The baby was turned the wrong way, which could make for a dangerous situation if the issue didn't resolve itself. According to Catreeny, it usually did.

"I'll let Sender know we've got another birth this evening," Catreeny said as they made their way back to the lane. Ordinarily, the only male allowed in the room was the baby's father, but Catreeny liked to keep Sender aware as a precaution. Prior to the return of their magic, there wasn't much he could do in an emergency. Now, if a problem arose, Sender's healing magic might mean the difference between life and death.

"I think he's at Arlo and Fay's," Wynne said.

"O'course he is, that man." Catreeny shook her head. "Heart of pure gold. Shame he never remarried after Bekka died."

"Bekka was his late wife?"

Catreeny hummed. "Sweet girl. Don't know why gods claim some of us when they do. Seems an injustice for the world to be deprived of her. Your hair looks pretty today."

Wynne's fingers traveled to the braid woven across her hairline. "Thank you. I'm going to make my way toward the boarding houses."

"Yes, you've mentioned wanting to be the one to bring the cart there four times."

Wynne's cheeks grew warm. "I have not."

Catreeny glanced at Wynne, as though suspecting there was more to her eagerness than bringing food to a handful of women and children. Wynne realized a moment too late, her defensiveness only aided this supposition.

"Don't be like those silly girls who lost their heads," Catreeny said.

"What are you talking about?"

"The men are finishing one of them buildings today. Quite the hullabaloo, from what I hear."

Wynne's curiosity roused even as she grew hot in the face. She felt mildly affront at Catreeny's insinuation. Especially because it cut too close. "That's not why I want to go by."

If Catreeny doubted her, she said nothing. "We'll come collect you when we're ready to move to the south side."

They parted, and Wynne mentally chided herself. How obvious was she?

She knew the visit to the family house would bring her near the site where Kal was still working. Which meant there was a chance, however small, of seeing him.

It was a nice thought.

In the week since they made peace, they'd crossed paths several times. To his credit, he never overstepped his bounds, though he pushed the limit, flirting whenever he got the opportunity. She tried to be careful. To avoid unintentionally raising his hopes. Still, she did nothing to discourage him. She didn't know whether this was right or wrong.

While flattered by the attention and persistence, she couldn't shake the nagging feeling that he was only trying to lay with her. What was clear was that she – out of anyone – had his interest. It was hard not to enjoy it.

As she rounded the bend which brought the boarding houses into view, she checked her sweater for stray bits of hay or smudges of dirt she may've acquired during the first part of her rounds. It was the pink one which he complimented earlier that week.

Catreeny's mention of hullabaloo took shape. The area where Wynne usually stopped the cart teemed with more activity than normal. People mingled in the grassy space on either side of the road, or spilled into the lane itself. She noticed the crowd included an inordinate number of young women. Concluding building projects were often a cause for rejoicing, but not the sort of thing Baldomar women grew excited over unless they directly benefited. They were practical people.

Wynne threaded the donkey through the congested lane, noticing Tawna and Simone amongst the idlers. Tawna twiddled her fingers in greeting, while Simone gave Wynne a brief glance and said nothing.

"Hi, Tawna," Wynne said, since Simone was too busy ignoring her. "Quite the congregation here."

"Oh, we're just enjoying the weather," Tawna said.

"And the view," Simone added. She leered past Wynne, making no attempt at subtlety.

Wynne followed their glances to the area between the road and the newest building. A handful of younger men were out front, milling around, moving supplies, or chopping wood.

Including Kal.

He'd positioned himself front and center. He was apparently so hard at work splitting logs, he'd rolled the sleeves to the elbow and allowed the front of his shirt to hang wide open. He spared the quickest glance toward the road, wearing that charming grin of his. The way he carried himself and angled his body told Wynne that he was keenly aware of his audience.

Aware, and enjoying the attention.

Wynne's stomach lurched into a knot. A spike of pique roused itself within her. "You two have nothing better to do?"

"Nope," Tawna chirped, like it was all a big joke.

"You're embarrassing yourselves."

This grabbed Simone's attention. Her face bent and she gave Wynne a contemptuous up-down. "Excuse you."

Tawna rolled her eyes. "It's not like he minds. He keeps looking over here."

Wynne said nothing. It was one thing to put this together herself, and another to hear it from someone else. Her eyes drifted to Kal. She thought his interest was reserved for her. Her mind washed over the interactions which made her believe him. What did he say? *I think you're lovely.*

She gritted her jaw.

"I've seen you two talking." Simone wagged her finger to indicate Kal. "Does this bother you?"

She spoke as though this was equal parts adorable and pathetic. A nasty smile curled onto her face. Or maybe it was a veiled threat. *What about Harek?*

Heat rose to the surface of Wynne's skin. She couldn't avoid serving the women and children, but she couldn't stay here. Not with the spectacle, reminding her that she was as gullible and silly as the rest of them. Not with Simone here, reveling in it. She didn't want to be anywhere near these girls, or she was bound to do or say something to embarrass herself further. She was embarrassed enough, and had no right to be.

"I'm talking to you," Simone said as Wynne pulled away without another glance or word.

The wagon creaked and jostled as the wheels rolled over a divot. Wynne's breath came heavier as the knot in her gut turned to stone. She wanted to crawl under a rock and leak a few tears, which made her even angrier with herself. *Why should you be hurt by this? You have no business letting your heart snag on this man. What's wrong with you?*

Wynne leaned into the anger. That was easier. As she separated herself from the throng, the cold trembly feeling in her limbs shifted into a pulsing heat.

Get it together, Wynne. What did you expect of an outsider?

"Wynne!" Kal's voice boomed over the hubbub. He lodged his axe in a stump and abandoned the workyard to catch up with her. "Wait."

Wynne slowed as he jogged past Simone, Tawna, and the others. Over his shoulder, she noticed her old friends glance their way with envy. His smile reached his eyes as he closed the distance. Wynne reflexively returned the grin, prompting a new twinge of irritation at herself.

Kal carried himself with easy confidence. It was impossible not to notice he was lean and strong, with muscular chest and arms. Attractive, and distracting.

Which, of course, he knew. It burrowed under Wynne's skin like a splinter, and kicked up her ire. She made the deliberate effort to keep her focus anywhere else.

"I'm glad I caught you." He touched her lightly on the arm. "You look pretty. How's your day?"

It was the same way he greeted her two days prior. Then, the words stirred up all kinds of pleasant feelings. They made her feel special.

Now, they sounded rote and hollow.

Wynne bit her tongue and resisted the initial impulse for snark. But not for long. "I see you learned how to use an axe."

Kal caught the edge in her voice. He gave her a funny look. "Something bothering you?"

"Yes. You." The words came out before she could form a better response.

He pulled his chin inward. "What did I do now?"

Now? She wasn't sure what it was about that little word, but it made it worse.

"Do you think I'm blind? I saw you over there, putting on a show."

"Putting on a show?" he sounded taken aback and offended.

Wynne's frown tightened. Without breaking eye contact, she made a sweeping gesture down the length of him, then waved gracefully toward the young women stealing glances in their direction. Her eyebrow twitched in question. *Answer that.*

He released a breath and jabbed his thumb over his shoulder. "You think this is for them?"

"You knew they were watching you. You kept glancing their way."

"I was looking for you," he said with emphasis. "You told me you were making the rounds today." He took a step closer to her and looked into her eyes. "I was out front working like this – for you."

Wynne said nothing.

"When I saw you, what did I do?"

Wynne said nothing.

"What did I do?"

"You came over here."

"I came running."

Cheeks burning and feeling chastened, Wynne pressed her lips into a line. Her attention dropped briefly to his bare chest.

If he was after her attention, why invite the eyes of the other women? His words held some credence, but he knew what he was doing.

Kal's eyes searched her for a response. "You don't believe me?"

"I don't know if I should."

"I'm not lying to you, Wynne," he said, looking so heartfelt, her anger receded.

She released a conflicted sigh. *I wish I knew what to think about you.*

Kal glanced away and shook his head. His expression tightened. "You don't like me very much, do you?"

"I want to," she said, surprising herself at the force of her words.

And the truth in them.

She bunched her eyes shut and rubbed the space between her eyebrows. She huffed. "My feelings are complicated."

"What does that mean?"

"It means I don't know if I should. One moment you're sincere. The next you act like the biggest chancer I've ever met. Then I see all this –"

"All this? As in, me trying to look good for you?"

"You're out of your head if you expect me to believe it's as simple as that."

They squared off with each other for a breath.

"You know what I think?" she said.

He cast a hand into the air, exasperated. "Tell me."

"We're after different things."

"What do you think I'm after, exactly?" he said, almost as a challenge.

"Yourself. Whatever you can get, from whoever'll give it to you." Wynne threw her hands in the air, showing both palms in a *No, thanks* gesture. She took a step back from him. "Enjoy your audience. I'm sure they're lovely too."

18

Kal sat at the bar in a foul mood, one hand on his drink. He didn't understand what he kept doing wrong. Trying with Wynne felt like running into a wall.

He scoffed. *More like stumbling down a flight of stairs.*

So he knew he was being watched. Drawing the eyes of other women was a crime akin to adultery now? He hadn't touched or flirted with anyone else since he'd been here. In fact, he'd been resisting a whole lot of temptation lately, all because of her.

You think that makes you worthy?

Though the ale blunted his critical reasoning, this back-of-the-mind challenge felt like a jab to the ribs. His natural desire to defend himself to himself ebbed.

Reevaluation. That's what he needed. The same-old wasn't going to cut it with Wynne. Is that what he wanted anyway? More of the same? Mindless distraction until work called him to the next place, then alone again?

He nursed his drink as a familiar ache tugged behind his ribs.

Wynne didn't feel like more of the same.

She said she wanted to like him. But what did that mean? She didn't? Part of her did? If that was so, why wouldn't she just listen to that part? It was so simple. Maybe she'd enjoy herself, and he wouldn't be sitting alone at the bar right now.

It means she wishes you were better than you are. Look at you.

The little voice at the back of his mind felt like a slap. A pointed finger, directed inward.

Like he needed more of that.

He signaled the barman for a refill, to treat the barren angst accompanying the indictment. As he waited, the little voice whispered again.

This is what she's talking about. She wouldn't even like you if she knew half of it.

His thoughts flicked involuntarily over the series of decisions which landed him here.

He'd seen more of the world than most people, met his fair share of pleasant and unpleasant figures, and while he wouldn't have characterized himself as rich, he was better off than many.

He left Austerholt for Hollis bankrupt in spirit, only to leave Hollis with next to nothing in his pockets. He was bunking in a tenement house with nothing to his name. Here, he was no one. To no one. He could die tomorrow, and no one would mourn him.

He tried not to idle on what his life might've been like if Isolde hadn't done what she'd done.

He took a pull from his drink, unable to smother the self-contempt which was usually content to lie quiet if he had a way to amuse himself. But the ache pressed against him with a weight impossible to ignore.

It was this place. A village full of families, constantly reminding him what he didn't have. The cities of Austerholt and Hollis were different. Brutal and filthy, but easier to float from one distraction to another without making himself a stink amongst the people. Sure, he'd deal with after-effects of a night of heavy drinking. He'd occasionally get a night of fun. Maybe a few weeks of it. Then alone again.

More than this place, it was Wynne.

She floated to the back of his mind. Challenging him. Baring her heart, in a way. She said she wanted to like him.

Wanted to, but didn't. Not as he was.

Her reason? *You're for yourself.*

No kidding. Who else was going to look out for him? The buzz of irritation returned with her parting comments. *My feelings are complicated.*

He scoffed as he brought his cup to his lips. "I'll show you complicated."

"What did you say?" asked a woman to his left.

"Nothing," he said, the effects of the drink blunting the embarrassment. "Talking to myself."

He cast her a sideways glance and recognized her from among the spectators earlier that day. The sheet of red hair stood out. Her nose was too long for her face, but she was otherwise pretty. Well, passably pretty, but everyone looked prettier after a few drinks.

She gave him an inviting smile. "I'm Simone." Her voice was low, pleasant, and smooth.

"Kal."

She slipped onto the stool beside him with her pint of ale and shook the hair away from her shoulders. Some folks said women just wanted to settle and have a family. Wholesome things. In Kal's experience, there existed a whole subset of women who were anything but wholesome. He wondered what type she was.

She caught him looking. Leaning closer, she spoke into his ear and effectively answered the question. "Do you want to go somewhere?"

Kal hesitated.

She placed a hand on his leg, which made the decision for him. Not his first choice, but how picky was he gonna be? He rested his drink, took her hand, and led her to the back hall of the tavern. It was empty. He backed her against the wall and kissed her.

She was not a good kisser. Her lips were tight and awkward. She used too much force in the wrong kind of way. It was so bad, Kal pulled his lips off hers to avoid them. He used a hand to brush the hair away from her face. He kissed her on the cheek instead.

She laughed deep in her throat.

"What's funny?" he asked. Not really caring. He kissed her again, moving closer to her neck.

"I was thinkin', wait until Wynne hears about this," she said, as though she relished it. "Don't worry. She doesn't know how to please a man like I do."

Kal stopped with his nose an inch from her ear. Jarred by the off-putting meanness in her tone, he pulled back.

The thoughts of Wynne which had been dancing around his mind, making him miserable, rushed to the forefront and pressed against his conscience, framing the issue in the clearest of terms. The Enclave was a small village. People talked. He could have Simone now, but if he followed through with her, his chance for anything of substance with Wynne died.

Is that what he really wanted? Passably pretty, low-hanging fruit, or Wynne – the best of women?

Kal pulled back further, turned his face away, and brought his fist to his forehead. He clamped his eyes shut and took a steadying breath.

He wanted to indulge himself. Badly.

I want to like you.

He wanted that too. More than that, he wanted to be the kind of man Wynne would like. He wanted her approval. Her affection. Her respect.

He wanted Wynne.

Kal set his mind with every ounce of resolve he possessed given his slightly drunken state. To his surprise, a deep inner well of determination seemed to flood his veins, lending him the strength to move, as long as he moved now.

Before temptation ensnared him, he removed Simone's hands from his waist. Without another look at her, he pushed away from the wall and proceeded toward the back door. "I gotta go."

"Where are we going?"

"Nowhere. Goodnight."

"What?" She sounded hurt and offended. Angry. "Because of that comment about Wynne? She doesn't even want you. She's not here. I am."

Kal pressed his hand against the swinging back door and shoved it open. The cold night air seemed to swallow him whole as he stepped outside and left the tavern behind.

19

At Fiona's side, Zak's voice was tight with stress. "You're hurting her!"

"It'll be alright," Wynne said as diplomatically as possible. "She's only trying to turn the baby. It's uncomfortable, but –"

"Uncomfortable? My wife is in agony."

"She's in labor." Catreeny's harsh voice cut into the argument.

Fiona whimpered and gritted her teeth as Catreeny attempted once more to coax the child in the right direction by pressing the belly.

Zak bit back another outburst. Tears leaked from the corner of Fiona's eyes. She rested a weary head back against her pillow.

In the last ten minutes, Fiona's pains intensified, coming in closer waves, signifying the imminence of birth. Despite the prayers and waiting, the baby hadn't assumed a head-down position in the hours since their morning visit. They all felt the looming question deeply. *What if Catreeny couldn't fix this?*

At some point, the attempts to turn the child could do more harm than good, and the effort had to be abandoned. Wynne maintained faith. Catreeny could do it.

Catreeny swore and shook her head. "It's not working."

She motioned for Wynne to feel the area below Fiona's ribs.

Wynne obeyed and laid her hand gently atop the pregnant belly, using gentle pressure to feel for what Catreeny wanted her to sense.

Wynne met Catreeny's face and new sobriety stole over her. "That's the head."

"Get Sender," Catreeny said.

Already anxious, the panic in Zak's voice spiked. "What's going on?"

Wynne didn't hear Catreeny's response. A blast of chilly night air enveloped her as she burst from the home and took to the road at a sprint.

✧

Wynne shouted Sender's name as his home came into view. Her lungs burned and her breaths came ragged as she raced down the lane in the dark.

When she reached the edge of his yard, his door flew open, silhouetting him with the light inside.

He took in the sight of her and grabbed his healer's bag from just inside the door. "I'm coming."

✧

They crashed into the house without knocking to find Fiona in the throes of labor. Catreeny's harsh voice filled the room. "Wynne! At my side. She's almost out."

Wynne swooped to Catreeny's side and knelt beside the heap of dirty rags. She scrubbed her hands with the clean cloth, listening as Catreeny relayed relevant information to Sender. Fiona cried out again, and it was over.

Catreeny gave the baby a pat and immediately passed her into Wynne's waiting hands. She turned her full attention to Fiona, who teetered on the edge of consciousness.

Wynne lost focus on what else was taking place around her. She knew the toll on Fiona's body had been severe. The loss of blood, too great. Zak was beside himself, frantic and helpless. And in Wynne's arms, the baby was limp. Her skin had a bluish cast. She wasn't breathing.

Anguished, indiscernible prayers from Zak filled the room, along with the curt, businesslike directions between Catreeny and Sender. Wynne half-listened, trying not to grow emotional and failing. She tried to warm the child and encourage breathing.

"Come on, little one. Please, take a breath." Her eyes clouded with tears. "Come on..."

Sender's hand appeared in Wynne's field of view. He rested it upon the child's head, and his other on Fiona's midsection. "*Fyrir therr hondum ae fyrir therune.*"

The glow of his runes brightened with an intensity which lifted more than the physical darkness hanging about the space. The room fell completely quiet, as if a heavenly force had touched earth, penetrating the little cabin, and brought with it a surreal peace to hold panic at bay.

The weak cry of an infant pierced the silence. Warmth and color returned to the baby. Relief collided with Wynne, making her weak.

She brought the baby to the new parents and laid her on Fiona's chest. Exhaustion and unspeakable solace mingled in Fiona's face as she shared her first moments with her daughter. "Hi, baby..."

Zak planted a kiss on Fiona's forehead and laid a hand gently over his little one. He leaned forward to rest his head on his wife's shoulder. His shoulders shook.

Wynne stepped back to give them space. She held her filthy hands away from her body to avoid touching anything.

A weary smile flickered across Sender's face. Sweat dampened his forehead and drenched his hair and the collar of his shirt. He was catching his breath as he nodded to Wynne. *It's over.*

Catreeny closed her eyes and tipped her head back, uttering a silent prayer. For once, she had no other words.

✦

Healer and midwives left together with promises to return the next morning for their payment, which was to be the agreed-upon young rooster from a recent clutch for the midwives, and to see how mother and baby passed the night. It was dark outside. Lanterns in hand, Catreeny and Sender chatted as if they'd lived through yet another day's work. Wynne trailed a few paces behind. A haze blanketed her mind like a dense fog. She felt as though she were moving through molasses.

She'd watched Sender pull two people from death's clutches. It almost didn't feel real. The events of the evening washed over her, with specifics ebbing in and out of her thoughts like waves against the riverbanks.

"You alright back there?" Sender said, glancing over his shoulder. He slowed enough for her to come alongside.

"Yes," she lied. She wasn't really sure how to feel. She was glad she'd been there. At the same time, a cold, gnawing apprehension had taken residence in her chest. She didn't want to talk about it. She wasn't sure she could.

"I'm glad this happened," Catreeny said over the squeak of her swaying lantern.

Horrified, Wynne gaped at her. "You are?"

"Yes. You'll learn from this."

Sender hummed in agreement.

Wynne said nothing.

✧

As Wynne plodded toward her front door, bone-deep exhaustion enwrapped her. She shuffled inside and leaned against the wall as she removed her shoes. The house was quiet except for activity in the direction of the kitchen.

"Wynne?" Susi's quiet voice carried from out of sight.

"I'm home." *Please don't come here...* Wynne's uniform was more of a mess than usual. She wasn't sure what her face would betray at that moment. She didn't want to rehash the details.

Susi's footsteps drew closer. She rounded the corner, face bright until she saw the state of her daughter. "Are you alright? You look like a ghost."

"Everyone's alive," Wynne said, lacking the energy for any inflection of enthusiasm. "Baby girl."

Alone in her room, Wynne shut the door and slid to the floor. With both hands, she pushed the hair away from her forehead. She drew a shaking breath through her nose, and started to sob.

When the tears dried up, her face felt puffy and a dull ache set itself behind her eyes. She wiped them on the back of her hand, sniffled, and released a cleansing breath. She tipped her head back until it rested against the door. When she shut her eyes, snippets of the evening returned.

Pain. Exposure. Death.

Was this what she had to look forward to nine months after marriage?

For the first time, she felt glad that Harek was neither here, nor ready.

Glad that there was no one else.

Her thoughts jumped briefly to Kal, before dismissing him entirely.

Dearest Wynne,

I enjoyed reading about your vision for a future home. I'm not all surprised by your desire for a stretch of land. I can almost picture little Jaegers running around the grass outdoors, picking flowers and chasing the hens.

At present, having the space for me to train horses sounds like a dream. It would cost a fortune. I also question whether it would provide enough income to support us – at least in the Enclave. Such work could prove profitable with the growth of the Gren.

It's difficult to imagine anything more than farming or following my father's trade. For most of my life, I assumed I'd continue helping my folks. Now, it seems the future is open. We might have a little niche at the Enclave, but at the Gren, we might do anything.

Don't think me selfish for these musings. And please don't mention this to my parents. I don't want to crush them. I'm certainly not advocating that we busk away to the Gren. Still, I must consider the footing of our futures.

The gods have looked upon us with favor, given the milder winter. The absence of snowfall means work can continue. Though we've experienced great progress, new challenges have presented themselves in the form of illness and interrupted supply chains.

Taige Goodhill is expected with another group of Enclavers by the end of the month, which means we'll have two medics instead of one. Neither bear runes to aid in healing. (It's difficult to match Sender's capabilities.) Still, I'm sure it'll help. The most recent group of our kinsman from the Enclave brought along a handful of non-runebearing Northerners. Other Northerners and Heartlanders have come on their own. It's impossible to vet everyone. If they're willing to contribute and work an honest living, leadership is remiss to reject them. In this way, the Gren has become something of a beacon of opportunity for those hoping for a fresh start. We need the extra hands for the work ahead, but it has resulted in more mouths to feed and a strain on resources.

Mother wrote that the family's experienced a spike in business due to the increase in pigs but not to worry. I question whether she's completely frank. I don't know how it's possible for me to return at this time, but I don't want to leave them struggling. I hope this isn't asking too much, but would you check on them and tell me how they are? I know you'll be honest with me. If all's well, it would set my mind at ease.

My mother also mentioned that my pops has a new wooden leg he's rather proud of. I'm more than a little curious about that!

On the topic of family, something happened this week which I hope brings a smile to your face. We were gathered for breakfast. Cain, slurping his tea. Me, attending the bacon. Finnion, dishing out the porridge. Grigory, cutting an apple for himself.

Without warning, Grigory fumbled the fruit and started yelling.

Startled, Billy nearly fell off his bench. "What is it?"

Grigory held up a hand with an expression of shock and horror, showing the stump of two fingers. The group relaxed with a groan, which he seemed to enjoy.

"Again?" Cain said.

"I got yeh."

"You've done it twenty times. You're foolin' no one at this point."

Grigory snickered, drawing a smirk from Finnion.

Cain just shook his head. "You got no shame."

"Look, I'll stop when Billy-boy ain't so jumpy." Grigory held up the hand, turned toward Billy, and hollered again.

Billy flinched at the shout. "For the love of all things sacred, stop yellin'. It's dawn."

"Josef!" Grigory hollered across the way where your brother was passing through.

Josef joined our circle. The conversation turned to his mechanical arm, and he made a comment about the injury preceding it. "I thought it might be the reason I couldn't use my runes for a while."

This grabbed Finnion's attention. "You couldn't use your runes?"

"For a bit. On that topic, what are yours?"

Finnion shifted in his seat, looking uneasy as every eye darted to him. "I don't know. It's alright."

"You haven't had them read?"

"No. It's fine."

"C'mon. We gotta find out what those mean." Josef beckoned with a flick of the hand, all four fingers together. I hesitated to speak up, not wanting to cause undo embarrassment. I could see that Finnion was fighting his distaste with this situation. He must've figured that Josef was not the sort of man to say no to. Reluctantly, he turned the back of his hand to show his runes.

Josef squinted and leaned in. "Huh. Never seen these combinations before. Interesting."

Finnion drew his hand back to himself and resumed his breakfast without a word. Josef tapped me on the arm and asked if I had parchment and something to write with. I did, I said. "Then you're my scribe," he said. With a snort, he turned back to Finnion. "I would write them, but learning how to read and write isn't something they teach you when you grow up a slave."

Josef's history was news to Finnion, and grabbed his full attention a second time. "You were a slave?"

When Josef explained what happened to him as a child, about fighting for his freedom, and making his way to the North where he belonged, I watched a change come over Finnion. A strange sort of comfort. Encouragement. I still don't know how the allur will manifest for him. He kept the paper, and I'm inclined to believe that he'll be studying.

I look forward to news from home.

Yours,

Harek

20

Kal wasn't going to wear Wynne down. That was certain. As counterintuitive as it sounded, he figured it best to give her space while he sorted himself. If he wanted to be with her, then he needed to prove himself a worthy option. The best option.

At minimum, this involved laying down roots.

It was the second time in his life he'd seriously considered such a thing. Circumstances with Isolde made him willing. But circumstances with Isolde were different. For one, Wynne was different. Kal wouldn't have his heart set on her if he had any doubts about that. For another, he was starting from scratch here. He was a master in his craft, and here, he was no one.

At his time of life, it wasn't a great feeling. But it wasn't going to get easier.

A group of men was preparing to leave for Goldbur Gren. Which meant, available houses. Kal bought one from a man named Taige Goodhill. It cost almost everything he had left in gold and silver, but it was his. It also got him out of the men's boarding house, which made him feel like he had to sleep with one eye open. He'd had enough of that.

The house was a glorified shed. Timber framing supported wattle and daub walls and a thatched roof. A fire pit occupied the center of the floor. There was no window, save the hole in the roof which allowed smoke to vent. The door was set low and the ceilings high to accommodate a platform overhead for storing food. This was theoretically reachable by ladder. The house came with a broken one.

Goodhill also left behind a saggy cot and an empty barrel which doubled as a stool or a makeshift table. It beat sitting or sleeping in the dirt. He'd had enough of that too.

Improvements could come later. Maybe he'd build additions. A workshop. A tool shed. A hutch for animals. He could get a hog or goat. A few turkeys. Here, most people kept animals in a barn or shed, but back in Austerholt, creatures were brought indoors and confined to a section of the house during winter. Extra body heat. Practical.

All this presented him with the next natural problem to solve.

He needed income.

Wynne wanted to perform good deeds to care for the needy. That was fine. He liked that about her. But food and other commodities weren't free.

The morning after his first night in his new house, he threw on several layers of warm clothes, a ratty knit cap, and set out to find Omri in hopes the young man could point him in the right direction. He wasn't disappointed.

✧

Kal crunched up the front walk to a stout cabin nearabouts the site Omri planned to build his own. An assortment of shriveled plants and overgrown holly dotted the front of the house in prickly, misshapen lumps. Thatching on the roof looked weather-worn, but the house appeared well-built. He stepped beneath the overhang and rapped his knuckles on the door.

The voice of an older woman carried from inside. "Arlo! Arlo, there's someone knocking."

An older man replied with more amusement than annoyance. "I have ears, you know."

Kal heard shuffling inside and a moment later the door creaked inward to reveal a man with tufts of white hair encircling his head. He had bright eyes and a friendly face. Kal laid a hand on his chest and introduced himself as a new neighbor.

"New neighbor, eh? Must be why I haven't seen you around yet. Name's

Arlo." The older man shifted in the doorway for Kal to see inside. He jerked his thumb over his shoulder and Kal noted the absence of runes on his hands. "My wife, Fay."

The old lady swayed in a rocking chair, bundled to the nose in warm layers. She held a pair of knitting needles and appeared to be halfway through a project. A heap of wool yarn sat in a basket by her feet. Her wrinkled face creased into a sincere smile. "Hello, dear."

"Now what do you want?" Arlo asked, not unkindly.

"Omri mentioned you may have work which needs doing," Kal said. "Is there anything I can help you with?"

"Omri sent you?"

"Oh, he's a good boy," Fay interjected. "Building his house on the plot of land behind ours, he is. Plans to marry Waylas and Pia's daughter, Lara. She's a nice young lady. Very kind and very beautiful. They'll be good neighbors, I'm sure. I can't wait until they fill their house with children." She placed a hand over her heart. "Oh, what a joy."

Kal smiled, unsure how else to respond beyond, "Yes, Omri sent me."

"Well, if Omri sent you...." Arlo thought for a moment. "Matter of fact, I could use a hand."

"Arlo, tell him about the leaves," Fay said, glancing up from her stitches. "They're going to rot our cabin from the bottom up if they stay piled against the house."

"I noticed those," Kal said.

Arlo raised a finger for him to wait a moment. He unhooked a coat from its peg just inside the door, and stood in the opening as he shrugged it on. He stepped outside with Kal. "Where you from?"

"Austerholt. Yourself?"

"Heartlands. Little ol' place called Tick Hill." Arlo waved for Kal to follow him around the side of the property. "Fell in love with a Baldomar girl out in the wider world. We came here together about fifty years ago."

"You built this home?"

"Aye. It's seen better times. Nearly burnt to the ground two years ago."

"What happened?"

"A raid." Arlo shook his head. "Awful. We lost a lot of friends."

Kal never experienced such a thing. His mother survived one when she was a girl. She said it was horrific.

Arlo cast his eyes toward the easternmost mountain bordering the village. He wagged a crooked finger toward it. "The fight went up that mountain. Did you know they found Silversaar there?"

"I thought that was the dragon-queen's mountain?" He'd yet to see her, which leant to some speculation amongst other non-natives in town that she was a myth. He didn't take these whispers seriously, in part because he had no reason to doubt the folks who'd told him otherwise. Omri, Leland, Wynne, and the other Baldomar men at the building site seemed more credible than some of the tavern-goers and boarding house residents who'd circulated the rumor.

Arlo hummed. "It is, now. She's Silversaar's daughter. His heir. We like her. Suppose if you got yourself a house, must mean you like it here?"

"I like the people. It seems like a good place."

Arlo hummed again. "The people make it. Well, good for you. Welcome." He gave Kal a fatherly pat on the arm. "Now, I'll find the rake, for the wet leaves. In the meantime, bring a stack from the wood shed to the porch. I'd do it, but my joints are a bit stiff with this cold. My wife handles it better than I, believe it or not." He chuckled. "She's a Baldomar, not me."

✧

When Kal returned to the house after completing the work, Fay beckoned him inside. He scraped his boots before entering and was met by the scent of woodsmoke mingled with savory pork and vegetables rolling off the hearth. "That smells fantastic."

Fay looked pleased. "Thank you, dear." She forced a piping cup of tea into his hand. "Here. Warm yourself."

"Many thanks." He blew a waft of steam across the surface and took a sip.

His eyes passed over the quaint lodgings. A set of rocking chairs were positioned near the fireplace. There was a square table with a lacy knit covering. A circular rag rug covered part of the floor. He noticed a modestly stocked pantry shelf. A crossbow hung from a rack within arm's reach of the door.

Though clean and cozy, the space showed signs of disrepair. There were cracks in the plaster walls of the cooking area. Floorboards, warped with age, curled in the corners. A ferocious draft rolled off the window nearest Fay's rocking chair and gave Kal a chill from six feet away.

"Finished so soon?" Arlo pattered into the room and narrowly avoided catching his toe on an uneven floorboard, making the muscles around Kal's ribs tense as he prepared to catch the old man, should he trip. He almost spilled his tea on himself.

"Yes, sir. I noticed a flapping shutter along the side, there. Nothing a nail won't fix. I could take care of it, if you got one."

Arlo's face fell. "I'm afraid I don't."

"Where can I buy them?"

"You'd want to see Bera and Dominik. They run the smithy."

"Alright." He downed the rest of the tea. "I'll be back."

✦

Kal returned to Arlo and Fay's with a box of nails and promptly used two-thirds of them to batten down the floorboards and repair the shutter. He also spent time shoving moss in the gaps surrounding the drafty window. The difference was significant.

While he worked, Arlo and Fay chatted with him about all kinds of things. The repairs they wanted to get to, but couldn't. The sweater initiative for the men in Goldbur Gren. The engagement of Omri and Lara which was taking a while due to difficulties of affording the materials to build a house these days, and how many young folks were having to rethink their housing aspirations. It made him realize how fortunate he was to snag Goodhill's hut when he did. Arlo was a conversational man, though far less talkative than his wife. She carried the bulk of it. She struck Kal as extremely knowledgeable about the goings-on in the Enclave.

They asked him about his life and plans. While he spared the more-personal details, he found he genuinely enjoyed sharing stories with them. They laughed together, and the afternoon flew.

When Kal finished, Arlo dropped several silver coins into his palm. More pay than Kal expected. More than he felt comfortable taking, considering their humble estate. Fay insisted he stay for supper, which was easier to accept. The smell had been taunting him all day, and he'd skipped lunch. He would've been satisfied with a hunk of bread and a cup of milk given the good company. He was low on food, and his only other option for a hot meal involved returning to the tavern. Which seemed like a bad idea.

"If you're looking for additional work, you should check with the Haranae brothers, Samuel and Elion," Fay said as she ladled the chowder into a bowl. "I was talking with Verelle – she's their mother – and she says a tree fell on the roof of the tannery during the storm we had the other night. It done crushed half the building. It's a miracle no one was inside at the time."

"How much work could they be doing in the dark?" Arlo said. "It makes sense no one was there."

"They're elves. They can see well in the dark. They could've died."

"If you say so."

Fay passed the bowl to her husband and started on the second dish. "Anyhow, the tannery is a disaster. They can't work until it's cleaned up, which is a problem because Samuel and his wife are having a baby in the spring. Elion and his wife...well, I don't know of any baby yet, but they're newlyweds, so it's only a matter of time. Anyhow, they need to get back to work. The tree is still there. They can't find anyone to help."

"I'm surprised by that," Kal said. The Baldomar seemed like a tight-knit community.

"I'm not," Arlo said. "Folks got their hands full with their own business.

The tannery is downstream, beyond the outer edge of the settlement. And it reeks."

Fay passed the bowl to Kal and he thanked her. He took extra care to avoid dripping on the lacy table covering.

"You're welcome, dear. Verelle said Hleni – Elion's wife – told her that Elion intends to ask Omri to bring tools tomorrow, bright and early. They're basically family. I'm sure they'd welcome any additional help they can get."

Fay took a seat with her own steaming dish.

Kal prepared to tuck in but stopped when Arlo began to pray a blessing over the meal. It caught him off guard. He'd been out of the habit for so long, but out of respect, he bowed his head and waited for Arlo to finish.

Kal dove his spoon into the creamy broth and watched the hunks of bacon, potato, and peas bob around in the liquid. A bite instantly brought him back to his childhood. He eased against his chair and sighed.

"You like it?" Fay asked.

"This is the best thing I've ever tasted," he said. "Reminds me of my mum. We ate a lot of potatoes growing up."

"That's the nicest thing anyone's said to me all week," Fay said, eyes twinkling. "You just made my day."

Kal fished the money out of his pocket and rested it on the tabletop. "I feel like you should keep this," he said to Arlo.

"Things cost money, son." Arlo patted the air. "You did the work."

Kal considered and a mutually beneficial idea came to his mind. "How about this? Keep the money. I'll come back to take care of all these repairs." He gestured to indicate the house. "For every afternoon I work, you can pay me with more of this." He tilted his dish to indicate the chowder.

"You like it that much?"

"I do."

Fay sat a little straighter. "It would be my pleasure, and we enjoy the company. I hope you don't mind if I make other dishes besides this. We do like a little variety."

21

The day Jairus was born, Wynne and Omri found themselves responsible for all the chores. A big task for an eleven and thirteen year old. They fell to with enthusiasm. There wasn't anything they could do to help with the birth. It turns out, those took a long time.

After finishing with the animals, they took refuge in the barn and swung on the rope swing attached to the rafters.

"Do you want to go inside and see if it's over?" Wynne said. She was antsy to meet her new sibling and after learning about Inorra, she wanted to make sure Susi was alright. Catreeny was capable. Still, births could be risky.

"I don't wanna go back in yet," Omri said.

Wynne decided not to push. Inside, they could hear their mother in labor on the other end of the house. It got to Omri in a way which it didn't to Wynne.

"Are you hoping for a brother or sister?" she asked.

"Brother," he said without a moment's hesitation.

"I'm hoping for a sister." She already had a brother in Omri. There was also the brother she never met, Josef. He would've been eighteen or nineteen now, if he was still alive.

They swung from the rope swing until the temperature dipped. Wynne decided they'd waited long enough. "We should go inside and boil water."

"Why?"

"I don't know. I heard Catreeny talking about it. I think it's for cleaning.

For after."

"Boil water if you wanna. I'm gonna stay in the kitchen." As far from the bedroom as possible.

They stepped through the back door and listened. The house was quiet. Too quiet. No sounds of Catreeny's harsh directions. No yells of pain. Wynne's heart clenched with a spike of dread.

A door opened on the far side of the house and Elric's heavy tread drew close. He appeared in the kitchen door cradling a bundle against his chest. His eyes were red with fatigue, yet he radiated a peaceful calm. "Come meet your brother."

Despite the brief tug of disappointment, Wynne beamed at the sight of the baby, tiny against the vastness of Elric. She elbowed her way past Omri, arms extended to hold the child.

Elric hesitated. "Why don't you sit down, first – and keep it down," he added as she barreled into the greatroom and threw her backside into the nearest rocking chair. "Your mother's resting."

Any disappointment she felt was forgotten the moment she held Jairus. He had the somewhat squashy appearance of a fresh newborn, with rounded cheeks and eyes squinted shut with drowsiness. His tiny, rune covered fingers gripped the edge of his swaddling cloth.

Wynne planted a kiss on his forehead.

She hadn't stopped wanting a sister. It seemed almost a tease that Aeryn had lived with them for such a short time, and now that she and Josef were married, she didn't live in the Enclave anymore.

Now, there was Lara. Or, there would be soon enough.

Wynne wrapped the new cherry-red scarf around her neck with a swell of sisterly affection. It had been a gift from Lara, who'd been making more effort to befriend Wynne. It was easy to see why Omri adored her. It was also her favorite color.

She found Elric and Susi sitting at the table.

"Where are you going?" Elric asked as she pecked him on the cheek.

"To visit Tess. My watch doesn't start until noon."

"You've got the early watch tomorrow?"

"Yes. Why do you ask?" Wynne moved toward her boots lined up near the door.

"I needed to know you hadn't switched with anyone," Elric said. "Don't. Corbin is coming to dinner tomorrow."

Wynne's feet drew to a stop. Her smile faltered, sticking to her face with an awkward, frozen quality as she rotated to face her parents. "By dinner...?"

"Yes, dear," Susi said, her voice bright and happy.

An invisible belt constricted around Wynne's ribs. Out of respect for her father, she kept herself from a vehement refusal. Still, her mind raced for a way out.

No obvious objections came to mind. Corbin was healthy, strong, and industrious. He was modestly handsome, as long as he kept his mouth shut. The few times they'd interacted, he'd been nothing but courteous.

Susi noticed the uneasy shift in Wynne. Her eyebrows drew together and pitched in the middle. "What's the matter?"

Wynne's frozen smile turned into a wince. "Do we have to?"

The line of Susi's mouth hardened. She cast Wynne a tired glance. "This is not a debate."

"You don't like Corbin?" Elric's bushy brow bent in an effort to make sense of Wynne's apprehension.

Wynne struggled for a response. "I barely know him."

"What do you think the dinner is for?"

Susi moved the basket of blackberries away from Jai. "Wynne, from the dawn of time, folks have been marrying without knowing the depth of the other person. Do you think I knew everything there was to know about your father when we married?"

Wynne tugged the scarf away from her neck. Why was it so warm in here all the sudden? "I understand that. It'd be nice to know a little bit. We've barely ever spoken."

"True, but your paths have crossed enough. You make an impression," Susi said. "You're a Thar, and a beautiful young woman. Hard-working and kind. Men notice these things, even if they have the manners not to be obvious."

"Ned speaks well of him," Elric said, as if more information would solve the problem. "He's made sure his mother and sisters were provided for after his father died. He's got plenty of sisters, so he's well-accustomed to relating to women. What more do you need to know?"

Wynne's heart ticked against her ribs. The mention of Corbin's family brought a potential objection to mind. "He lives with his mother!"

"He lives in a large home built to accommodate several generations. That's how they do things where he's from," Susi said matter-of-factly. "They'd build on to accommodate your family."

"Mother, you're speaking like it's decided already," Wynne said, trying to keep the panic out of the edge of her voice.

Susi flashed a palm. "I didn't mean to. But you know how these things go. Wynne, you might be engaged tomorrow night." Her eyes crinkled into a smile and her whole face brightened. "It's a special day. You should be excited."

Wynne tried to return the smile. The half-hearted effort only made her look sick. A hot wave of stress prickled over her scalp as the dinner played out in her mind. Corbin, eager. Her parents, delighted. A decision, that night. His teeth, closing in as he tried to kiss her.

Wynne blew a steadying breath through her nose. This was too much.

Susi's tone softened, and she placed a hand flat on the tabletop in Wynne's direction. "Wynne, dear, I understand you're nervous. What you're feeling is completely normal. I was nervous too when your grandpop announced my dinner with your father."

"That was different," Wynne said. She sincerely hoped it would be. Grandpop had been an elder, too, which meant he could officiate a marriage, and he did. That day.

"It wasn't that different," Susi said.

"She didn't like me," Elric said, which drew a curious look from Wynne. She never heard that detail before.

"Stop it. I wasn't sure about you."

Elric made a doubtful hum but his eyes twinkled.

Susi tossed up a hand. "You had a habit of pushing me into the Bekker, Elric. I had reservations."

Elric inclined his head toward Wynne with a little chuckle. "That, she liked."

Susi fought back a smirk. She smoothed the front of her skirt in a dignified manner. "I came to the dinner with an open mind. Your father impressed your grandpop and won me over. I want you to promise me that you'll give Corbin a fair consideration."

Wynne turned to Elric for help and found none. Elric heaved a sigh and fixed her with a thoughtful, fatherly look. "Do you trust us?"

"Yes."

"If we think Corbin's worthy of consideration, doesn't that count for something?"

Wynne understood his point and agreed in principle. She still felt like a rat trapped under the claw of a cat. "I suppose."

"Then will you agree to give him a fair consideration?"

It wasn't an unreasonable request. Still, it felt like surrender. "...Alright."

Satisfied, Susi nodded. "Good."

"What if I don't think he's a good match?" The words burst from her, like getting them out was the only way to save herself from heading to Corbin's large multigenerational home as his new wife at the end of tomorrow.

Susi placed her hands on her hips. Not a good sign. "You just promised you'd participate without having made up your mind from the start."

"I will keep that promise. I mean, when the dinner comes to a close. Pops, is it safe to assume he'll say yes if you ask?" To drive home her earlier point, she added, "You know him better than I do."

Elric drummed his thumb on the tabletop and took a patient breath. "Highly likely."

"I thought so. What if I desperately don't want you to ask?"

Elric and Susi exchanged a glance.

Wynne pressed ahead. "What if he gives me a bad feeling in my gut?"

"Wynne, is there something about Corbin you know that I don't?" Elric sounded concerned.

"No, that's not what I meant," she said, realizing she sounded like she was hinting he wasn't as upright as assumed. She wasn't trying to impeach his character. "I mean, what if I find him repulsive?"

"Do you?"

"Well, no. What if I do by the end of the dinner?"

"Wynne."

"What if I know that I could never love him?"

Elric watched her for a long moment. "Should I worry about you sabotaging this event?"

"I wouldn't do that to you," Wynne said, a little wounded. "Try to understand, Pops. Your choice to ask or not affects the rest of my life. Once I'm married to him, we're stuck together forever unless one of us dies." *Say, in childbirth.*

"Heavens, Wynne. Stuck?" Susi said. "You make it sound like marrying him is a punishment."

Wynne shook her head. "Not what I meant. Only, marrying the right person matters."

Elric shifted in his seat. He folded his hands and leaned onto his forearms. Same intent posture she'd seen dozens of times, for dozens of serious father-daughter conversations. "Daughter of mine, look me in the face. I consider myself a good judge of character. You know I wouldn't pose the question if I doubted whether he'd be good to you. I won't force you into a marriage you don't want. You have my word. But I want yours that you'll be fair. We're Thars. We're brave and fair."

Some of Wynne's apprehension ebbed, replaced by a pull of affection for her father. She nodded. "Alright."

"We'll work out some kind of signal," he said with a wink.

✧

Tess opened the door holding a finger to her lips. She allowed Wynne to peer into the house where Skeggis dozed atop a bearskin rug, stretched before the fireplace. Asmund slept soundly on his chest. The child gently rose and fell in time with Skeggis' breathing, while Skeggis' hand rested on his back to keep him from rolling off. The show of tenderness was such a contrast to the boisterous, destructive man Wynne knew. She couldn't help smiling and placed a hand on her heart.

"I know. Adorable," Tess said in barely a whisper. "Don't wake 'em." They stepped into the yard, and Tess closed the door quietly. "I like your scarf."

Wynne reflexively touched the soft wool at her neck. "Thank you. It was a gift from Lara."

"Why you look like your cat died?"

Wynne's face fell. "My parents are hosting a special dinner tomorrow."

Tess gasped. "With who?"

"Corbin Unger."

Tess thought for a moment. "The one with the feral front teeth?"

"It's more than just the front."

"Heh. Apart from the mouth, he's not bad."

Wynne followed her around the house toward the cowshed. "I don't know what to do."

"It's not complicated. You don't even gotta go nowhere."

"I mean, I don't want to marry him."

Tess shot her a funny look. "Wot do you got against Corbin?"

Wynne's shoulders inched toward her ears. "The fact that I don't want to marry him is enough."

Tess hummed in the negative. "That don't answer the question. Second, you don't know that. You haven't done the dinner yet."

"I don't need to do the dinner to know that, Tess."

"Well, don't snap at me about it."

"Sorry." Wynne kicked a rock out of the way as Tess unlatched the cowshed door. "It's been an awful week."

"I heard you saved Zak and Fiona's baby. That don't sound awful."

"I didn't. Sender did."

"Well, Sender's goin' around, givin' you credit." Tess gave the door a yank. The potent aroma of barn animals met them. Inside, Tess kicked a milking stool into place beside the cow, positioned a bucket, and got to work. "So wot's the issue with Corbin? Does he smell? You know, more than the average person?"

"Not that I can tell."

"Wot then? He's too poor? We're all barely scrapin'."

"I know," Wynne conceded with a groan. She sank on to the spare milking stool and rubbed her hands over her face. "He's not horrendous –"

Tess threw back her head and released a bark of laughter. "There's a compliment if I ever heard one."

"Glad you find this funny."

"Is it that newcomer you been flirtin' with?"

A flush of indignation made Wynne's face hot. "I haven't been flirting with Kal."

Tess made a noise in the back of her throat.

"Alright, I've flirted with him a tiny bit."

"He's a handsome one."

"He knows it," Wynne said darkly. "I'm not impressed."

Tess shrugged. "Harek, then?"

With a pang behind the ribs, Wynne's thoughts turned toward the letters stowed in her room. To the complicated set of feelings he always tended to elicit. "Maybe that's it."

Tess cast her a funny look for the second time.

"He wrote to me again."

"Why didn't you start with that?" Tess' face cracked into a gap-tooth smile. "Wot did he say?"

"He told me about his progress at the Gren. His friends. He's working hard."

"He tell you he loves you yet?"

"He says he misses me."

"That's it?"

"He signs his letters, *yours.*"

"Oh-ho-ho."

"Stop teasing," Wynne said, blushing.

"And how have you been signing your letters?"

"With my name."

"That's it?" She sounded outraged. "Gods. I can't read, but even I know you should be signin' more than that." She stopped milking and wrote in the air in exaggerated loops with an imaginary pencil. "Like, *I want to have your babies, Wynne.*"

A cold sinking gripped Wynne from the inside, pulling fun out of the conversation. "Yeah, well...we'll see."

"Suppose we will. 'Specially with the dinner tomorrow."

Wynne rubbed her hands over her face again and groaned.

"Just do the dinner," Tess said, coaxing. "See how it goes. You might be surprised."

22

Kal supposed the tannery's proximity to the southern woods shouldn't surprise him. The Haranaes were elves. Still, tree-people near the woods might've been coincidence. Tanneries usually weren't a welcome fixture in town. Necessary, but they stunk.

He wasn't sure what to expect of the brothers. He'd seen them around on market days. Neither were overly outgoing, though the shorter, younger one seemed like the happier of the two.

He'd also heard more than a few stories associated with their name. Their sister, Aeryn, was some kind of dragon-slaying freedom fighter who'd joined herself to the Baldomar clan through marriage – to the guy responsible for defeating the dragon who'd fashioned himself king of the Empire.

None of it sounded real. But these were weird people.

As Kal drew up to the property with Omri, he whistled long and low. Fay hadn't exaggerated. Normally a well-supported tree possessed enough give to withstand the battering of Noemar weather. Not so in this case. The offending tree appeared otherwise healthy, though fell at just the right angle to demolish the roof. Its main shaft was over a foot in diameter with several thick offshoots. Long enough to stretch the full width of the building and beyond. Some effort had been made to cut away the branch, as evidenced by the tools resting unattended nearby.

Two elvish men came around the side of the building. Kal identified a familial resemblance in the slope of their nose, the pointed ears, and the green eyes.

The taller one shook his head about something. His skin had a pale cast and he moved with a stiffness to his gait.

"Morning," Omri said with too much enthusiasm for the early hour. "I brought an extra set of hands. Meet Kal. Kal, the brothers Haranae."

The shorter brother moved forward with an amiable expression, hand lifted in a wave. "I'm Elion. This is Samuel."

Up close, Kal noticed pronounced bags under Samuel's eyes, along with coarse stubble on his lip and chin. His dark hair had been slicked into a knot at the back of his head, and several shorter whisps had come loose.

"Many thanks for coming out," Samuel said. "We'll take any help we can get. And we haven't been able to get much."

"I thought the Baldomar worked for fun," Kal said, keeping it light.

Samuel's mouth twitched into a cynical smile. "Not much incentive."

"Well, I've got a handsaw and an axe. Point me in the direction of what needs doin'."

"Gladly."

With a wave, the brothers directed them in through a gap in the wall. A barrel of urine had been knocked over during the incident, making the building reek worse than a typical tannery. The remains of damaged hoops, splintered wood, roofing material, and dead leaves littered every surface.

"Thankfully, half of our equipment is still intact," Elion said.

"Thankfully, no one was inside the building when this happened," Samuel countered. "Which is a miracle, the luck we've had lately..."

"We need to clear the tree and rebuild the roof as soon as possible," Elion said. "You may've seen our stack of logs out there. We got started."

Kal had noticed. *Stack* was generous. It was difficult to imagine the Haranae's accomplishing much more without significant help. Samuel and Elion both appeared wiry and strong, but diminutive in comparison to their Baldomar neighbors.

"It's going to take weeks," Samuel said darkly.

"Let's be sunny." Omri clapped him on the shoulder. "With all four of us?

I recon, less than a few days."

✧

The Haranaes presented a stark contrast to the few elves Kal met during his stay in Hollis, who were lovely in appearance but haughty. The Haranaes were people of the earth. Decent, direct, and without airs.

Kal sat in a loose circle with Omri and the brothers while he devoured a midday meal. The group conversed with an easy dynamic which facilitated frank banter, in the same spirit which characterized the last several hours of strenuous work. Samuel, however, stared at an indistinct patch of ground as he chewed a hunk of bread. He had scratches on his hands and face from sheering branches.

"You alright, friend?" Kal asked.

Samuel shook himself. He rested his bread and drew a thoughtful breath, as if deciding whether he possessed the energy to elaborate.

"It's been a rough week," Elion said by way of explanation for his brother's misery.

"It's been a rough year." Samuel ran a hand over his weary face and Kal recognized more clearly a man hanging on by a thread. He'd been there himself. Samuel cast a weak nod toward the growing pile of firewood. "This, added to everything...."

"What kinda things?" Kal asked.

"We fled the South under less than ideal circumstances," Samuel said after a moment's consideration. "We left a well-established family business. Our homes. Friends. In-laws – not that mine thought much of me to begin with. Still it's a shame they'll likely never know their grandchildren. Now, make no mistake. My family is together. We're alive. I'm grateful. But to say it's been difficult is an understatement. We're starting from the ground – in *Noemar* of all places. You cannot describe a place more different from Thoen. The cold alone feels like grim death breathing down your neck. It was here, or dead anywhere else."

"Why were you dead anywhere else?"

Samuel lifted his sleeve and showed the brand on his forearm. A shimmery purple crescent along with the number three.

Kal knew what it meant. *Conscripts.* "You were in the Empire's army?"

"Only for a short time, thank the gods," Elion said.

"No, thank our sister," Samuel said.

"The elvish freedom fighter?" Kal had been wanting to ask but held back for lack of natural opportunity.

"I know. Hard to believe." Samuel snorted. "I recall when she was waist high, shooting half her arrows into the pond. Then me, having to fish them out before our parents returned from work."

"I recall you falling into that pond," Elion said with a straight face.

Samuel cast him an unamused glance.

"There was a great splash."

The brothers locked in a stare-off for a beat, then Samuel's smile cracked. He snorted and shook his head. "So what brought you here?" he said to Kal.

"Funny enough, I was dead meat if I stayed where I was, too."

Omri crunched into an apple. "I haven't heard this story."

"Did you escape the Talons also?" Elion said.

"No. I left Noemar for Gallendahli before things grew turbulent. I missed the conscription." He fished around the bottom of his burlap sack for a bite-size hunk of brick which had come loose. "The war didn't touch the East in the same way it did other parts."

"Why go to Gallendahli?" Omri asked.

"Mainly, because it wasn't Austerholt," Kal said with a bitter laugh. "It's gorgeous. They got an appreciation for beauty, which helped me find a good job."

"You're an artist, I hear," Elion shifted his bite of food into his cheek, and covered his mouth as he spoke. "I've seen Leland Jaeger's new leg."

"Everyone's seen Leland's new leg," Samuel said. "He can't stop showing it off to anyone with sight." Samuel altered his voice in an imitation of the butcher. "*Go ahead, kick it. Solid as an oak tree. Go on!*"

There was a round of laughter. Samuel raised his canteen to Kal. "You've skill."

"Many thanks," Kal said. "I was hired to work on a new palace in Hollis for a nobleman named Isak Fasthelm. I was responsible for much of the detail work. Crown molding. Carved fixtures."

"Sounds like quite the opportunity."

"It was great. I wish it ended better."

"What happened?"

"I slept with Fasthelm's wife."

Kal was met by a stunned silence. Worried he'd strayed too frank for present company, he flashed a palm before elaborating. "In my defense, she was not forthright about her identity."

"You slept with the woman, not knowing who she was?" Elion said with a mix of curiosity and honest concern.

Kal turned up his palms. "She approached me, presented herself as available, and offered me the night of my life. Difficult thing to say no to, my friend. Also a tremendous mistake."

"I take it the nobleman found out?" Omri said.

"The next day," Kal said. "She went to her husband and told him. Apparently to get back at him. As you can imagine, he was livid."

"I bet."

"A friend got wind and warned me that I was about to be crucified, so I left Hollis as quickly as I could," Kal said. "Fasthelm had a lot of resources at his disposal. I figured going back to Austerholt off the beaten path was the safest course. Except I ended up getting robbed at one point."

"By the nobleman's guys?"

"Outlaws. If it was the nobleman's guys, I'd be dead," Kal said. "Then I stumbled across this place. Sort of."

"Sort of?" Samuel said.

"I didn't realize how close I was to civilization. A scout ran me over in the woods." Kal smiled to himself at the memory. "It was a great day."

"This scout – you're talking about Wynne?" Omri asked. "She ran you over?"

"Knocked me flat on my back. She was being chased by a boar at the time."

"A boar?"

"Hunting gone wrong, I suppose."

"She was hunting boar by herself?"

"Yeah. What's the look?"

"Nothing. Just hunting alone, tackling strangers in the woods...." Omri smirked. Bringing his canteen to his lips, he gave a little shake of the head. "Kal, you've given me a gift."

"Go easy on her."

"She can handle it."

"I believe you, but if you mention it, I'll be in bigger trouble. She's mad at me as it is."

"What did you do?"

Kal released a breath and rubbed the back of his head. "Made a pronk out of myself showing off."

Omri hummed, as if empathizing with an all-too-familiar predicament. "So how many women have you been with since you got here?"

The question caught him off guard. The circle waited for Kal's response.

"None," he said. "That whole ordeal with Fasthelm's wife? It cost me a good job. Even beyond that." He shook his head, feeling a little disgusted with himself. "No. I can't be doin' that. Not if I want somethin' better for my life. And I do."

23

In Baldomar society, the dinner was every bit the social negotiation. If a man wanted to marry, he needed to win over the head of the household. Fathers reserved the right to withhold the question if the would-be suitor failed to impress. Similarly, the woman's family needed to win over the man, who reserved the right to decline the marriage if asked.

At present, with a disproportionate number of available women, the balance of negotiation favored the men. This left families with eligible young ladies the unenviable task of persuasion. *Pick my daughter, not someone else's, despite plenty of other options.*

The dinners were also a cause for gossip, especially amongst the women of the Enclave. People were judged upon them. While a lackluster dinner reflected poorly on a woman's family, an over-the-top event – especially if folks drank too much – invited whispering. No one wanted to be accused of putting on notions, or acting in desperation.

It was a delicate, high-pressure affair.

Wynne had been feeling that pressure all day.

"You look sick," Roran said when he relieved Wynne at the lookout hutch at noon. Roran was a man without subtext. Genuine, loud, and like his sister Tess, as subtle as a lightning bolt. He wasn't nice, but he and Wynne got along fine.

"Thanks, Roran," she said with a roll of the eyes. "You bring your own rope today?"

"Yeh. I heard you got a dinner with Corbin tonight."

"Who told you?"

"Tam," he said, meaning his wife.

Wynne took a slow breath. She hadn't mentioned anything to Tam.

"Wot?"

"I barely know him," Wynne said.

"So? I barely knew Tam when her pops invited me." Roran shrugged. "She was pretty. Seemed like a good woman. I said, yes."

He made it sound so simple. Maybe it was that simple for Roran.

"What do you know about him?" Maybe more information would help, though she doubted it.

"I hear he's got a rivalry with Lugh Bendick."

"Over what?"

"Cows."

Wynne dipped her chin. "Cows?"

"Man's a farmer. Wot do you expect?"

When Wynne arrived home, she was surprised to see fewer in-progress dishes arrayed across the table than expected. Susi bustled into the room wearing an apron and a dusting of flour. "How was your watch?"

"Uneventful. What are you planning for tonight?"

"Beef stew and barley rolls. I'm also making a cake with blackberry and goat cheese filling."

It sounded like a normal supper, dressed up by the promise of a treat. "That's all?"

"It's a nice, family meal," Susi said with an air of dignity. "I won't be serving a seven course feast. Nor will we provide more than one cup of hard cider."

Wynne hopes pricked up. "Really?"

"I will not have it said that the Thars bent over backward in desperation, nor that we acquired an arrangement by intoxicating our guest."

The stifling sense of formality eased, relaxing some of the knots which had taken residence within Wynne since the announcement.

"Still, this is not a casual dinner, so choose a nice dress," Susi said. "I'll help you braid your hair as soon as I finish with this cake."

Normally, Wynne enjoyed the opportunity to dress up, but today it felt like giving in. Despite the remnants of dread clinging to her, she wanted to make a good impression and reflect well upon her family. She gave careful thought to how she presented herself. It took an hour to decide what to wear.

The blue dress with the embroidered flowers reminded her too much of Harek. She'd worn it on the day of the last feast she spent with him. It gave her an uncomfortable feeling she struggled to name. She set it aside.

Her slate gray dress was out of the question. Though far from drab, it didn't strike the right mood. Better for a memorium or somber occasion. Though part of her considered wearing it just to make a point, she set it aside.

She considered the dress given to her last year for her day-of-birth celebration. It was the color of a ripe apple. The dress looked good on her. Maybe too good. The vivacious color, while pleasing to the eye, evoked a sense of intensity. She didn't want to risk sending the wrong message.

In the end, she chose the dress dyed a rich, spruce green with a long skirt, a fitted top, and a wide neck. Flattering and respectable.

Wynne consented to an elaborate braid. Nerves crawled around inside of her as her mother wove strands of hair over and under. She barely spoke. She hadn't decided what *giving Corbin fair consideration* looked like. Promise notwithstanding, she foresaw this evening ending one way.

She wondered what he'd be like, and a terrible thought occurred to her. What if he found *her* unpleasant? She might not want to marry him, but she didn't want to be rejected either. It was one thing to end the dinner with no agreement because she could do better. It was another matter to end the dinner with no agreement because the man in question thought he could do better. She was Wynne Thar. An elder's daughter. What did *better* look like for Corbin?

The sun resigned itself in late afternoon, when the knock on the door came.

Corbin entered the home, carrying himself with a cautious, albeit collected air. If he felt as nervous as Wynne, his self-mastery left her envious. For the first time, it occurred to her that he had reason for confidence. Elric chose to consider him, of all people, for a possible son-in-law.

The toes of his boots were clean. He wore a dark blue sweater with leather ties at the neck. The scent of cloves hung around him and he held a bundle of flowers. The clusters of cherry-red petals caught Wynne's attention immediately.

"These are for you," Corbin said.

"Thank you," she said, genuinely touched. It wasn't expected – or customary – for a man to bring a gift, especially considering the circumstances. "This is my favorite color. How'd you know?"

"I didn't." He sounded pleasantly surprised. "I remember you wore a dress in that color at last year's Ice Throw feast. The color looked so good on you, I wanted to bring you something in the same shade."

The comment caught Wynne off-guard. She couldn't keep the grin off her face if she tried. This seemed to please him. He exposed his crooked teeth in a smile, which brought her back to earth. She cringed inwardly, then caught herself.

We're Thars. We're brave and fair.

Something inside her shifted, and she found herself able to see past the crooked teeth, to the happy eyes and the generous, humble spirit she was told about.

Susi cast Elric a glance, which was as much to say, *We're off to a good start.*

"I can turn into a bear," Jai announced as soon as they were seated.

Corbin inclined his head. "A bear, you say?"

Jai hummed and nodded. "Do you wanna see?"

"Not now," Susi said. "You can't eat your supper as a bear."

Elric took the cue to cut off further debate on the matter, and prayed a blessing over the meal.

"If I finish eating fast, can I show my trick then?" Jai asked.

"Not tonight," Elric said with a chuckle.

"Children are a joy," Corbin said. "I'm sure you feel the same way, Wynne, with the work you do."

Wynne hummed in the affirmative. "I love helping the new babies. The moment the parents get to meet the little one for the first time? It's the best part."

"What do you think about all these men goin' to the Gren?" Elric asked. Wynne's thoughts turned with an ache to Harek. They shouldn't be having this dinner when he was out there, working to come back to her.

"If what they're saying is true, it's hard to blame them," Corbin said. "I'm interested to see how many folks'll take root there or come home. From what I hear, it seems like the Enclave is a better place for families right now. But as the Gren matures, that might change."

"Would you ever consider moving there?" Susi said.

"No, ma'am. My place is here," he said. "I want to continue to work my land, and be around to help my mother and sisters. My parents built a large house when they arrived here. It's feeling emptier and emptier as my sisters get married, and go live with their husbands. Someone needs to care for it, and I don't plan on leaving my mum to do it alone. Don't seem right."

Elric hummed.

"Really, I hope to fill it with my own family. A wife and many children, if the gods are willing. That's my highest hope. A family of my own."

There were smiles and nods from Susi and Elric. Of course they were pleased to hear this. Part of Wynne was pleased too. In the short time he'd been here, Corbin had grown in her estimation. He was a good, hardworking man who wanted to build a life with someone. He was ready.

Corbin met her face, seeing how his words struck her, with a gentle confidence which invited her to cast aside her fear and join him.

Sweat pricked along Wynne's hairline. A sudden queasy wave swept over her. Vivid images skipped across her mind. Fiona, exposed and in agony. The baby, discolored and limp. Zak, frantic.

It took everything she had to keep from popping out of her seat and fleeing through the back door.

She forced a smile. "That's great," she said, trying to keep the choked quality out of her voice. She realized she'd been clenching her teeth.

"You want a big family as well?" Corbin said.

"Of course," she said with a complicated wrench in her conscience.

Wynne stirred the food around in her dish and tried to quell her rising stress. *You need to set this aside. Change the subject.*

She wasn't sure how she managed it, but she did. As the dinner progressed, conversation flowed naturally. Wynne found she enjoyed speaking with Corbin, as much as anyone. Maybe more than the average person. Despite earlier reservations, the hours flew. The only other aspect which threw her was Corbin's laugh. It was higher-pitched than she expected.

"I'm told you have a rivalry with Lugh Bendick," she said as she used her spoon to cut into her treat. "How'd you two get so adversarial?"

Through a grin, Corbin groaned and cast his eyes toward the ceiling. "There's no rivalry. He's just...well..." He trailed off, clearly wanting to avoid speaking ill of his neighbor.

Elric patted the air. "You don't have to say it, son. We all know."

There was a round of good-natured laughter.

"Let's settle on *peculiar*," Corbin said.

"Good word." Wynne took the last bite of the blackberry treat.

"What happened is this. I was coming in from the fields one day. Sun's setting. Sky was all orange and purple." Corbin waved a hand, as though painting a picture with a sweep of his palm. "I had a stack of hay bales situated near my stable. As I'm passing, I noticed the silhouette of a cow in leather barding atop it. Just standing there, sniffing the breeze, with the setting sun behind."

Wynne tried not to choke on a laugh. "Peig?"

"The one and only."

"What was she doing?"

He turned his palms up. "She must've gotten loose and wandered onto my land. The real question is how she climbed up there. They're not the most nimble of creatures. I stopped to stare. Then I heard Lugh hollerin'."

"Oh, no."

"He marched up the lane." Corbin altered his voice in a spot-on imitation of Lugh. "*Corbin, you tryin' to steal my cow? I shoulda known when I saw you pilin' all this hay. You know she can't resist a regal perch!"*

The family broke into another round of laughter and Wynne covered her mouth as tears came to her eyes. Corbin finished his story. She rested a palm against her cheek. Her face hurt from grinning.

Elric cast her a searching look. She smiled back at her father, enjoying the tide of mirth and good spirits.

With a look of pride, Elric gave a satisfied little nod. He returned his attention to Corbin. "Thank you for joinin' us this evening. I think I speak for us all when I say, we've enjoyed the time."

"Thank you for inviting me," Corbin said. "Dinner was very good, and the company, even sweeter."

With a jolt, Wynne understood Elric's glance. Her stomach lurched at what was about to happen. She sat bolt upright, scrambled for the napkin in her lap, and threw it onto her empty plate.

Susi noticed first. Her smile slipped. Before Elric pressed ahead with the question of the evening, she placed a hand on his forearm and gave it a light squeeze. "Husband?"

Elric's attention jumped to Susi, who made a subtle nod in Wynne's direction. He noticed the napkin.

The signal.

Elric met Wynne's face with a mixture of surprise and disappointment.

And frustration.

He drummed his thumb against the table and drew a slow, deep breath.

Corbin's focus jumped between them. "Is everything alright?"

"Yes." Elric cleared his throat. "I just remembered. The cheese, in the treat. Brought the goat to mind. She's been gettin' out, and I need to make sure she's secure before it gets too late. Why don't I walk you outside?"

Corbin seemed confused for a moment. Then insecurity rippled behind his eyes, his former confidence forgotten as he realized what wasn't happening. He offered a tentative smile to Wynne.

With a stab of guilt, she looked away.

24

Wynne expected a diatribe from Susi as soon as Elric and Corbin stepped outside. Susi said nothing, which was worse.

Wynne helped collect dishes and cups without speaking. The temperature in the room seemed to spike in the aftershock over her narrow escape. That, and the storm to come.

Elric returned. "Why did I just send him away?"

Wynne's mouth opened. No sound came out.

He pointed at the door with all four fingers. "Any woman would be lucky to have that man. What happened?"

Wynne's eyebrows pitched in the middle. "I don't want to marry him."

"I don't understand. What was wrong with him?"

"Pops, I don't like him."

"You seemed like you were gettin' along fine. What did I miss?"

A wife and many children...

Wynne grimaced as her mind stretched to avoid admitting that this remark, more than anything, made her most uncomfortable. "He laughs funny. And his teeth are terrible."

"Wynne."

"They look like warring tribes."

Elric clamped his mouth shut. His nostrils flared as he released a controlled breath. He shook his head and turned to Susi. "Is his laugh really that bad?"

Susi made a non-committal hum. Holding her hand level, she tilted it back and forth. "Wynne, I'll grant, his teeth aren't pretty. But you can't be so picky about inconsequential attributes."

Flustered and feeling cornered, Wynne wrung her hands. She tried to avoid looking either parent in the eyes as a rush of water came to her own.

"Why are you crying?" Susi asked.

Wynne covered her face with her hands and shook her head. "Can I just go to bed?"

✧

Don't pry. It was the unspoken rule surrounding the dinners, to avoid embarrassment and protect both parties. A declined betrothal didn't make the rejected individual a poor fit for someone else. Disparagement could ruin a person's reputation and their chances in the future. The Enclave was too small to burn bridges.

Wynne wasn't overly concerned about busybodies plying her for information. Still, she wasn't entirely safe. Despite the custom, chatter was to be immediate and expected. It was tactless, but it happened. Scouting would provide an escape from whatever social repercussions awaited her in and around town in coming days.

There would be no escape tonight.

Wynne dumped her clothes on the floor and pulled on a loose-fitting tunic. The hay mattress crunched beneath her weight as she sank on to the edge of her bed. With a chirp, her cat Gretta picked her way over the lumpy blankets and settled on Wynne's lap. Wynne stared at an indistinct spot on the floor, stroking the mangy cat's rough fur. On the other side of the house, she could hear her father's agitated rumble as he banged around the kitchen. Susi's voice had a tight, measured quality, like she was trying to calm him.

Wynne's eyes drifted to the pendant hanging beside the door. Inorra's pendant.

She'd learned how she came to the Thars by accident. She was ten at the time. Back then, the only newcomers were the rare Baldomar family whisked from the wider world and ferried along by the Silver Shadow. It was an infrequent occurrence which only happened once before in her lifetime, and she barely remembered it. This time, the family had girls around Wynne's age. Two of them. Omri might've been good company, but he was a boy. The gulf between them widened the older she got.

The whole Barliman family was brown-haired and scruffy. There was no mother, and the eldest of the four kids – if he could be called that – was a young man nearing his second decade. Wynne remembered with embarrassment that she found Roran cute at the time, but was cured of the notion once he opened his mouth.

She'd begged to tag along when her grandfather and Aunt Teagan went to see how they were settling. She was nearly crawling out of her skin by the time they reached the one-room cabin designated for newcomers. She stood patiently by, trying not to bounce on her toes or fidget as the adults made introductions.

"I'm sorry, we don't have anyone here by the name of Barliman," Teagan had said in response to a question about relatives. "Still, you may have other family here. I'm sure there'll be no shortage of folks checkin' in, and introducing themselves. You can compare runesets for a match. You never know."

The remark struck Wynne as a little strange, but no one questioned it except for the plucky girl with an animal tooth necklace. Tess was two years older than Wynne, with a gap in her smile where her upper left canine ought to be. She carried herself with competence – about what, Wynne wasn't sure yet – but was otherwise without airs. Her eyes were bright with the spark of good humor. From the little Wynne had seen thus far, she had the frank disposition of a girl who said exactly what she meant and didn't give two figs whether you liked it or not. Wynne liked her immediately.

"Wot does that got to do with relatives?" Tess asked.

"Runes run in families. You may've noticed amongst yourselves," Teagan said with a gesture toward her hand. "Everyone's set is different, but like-groupings are often seen amongst blood-relatives. Granted, lots of people share a rune or two. It's not a foolproof way to determine whether you're related to someone. But closer relations tend to have more matches. You might be surprised who you meet here."

Something cold and solid settled in Wynne's belly, threatening her enjoyment of making new friends. She stole a glance at her knuckles. She already knew her runes didn't match any of Elric's, or Susi's, or Omri's. It hadn't bothered her before.

Of course, she didn't know what most of them meant. No one did, apart from a handful of symbols. Wynne happened to know one. On both index fingers sat a little arrow pointed toward the tip of her finger. She was told it had to do with direction. Which felt right. She had a head for whereabouts, and it made her proud when Elric verbalized his appreciation on a hike. *Alright, Wynne, which way back to the trail?*

It set her apart and made her special.

Now, doubts and questions chewed into her conception of herself. The things which made her unique were things she should've paid better attention to before.

Like her family's disposition. Elric and Susi seemed to possess an innate sense for other's needs and motivations, along with the ability to harness wisdom and compassion in their role within the community. Even Omri had his own effortless charisma. People liked him. He played well with others in a way Wynne envied. As much as she enjoyed the company of others, she was an over-eager puppy by comparison. Full of spunk and vinegar.

She didn't even look like them. She was blonde; they were not. Her nose was wide, not short and straight. The shape of her eyes when she smiled was all wrong. They were all on the short side, so they had that in common. Even then, they were stout and solid where she was slight and increasingly coltish. Even her neck was longer.

More than ever before, she felt like the odd turnip in the carrot patch. Of course it was possible. She wouldn't be the only person to have been raised by someone other than her parents. Rakel lost both of hers when she reached her teens. Tess didn't have a mother anymore.

"Mum, why are my runes different from yours?" she asked after supper that night, too afraid to wound Susi by asking the thing she really wanted to know. Perhaps it was all in her head.

Susi's shoulders tensed and her gaze jumped to Elric in his rocker. A silent conversation passed between them and something clenched behind Wynne's ribs. Her worrying and overthinking ought to have done more to prepare her, but she still felt like the floor swung out from beneath her.

"Am I adopted?" she asked, unable to hold it in any longer.

They told her the story in full.

Inorra Erlander had arrived at the Enclave pregnant, having survived a raid in the Heartlands. Her husband, Markus, and their then-eight-year-old son, Josef, never made it here. Inorra was a fragile thing – petite like Wynne, and strong in spirit, but leaving them behind had broken something inside her. Susi befriended her in a loose sense, and looked in on her as much as she could, having a one-year-old of her own.

They told Wynne about the hungry winter and the sickness which swept through the village. About checking on Inorra and discovering that she'd died during the night. Finding Wynne beside her, crying, hungry, chilled.

Susi and Elric brought her home and cared for her. They waited to see if family would turn up to claim her. When it became clear that no one was coming, they made the choice to keep doing what they were already doing, and raise her.

Wynne remembered sobbing at the story. Not out of self-pity. The thought of any baby in desperate need of comfort was enough to move her to tears. Her heart broke for Inorra, who loved her to the end. For the father and brother she never knew.

Wynne had been lucky.

Emotions chased her thoughts to the images of childbirth she'd witnessed recently, and expounded on them, pressing them onto her future.

Humiliation. Helplessness. Pain. Her dying thoughts, fearing what would happen to her child.

She closed her eyes and took a breath to steady herself. It didn't help.

She was expected to continue these dinners and find a husband, which meant pregnancy and childbirth was only a matter of time. It was probably going to kill her.

You have to be brave to give birth.

Wynne didn't feel brave.

The amorphous dread which had been clinging to her about these matters came into sharp focus. Cold sobriety settled in its place as realization struck, clear as a bell.

I want many children, Corbin had said.

Wynne didn't.

She didn't want any.

Admitting this to herself produced a sudden twist of grief. For so long, that's what she wanted. Yet there was no denying it to herself.

This acknowledgement was immediately followed by the implications. She still wanted to be loved by a good man. Yet who would want her, if they knew the truth? *What self-respecting man doesn't want to be a father?*

Susi knocked on the door, halting Wynne's inner spiral. She slipped inside and offered an empathetic smile. She sat beside Wynne on the edge of the bed.

"Is Pops upset with me?" Wynne asked.

Susi took a thoughtful breath.

"That's a yes."

"He doesn't understand. We thought Corbin was a good option."

Wynne said nothing. Truth was, if circumstances were different, he might've been. She considered divulging her fears to her mother. She didn't know what to say, and she felt ashamed.

"Be truthful with me." Susi looked her in the eyes. "Is your reluctance because of Harek?"

Would Harek even want her if he knew how she felt?

The stress of the evening, Wynne's anxieties, her ongoing, complicated feelings about Harek, and thoughts of a future spent alone coalesced. They rose within her like a plume of smoke. She crinkled her nose as she tried to fight back another rush of tears. She released a whimper.

Susi's face softened. She placed a comforting hand on Wynne's arm. "You're waiting for him. I had a feeling. I saw you two at the feast last year, and I've seen how many times you've read and reread his letters." She gave Wynne's arm an affectionate rub and the tiniest smile eased onto her mouth. "I'll talk to your father."

Wynne's conscience squirmed as Susi hugged her. *You could just tell the truth.*

Or you could lean into the misconception and avoid more nights like tonight. It wasn't entirely false.

Wynne said nothing.

25

Kal scraped the last of his coins out of his belt pouch and counted the equivalent of forty coppers. Enough to last through week's end.

Afternoons with Arlo and Fay had been a win-win situation. It kept him out of trouble. He got a delicious meal he didn't have to prepare himself two nights a week. Their cabin was looking better. They all benefited from the company.

He'd spent several days over the last two weeks at the tannery, clearing debris and helping reframe the roof. They didn't need his help anymore. Which was just as well. Apart from sore muscles and new friendships, Kal had nothing else to show for his efforts. Not yet. They lacked the funds to pay him. They promised him a new furry leather coat, and he trusted they'd be good for it. It was a better trade in the long run. Still, it didn't help him today.

As he felt the weight of his remaining coins in his palm, hopes of making significant improvements to his home receded in the distance. Bartering would only get him so far.

He decided to stop at Leland Jaeger's first. Perhaps the favor Kal garnered with the ol' butcher would carry over to a discount on meat. One could hope. Kal was too proud to ask, and he didn't expect something for nothing.

Leland stood in front of his counter with a formidable man layered in fur and hide clothing. The shock of white-blonde hair and the short white beard betrayed his age. His most prominent feature was the crescent-shaped tattoo around his left eye. Time had smudged the once-crisp edges. Kal knew it was a ceremonial custom for some nomadic tribes further north than Austerholt.

Nialls.

"Ah!" Leland broke off the conversation when Kal entered. With a jovial grin, he spread his arms as though welcoming an old friend. "The man himself! I was tellin' Nialls here about my new leg."

"Is it treating you well, friend?"

Leland pushed a breath through his teeth. "Is it? Look at it. I feel like a king. I'm wearin' a piece of art. And it's sturdy as a brick. Give it a kick. Not too hard. Don't want mud crustin' up the detail-bits."

Kal chuckled and gave the false leg a tap with his toe. He'd carved it to look like a dragon coiled around a pillar. Every inch of wood was scales, bumpy leather of wings, snout and teeth, sharp paws, and pointed tail. Kal was proud of his work, and it pleased him that Leland was enamored with it.

"Have you met Nialls?" Leland asked.

"Not personally." Kal placed a hand on his chest. "Kalomir. Or, Kal."

Nialls' gaze jumped between Kal and the leg. His eyes were so light they were almost colorless. "Northman, yeah?"

"Yes, sir."

"Where?"

"Austerholt."

Nialls said nothing.

Kal spent a third of his coins on enough cheap meat to last him the week. Nialls lingered like he was waiting for him to leave. For reasons Kal couldn't fathom, Nialls gave him the uncomfortable sense that he was about to land himself in trouble. Like the guy was one false move away from confrontation.

Of which, there was no doubt who'd be the victor. The man might be in his fifties, but he looked like he knew how to handle himself.

Kal collected his purchases and bid the men farewell.

Nialls followed him out.

Kal tried to avoid overthinking the prickles on his neck. He'd been behaving himself lately. Surely, Nialls wasn't hounding him.

Nialls called to his back. "Northman."

Kal's feet slowed to a stop.

"Come with me."

Nialls didn't look happy.

A nudge of concern pressed against Kal. "Where?"

"Something I need you to see."

That doesn't answer the question. "...Alright."

It was an anxious trek through town. Kal wondered if he was being led to a back-alley where he'd unwittingly walk into a beating. Or be presented with evidence of a crime and accused. He wanted to ask, but they walked without speaking for so long, it felt awkward to strike up a conversation after the prolonged quiet. So he said nothing.

Eventually, they turned up the front walk of a little farmstead. A cabin and barn sat away from the lane. Each bore evidence of recent repair. Char-blacken swaths marred one side of the cabin, but the door was new. A horse grazed in the grass of the post-and-rail yard at the rear, while a handful of turkeys scratched in the dirt out front. Upon noticing Nialls and Kal, the turkey gobbles took a louder, faster quality. As one, they rushed toward them.

Kal tensed. He lacked experience with livestock. Still, he knew male chickens were testy, and these were four times in size. To his relief, they ignored him entirely and trotted alongside Nialls all the way to the house. Like they were excited by his arrival. Pleased, even.

Inside, scorch marks discolored a portion of the floor and wall. There was a fireplace, an empty suds bucket, and a table with two chairs. One was piled with Nialls' clothing, which gave Kal the impression it wasn't often used. Nearby stood a bed, heaped with fur blankets, and a chest along one wall. No rug.

What drew Kal's attention most was the dismantled rocking chair in the center of the floor. The seat itself was intact, though separated from the rest of the chair. The rungs and arms were a mess of splintered wood. It was obvious repairs had been attempted and made it worse.

Nialls stopped. For a long moment, he gazed upon the wreckage, as though disappointed by it.

Was this what I needed to see so badly?

Kal's eyes traveled from the broken chair to Nialls. His presence filled the room. Not just physically, though there was that.

He broke the quiet by chancing a joke. "Got to be too much for it, eh?"

Nialls eyed him. "How'd you guess?"

Kal jerked his chin toward the mess. "Stress points on the chair look like they gave out under a heavy load. See where the joints failed. The splitting. But it could just be the wear and tear of time."

Nialls' stern expression broke. He smirked and conceded with the tiniest dip of the head. "I am not as slim as I used to be." He rested a hand on his gut and gave it a pat. "It saddens me. This is my favorite chair."

Kal hummed.

"I realize this is beneath your skill level, but do you think you can fix this?"

Sounded like a paying job to Kal. "Let's see."

Kal rested his bag and crouched beside the broken piece of furniture. The seat, arms, and backrest appeared to be made of solid cherry wood. The seat bore dents along the edge from its impact with the floor. Nothing a block plane couldn't handle.

A deep crack ran down one of the arm rests. Holes had been poorly widened to reassemble connecting rungs. The joints themselves suffered under the strain and shoddy repair. A rope had been tightly bound along the foot rungs. Instead of a straight beam, it sagged in the middle.

"Is there a brace beneath the rope?"

Nialls shook his head. "There is a crack. I thought the rope could hold in place."

Kal tapped the foot run. "These parts look like ash."

"Yes."

"Is this wood available here?"

"I can find out."

"If not, I can use birch. It has a similar workability. The color is close, but the grain won't match. You shouldn't need to replace the seat, but there's a crack in the arm, here..."

Nialls patted the air. "I will get you whatever wood you need. But you must not tell Elric."

"That's a strange request, but alright."

"Northman, I will never hear the end of it."

They spent a few minutes negotiating a price. As Kal collected his belongings with plans to return with tools that afternoon, he noticed a charred statue on the mantle. It looked like it was a bust at one point. What remained was blackened and misshapen.

Still, Kal recognized northern-style artistry when he saw it. "What is that?"

Nialls' expression softened by a hair's breadth. "That was my wife. It burnt in the fire."

It was obvious no woman lived in Nialls' house. Probably not for a long time.

"Did you make it?" Kal asked.

"I did."

Kal hoisted an eyebrow, intrigued.

"I am a Northman. Like you. I knew how to carve, back in my day." Nialls gave a little shrug. "Unlike you, I haven't picked up the tools in twenty years."

"Why so long? You lose them, friend?"

"No. I lost Saffronia. She died on the way here." Nialls nodded toward the lumpy statue, a little more somber. "That is the last thing I have to remember her by."

It was quiet for a breath. Kal followed Nialls' gaze to the bust. Something pulled behind his ribs. "Do you want another?"

"Another?"

"I could fix it for you."

Caught off guard, Nialls studied Kal for a moment. Tempted. Probably weighing the offer against what he'd seen of Kal's skill and an unwillingness to risk parting with the statue if something went wrong.

Finally something resolved behind his eyes. "How much?"

"We don't have to settle on a price yet. It's important you're completely happy with it. You don't have to pay me if you're not." Kal was, of course, relying on Nialls to be honest. It was a risk he was willing to take.

"Done."

Dearest Wynne,

I have some exciting news.

We have established a space similar to the Enclave's training grounds here. While there's not much time to practice, those who've made it a habit have stood out to leadership. I've found myself in this group.

Last week, they asked me to select a band of brave, capable men and begin a training regimen, with the understanding that there may come a time when we're called upon to protect the Gren. I've been granted a good deal of freedom as to whom I select and how I approach organizing and training. I've elected to keep the team small. I've chosen six men who've proven themselves and work well with others, including Cain, Finnion, Lara's cousin Billy, Dorian, your former fellow scout Oleksy, and Grigory, Catreeny and Ben's son.

It's reassuring that my efforts haven't gone unnoticed, and I'm glad to do my part, though I feel unqualified. I'm trying to absorb as much wisdom as I can from my betters. The work is difficult in a different way, though satisfying, and the pay is better.

It seems like a matter of time before we're called upon. We've had word of folks being accosted on their way to the Gren. Without the Empire's sword to maintain law and order abroad, the roads have become increasingly perilous.

Some in the Gren believe these malicious activities may be deliberate efforts by resentful actors to sabotage us. Others speculate it's nothing more than opportunistic brigands. It may be both. Regardless, leadership (almost all of whom are Baldomar) believes this is a ripe opportunity for our people to distinguish ourselves. "No More the Hunted" has become something of a rallying cry. I'm inclined to agree. I'm curious how this strikes you.

I hope you haven't experienced trouble at home. We've received a bounty of sweaters from the Enclave, and what a welcome reminder of home they've been. My father recently sent me a slab of pork belly, which has made me quite popular amongst my comrades.

I don't mean to be a bother, but your most recent letter stuck with me in an uncomfortable way. Your reply seemed uneasy, or sparse. I fear I may've said something to bother you in my last letter. I was only thinking on the page. Perhaps I'm mistaken and misreading your tone entirely. If so, forgive me. It is difficult not being able to see you face to face and discuss these matters in person.

Thinking of You,

Harek

26

Kal tugged his hat over his ears as he stepped into the brisk winter air. He turned his attention to the box on the pedestal situated beside the door and swatted the thin coating of powder off the top. It was the first addition to his property, and he hadn't even wanted it. Last week, he helped a wheelwright named Cedric with a roof repair. The box was his repayment. Cedric insisted it was necessary. *What if your neighbors want to bring you something, and you're not home? They can't leave it on your doorstep. Animals'll get it.*

Kal wasn't so sure, but the next evening, he returned from Arlo and Fay's to find it in place.

Since then, it'd proven its worth. Earlier this week, he found a few apples and one of the tools he'd accidentally left at Nialls' house. Today, there was a braided loaf of raisin bread from Samuel and his wife – cold and a little stale, but edible. Kal guessed it had been put there the day before. He made a mental note to check the box more often.

He tore the bread in half, tucked the rest back indoors, and remembered his cup. He ate as he made his way toward the meeting hall. He'd never had reason to come to the hall specifically. It stood near the village center, proximal to the market grounds and close to Wynne's residence. It was huge. Impossible to miss. From what he understood, the building was community-owned and used for meetings, memoriums, and weddings. Today, it hosted a men's gathering called The Craftsmen's Guild.

He entered through the large double-doors at the front and the temperature change was immediate. Roaring fires blazed along the sides of the room. A handful of tables were positioned throughout the spacious floor. One for a keg of beer. Another held what appeared to be building plans. Forty-or-so men milled around, conversing.

He scanned the area for a familiar face. Apart from the Haranae brothers, Kal was the only non-Baldomar present.

He found Nialls and Omri in a cluster with a few others, discussing the Ice Throw.

"Be honest, Nialls," Omri said with a wry smirk. "Did you banish the snow just to keep from bein' beaten this year?"

Nialls spread his arms as if welcoming the challenge. "Who would beat me?"

"Me!"

Nialls released a booming laugh, which caught on. Omri shook his head, not really mad.

The other men noticed Kal approach and the circle expanded to include him. Nialls threw out an arm in welcome. "Northman!"

Kal returned the gesture with a grin, which Nialls took as an invitation. He clasped him in a rough hug, slapped Kal's back, then released him to address the other men. "This is the one who fixed my Saffronia. No – fixed is not the right word. It is even better. Looks more like her than before. It's beautiful."

"You're the one who carved Leland's leg," said a mountain of a man who spoke at an energetic volume a tick above everyone else. He lifted a pint to him. "Well done."

Dominik the smith extended a fist to bump knuckles with him. "I've seen it."

"We've all seen it," the big loud guy said with a chuckle. "Ol' Leland's made sure of it."

Kal dipped his chin, both proud and humbled by the praise.

Elric, the bushy, barrel-chested elder approached the group with an armload of rolled papers. "Nialls. Tomorrow mid-morn. Omri, you'll come?"

"Yes, sir," Omri said.

"Skeggis?"

The big loud guy rumbled in the affirmative.

"Kal should come," Nialls said.

"Come where?" Kal asked.

"We're plannin' an addition to the meeting hall," Elric said. "Remind me. You worked on the boardin' house?"

"I did."

"You've got much experience with buildin'?"

"I'm a master carpenter."

"That's right. I remember Visenny mentionin'."

"I mostly focused on indoor projects, rather than new construction, but I can do both. I'm good for labor and detail work."

"Good?" Nialls sounded outraged. He gripped Kal's shoulder. "This man's an artist. We need him."

Elric turned his attention to Kal with interest. "We hope to continue the work steadily, best we can, until it's finished. You got the time?"

"Sir, if it's paying work, I'd make the time."

Elric's bushy mustache twitched. "Tomorrow mid-morn. Plannin' meetin'."

"I'll be there."

✧

The Craftsman's Guild struck Kal as more of a good excuse to get out of the house, drink beer, and discuss upcoming projects. There were no dues, speeches, or officials seeking the favor of influential members. A stark contrast to guild meetings in the large cities. Kal liked it.

He made a point to introduce himself to a handful of folks he didn't know. A good way to learn who was who, and potentially drum up future work. Helping himself to a pint, he joined a handful of men including Omri and the Haranae brothers at a grouping of benches near one of the fires.

Elion noticed his approach first and stood to welcome him with a hug. Turning to the group, he gestured to a talkative older elf with shoulder-length, peppery gray hair. "Kal, this is my father, Bartholomew." He pointed to a middle-aged farmer and the younger man at his side. "My father-in-law, Ned. That's Corbin. Willem, there. Ben Hodd. You know Omri."

Kal flashed a palm and got comfortable as the men continued their conversation about spring planting. He listened and made comments as the opportunity rose. Kal wasn't much for agriculture, but the men were easy to talk to.

They hadn't been seated for long when Cedric approached the circle. He plopped beside Kal and angled toward him. "I'd like to invite you to dinner tomorrow."

"Dinner?" Kal was intrigued. Another meal he didn't have to prepare himself.

Cedric seemed pleased by Kal's reaction. He dipped his chin knowingly and his voice took a particular tone. "Regarding my daughter Tawna."

Kal hesitated, momentarily caught off guard. He barely remembered saying hello to the girl when he went to Cedric's for the repair.

Cedric gave Kal a fatherly pat and a meaningful look. "You've made an impression."

His tone left little question about the kind of impression Kal made. Which made this simple, if not easy.

"I appreciate the invite, but if this is related to your daughter, I have to decline," he said. "She's a lovely girl, but I've got eyes for someone else."

Cedric stiffened. Flustered and offended, he glanced aside and huffed. Shaking his head, he rose and departed their company without another word.

A thick quiet fell over the circle as several sets of eyes watched him go.

Elion leaned forward in his seat. "We should talk about that."

"You mean, what's his problem?" Kal said, jerking his head in the direction of Cedric's departure.

"About that dinner invitation. It's a bit more complicated than a meal."

"How so?"

"It's a custom – more of an event – to determine whether you'd make a good husband for their daughter."

Kal's eyebrows shot up. "Serious?"

"If the parents like you, the father asks if you'll accept her hand in marriage," Elion said. "You don't have to say yes. However, refusing to attend is considered extremely rude."

"...I had no idea."

"Honest mistake."

"Cedric should know that," Omri said. "But that's why he's chafed."

Kal took a moment to piece this new information together. In Austerholt, family approval was important, but not like this. Nowhere was it like this.

New questions presented themselves. "How do I know the difference between a normal dinner invitation and...the special kind?"

"You'll know," Omri said.

That wasn't helpful.

"Who've you got eyes for?" Elion asked with a smirk.

The thought of her brought a smile to Kal. "Do you know the scout, Wynne?"

"Of course."

A shadow passed over Corbin. He took the expression of a man making a valiant effort to bite his tongue. Without a word, he stood and crossed the room.

In the silent lull which followed, Kal caught glances amongst the other men. Like they knew something he didn't. It wasn't a nice feeling.

Omri focused on Kal. "Can I share something with you? To inform your approach."

"Please."

Omri pointed across the way where Elric was currently arm-wrestling Skeggis, and winning. "See him?"

"What about him?"

"That's her Pops."

"Wynne's an elder's daughter?"

"Yup."

Kal could've shook himself for not putting that together sooner. He thought she rented a room at the Thars'.

He gave Elric a second appraisal. He wasn't tall, but he was wide. The marks creasing his face seemed to take a new shape. No longer the lines of a wry, direct man, but of someone not easily impressed. Someone who wouldn't hesitate to confront anything or anyone should he harbor questions. "He's kind of imposing."

Omri laughed. "If you think he's imposing, you should meet her brother."

"Her brother, the bear?"

"Her other brother."

"Who's that?"

"You ever heard of Grim Stonebreaker?" Elion asked.

"No."

"Josef Erlander?"

It took Kal a moment to place the name. "That's the same person, right? The one who killed Malachai, the dragon king? Your sister's husband?"

"Pretty much."

Kal's voice tightened and he dipped his chin to look at Elion level. "That's Wynne's brother?"

Omri and Elion both nodded.

"I'm her brother, too," Omri said.

"Now I know you're joking," Kal said.

"I'm not. Wynne Thar is my sister."

"You look nothing alike."

"She's adopted."

Kal watched Omri for a moment. He was telling the truth. Relief and embarrassment competed for dominance in Kal's chest. Kal ran a hand down his face, grateful he hadn't been more explicit about his interest. "You're telling me this, now?"

"Yeah. Figured, the way things are going, you should probably know."

"Are there any other brothers? Warlords from foreign lands? Executioners?"

"Just me, the dragon-slayer, and the bear. Oh, and him?" He pointed in Corbin's direction.

"Another brother?"

"No. Corbin had one of those special dinners with Wynne. She turned him down."

"She did?" Kal couldn't keep his interest in that nugget of information out of his voice. At least Kal wasn't the only one to be turned away. "When was this?"

"Couple weeks ago."

"It's still a little raw for ol' Corbin," Ned said. "Don't take it personally, Kal."

"What was her reason?" Kal asked, hoping he wasn't pushing too far.

"Rumor is she's waiting on Harek Jaeger."

"Who's that?"

"Leland's eldest son. He went to the Gren to make something of himself. He's been writing to her."

"Huh."

A competitive instinct roused itself within him. *She's waiting for Harek?*

Not if Kal could help it.

27

After the conversation at the Craftsman's Guild, Kal hesitated to mention Wynne in Omri's presence. Turned out, he and Harek were old friends. As far as Kal could tell, Omri wanted to remain neutral. Or perhaps he thought Kal had no chance with his sister and was none too concerned. Regardless, Kal didn't want to press his luck. Though he'd been itching to ask about this Harek character, he said nothing.

He got his opportunity toward the end of the week.

The Baldomar were an industrious lot, and work on the meeting hall began immediately. They constructed framing in a day and a half. Kal labored alongside a dozen others until dusk. As he packed up his tools for the day, Omri sauntered over.

"Goin' to supper at my parents' house," he said while stretching his shoulder. "Wanna come?"

A meal Kal didn't have to prepare after a long day's work, and the possibility of seeing Wynne?

That didn't take long to think about.

The sun gave up early these days. Any lingering daylight reflected off the meager coating of snow, making the twilight seem brighter than the hour called for.

"I noticed Elric left in a hurry earlier," Kal said as he tugged his hat over his ears. His breath turned to a cloudy fog before him and quickly dissipated. The blast of chilly air initially felt refreshing, but it was Noemar. Refreshment quickly gave way to the bitter cold.

"He needed a sit-down with Nialls and Rakel. They're about ready to knock some heads together."

Kal had since gathered that Rakel was the icy woman he'd met on his first day. He knew she was responsible for scouting and patrol, which meant she worked closely with Wynne. Based on the handful of stories he'd heard, she wasn't the sort of woman he wanted to provoke.

Omri continued. "They've been talking about starting a watch for months."

"A watch, like town guards?"

"Yeah. Mainly due to issues at the tavern."

"What kinda issues?"

"Fighting. Disorder. People leaving drunk then doing stupid things." Omri hiked up his bag to adjust it on his shoulder. "Last night, there was a huge brawl. Some bloke got stabbed."

"Good gods."

"He lived."

"Did they catch the guy who did it?"

"Narrowing it down."

"What happens when they do?"

Omri shook his head, at a loss. "We really haven't had these problems before. Which isn't to say we have no problems. Mostly we sort 'em amongst ourselves. Elders only get involved, depending on the severity. If it's really bad, justice is swift and severe."

"As in, death?"

"Yeah. Certain things, we don't put up with. An execution only happened once in my lifetime. Some lady started trying to contact a dead relative."

"They killed her for that?"

"No, they executed her because she lost her mind and murdered two people."

Kal made a face. He'd heard about that sort of thing and how, despite being initially comforting, it usually ended badly.

"Communing with the dead – strongly discouraged around here." Omri snorted, joking but a little serious. "So in case you ever get the notion…"

"Nothing to worry about here." Something tweaked behind Kal's ribs as his mind skipped involuntarily backward in time. "When someone's gone, they're gone. I know."

All the talk about the dead sobered Kal. As they turned up the narrow front walk of the Thars', he felt suddenly nervous. He tried to push the remnants of the conversation from his mind. It wasn't going to help him. He hadn't crossed paths with Wynne since their confrontation weeks prior. He wasn't confident she'd be happy to see him. He fell in behind Omri and took the opportunity to pull off his cap and smooth his hair. He straightened the leather strap over his chest, and brushed the sawdust off his sleeve.

Omri led the way indoors without knocking. Kal was immediately greeted by an inviting warmth, the glow of lantern light and fireplace, and the savory aroma of supper. Multiple conversations came from further in the house.

Kal and Omri lingered at the alcove by the entry, where coats and hats hung on pegs. Assorted gear leaned against the wall beside the door. Satchels. A shortsword in a scabbard. A strung bow and quiver. From this position, he caught a glimpse into the greatroom, which had an enormous plank table, a set of rocking chairs at one end, and a roaring hearth. Nialls stood by, listening to Elric who tossed another log on the fire. A young boy who looked like a smaller version of Omri sat on the floor, stacking a set of blocks into a tower.

Along the side of the room, an open doorway led to an otherwise closed-off kitchen. The icy woman, Rakel, leaned against the doorframe, arms crossed. She rocked back a few inches for a better view of who'd just entered the house. Her piercing eyes made a disinterested sweep of Kal and Omri before she returned her attention to the open conversation taking place amongst the women in the kitchen.

"Your son and a pal," she said. "Continue."

Out of sight, another woman picked up her thought. "Part of the dilemma is that so many of the newcomers are women and children. From what they tell me, their opportunities for furthering their skills are limited where they're from. So here they are, and what can they do? The village only needs so many seamstresses and washerwomen."

"It's the same problem with the men," Rakel said. "They can chop wood, or dig a well, but they can't lay stone. Or work a forge. Or make shoes."

Kal heard Wynne's voice amongst the ladies. "There's some talented craftsmen among them."

Kal wanted to think this comment was about him. That time had cooled her wrath.

Rakel flashed a palm. "Mostly, they're unskilled. Most don't got land of their own, so they're not producing food. Unless you count beer. I don't."

"They got pigs," Wynne said.

"Heavens." The other woman's voice had a wry note to it. "That, they do."

"Northman!" The booming voice of Nialls filled the space as Kal followed Omri into the greatroom and greeted his father. Nialls spread his arms and clapped Kal in a hug.

Rakel took a basket overflowing with bread, and the women entered as a pack.

Wynne wore a heavy blue sweater with a narrow leather belt around her waist. Her beige trousers were free of hay and debris. She'd used a strip of cherry-colored cloth as a headband, while the loose ends rested over her shoulder. She looked fresh-faced and pretty.

Kal recognized the lady who'd chased the bear cub. She had a sweet face and a commanding presence, and appeared far less frazzled.

Omri pecked her on the cheek. "Mum, I hope you don't mind, I invited a friend for supper."

"The more, the better." Her eyes twinkled up at Kal. "Welcome."

"Thank you."

"Everyone, this is Kal. Kal, my mother, Susi. You know my Pops. Nialls." Omri pointed at the boy with the blocks. "That's Jai the bear-child. Rakel. And you've met Wynne."

Wynne watched the greeting party with thinly veiled apprehension, and eyed Omri, like she wondered what he was up to. Then she offered Kal the briefest obligatory smile.

So that's how it's gonna be? It was better than contempt, though less than satisfactory. Her presence roused some deep-seated feral drive inside Kal. He took the cool gesture as a personal challenge. *We'll see about that.*

When it was time to sit, Kal waited to see where Wynne settled herself, then selected the spot beside her. Color rose to her cheeks, and he noticed her nostrils flare. For a moment, he wondered whether the move was too bold. It was also a dare. *Do you dislike me enough to move?*

She stayed where she was but refused to look at him. After a prayer, everyone served themselves from the food arrayed down the length of the table. The pottage made its way around, and Kal scooped a portion of lentils, garlic, greens, and carrots onto his tray while he half-listened to the conversation around him.

"Pottage, Wynne?" he said.

She took the crock from his hands, still without a glance.

Kal supposed he should've expected to fight an uphill battle. Regardless, the chill felt more discouraging than he anticipated.

He needed to adjust his expectations. If they could simply get on solid footing, that would be a move in the right direction. Amiable speaking terms would suffice. He had to start somewhere, and he resented that he felt like he was starting from scratch.

No, not scratch. Scratch was easier, but he'd botched that. This felt like beginning a foot race a hundred yards behind the start line.

"I hear the tavern's been a rife boiling pot," Wynne said, still without looking. Her tone was loaded, but she'd initiated. That was something.

"I heard a bit from Omri. I wouldn't know firsthand," Kal said.

"I thought you went there every night."

"I haven't been in weeks."

Wynne paused briefly with her hand in the bread basket. She shot him a curious glance.

A thread of conversation about a meeting caught her attention. She straightened up and turned her focus toward Elric. "What's the gathering about?"

"The increase of needy persons," Elric said. "We've got our own strugglin' to get by – more than usual now – and many times that in newcomers." Elric nodded toward Kal to include him in the discussion. "The ways you've planted yourself, you've been more the exception than the rule."

Another curious glance from Wynne. She returned her attention to her father. "When's the meeting?"

"Soon, I hope," Rakel said.

"The hall is a building site right now. Most of it, not fit for laymen, and Sender's away. I intend to ask Leland, too. Dominik. Other folks whose lines of work have been impacted. I'd like as many to attend as possible."

Rakel's brow furrowed. "Even newcomers?"

"If they like. Kal, you're welcome to join."

"Do they get a say-so?" Rakel seemed bothered. "Seems awfully generous to give them a say on how to spend community funds they haven't paid into."

"They've only been here so long. Most aren't in a position where they can contribute even if they wanted to."

Kal raised a tentative hand. "Pardon my ignorance. What's the community fund?"

Rakel gestured to him without looking. "My point."

"The community fund is a completely voluntary collection," Susi said as she dished a portion of turkey and gravy onto Jai's plate. "Rents from the boarding houses go into it too. We use the funds to help those in need. I don't know how familiar you are with Baldomar history, but some of us came here in dire straits, with little more than the clothes on our backs. The Enclave was to be a refuge for Silversaar's people. It's grown since then, but the spirit behind its founding is part of who we are. Where there is true need, we seek to meet it. If we can."

"The community fund isn't for the needy alone," Elric said. "We use it around town for that which benefits us all. The flumes, for example."

"Or the addition to the meeting hall," Omri added.

"Another example," Elric said. "Wynne, I want you to be there, when this happens." Elric dove his spoon into his food and scooped an enormous mound toward his face. He paused with the spoon hovering midair before he took a bite. "You're in a unique position, goin' with your mum weekly, scoutin', and midwifin'. The gatherin' would be well-served by your insight. I reckon you have a good idea of how many babies will be joinin' the Enclave come spring and summer."

Wynne sat up a little straighter. "I do."

"Good."

Wynne squared her shoulders and smiled into her tray.

It got better after that. The tension she'd been harboring eased. She'd warmed up and laughed at a few of Kal's jokes over supper. It sparked hope within him.

After the meal, he pitched in with the cleanup by bringing a stack of dirty trays to the kitchen where Wynne was at work at the suds bucket. She spared him a glance as he came alongside her. "Set those there."

"I'll help."

"It's alright."

"Least I could do. I remember how much you love this chore." *Remember you told me back when we were speaking?* He hoped he wasn't pushing too far.

Wynne hesitated, then nodded toward the nearby towel. "You can dry. Thanks."

It felt like a step in the right direction.

"What did you do?" she asked after a quiet moment.

"Pardon?"

"I've never seen Nialls so friendly with anyone so new here."

"I helped him with something." Kal rested the first trough aside, and plucked another out of the drippy stack of clean cups and spoons. "Question."

"Ask away," she said without looking up.

"Who's Harek?"

Wynne stopped scrubbing and cast him a side-eye.

Kal waited.

"He's Leland Jaeger's son," she said. "Why?"

"Who is he to you?"

Wynne said nothing for a moment. She dropped her eyes to the dishwater. She looked like she was struggling to answer, so Kal threw her a bone.

"I hear he's the reason you rejected Corbin at your special dinner a while back."

"Oh, you heard about the dinners?"

"Of course. I was invited to one."

A shade of jealousy swept over her. She was trying not to show it. She scrubbed a little more industriously than before. "How special."

Inspiring jealousy wasn't Kal intent. Still, it was telling. It encouraged him more than he expected.

"I said no," he added.

"At the end of the night, or you refused to go?"

"I refused to go."

She paused again. She seemed surprised, and a little concerned.

"I didn't realize how offensive it was at the time. Don't change the subject. Tell me about this Harek fella. He's gotta be pretty special if you turned down Corbin for him. Because I met Corbin. He's a fine fella." Kal hoisted an eyebrow. "Unless I got that part wrong?"

Wynne resumed scrubbing. She said nothing for a beat. She cast an eye to the kitchen doorway to make sure there were no evesdroppers. When she spoke, she kept her voice down. "There's a little more to it than that."

"Enlighten me."

She cleared her throat. "Harek left for the Gren over a year ago. Promised he was coming back. He's still gone. So, we'll see."

"You're waiting for him?"

Wynne handed him a clean plate and hoisted an eyebrow. "Would it bother you if I was?"

"Not at all." Kal took it from her and wiped the towel over it. "He's not here. I am." Without breaking eye-contact, the corner of his mouth twitched upward. "I don't think he'll make it back in time."

Wynne pulled her chin inward. Color rose to her cheeks. She tried to pin back a smile and failed.

Feeling emboldened and riding the wave of encouragement, he gave her a playful nudge. "So, when am I invited for dinner?"

Wynne recovered and laughed. He'd missed her laugh. "I don't know, Kal. I'm a little concerned about your table-manners."

"I used a napkin," he said, playing along.

"I'm more surprised you know how to use a spoon."

"Come, now." Then he added, more demure, "I'm very good with my hands."

Wynne rolled her eyes, but she was still smiling. "You can't help yourself, can you?"

"I said nothing untoward."

"Uh-huh. You better mind yourself. My Pops or Nialls hear you talkin' like that, they'll sick Rakel on you."

"She's the attack-dog?"

"Pretty much."

"Good to know."

28

Dear Wynne,

I appreciate your idea about writing to your father to state my intentions for our future. With a matter so serious, I'd much rather speak to him in person. If I'm to address this with Elric, then I'd better be ready to marry you that day. I haven't forgotten who he is. If you are in any way reflective of him, I doubt that he'd be thrilled about approving a union between us when I'm not fully prepared. You know I left without the means to provide a home. Even now, though I've made great strides, I have not reached the goal – something which keeps shifting due to the increasing expense of affording the means to live.

I know Omri and Lara have pledged themselves with her parent's approval before acquiring all they need to establish themselves in the way they want. I admire their willingness to wait. I urge you to remember that Omri does not seek the hand of an elder's daughter. He's afforded some patience.

I wish I could speak to you about this, face to face. I'm doing the best I can. I do not intend to return until I've earned my keep. Please be patient.

H

Wynne's mind skipped over the evening as she lay in bed that night. Over the news about the brawl which nearly killed a man, and Rakel's anxiousness to get a lockup built. She and Nialls had been drumming up interest in a town watch. Most folks couldn't afford to spare the time to participate on a volunteer-basis. With pay, there were a dozen men prepared to start tomorrow. It was an interesting, albeit unsettling, development. Life in the Enclave was never without danger, but they'd never needed something like this.

As Wynne turned these matters over, she found herself distracted. Her thoughts repeatedly strayed toward Kal.

He's not here. I am.

When Omri showed up with him, Wynne questioned her brother's motives. She never let on about their previous dealings. Still, Omri was involved in everything. She wondered how much he knew. She wouldn't put it past him to invite Kal simply to make her squirm. He'd find the whole thing funny.

Though tempted to confront Omri, it felt tantamount to admitting that there was something between her and Kal. There wasn't. So she said nothing.

I don't think he'll make it back in time.

She found it highly unlikely Kal would somehow win her over before Harek got the chance. Yet, the thought stirred a pleasant lilting through her. It flattered her. It shouldn't. After what she'd seen, she knew better than to take the remark too seriously. This was Kal. He was suggestive, a little mouthy, and too handsome for his own good.

Wynne snorted. Too handsome for *her* own good.

As far as she knew, he wasn't actively pursuing anyone. Apparently, he'd been working hard to make himself useful. He'd garnered the favor of Nialls, which was no easy feat.

The improvement in behavior didn't make him less of a roguish chancer. It might be an act. Surely by now, he'd figured out that most Baldomar thought poorly of drunken philanderers. He wouldn't get into anyone's good graces acting like a lout.

Yet, here he was. Once again, snagging her attention for too many reasons to dismiss out of hand.

What if Harek didn't make it back in time?

She felt a little guilty for entertaining this thought. Disloyal, even.

Furthermore, she knew that entertaining interest in anyone led one place –
the eventuality of childbirth.

She found herself beset with a familiar frustrated ache as her thoughts
turned to Harek and kicked around inside her like a gust of wind stirring the fallen
leaves. She rolled over and fished his letters from beneath her mattress. His last one
– the one she was unhappy with – was written on half a sheet of paper. After the
previous letters, it felt like little more than a scrap. She'd written back, and never
received a reply. She didn't know what to make of it.

She reread the letters by candlelight wondering where she'd gone wrong,
then rested them on her chest to stare at the ceiling. He was her sweetest friend. She
was proud of him. But what sense did it make pining after someone who wasn't
ready and might never be?

How long am I supposed to wait for you?

She never promised anything to Harek, but the notion that she was waiting
for him wasn't false. Susi seemed to find the whole thing romantic. She
occasionally fished around for any indication about Harek's timeline. Wynne
didn't have an answer.

At the moment, Susi and Elric were content to let the special dinners lie. It
wouldn't last.

29

The first time Wynne received a message from Harek, there was no paper involved. A twittering pigeon waddled after her during her morning chores, making puttery noises. Cute, at first. When it wouldn't leave her alone, she worried there was something wrong with the bird.

Then Omri noticed. "Why's that pigeon hounding you?"

"I don't know. Maybe it likes me."

"I doubt it."

"That's not nice."

Without warning, the pigeon flapped a circuit around the barn and made a dive for Wynne. She yelped and covered her head as it fluttered around her shoulders.

"I stand corrected," Omri said with a laugh. "I think it likes you too much."

The coos grew insistent. It grazed the top of her head on a second pass.

"Omri, help me!"

"What do you expect me to do?"

Omri's attempts to help were pitiful, as he laughed himself sideways. Wynne dashed for the open barn door. The pigeon pursued. She cleared the row of outbuildings, managed a meager lead, and rounded the corner in a race for the front of the house. Harek jogged up the front walk.

Despite the embarrassing predicament, Wynne shifted course immediately and ran at him. "Help me, Harek!"

He took in the scene with bemusement. Extending his arms, he grabbed the bird on the first try and gently held it in front of him. Beaming, he searched her face. "Did it work?"

She stared askance as her heartbeat settled into a more natural rhythm. "What are you talking about?"

"I used my runes to have the pigeon bring you a message."

"...That's what that was?"

Harek nodded.

She gaped at him for the length of a breath. "Harek, I can't speak with beasts."

His face fell, as if this was just occurring to him.

"What did you want to tell me?"

She never found out. Omri came to the front yard, holding the stitch in his side. "Oh, Harek, you missed it..."

This first attempt at an animal messenger was replaced by better ones. Clever jokes, little illustrations, a plucked wildflower. One time, Yamma scratched at the door with a soggy curled parchment in her teeth. Another time, a crow brought a less-soggy curl of butcher paper, but wouldn't give it until Wynne offered a button in exchange.

It had been a long time since she'd received a message from him in this manner.

It had been a long time since she'd received anything.

Most days remained too full to overthink it, and the unseasonably mild winter marched on with no shortage of activity. Kal had been a regular fixture at the Thars' table. Due to the project at the hall, he was brought along nearly any time Omri came for the evening meal. Wynne wasn't always present for these occasions. Still, she'd be lying if she claimed she didn't enjoy them. If nothing else, their good-natured verbal sparring made her days interesting.

Wynne kissed her fingertips and touched them to Inorra's pendant as she left her bedroom. Her parents' terse voices carried from the other end of the house. They were making an effort to keep it down. It brought Wynne to a sudden halt in the narrow passage outside her room. She pricked her ears, ignoring the prod of guilt for eavesdropping.

"Last I checked, it sounds like he'll be done when he's done," Susi said. "It might be a while."

"How set on each other can they possibly be?"

"You'd have to ask Wynne, and good luck. She's been rather guarded about the whole ordeal and difficult to catch."

Dread prickled over Wynne as she envisioned herself cornered for information regarding Harek. Not that she had anything new to report. That was part of the problem. The courier arrived yesterday, as expected. Once again, nothing from Harek, yet she'd received a letter from Aeryn. So apparently, paper wasn't in too short of supply. At least not for Aeryn.

Susi continued. "I tried getting an idea from Micha. I didn't glean anything we don't already know."

"Don't go a-gossipin' with Micha. I don't want her hopes raised. What if she spreads word?"

"Elric, I know how to speak to people," Susi said, peeved. "I was subtle, and Micha isn't a busybody. Regarding raised hopes, it's too late for that. The Jaegers adore her. Wynne and Harek have been fond friends for a long time. It's only natural for his mum to hope. She'd be a wonderful daughter-in-law to them."

"I never thought the feeling's were...strong, between them."

"They're young. You know how rapidly that can change."

Elric grunted.

"You saw them at the feast."

"One feast."

"Sometimes that's all it takes."

"It was over a year ago."

"He's been in the Gren, and she's waiting for him. He's been writing to her, and she's been writing back."

"What do they say?"

"How should I know?" It was quiet for a beat. Then Susi added, "Not his timeline, evidently."

"I don't like it."

"You dislike Harek?"

"I like Harek just fine. He's a good young man. But he can't make her wait forever."

"He's been away, and for good reason."

"With no end in sight."

Susi sighed.

"He's slow."

"Elric."

"She'll be eighteen this year, Susi."

"I was eighteen when we married. There's nothing wrong with eighteen."

"That's not the point," Elric said. "It's my duty to make sure she marries well. The longer it stretches, the more it seems I'm dishonoring my daughter."

"I promise you, Wynne does not see it that way."

Elric's voice strengthened. "Wynne is not the only person in the Enclave."

It was quiet for a beat.

Uneasiness settled in Wynne's chest. She hadn't considered how her stance reflected on her father. She could only spare so much remorse. What alternative did she have? Settle? No. She was an elder's daughter. She did not settle. Besides, marrying meant babies, and that was going to kill her.

"They're not intended," Elric said with finality. "I can't be expected to pretend they are. I won't."

"What are you going to do?" Susi asked.

It was quiet for a long moment.

Elric grumbled. His heavy steps moved toward the back door. "Right now, I'm going to hitch up the donkey for you."

"Thank you, husband."

"You're welcome. C'mon, you little goat."

Jai's voice piped up as his little feet pounded across the floor to keep up. "Pops, don't call me a goat. I'm a bear."

The back door clattered shut.

Wynne closed her eyes and forced a long, slow breath through her lips. She gave herself a little shake and took the rest of the hallway at a normal gait, hoping she didn't look as unsettled as she felt.

She entered the room and thoughts of Harek fled. She let out a low whistle. The table was loaded with food to distribute. Fresh bread, bundles of dried, smoked meat, baskets of carrots, cabbages, and apples, and hard boiled eggs. Stacks of freshly folded sweaters, blankets, and bandages filled the benches.

Susi stood before it with palms pressed together like she was praying as she scanned the array. "I think this is everything, for now."

"This seems like more than usual."

"You noticed." She sighed and brushed the loose strands of auburn hair away from her forehead with a palm.

"Who else is joining today?"

"Catreeny and Ben as usual. Pia, Lara, and the girls…"

"Ah. Your favorite people."

"I don't have favorites."

Wynne made a noise in the back of her throat and Susi cast her a wry smirk.

"I'm surprised no Sender today."

"He's preparing for another trip to the Gren. They've had an outbreak of sickness. Leadership there requested that he go at once to train medics and help the sick."

Wynne's thoughts thrust toward Harek again, along with Josef and Aeryn. Suddenly sober, she wrapped an arm around her mother's shoulder as she came alongside her. Susi leaned into the hug and sighed as she continued to survey the table. "I'm glad we've been able to spare him. Still, this many new folk, I worry."

Susi wasn't the only one. The most recent group of newcomers was halved after they got here, took one look at the place, and decided to take their chances in Goldbur Gren, perilous and unfinished though it may be.

"It's been a healthy winter so far," Wynne said, trying to remain hopeful.

"It's been mild. Which has helped. Frankly it feels like a miracle."

Susi hesitated and eyed Wynne for a beat. Something stronger than curiosity passed over her and Wynne heard the next questions about Harek – his timeline, the sincerity of their feelings for one another – before Susi asked.

"Do the men at the meeting hall have an end date?" Wynne asked, desperate to veer the conversation elsewhere. She already knew they did, thanks to Omri and Kal, but couldn't think of anything else.

"Oh." Susi gathered her thoughts as they shifted track. "Some time next week, I think."

✧

A nameless dread clung to Wynne throughout the outing. It intensified whenever she interacted with mothers who were trying to raise their children alone. Seeing the desperation which had driven them here, the loneliness they contended with, left her feeling sunken and melancholy.

Helping others usually lifted her spirit. Not today.

It was difficult to acknowledge Elric's sentiments without a twinge of irritation. Harek left with little indication about his future plans beyond general intent to return. If he was sincere, why hadn't he discussed *anything* with Elric before leaving for the Gren? It was difficult to empathize with his rationale. He had to have known that delay would leave Wynne in an awkward position. She couldn't help but wonder if perhaps he'd neglected to because it gave him an out if he changed his mind.

A year ago, she agreed with Tess. *He's a too-shy butcher's boy, and you're Wynne Thar.* Now, things felt different. His letters painted the picture of a respectable man quickly outpacing her.

Perhaps her gauge of his affections stacked against her own were faulty. Maybe they always were.

It inflamed her. It hurt. Wynne's dignity prevented her from baring her heart or badgering him. Still, something had to give.

That evening, she scrounged up two pieces of parchment and a well of ink.

The courier, Paul, was leaving tomorrow with Sender and care packages for the Gren. She had one more strongly-worded letter to add to his load.

30

At first, it was only a cough, mild enough to go undetected. One sick person turned into six, then twenty. Then a hundred.

Wynne spent three days in bed, burning with fever while she slipped in and out of restless sleep. Throat, raw. Head, pounding. It hurt to breathe and to move. The hardest part was not knowing what was taking place elsewhere. She knew Jairus was sick, two rooms away. That Omri was ill and coping, more or less alone, at Josef's cabin. She didn't know about Lara's family. Tess' family. The Jaegers. The Hodds. Or Kal.

When the fever broke, improvement was immediate, but it still took a week for Wynne to be pronounced well-enough to leave the house. The physical toll exacted on her body left her keenly aware that she'd feel the effect for a while.

Wynne rejoined the distribution as soon as she was well enough. The day was damp, with lumpy drifting snowflakes which melted the instant they touched the muddy earth. All morning, the suffering she witnessed nearly brought her to tears. Corbin's family and others opened their homes to the dozen children who now found themselves without parents.

Needing a reprieve, she loaded her basket with bread, a bundle of salt pork, and a few root vegetables, and hauled it to Arlo and Fay's cabin. A tidy stack of firewood sat beside the door. She freed a hand to knock, when she noticed the new fixture. Roses, leeks, and thistles decorated an ornately carved knocker, secured at eye-level.

She'd seen workmanship like that before.

She thunked the knocker and Arlo opened a moment later. He waved her inside. "Come in, come in."

"Wynne, dear! I'm so glad you're feeling better." Fay shuffled across the room in her house slippers. She pulled her chunky knitted scarf and a shawl more tightly around her. "It's been too long since we've seen you. Is Jairus recovered?"

"He is. He's been a big help with some of the kids, lately. His bear-trick – the other kids love it."

"Bless him. It's so sad, all these children. What they've been through already, and now to lose their caregivers to disease."

Wynne nodded and tried to keep her mind off it, or the lump in her throat was bound to return. "Have you been well?"

"Oh, yes. We haven't caught the sickness. We've been careful, and we've had help."

"I'm glad." Wynne carefully passed the items from her basket into their hands. She pointed over her shoulder to indicate the door. "That's a pretty knocker."

"You like it?" Fay said as she laid the loaves of bread on the table. "It was a gift. Have you met Kal?"

"I have. A gift, you say?"

"Oh, yes. He's very generous. A wonderful boy."

"Boy?" Arlo gave his wife a funny look as he took the beetroot from Wynne.

Fay patted the air. "You know what I mean. He's been coming by, helping with some projects."

"Kal?" Wynne said, hardly believing her ears. "As in Kalomir, from Austerholt?"

"Yes, him. Tall with the dark hair and the beard. Very strapping."

"He's been helping you?" Wynne chose her phrasing carefully. Part of her worried about what he was getting out of this arrangement. She didn't expect him to volunteer his efforts. Still, Arlo and Fay didn't have much to give. She prayed he wasn't taking advantage of them. "For pay?"

"Well, we tried to pay him, but he wouldn't take it." Fay straightened her posture with a measure of pride. "He said my cooking reminds him of his childhood, so he stays for supper whenever he's here. We like the company."

Wynne made a visual sweep of the cabin. Fay ordinarily kept a tidy space. The floors, shelves, fireplace, windows, and rafters were in better condition than she'd ever seen. Better, even, than her parents' house.

"Last week, he finished repairing the plaster on the walls in the kitchen," Fay said. "He fixed our drafty window and the shutter."

"Floorboards," Arlo said as he eased his bones into his rocking chair. His knees cracked as he half-sat, half-collapsed into the seat with a sigh.

Fay straightened the fruits atop the table as she continued. "He nailed down the loose floorboards. It's much safer, and less creaky. Such a relief to my mind. You know how dangerous a trip and fall can be at our age. Two days ago, he brought his ladder and cleaned out the rafters. A squirrel got up there and done made a nest. Can you believe it? Well, he took care of it, and stopped up the hole where the critter got in. He's needed to scale back to once a week, due to the project taking place over at the meeting hall, but we don't mind. He still comes by regularly to make sure we have plenty of firewood near the door, so we don't have to go out in the damp and the cold to fetch it from the woodshed. We never asked him to – he just does it."

A newfound warmth bloomed in Wynne as she listened to Fay's recounting. Kal had never mentioned any of this.

She chatted with Arlo and Fay for a couple minutes, and left their home feeling lighter than she had in weeks.

✧

The next morning, Wynne grabbed Splitter and headed to the training grounds in an effort to clear her head and untangle her heart. The grounds were sparse. They'd been less-frequently used lately, but Nialls was there, overseeing. She didn't need to wait for an opening before she jumped into practice.

She'd barely begun when she spotted Maeve, who was supposed to be on watch. Her hair was disheveled and she cradled her wrist. Wynne's eyebrows dipped into a frown as Maeve scanned the fields, almost like she needed help.

Wynne jogged toward her. Up close, she noticed the scuff on her chin. "What happened to you?"

"Group of men decided to go up the mountain. I tried to stop them." Maeve indicated the wrist. "This happened."

"They hurt you?"

Maeve rolled her eyes. *Dumb question.*

"Why were they going up the mountain?"

"Why do yeh think?"

Wynne's eyes widened.

"I told them the mountain is warded. They don't believe there's any real threat."

Wynne craned her neck as her eyes swept the grounds in search of Nialls. She located him on the opposite end, in conversation with Kal. She didn't know what he was doing here, but she could deal with that question later.

Queen Kalane and the Baldomar lived trustfully near each other. She was just, and wouldn't punish the whole village if those men attempted, or succeeded, in raiding her treasure hoard.

But she would blame the Baldomar for not stopping them.

Who knew what repercussion that entailed?

"We need to tell Nialls."

31

The project at the meeting hall brought together an assortment of Baldomar men. Kal brought his carpentry skills and artistic talents to bear and the potential for new opportunities presented themselves. One man, Anders, enlisted him in helping to raise a barn come spring. Another, Willem, bought one of Kal's carved pieces to give as a gift for his wife. It made Kal feel like he was starting to find his place. The regular pay meant he could afford basic necessities and begin planning modest improvements to his home.

His friendship with Omri resulted in regular invitations to supper at the Thar house. Despite living alone, Omri shared meals with his parents so often Kal wondered if he knew how to cook for himself. He joked that Omri's eagerness to marry his lady was equal parts her beauty and the desire to avoid starving to death. Kal had no complaints. Susi was a great cook, and it offered him opportunities to see Wynne. He found himself looking forward to her face and the chance to tease her about one thing or another.

Then the sickness hit.

The abject suffering was nothing short of the challenges he witnessed growing up. The mindset of the entire village swung to one of survival. As expected, families pulled closer together. Unlike what he'd seen growing up, the Baldomar fought the temptation to isolate. Neighbors looked in on each other. Efforts were being made to house the fatherless and treat the sick.

The outpouring of goodwill staggered him.

Kal considered himself fortunate. He remained healthy and employed as the unseasonably mild winter crawled to a close. No one he knew had succumbed.

With the project complete and most folks on the mend, Kal decided to take Anders up on the offer to visit the grounds. He wasn't sure Anders would be there, but days off didn't come around that often.

The day felt more like early spring. Windy, overcast, and pleasantly gray. The grounds were far from crowded with fewer than twenty people spaced throughout muddy fields along the edge of the village. Kal was more than a little curious to see some of the famed Baldomar magic in action.

He entered the grounds near a bare-dirt and gravel area where one man stood before a campfire, hands extended. The fire bloomed in breadth and intensity, then climbed higher into the sky. Like he was controlling it.

Kal stopped to watch, hoping to strike up a conversation with the man when he was finished concentrating.

"Kal!"

At the sound of his name, he turned toward the exceptional sparring match taking place a third of the way across the field. Dominik the smith and Willem were at it like mortal enemies. Amongst the knot of onlookers standing along the fringe, Anders lifted an arm in a friendly wave. He was gathered with a handful of familiar faces, including Nialls, Ben Hodd, and Dominik's wife Bera.

On the short walk to join them, his gaze reached the far end of the grounds where targets stood ready arrows or hatchets. At a distance, Kal recognized the profile of a petite blonde woman as she hucked a handaxe toward a heavy wooden target. He found himself involuntarily straightening his spine.

The sparring match came to an end with Willem as the clear victor, and both men struggling for breath.

"Oy. Dom!" Ben turned up a palm. "What was that?"

Still breathless, the burly smith made a rude gesture in response, but he was smiling.

Anders clapped Willem on the back in congratulations while he got in on the teasing. "Yeah, who's gonna to keep ya from gettin' rusty when ol' Willem leaves for the Gren?"

People heard *the Gren*, and their ears pricked up. Kal amongst them. For the Baldomar, it was personal and patriotic. Everyone knew or was related to someone who'd gone to establish the city. Word was that it was progressing, though not without difficulty.

For Kal, it was selfish. Interesting, but also selfish. The Gren was where this Harek fella had gone, and he had no idea where things stood in their little competition.

Willem took a swig from his canteen. "You know Paul?"

"The courier?" Kal asked. "I've seen him a couple times. Never met him."

"My cousin. Says it's gotten real dangerous."

"The Gren?"

"Nah. Folks ain't dumb enough to attack it directly. Raiders been going after supply lines. Harassing folks to and from."

Huh, Maybe this Harek fella won't survive. The thought entered Kal's mind. He didn't wish ill on him, and felt a little bad. But only a little.

"Nialls!" Wynne's troubled voice carried as she hustled across the grasses in their direction. She was shoulder to shoulder with a second woman who held her wrist as though nursing a sprain.

Nialls peeled away from the group and strode toward them.

Bera squinted in their direction. "Wonder what's the fuss?"

"More newcomers?" Willem said.

Anders groaned. "Just what we need."

Kal and the others watched from a distance. As Nialls listened, his face hardened. A few Baldomar from the target-practice area stepped in to listen and seemed to swell with indignation.

"Nah, somethin's ain't right," Dominik said.

Kal followed the pack. As they drew up, he caught the tail-end of the animated discussion.

"How many?" Nialls asked.

"Four," the second woman said. She was in her late thirties with chin-length brown hair and a scrape on her chin. Kal was pretty sure she was one of the scouts.

"Baldomar?"

"No."

"Armed?"

"Probably, but I saw no swords."

"Where's Rakel?"

"On watch in the southern wood."

Nialls' eyes passed over the growing crowd as he gathered his thoughts. "Maeve, find Elric. Tell him what happened. Then go to Sender for your wrist. I'm leading a party up the mountain."

As Maeve hurried toward the village, Nialls turned to the gatherers. He cast a finger toward the easternmost mountain and spoke in a powerful voice which sent a chill over the group.

"Four men have ascended that mountain. They have laid hands on our scout and intend to steal from our dragonish neighbor. This cannot happen."

Ripples of outrage worked throughout the crowd. "What are we waiting for? Let's get 'em."

There were rumbles of agreement to this. The man at Kal's right cracked his knuckles.

Nialls lifted a palm for order and continued. "We will find them, and bring them back to answer for what they've done. Who volunteers?"

Arms shot up as folks jockeyed for Nialls' attention.

The dragon queen and her hoard were a popular topic of conversation. Kal had been here for months, and still hadn't seen her. Still, he believed she existed. While he wasn't quite sure what measures she'd take to protect her treasure, he trusted those who insisted she would.

Which meant those men were in grave danger and didn't realize it.

Kal lifted his arm and stepped forward. "I'll help."

Nialls pointed at Wynne, who'd done likewise, then beyond her at another man. "Wynne, Roran, with me." He took notice of Kal and waved him forward with a flick of the fingers. "Northman."

They separated themselves from the group as Nialls selected three others. Kal met Wynne's eyes and was more than a little encouraged by the sudden brightness in them, given the situation. Before they exchanged a word, Roran sidled up beside her. He was a lean, scruffy man near Kal's age, dressed in matted fur, heavy canvas, and worn boots. He carried a bow and quiver. An animal tooth dangled from a cord at his throat. He exuded a quiet intensity which reminded Kal of a predator anticipating the hunt.

Roran picked something out of his teeth and spat at the ground. He dropped his voice to a low growl. "If I find out which one of them roughed up Maeve..."

"I know," Wynne said. By contrast, she radiated a calm readiness. No fear. No thinly-masked rage.

"You don't touch the scouts."

"No, you don't." She made a brief visual sweep of Kal. "You have a weapon?"

"A knife." He always carried one. He'd brandished it a few times in his life, though never used it against another person. He hoped he never needed to.

Willem joined the group, along with Anders and Ben Hodd. With a colorful string of expletives, Anders positioned himself between Kal and Roran, forming a loose circle. He shook his head. "Outsiders." He spat the word like it was a curse. "We should just round 'em up and boot 'em. Them and their pigs." He glanced toward Kal in search of agreement. "Nothin' but trouble."

Kal said nothing. He felt like he was perched on a tightrope. Part of the group, yet standing on the outside. Not a Baldomar, but nonetheless one of them.

"What protections lay up the mountain?" he asked.

"We don't know," Ben said.

"No idea whatsoever?"

"We don't go up the mountain. That's the rule."

"What do wards normally do?"

"Depends on the ward. Some cloak and deter. The woods to the south of town used to be real spooky."

Roran grunted. "Don't miss that."

"Kalane pulled those back a while ago," Wynne said to Kal. "To focus her energy on guarding her hoard."

He cast his eyes toward the heavily wooded mountainside. An uneasy trickle ran over his scalp, but he managed a smile. "I'm not sure whether that's comforting."

"It's not."

Nialls joined the group and took command immediately. "Scouts, move ahead and observe. Keep your wits about you."

Without a word, Wynne and Roran jogged ahead at a quick, silent pace and melted into the wooded mountainside.

32

Kal and the others followed over tangled roots and a coating of pine needles. Around brambly undergrowth and boulders the size of cattle. There were trails which weren't really trails and evergreens in all directions. No squirrels nosed in the brush. No bird sang.

No one spoke.

The prickle of anticipation gripped Kal by the heart, keeping him alert. He'd never contended with magic before and felt woefully unprepared in comparison to the Baldomar. He had a working set of eyes and ears. Another set of hands. He was another presence to outnumber potentially hostile men who couldn't use magic either.

They'd trekked uphill for half an hour when Wynne reemerged ahead, seemingly from nowhere. "We found two of them."

"Where's Roran?" Nialls asked.

"Watching at a distance. They don't know he's there."

"Hostile?"

"Not yet. I think they wandered into a warded area." She tapped her head with a finger. "They're not right."

"How so?"

"They're moving around like a couple of sick animals. Come see."

Wynne led them off the path to Roran. He held his bow and arrow in the rest position as he observed a pair of men forty feet away from behind the cover of a tangled shrub.

Kal recognized both from the tavern. He didn't recall their names. One had too-long hair like hay and the start of a drinker's belly. Muttering to himself, he ambled in no particular direction in a wobbly manner which made him look dizzy. Or drunk. Not much different from the other times Kal saw him.

The second man was as thin as a rod, with weak, gangly arms and a hook nose. He stood six inches before a tree, inspecting the bark like it was the most interesting thing in existence.

Willem grimaced. "They look confused."

"Where does the ward begin?" Nialls asked.

Roran's shoulder twitched upward. "Somewhere between here and them, I reckon."

Nialls watched the two men for a long, silent moment.

"You think if we step into the ward, we may not come out on our own?" Ben said.

Nialls dipped his chin. "Possible."

"Anyone got rope?" Ben asked the group. "We could attach a line to whoever goes to grab them, and pull you back if needed."

Wynne had ten feet of line. Roran, twelve.

Nialls sucked his teeth and shook his head. "Not enough."

"Enough to bind them, if they're difficult," Ben said. "Maybe if we're quick, it won't affect us."

Anders straightened and snapped his fingers. "I know. We tie the lines together, lure one of 'em closer, and snare him with the lariat. Then drag him out, and do the same with the other guy."

Ben looked at him like he was an idiot. "You expect that work twice?"

"Look at 'em. I bet they were none-too-bright to begin with."

Willem wrinkled his eyebrows in serious consideration. "Can you tie a lariat?"

"How hard could it be?"

"Stop talking," Nialls said, and the men obeyed. "Here's how this is going to go. We show a united front. Call them to us. If they do not cooperate, then a few will go in to get them."

"I'll go, if it comes to it," Ben said.

"Me too," Anders said.

Willem added, "Count me."

Brave men.

Before anyone had time to overthink, Nialls signaled. As one, they stepped out of the brush.

The threat of violence thickened the air with an unspoken tension, and Kal felt it thrum in his veins and stiffen his backbone. Resolved to do his part, he drew himself to his full height and spread his shoulders. He hardened his face. Concerns about magical interference set him on edge, but he forced himself to focus.

Nialls bellowed. "You two. Come."

There was no mercy in his voice. It was the sort of command no rational person disobeyed.

Drinker's Belly winced at Nialls while Skinny blinked in their direction, dazed.

"I don't know," Drinker's Belly said.

"It's not complicated," Ben said.

"They said she's not home. The dragon. They said she's never home."

"You can't be up here."

Skinny said nothing.

Drinker's Belly stared at Ben for the length of a breath. His eyes swept the group. Two on seven. All persons, armed. Their presence, persuasive. He craned his neck to take in his surroundings. Without another word, he staggered in the opposite direction.

Ben and Anders broke rank and overtook him with ease. Each grabbed him roughly by an arm. Kal tensed as Drinker's Belly pulled to get away. He wasn't a match for the Baldomar, especially in his current condition. Though grumpy, he gave up the struggle quickly, and allowed himself to be steered toward the group.

Willem took charge of Skinny, who'd remained stationary to watch the exchange unfold with a look of vacant confusion. Willem cringed and shook his head as he returned. "It's like stepping into a fog."

"The ward?" Wynne said.

"Aye," Anders said as he, Ben, and Drinker's Belly rejoined them. "Was cloudy straight away. Had to keep telling meself what we were doing."

New stresses roused in the back of Kal's mind as he considered the power and span of the wards. Anders, Ben, and Willem were only in the area for a few moments. He wondered about the likelihood of accidentally stumbling into it and starving before anyone knew what happened.

"Do you have command over yourself?" Nialls asked.

The Baldomar nodded assurance.

"Then haul them back."

Two to go.

33

Wynne and Roran directed Nialls and Kal away from the cloud of confusion. They pressed up the mountainside as a group this time. The sounds of breathing and the faint swish of fallen leaves felt like a cacophony. It made Kal prickly. He figured it was the stress of the situation until Nialls bumped his shoulder. Feckless rage surged inside him. He gritted his teeth and tightened his muscles, ready to shove Nialls and bark at him to mind himself.

Which jarred him.

He didn't want to tussle with Nialls. Regardless of the sudden spike in confidence which made him feel like he could go unscathed, he knew how it'd end if he picked a fight with Nialls.

He chanced a glance at the others. Jaws were tight. Sweat beaded Nialls' brow. Wynne looked agitated. Her mouth was a tiny line, and her nostrils were flared.

Another ward?

As he acknowledged the question, the surge of aggression lessened its press. Though far from dissipating, the shift was immediate.

Wynne broke the quiet. "Anyone else feeling weirdly aggressive?"

Roran growled. "How'd you guess?"

"It's the ward. Resist it."

The fact that Kal had come to the same idea moments earlier bolstered his resolve. He felt less inept. It was a strange comfort to know he wasn't the only one struggling to maintain focus.

Roran pushed a breath through his teeth. "I can barely think. Feel like I could fight a bear right now and win."

Kal shot him an amused look.

Roran's scowl cracked. "Wot? You don't?"

Kal snorted. "Didn't say that."

"Nialls, should we go back and try to find another way onward?" Wynne asked. "To get out of it?"

Roran shook his head. "For serious, part of me'd rather lean into this, once we find these last two...."

"Careful, friend," Kal said. "If a ward alters your state of mind by magic, better not to test the limits. You don't know how deep that well is. You dive in, you might not make it back out."

A shout in the distance cut off further discussion.

As one, they moved cautiously toward the yelling until the trees thinned and they saw a man standing on the ridge of a gully sixty feet ahead. Kal recognized the short dark hair which grew thicker on the sides than on top and the single hoop earring. His name was Gunther. *Non-Baldomar. Unpleasant.* He proceeded to shout his defiance in the foulest terms possible.

The group drew to a stop.

"Well, he knows we're here," Kal said. "Where's the fourth man?"

"Can you find him?" Roran asked Wynne.

Kal kept his eyes on the obvious problem as Wynne murmured the allur. She cringed like she was in pain and shook her head.

"I can't focus. I'm sorry." She swiped the back of her sleeve across her forehead.

Kal pricked his ears and made a visual sweep of their surroundings. With the press of the ward and irate jabber of their would-be confronter, he found it difficult to concentrate, too. He could only imagine the challenge of directing magic in this swamp.

Gunther's roars escalated. He advanced and Kal tensed in anticipation of a clash. "I know what you here about!" Gunther drew to a sudden stop after only a few paces. "Think you can kill me and keep the treasure for you-selves? Why don't I fight you for it? Then we'll see."

Nialls spoke rapidly to the group. "We're not here to kill. Wynne, keep your axe at hand. Do not fight unless you have to."

He drew himself up, somehow managing to look even more intimidating. He extended a hand toward the ground. "*Fyrir therr hondum.*"

A rustle of dead leaves drew Kal's attention. A trickle of water ran over them, as though drawn by an unseen force. Liquid pulled from the earth rushed upward toward the outstretched hand in a cloud of sparkling droplets. At Nialls' touch, the droplets crystalized into a warhammer.

Baldomar magic.

Kal gaped for the length of a breath.

Nialls marched. He pointed his ice hammer in Gunther's direction like a king with a scepter. "Shut your mouth."

"Get on the ground!" Roran swept wide and took aim with bow and arrow. "Face down. Hands to the sides."

Suddenly feeling more under-armed than he was comfortable with, Kal snatched a sturdy branch out of the dead leaves at his feet. It was three inches wide and as long as his forearm.

"Drop your bow first!" Gunther spat back.

Roran jerked his head to indicate Nialls. "Do what he says, or get an arrow in the chest. Your choice."

A new wave of stress rolled into Kal. He wanted to hope the threat was a bluff, not Roran disregarding orders. It could've been either.

"What's to stop you from shooting me anyway? You already think we outsiders are rubbish –"

"Good point." Roran raised his aim. "Which one of you touched our scout?"

"Get on the ground!" Nialls said.

Gunther hesitated. He made a face like he'd tasted something bad. His gaze darted beyond Wynne, and up where branches rustled and a stick snapped. Kal followed Gunther's line of sight. Wynne whirled around with a gasp. A second dirty individual with a messy ginger braid leaped out of a tree with a battle-yell. He landed hard in the brush, fifteen feet from Wynne. He righted himself and his eyes landed on her with crazed malevolence. Teeth bared, he whipped a crooked knife from his belt.

34

Something feral and protective surged to life inside Kal. He forgot Gunther. Nialls. Roran. All that mattered was putting himself between Wynne and that knife.

Kal sprinted toward her.

The second man snapped into motion and closed the distance with an alarming burst of speed. Barely slowing, he drew his knife arm across his torso and threw his weight into a hard, backhanded swipe with enough force to lob off Wynne's head.

Kal crashed into her and shoved her out of the way before the slash intended for her found purchase. She hit the ground hard while Kal barreled into the knife's path. A hot, stinging slice bit deep across his upper arm. The pain was more of a factual acknowledgement than a present problem. He pivoted, anticipating another slash, and squared off with the attacker.

Now focused on Kal, the guy with the braid redoubled his efforts. He slashed blindly. Wildly.

Kal threw his upper body back to avoid another cut. Remembering the branch in his hand, he brought his makeshift club to bear. He swung at the knife hand as it flashed in another attempt.

The guy with the braid screamed. The blade dropped somewhere in the dead leaves. "You broke my hand!"

"Stand down!" Kal said.

The guy swung his good fist and missed. Kal returned with a left hook to the gut. The guy staggered backward two steps, disoriented and gagging. He gave himself a moment. Kal realized too late that he was only buying time while he scanned the leaf litter for the dropped knife.

Their eyes landed on it at the same time. A breathless pause gripped them.

At the first twitch of the guy's muscles, Kal plowed into him. He grabbed him around the middle and knocked him off his feet.

The guy thrashed like a trapped animal. Kal took an elbow to the face. Somehow, he managed to keep his weight on top.

The physical struggle intensified the raw, aggressive press against his mind. It took every fiber of strength to resist. Through the guy's yelling and the murk of the ward, he heard Wynne's voice.

Help was coming.

Kal marshaled his fortitude, clenched his eyes shut, and held fast. Anything beyond that, and he knew the dam would burst. He'd lose control. He willed himself to hold on.

A little longer.

Help was coming.

The guy squirmed and freed an arm which he used to pound against Kal's knife wound. Once. Twice. Kal yelled and eased up involuntarily. The guy contorted himself and kicked. A sharp, snapping pain exploded in Kal's ribs.

Then Roran was there.

It was too tight and chaotic for Roran to take a shot, so he dropped his bow and threw himself into the fray. After a frantic moment of two-on-one struggle, Roran cried out in pain. "You bit me!"

Roran's fury spiked. He pulled back briefly, then beat the guy over the head without mercy.

"Roran!" Wynne's voice again. "The ward – resist it!"

The words entered Kal's ears as though through water. They evidently reached Roran, too. He gave a moment's pause and the wrestling match stilled briefly. Long enough for Kal to see that the guy with the braid teetered on the edge of consciousness.

Taking the opportunity, Kal struggled to turn him over. "Gimme rope!"

With effort, he and Roran flipped him the rest of the way onto his stomach. They wrenched his arms behind his back. Wynne dropped to her knees beside them and worked quickly, tightening the knots over the man's wrists.

Disheveled and bloody, with one eye swollen shut, the guy craned his neck for a look at her face and cursed at her.

"Shut up." Kal's thoughts were thick with a brazen aggression. It took everything he had left to hold the guy in place and keep the physical distress of his body at arm's length while she finished.

The dull smack of a landed punch drew Kal's eye across the clearing. Nialls flung Gunther face-first into the dirt, contorted his hands behind his back, and knelt on him to hold him there.

"He's bound," Wynne said.

Roran and Kal eased their weight against the guy. With difficulty, Kal leaned back on his haunches. Resting his hands on his knees, he caught his breath. The gash across his upper arm slid to a stinging ache. It bled profusely. His knuckles were torn. His cheek felt swollen and hot, and he had a fat lip. All this was small beans in comparison to the pain in his side. It was bright and expansive. Worse when he drew a breath.

Roran gave the guy a kick.

"Roran! It's over. Help Nialls," Wynne said.

With a growl, Roran peeled away.

Wynne turned to Kal. "You're bleeding."

"I know." He winced as he held his arm away from his body and rotated it for a better look. He displaced the torn fabric. The knife had sliced into the meat of his arm and ran several inches across. It hurt to move it.

Wynne rooted through her bag. "I have bandages."

He shifted his body and felt the scrape of bone against bone. Gritting his teeth, he bit back a grunt and braced a hand gently on his side. Something moved which shouldn't. He released a slow breath.

Wynne found her bandage. With shaky fingers, she came alongside him and wrapped it over the cut. Blood soaked through immediately. Kal's face tightened as she tied it snug.

"I'm sorry," she said. "I'm only trying to slow the bleed. It needs pressure."

"It's fine."

"I have more bandages."

"Don't know if that'll help."

Wynne's attentive gaze swept briefly over Roran and Nialls in search of grievous injuries as they drew up with Gunther, now bound. "Is anyone else hurt?"

Roran jerked his chin toward the guy on the ground. "This bad dose bit me."

"Are you bleeding?"

He pushed up a sleeve to reveal a black and purple teeth-print. "Nah."

"Nialls?"

Nialls gave a single shake of the head. "Time to go."

Wynne returned her attention to Kal. "I'll take you to Sender."

"Who's Sender?" Kal asked.

"The best mate you didn't know you got," Roran said as he hauled the second guy to his feet more roughly than necessary.

"Village healer," Wynne said.

At this, Kal experienced an uneasy clench which had nothing to do with his physical pain. Healers were expensive and known for administering painful remedies which did more harm than good. He couldn't afford to waste his money, especially if his injuries kept him from work while he healed.

"As long as I can move the arm, it'll be fine." A stretch, and he knew it. As for the pain in his side, there wasn't much to be done except try not to make it worse.

"You don't know where that knife's been," Wynne said.

Kal wasn't sure why that settled it, but it did. Spawning an infection would kill him faster than no food. He supposed *poor* was better than *dead*. "Alright."

"What about us? Either of us get a healer after what you did?" Gunther said.

Nialls, who was holding him by the back of the collar, gave him a little shake. "Quiet."

The other guy piped up. "This is your fault, Gunther."

The return sneer made Gunther even uglier. "Mine?"

"Whose idea was this? *Draw them in, and we'll take 'em. The treasure will be ours.*"

"Not my fault you jumped when you did."

"You gave me away!"

Gunther scoffed.

"What good is an ambush when your idiot partner looks at your hiding spot? I woulda had her."

Roran jerked the guy by the arm. "Is that wot you thought? *Do you know who we are?*"

Wynne huffed as she swatted dead leaves from the legs of her trousers. "Clearly they weren't thinking straight."

35

Roran followed Nialls, each man in charge of a prisoner. Wynne lingered, waiting for Kal. The considerate sweetness of the gesture cut through the haze still leaning against his heart and lessened the weight of it further.

Still, Kal almost wished she hadn't. It had nothing to do with the ward and everything to do with his dignity.

He stood with effort. It didn't matter what he did – his side hurt. Less-so if he kept still and took steady, shallow breaths. Which would be a problem, hiking down the mountain.

Shoulder to shoulder, they took up the rear of the procession. The exertion tired everyone, and no one spoke beyond general factual communication. *The moss on that rock is more slippery than it looks.* Or, *Mind the hole.* Or, the welcome, *We're out of the ward.*

Kal felt it immediately. He'd been running over the fight and what he should've done differently. His fury burned against these men. They almost murdered Wynne, and his injuries would cost him time, money, and work. Justice was called for. It felt like it was up to him.

Then, it was like stepping into the brisk Noemar air after a prolonged stint in a dark and stuffy hovel. Relief washed over him and a new fatigue which bordered on euphoria sank into his body.

The last wisps of the ward abated, along with the necessity to personally take matters into his own hands. Not that he was in any state to administer justice.

He was pretty sure his rib was broken.

The hike down the mountainside was punishing. He only managed by moving carefully and slowly. Which resulted in him falling behind.

Wynne never left him.

✧

The fields standing between the dragon's mountain and the village came into view. Ahead, Nialls and Roran adjusted course with their prisoners, parting with Wynne and Kal. She directed them though less-congested lanes, past farmsteads, orchards, and the occasional loose hog.

"Thank you," she said once it was just them. She nodded toward the soaked bandage on his arm.

"Of course," he said.

"You saved my life."

"I feel bad. I knocked you on the ground, hard."

"Don't feel bad. That was the best part."

The remark gave him pause until he caught the spark in her expression. The little smirk. It took him a beat to catch the reference to their initial meeting. His genuine, albeit lopsided, smile built.

"You handled yourself well," she said, more sincerely. "A lot of folks would've beaten him to a pulp. Or worse. You kept your head."

Kal cringed a little as he shrugged. "He was under the influence of the spell. Don't make him innocent, but we all felt it."

They turned down the next muddy road wending through town, drawing a few inches closer.

"I'm concerned about what happens now," she said. "They're at the boarding house with you, right?"

"I'm not at the boarding house anymore."

"You're not?"

"I bought a home."

"You never mentioned that." She sounded pleasantly surprised.

He'd been wanting to mention it for weeks, and struggled to find a natural way to slip it into conversation when she was around. "On the south side, near the edge of town. About five minutes from the mill."

Wynne eyed him with a measure of newfound respect, which was easy to enjoy. "Good for you."

Kal considered inviting her to come by and see it sometime but thought better of it. Too big of a risk the remark would be ill-received. The conversation had been going well. He didn't want to stick his foot in it now.

"Does that mean you're laying down roots?" she asked.

"Like I said, not much to go back to. Whereas here?" He cast her a puffy-eyed glance. "I can think of a good reason to stay."

The color in her cheeks deepened and she tried in vain to pin back a tightlipped smile.

"Why the concern?" he asked, bringing her back to her original thought.

"There'll be consequences for those men. They know you helped catch them," she said. "What if they're the sort to retaliate?"

"I wouldn't be surprised."

"Me neither. And it'd be easier for them to try something if you were still at the boarding house. I think they all still rent there."

"Aw, Wynne. Are you worried about me?"

"I'd rather you not be murdered in your sleep, if that's what you mean."

"It sounds like you're worried about me."

She rolled her eyes and smirked. "Sure."

"I'm touched."

"Lock your door at night. Also, don't listen to Anders – what he said about newcomers."

Kal was quiet for a moment as it came back to him. "He didn't mean it. He was upset."

"Still. He's wrong."

They drew deeper into the village and the stress began to fall away in earnest. The quiet between them felt natural. Comfortable.

"I saw your handiwork at Alro and Fay's house," she said after a spell.

"Passable workmanship?"

"It's well done. They said you'd been helping them quite a bit."

"They need it," he said, careful to avoid a muddy puddle collecting in a divot. "I like them. So it's win-win."

This, more than anything else, seemed to touch her. It wasn't what Kal was aiming for. He was only stating the truth. Yet her color deepened a second time, and her eyes softened.

He'd never forget that look.

✧

The village healer's door creaked open to reveal a portly man nearing middle-age. He had a friendly face, despite the bags under his eyes. His questioning gaze swept over Kal and Wynne.

"We went up the mountain," Wynne said by way of greeting. "There was a fight."

"I got cut," Kal said stupidly.

"I see." The healer kept his voice light and even. He waved them inside as if he saw this sort of thing everyday. "If your adversary had a knife, you're mighty lucky it wasn't worse. Both of you."

"We have Kal to thank for that." Wynne offered Kal a sweet smile and a wink as she grabbed a stool at the clean table in the center of the room.

The space was well-lit by several glass-pane windows. A washbasin stood along one side of the room. Wall-mounted shelves held clean rags, linens, soap, tonics, and various healer's implements.

"I don't believe we've met face-to-face. Sender Fife." The healer placed a hand on his chest as he shut the door.

Kal couldn't manage the same gesture, so he dipped his chin. "Kalomir. Or, Kal."

"Well, Kal, take a seat. I'll see about that knife wound."

Kal's focus jumped to the seat beside Wynne. He knew what sitting in that stool entailed, yet it looked more inviting than his cot at the end of a long day. He eased himself onto it, careful to avoid sudden movement which might send his broken ribs grinding against each other.

"How's Maeve?" Wynne asked.

"A bit bruised." Sender grabbed a bar of soap and proceeded to scrub his hands and forearms in the washbasin. "She tweaked something in her wrist. Couldn't move it. Right as rain now."

"I don't suppose the others brought the guilty persons to you?"

"Ben, Willem, and Anders delivered two befuddled men. Nothing I could do for them."

Wynne's eyes grew a little wider. "They're permanently addled?"

"Oh, I doubt it." Sender grabbed a towel to dry his hands. "There's nothing really wrong. They're just confused. I'm sure they'll be fine once they sleep it off. Worst case, we'll ask Kalane to take pity and undo the effect when she comes back."

"You think she'd have mercy on them?"

Sender thought for a moment. "No. Now that you mention it."

"Where has she been?"

"Governing her dominion. No easy feat, from what I hear."

Wynne and Sender made small talk in the personable, businesslike fashion of old friends or long-time coworkers. Kal, once again, experienced the strange sensation of being on the outside of things, yet welcome. He decided he liked Sender, though he might feel differently depending how this treatment went.

Sender positioned a stool closeby and settled himself. "Let's see what we have here."

Kal picked at the bandage, trying hard not to move his trunk as he pried it away.

Sender frowned at the deep slice and hummed. "I've seen worse."

"What do you recommend?" Kal said, fearing he already knew the answer.

"I'm going to heal the cut and any deeper damage you might've incurred," Sender said. "Also, make sure this doesn't turn septic."

Kal cast Wynne a wary glance. He wasn't sure whether he wanted her to stay for this. A splash of alcohol might cause him to cry out or pass out. Stitches were known to make grown men leak tears.

Without further explanation, Sender pressed his hand over the wound. Kal flinched. Without an utterance, Sender's runes glowed orange. The throbbing sting diminished, then disappeared altogether.

Sender pulled his hand back, looking tired but satisfied. "All set."

The wound was gone.

As if it had never been there.

Kal's lips parted as he touched the healthy, smooth skin. He gave it a prod. No pain whatsoever. "I can't believe it."

Wynne's smile brightened. "That's right. You've never seen Sender work before."

"They said you were a healer. I didn't think they meant miracle-worker," Kal said to Sender. He cast Wynne a glance. "Why didn't you tell me?"

She turned her palm upward. "We're Baldomar. We use magic. What did you expect?"

"A splash of alcohol and sewing."

"I haven't had to do that since we got the allur, thank the gods," Sender said. "Most folks would rather take the scar, and I can't blame them. Although sometimes it couldn't be helped. It was the worst part of being a healer. Especially when it was a child." He blew out a breath and shook his head. "Wynne, I still remember when Omri split his knee open." He turned to Kal to include him in the conversation. "You could see the bone."

Wynne cringed and gave her head a little shake. "That was awful."

"What do you mean, got the allur?" Kal asked. "It went away?"

"It's a long story. A good one. Wynne's brother was involved."

"Omri, the dragon-slayer, or the bear?"

Wynne laughed. "Dragon-slayer and his wife, Aeryn. They set things right.

I'll tell you about it another time."

"Is there anything else I can help with?" Sender said.

"Can you do anything for broken ribs?" Kal asked.

"I can," Sender said carefully. "Why? Do you think your ribs are broken?"

"You tell me." Kal winced as he maneuvered to hike up his shirt. He paused and fixed Wynne with a semi-serious tone. "I promise, I'm not showing off."

Her jaw dropped. He wasn't sure whether he'd offended her, or provoked mock-indignation. Before she formed a response, he lifted his sweater to reveal the swath of mottled black and blue.

"Good gods, Kal," she said, whatever she'd been thinking evidently forgotten.

Sender moved the folds of fabric out of the way and gently prodded the swollen skin. Kal bit back an involuntary grunt.

"When did this happen?"

"Up the mountain."

"That man did that to you?" A fire blazed in Wynne's eyes. Her tone took a sharper quality. "Why didn't you say anything? Better question, how were you able to hike down the mountain like that?"

"Carefully."

She stared at him, incredulous. And, he thought, a little impressed.

"I had good company," he said. "It helped."

36

Wynne bounced on her toes outside Tess' door. She rubbed her hands together and blew into them to warm herself against the brisk wind cutting through the village that day.

Tess yanked the door wide, bright-eyed and expectant, with Asmund on her hip. "Get in here, and tell me everythin'. I'm makin' tea."

"You heard about it already?" Wynne asked as she bundled into the house and unwrapped her scarf.

"A bit from Brinja. She came by. Brought those." Tess nodded to a basket of cranapples on the table. She forced a hot cup into Wynne's hands and jerked her head toward the chairs. Wynne took a sip of tea as she settled. She watched Tess set Asmund up with wooden blocks on the rug.

Tess tucked her skirt beneath her and plopped into her chair across from Wynne. "I'm ready. Start at the beginnin'."

Wynne didn't make it far into the story before Tess interrupted with a raised palm.

"Nialls chose Kal?"

Wynne bobbed her head.

"You don't seem repulsed."

"I'm not. I'm glad he was there."

"I thought we didn't like Kal."

Wynne said nothing.

Tess hoisted an eyebrow. "We'll come back to that. Go on."

Tess was an ideal listener. She asked good clarifying questions and gasped in the right places. When Wynne explained how Kal stopped the man with a knife, Tess dipped her chin and her tone took a suggestive quality. "He saved you, you say?"

"I'm a little bruised, but he took a nasty cut and wound up with a broken rib."

"How did that happen?"

"He tackled the man with the knife."

"That don't sound smart."

"The man didn't have the knife at the time. Kal knocked it out of his hand," Wynne said. "They were fighting all-out. He went out of his way to stop the guy without killing him."

"Awfully merciful, considerin' the circumstances."

"Awfully impressive," Wynne said. "The ward was awful. Like an aggressive fog pressing against us, heavy as smoke. I can't tell you how tempted I was to slap your brother."

"He prolly deserved it."

"Point is, I'd never do that. None of us could focus. I couldn't even use the allur. Nialls could, but I couldn't."

"Wot did he do?"

"Ice hammer. I don't think it requires as much concentration."

"Wonder wot ol' Kalane was thinkin'."

"You and everyone else. Maybe sow enough discord so a group can't continue?" Wynne offered.

"Maybe. How'd Roran handle?"

Wynne considered how best to describe his behavior without slighting him. "He was worked up for a start."

"Well, yeah. You don't touch the scouts."

"It could've been worse."

Tess raised her cup in mock toast. "Sounds like Kal's got more fortitude than you reckoned."

Wynne bit her lip and tried to keep the grin off her face. "Did you know he has a house? And he's been helping Arlo and Fay during his spare time, for nothing more than a meal. Have you seen their home lately?"

Tess shook her head. "How's the workmanship?"

"Quite good. And you can stop the look."

"I didn't say nothin'."

"You were thinking it, very loud."

"Only wonderin' whether this means we like Kal now?"

"I don't know," Wynne said, not convincing herself. Her conscience prodded her.

"I'll take that as a yes. Wot happened to the four troublemakers?"

"They kicked them out."

New gravity settled between them.

"That'll send a message," Tess said. "Who handed down the judgment?"

"My pops."

Tess looked surprised. "It sounds more like Nialls. Though, I guess I'm none too surprised. One tried to kill you."

"One of the men had a wife and a couple kids. All of them had to go too."

"Shame."

"I know. I feel bad for the wife and kids."

"For all you know, she put him up to it."

"We don't know that."

"Possible."

"Speculation. Even if she goaded him into it, the kids weren't involved. It feels like they're being punished."

"Not to sound like an ice-woman, but they're not."

"The effect is the same as if they were."

"I agree, they're suffering. But their pop ought to have considered that before he went and did somethin' stupid. He's a parent. Wotever he does affects his whole family, for better or worse." She threw up a hand. "Wot if it was one of our own people, and he went and did somethin' heinous? Does he get a pass because he's got a wife or kids? No!"

Wynne tipped her head as she considered. "When you phrase it that way…"

"Wot other way would I phrase it?"

"I still feel bad for the kids."

"So do I. They deserve better from their pops."

"I wonder if they'll go to the Gren."

"They ain't the only ones. You heard from Harek lately?"

Wynne shook her head as a bud of uneasiness pressed heavier against her heart.

"I thought he was writin' to you nearly every time the courier came 'round."

"He was."

Tess caught the look in Wynne's eye. Sensing a change in Wynne, she rolled her hand. "Go on."

Wynne forced out a breath. "It's been weeks. The last few times the courier came – and you know there was a long stretch between some of those times because of the illness – there was nothing."

"Think he got sick?"

"I thought of that. Still, it's been long enough that I should've heard something if he was still interested in communicating."

"Wot makes you think he ain't? Apart from no letters."

Heat rose to the surface of Wynne's skin. "After the debacle with Corbin, I asked him about his timeline. I also asked if he'd write to my father to state his intentions. He won't do it."

"Wot? Why?"

"He'd rather speak to him in person. He feels he has to have everything in order before he goes to him."

"You did kinda make it a requirement."

"No, I told him there are certain things that need to happen before we marry. I never said he shouldn't speak to my father about his hopes for our future."

"Fair. But you can see how that puts him in a tight spot. If he's gonna buck the tradition and seek out Elric, rather than the other way 'round, then he's gotta have himself together."

"Who's side are you on?"

Tess flashed both palms in the air. "I'm only sayin'."

Wynne rubbed at the stress in her forehead. "What's worse, he seemed bothered that I'd even bring it up."

"Were you naggin'?"

"No. It was an honest request. I have not badgered him about this once."

"Chance you're misreadin' it, then?"

"Tess, my mother understands that I'm waiting on Harek in some sense, but my pops is gettin' antsy. He wants to see my life move in the right direction. He thinks he's failed to find a good man for me and that it reflects poorly."

"Oh," Tess said. "I guess I hadn't thought of it that way."

"Nor does he appreciate Harek's delay."

"Sounds like you got that in common."

"Harek's put me in a difficult position, and he doesn't seem to understand it."

"You ever tell him about your dinner with Corbin?"

"Initially, no. I didn't want to worry him."

"You might consider doin' it. Could light a fire under him."

"Well, I did in my last letter. I made it plain. I told him that I have no problem with waiting for him, and I mean it."

Tess gave her disbelieving glance.

"I'm serious, Tess. Marriage means babies, and..." Wynne caught herself.

Tess' eyebrows twitched in question.

Feeling flustered, Wynne shook herself and took a breath. When she opened her mouth, she chose her words with greater care. "I don't need him to rush home. But if he really wants to marry me, like he says, then he must make that clear to my father. Soon. I told him where my father stands, and what that means for my future. He hasn't written to me since."

Something twisted in Wynne's chest and brought a rush of water to her eyes.

"I think it's done between us."

She laid a hand across her face and started to cry.

"Oh, Wynne." Tess rested her cup, came around the table, and wrapped an arm over Wynne's shoulders.

"I was sharp. I know I was. What else was I supposed to say?"

"I know."

"His reluctance makes me wonder whether he ever meant what he said."

"Did you write that part?"

"No – it seemed mean. But I've thought it for a while. Maybe he wanted to give himself an out, in case he changed his mind about me, or got a better offer."

"I dunno if that sounds like Harek. Could be he's just not using his head."

"That's what I hoped when I wrote. That's why I did. Now he's silent? It makes me furious." Wynne sniffed hard and shook her head. Another wave of tears came unbidden. "I'm the fool who believed him."

Tess rubbed Wynne's arm and let her get it out.

37

"Something's not right with Finnion."

Harek looked up from the kindling he'd been nurturing and met Cain's wary expression.

"What do you mean?" he asked, more to draw out Cain's observation than out of disbelief. Cain hadn't taken issue with Finnion before now. Yet, Harek couldn't shake the ring of truth in his words. He couldn't put his finger on it.

"You disagree?"

"I'm only asking."

"He's more agitated. Quieter."

"Cain, we're in the middle of nowhere, huntin' down bandits. Everyone feels the strain."

"That's not it."

Harek pressed his lips into a tight line and waited.

Cain rubbed a hand over his face. "Maybe it is." He cast a brief glance toward the brush where Finnion disappeared a minute earlier. He lowered his voice. "I've heard him talking to himself."

"When he's awake or in his sleep?" Neither was unusual in itself. Sometimes people vocalized their thoughts in an effort to work through them. For Finnion, the night-terrors were a regular occurrence.

"On his watch. When he thinks we're sleeping."

"What's he saying?"

"No idea. I thought it was the language you lot use for your magic." Cain gave a tight shake of his head. "It's not."

"What does it sound like?"

"I can't repeat it. I wouldn't, even if I knew how. It sounds evil."

"Cain."

"I'm serious."

Harek turned up his palms. *What do you expect me to do with this?*

"Look. It's not the only thing. Dorian says he caught him eating a squirrel."

"Not my favorite meal, but I don't see the issue."

"Raw."

A nudge of uneasiness pressed against Harek. His expression betrayed the first signs of it. Not because of the squirrel – that was outrageous. The other day, Dorian made an off-hand remark about the allur. Harek had been there. At the time, he sensed no malice, but Finnion grew defensive and confrontational. Harek thought the matter was more-or-less over. Now, he wondered whether lingering offense prompted Dorian to spread a story out of spite.

They didn't have to like each other, but Harek needed his crew united. Anyone seeding divisions meant they'd struggle to work together. People died that way.

"Where's Dorian now?" Harek asked.

"Pitching tents."

"I want to talk to him."

"I'll get him."

"You can let him finish."

Cain trotted toward the far side of their camp. Harek returned his attention to the kindling. His mind felt a thousand miles from fire-starting. In his last letter home – far briefer than he would've liked given the limited supplies in the Gren – he'd asked Wynne to be patient. He hadn't received a response before he was called upon to resolve the supply chain issue. He hadn't allowed himself to think too deeply about this. They'd been away from the Gren for weeks already, and everyone was on edge. They were getting close.

Oleksy's last scout-ahead brought news of great plumes of black smoke some miles in the distance. Here in the uninhabited lowland moors of Noemar, it didn't bode well. That was where they were headed tomorrow.

A crunch over the gritty earth, much closer than Harek expected, drew his attention over his shoulder.

Finnion's mouth twisted into a grim line, and he slowed slightly to take in the scene. Harek crouched by the fire, Cain on his way toward the tents. He stared darkly after Cain, then refocused on Harek. "Were you talking about me?"

Harek hadn't been expecting that, and it set him on his heels. He hesitated a beat.

It was a beat too long.

Finnion's voice grew sharp. "You're my enemy now, too?"

Harek stood and extended an arm. "No one's against you, brother."

"Not true – it's not –" Finnion clamped his eyes shut and gave his head a tight shake. His breathing quickened and stress rippled across his face. He took a few steps away and rubbed his temple. "I don't believe you."

"When have I lied to you?"

Finnion said nothing for a long moment. Then, "I – it's not safe – I shouldn't be here."

"You knew there could be danger when you signed up. We all did." Harek leveled a serious tone and moved toward him. "None of us is in this alone."

Finnion scratched aggressively behind his ear and gave his head a second shake. Harek wasn't sure if he was listening. He looked miserable.

Harek understood that dread was a real, powerful force. He'd seen men similarly distressed before. A hearty meal and good rest often helped matters. He also understood that whatever he said or did next could push Finnion one way or the other. Finnion might just need an ear.

"You're an important part of this team. Tell me what's going on," Harek said.

The tread of boots over packed earth and scrubbly grass drew closer. Finnion's focus jumped beyond Harek to Cain and Dorian. A shadow passed over him. "I knew it."

"Knew what?"

"Him. Them." Finnion jerked his chin at Cain and Dorian with fresh ire. "I know what you're doing. I'm not playing your game."

Dorian gave Finnion a confused up-down. "What game?"

"You're always playing games –turning the rest on me – like I'm a freak who can't do anything –"

"Is this still about the other day?" Dorian asked. "Finnion, my comment about the runes? Not a jab. It was stating a fact. *Not all of us can use 'em.* It's fine. Cain don't got 'em. We don't consider him less-than."

"False. You're all false."

"You callin' me a liar?"

"You act like it."

Dorian grimaced and spat back a curse. "What's your problem?"

"You. You and the rest – think you're better because you've had your magic longer." His expression darkened and his voice strengthened. "You don't even know what I'm capable of."

"What you're capable of? Like eating squirrels, raw?"

"Try me, Dorian!"

"How about I try you right now?"

"Enough!" Harek surprised himself with the power in his own voice. The men quieted. Eyes darted to Harek. "You're brothers."

"He's not my brother," Finnion shot back. "He's probably wishing I was dead –"

"I said, enough." He gestured to Finnion. "Walk."

Finnion swatted the air and stomped back into brush. Harek took a controlled breath, then returned his attention to Cain and Dorian. "Dorian, I want a word."

✧

"Tell me what's going on," Harek said. "Keep in mind, I'm going to Finnion to ask the same question. Now's your chance if there's something you need to say."

"Harek, I swear I don't know what he's talking about," Dorian said.

"What's this about the raw squirrel?"

"I caught him eating one – like a corn cob. Fur was still on it. It was the most disturbing thing I've ever seen, and you were there with me in Nyassa. We saw some horrific things."

Harek said nothing.

"I mentioned it to Cain and Billy. Now Finnion's acting like I'm plotting to kill him." Dorian took a step forward, urging him to understand. "Look. I never took issue with him before. Now? I don't want to be near him."

"You don't have a choice. We're out here, and he's part of the team."

"He's not-right."

"I'll talk to him," Harek said. "Next time there's an issue, you sort it with him directly, or you bring it to me. You don't spread it around, sowing discord. If we're not functioning as a unit, someone could end up dead, with what we're doing. Understand?"

"Yes, sir."

"Good."

With Dorian dismissed, Harek ran a hand down his face and drew a deep breath in an effort to gather himself. He loved his crew like they were his brothers. Yet, for some of the hardest men on the continent, too many exhibited a prickly sense of honor. Harek's sisters had thicker skin.

He found Finnion a little ways off, chewing on his thumbnail and pacing. He looked more careworn than normal. Dark circles surrounded his eyes, like he was overtired or needed water.

"What's going on with you?" Harek said, conversational but direct.

Finnion shook his head and continued his distracted back-and-forth.

"Stop pacing and answer me."

"I should just go. I should leave."

"You can't. We're too far from the Gren. It wouldn't be safe for you to turn back alone, and I can't spare anyone to go with you."

"I shouldn't be out here. It's not safe for them."

Harek watched him for a long moment and found himself frustrated. Of course it wasn't safe, and Finnion's continued insecurity over his inability to wield magic made matters more precarious, not less. "Is this because of the runes? You believe you're a detriment to the crew?"

Finnion said nothing. He seemed distracted again. Shaking his head, he continued to pace.

Harek couldn't tell if this was a refusal of his question, or if something else troubled him.

"Stop moving," he said, firmer this time.

Finnion obeyed. He met Harek's face, looking tormented in spirit.

Harek's frustration ebbed, replaced by a tug of empathy for his friend. He took a breath. "If I thought you were a risk, I wouldn't have chosen you for this team. You need to believe that. Or else, start acting like you do."

Finnion said nothing.

"You agreed to come and complete the job. When it's done, if you need a break from all this, take it. I'll approve whatever needs approving. Right now, we have a job to do. We need your head in this."

Finnion's mouth bunched into a deeper frown. He rubbed both hands over his face.

"I need to ask you something."

"What?" Finnion said, voice muffled as he rubbed his face.

"The squirrel?"

Finnion lowered his hand, wary.

"Were you really eating it raw?"

"So?"

"You can't be doing that. Look, I don't care if you're not using the allur. Don't alienate yourself by doing weird stuff. It makes people uncomfortable."

Pain rippled behind Finnion's eyes. For a moment, Harek worried he'd been too harsh. He wasn't trying to grind him into the dust, but a little shame could do a person good. Some folks needed to be reminded that they existed in a world other people, and they were obligated to behave in a way which allowed them to fit into society. It was for his own good.

"You're wrong," Finnion said.

Harek took a slow breath. When he accepted this leadership position, arguing about the normalcy of eating raw squirrels was not a problem he thought he'd have to navigate. He had the nagging sense there was something Finnion wasn't sharing. "What am I wrong about?"

"The allur. You think I haven't been trying. They think I can't use it." Finnion looked him in the eye. "I've learned some things."

This surprised Harek. It felt like the conversation had shifted in the right direction, so he didn't understand the trickle of cold down the back of his neck. If Finnion was learning the allur, it should cheer him. "What'd you learn?"

"I can hear the spirits."

38

Wynne deserted the lane and hiked through the grass toward the post and rail fence surrounding Kal's property. Her eyes passed over the hut to the in-progress additional room just visible from the lane. As she drew closer, she heard superb whistling at the rear of the property.

She glanced over her shoulder, finding the lane still empty, except for the loose hog nosing in the brush on the other side. She wasn't concerned with the violation of the pig rule. Not now. Entering, or appearing to enter, a single man's home reeked of suggestion. Even if the visit was innocent in nature, she'd been taught that it was better to avoid any hint at impropriety. So she leaned against the fence and called.

The whistling continued, interspersed with the whack of a hammer.

What am I doing?

She fiddled with the gold disk dangling from her ear and cast a second uneasy glance up the road. She considered leaving before he realized she was here, or anyone strolled by and generated ideas about her interest in Kal. She wasn't sure she could articulate it, herself.

Yet, with the project at the meeting hall now complete, there'd be no Omri to bring Kal along for supper. If Wynne wanted Kal at the Thars' table, it was up to her.

She cleared her throat and tried again. "Kalomir!"

The whistling stopped. Kal appeared around the bend of the house and his face brightened when he saw her. It was difficult not to smile back.

"You first-named me?"

"I did. How's your side?"

"Much improved." He rested his tool and joined her at the fence, leaning against it from the opposite side. "You look pretty. And nervous. Why are you nervous?"

"I'm not nervous," she lied. "I had a question."

"You got my undivided attention."

"Do you want to come to supper tonight?" She caught the unspoken question behind his eyes and added, "Just a pleasant family dinner. We're having beef and barley stew."

Kal's shoulder's sagged. "I wish I could, but I can't. I'm having dinner with another lady tonight."

Wynne pulled her chin inward and tried not to look as flustered as she felt. "Oh."

A rush of warmth settled uncomfortably on her cheeks. She knew her spike in jealousy was telling, and wholly unjustified. Suddenly feeling supremely foolish, she cleared her throat in an attempt to buy enough time to bring her tone under control and keep her voice from betraying her. "Who?"

"A lady named Fay," he said. "Of Arlo and Fay."

"Oh!" Just as fast, relief rushed in to drown the sudden surge of contention. "Yes. I know that Fay."

Kal studied Wynne's face and his mouth hiked up in the corner. He had her, and he knew it. "Would it bother you if it was some other lady?"

Wynne hesitated. Feeling a little cornered and like she'd unintentionally exposed her heart, she opened her mouth, still unsure what would come out.

Kal continued. "Because it looked like it bothered you."

He waited for a reaction, clearly enjoying himself. The color in Wynne's cheeks intensified. She had to fight to keep a grin from crawling onto her face.

She conceded with a laugh. "Maybe."

His smile deepened. He nudged her forearms from his side of the fence.

"I'm glad I know that."

"So, Arlo and Fay tonight?"

"I told them I'd come by this afternoon. They need a hand getting the hay from the loft out back, and Fay said she's making some kind of lamb and potato mash."

There was a tweak in Wynne's chest. A hardness she hadn't realized she'd been clinging to melted further. "It's good of you to help them. And I don't want to take you away from supper there – Fay is a wonderful cook."

"You're tellin' me. She makes this one soup –potatoes, leeks, and bacon – it's like I'm a kid in my mother's kitchen again."

I'm gonna have to learn this recipe.

"Well, do you want to come for supper..." Wynne tipped her head back and cast around her memory for her last glimpse at the slate nailed to Rakel's door which listed the scouts' watch schedule. "...the day after tomorrow?"

"I can't think of a better way to spend my day of birth."

"That's the day after tomorrow?"

He dipped his chin. "This'll be my thirtieth."

Her eyes brightened. "We'll have to make it good, then."

"You don't gotta go out of your way. It's only another year."

"Tell me your favorite thing to eat."

He shrugged. "I'll eat anything. I'm more interested in the company."

Wynne's affection for him bloomed at this remark. She eyed him in a playful manner and made a conspiratorial hum. "I'll just have to surprise you, then."

39

The faint stench of charred human flesh carried from the nearby burn pits every time the wind shifted. It wasn't the first time Harek smelled such a thing, or the second. There was no getting accustomed. It stuck in the nose and chased away all appetite.

The day before, they'd observed blackened smears of violence along the main road. Signs of struggle left impressions in the earth. Tracks of all kinds diverted from the path, leaving no question as to the cause of death of the nine recently-deceased, smoldering nearby. From there, tracks continued in a northeasterly direction.

Discovering the bandits' handiwork drove a new focus into the heart of each man on Harek's crew. It burned with a quiet, grim intensity to set things right.

It was late when they gathered to listen to Oleksy's report. His detailed drawing in the dirt outlined the whereabouts of the bandits' encampment proximal to the pits and their bivouac. It made three points of a skewed triangle.

In a separate drawing, Oleksy detailed the encampment itself. He'd risked approaching far closer than Harek was comfortable with. Still, the information gleaned was invaluable.

"How many men, would you say?" Harek asked.

Oleksy scraped a hand over the stubble atop his head as he recalled. "I counted twenty one. Two on watch. There's probably more inside. Maybe thirty or forty in all, given the number of huts. Don't think their camp can support more than fifty."

Harek grabbed the lower half of his face as his eyes passed over the picture. The encampment consisted of fifteen structures – mostly small – including a dilapidated hunting blind utilized as a lookout hutch near the entrance, one medium sized building which was probably a barracks, and two storehouses. There, a number of well-crafted covered wagons butted against the side. A shallow trench encircled the camp, along with a fence which was little more than a series of felled trees on their sides. Climbable and shoddy workmanship, Oleksy remarked, but effective at preventing them from entering any way but one on horseback. The main entry was a ten-foot wide gap which presented the only break in the fence and the only interruption to the trench. No barred gate.

All in all, it spanned a manageable area, which was a mercy. Too spacious meant Harek's crew would be spread thin, or that the camp housed more men than they could handle. Too tight presented other hazards, especially once magic started flying.

The main question was whether taking the encampment was achievable.

If Oleksy's estimate was accurate – and Harek trusted his assessment – they were outnumbered six to one. Maybe seven to one. Harek faced worse odds in the battle of Nyassa. There was a vast difference between a battle fought in the open with a hundred of his kinsmen at his back, and infiltrating a camp of murderers and thieves.

If they were to succeed, they'd have to approach every aspect carefully, with each person well-positioned to utilize his skills to the fullest.

Harek looked up from the sketch and his gaze passed over the faces crowded around.

Grigory Hodd, with his constant bad jokes about his missing finger.

Cain, who'd been Harek's first friend after arriving in the Gren.

Billy, the only surviving son of his mother, and the youngest among them, though he carried a maturity which set him apart. He was always ready to help his fellow man.

Dorian, who was true as steel and zealous for good. In recent months, he'd kindled an affection with a striking young lady who'd come to the Gren from Proimos with her aged father. He'd been talking about marrying her.

Finnion, still fighting against his demons for a fresh start. He'd get there. Harek would do his utmost to ensure it.

Oleksy, their scout. A superb one, if a little reckless. He'd stayed with Jaegers after his immediate family was killed in the raid and his house burned to the ground. He was among the first to voluntarily leave for the Gren when the opportunity arose. Harek couldn't blame him.

He loved these men. He would not throw them to the wolves in a reckless grab for plunder.

They watched him, waiting for a reaction. For a plan.

"We're taking the camp," Harek said.

Grigory rumbled in his chest, approving. "No more the hunted."

Luka sprawled, docile and observant at Harek's feet. When Harek crouched beside Oleksy's drawing, Luka took it as an invitation to lick him in the face. Harek offered a pat, then planted his finger on the blind being used as a lookout post.

"Here's how we're gonna do this."

They listened as Harek laid out his plan, modifying it as necessary with their input.

"I want to be clear," he said as he finished. He let his eyes pass over the group, especially Oleksy. "This is not worth losing a single one of you. Don't take risks you don't need to take. If we have to retreat and send for help, then so be it. Any questions?"

Dorian snapped his fingers and straightened. "Should we, you know, take trophies?"

"What kind of trophies?"

"I dunno. Like, their ears."

Harek tried not to show his disgust. "Absolutely not."

"No? Oh, okay."

Cain shot Dorian a glance which was equal parts amused and disturbed.

"Ears? Really?"

"They think I'm crazy," Finnion muttered.

Dorian turned up his palms. "I thought it might be, you know, a sign of our strength in battle."

"No. That's gross." Harek patted the air, taking a firm but reasoning tone. "You want to go back to your lady with a string of ears around your neck?"

Dorian thought for a moment then nodded. "Oh. I see what you mean. That's smart. See, that's why you're the leader."

"I try," Harek said.

40

Egan whistled a customary hale as he and Gil passed the lookout tower on foot. Like footpatrolers, there was always to be two men in the lookout. The lookout was the preferable assignment – shelter from the cold and the rain. A body could usually get away with a couple hours of shut-eye undetected. Not so on footpatrol. Everything was out in the open. It was misery in the high sun, torture in the black cold of night, and gods forbid Captain Ammon find a body dozing whilst on one of his paranoid evening strolls. Footpatrol was the short stick. The punishment watch. The task all new recruits undertook until Providence granted them some seniority in the form of new men.

There was no response from the lookout.

Egan slowed and frowned.

Gil drew up alongside. He whistled.

Still no response.

"Not very friendly-like," Egan said.

Gil scoffed. "Prollly asleep."

"Not both. They's not supposed to be sleepin' at all, but how's you do it is by takin' turns. So one can shake the other if Ammon comes 'round. So no one gets in trouble."

"They're prolly both asleep."

"No." Egan shook his finger at the lookout. "That there's spite."

"Spite?"

"You know Zand said he'd never speak to me again over what I said about his mother?"

"What'd you say about his mother?"

"Not important."

Gil snorted. "Ain't likely. You can't be disser-spectin' a man's mum, now. You're lucky he didn' thrash you."

Egan just eyed him, disappointed Gil wasn't taking his side. He returned his attention to the lookout. It was completely dark. He made a rude gesture.

No response.

He swatted the air and kept marching. "Know wot? I hope they's did fell asleep. Let Ammon catch 'em."

"Actually, I think he was awake." Gil jerked a thumb over his shoulder. "I heard movement when we passed."

They made their way to the campfire on the opposite side of the camp. Tossed a log on top. Plunked down. Warmed their palms. Dipped into the liquor.

It wasn't long before nature made its demands. With a grunt, Egan stood and sauntered toward the wall.

"Where you goin?" Gil asked.

"Gotta fill the moat." Egan snickered. He hopped up onto the log, his back to Gil as he fiddled with his belt buckle. He relaxed and gazed out upon the shadowy moors, which hadn't yet taken shape and wouldn't for another couple hours.

The thwip of bowstrings carried to him a moment too late. By then, the arrow punched through his leather chestpiece like it was little more than wet paper. It sank deep into his lung and came to an abrupt stop. The force staggered him. He looked down to take in the fletched end of the arrow and the still-quivering shaft protruding from his chest. The delayed crack of pain exploded through his body as the shock took hold.

Unable to scream, his knees gave out. He tumbled headlong into the trench.

✧

Gil heard activity coming from the center of camp. Captain Ammon on another nighttime stroll, by the sounds of it. He jingled when he walked, like he was carrying a set of keys, or a heavy belt pouch, or had affixed spurs to his boots. It wasn't any of those things. No one could figure out why he jingled. Gil thought it was the gold chain around his neck which swayed when he walked, but that didn't seem quite right either.

A dull thud and the sound of a body hitting the earth drew Gil's attention over his shoulder toward the wall, where Egan had stepped away to relieve himself. He wasn't there.

Gil wasn't sure whether to laugh or groan. He hauled himself up and sauntered to the wall to investigate.

"Did you fall into the moat again? I'm not helping you out this time. But you best hurry, Ammon's coming –"

He hopped onto the wall for a better look. His ears picked out a wet gurgle, then a wheezing sound. Frowning, he peered over the edge, straining his eyes in the gloom.

"Egan?"

Gil heard the thwip of bowstrings a moment too late.

✧

Magnus Ammon was accustomed to being in charge. Hailing from one of Wolfwind's noble houses, he was also acquainted with the risks of political turnover, which became a hellish reality in recent years. When the dragon king Malachai ousted the former ruler of Errebos, it threw everything into flux. Ammon never liked the old king, but he was predictable, which kept life steady. The dragon king was a comparative lunatic.

Ammon hadn't survived five decades of nobility without cunning. He cared little for the dragon's ideological objectives – he'd bend the knee, vow fealty, pray to whomever he needed to. Under the new regime, loyalty promised wealth and security without measure. Besides, what was the alternative? The dragon would raze his city in minutes if he so much as smelled rebellious thoughts.

Then the Baldomar ruined everything.

The Empire dissolved. Cities and regions pitched into the chaos of newly acquired independence. The strong vied for control while the masses engaged in open revolt against the old leaders. Ammon found himself fleeing for his life with little more than the possessions he could carry. Once again, forced to adapt.

It was a new world. At least, for now. Widespread political instability had its advantages. If Ammon bided his time, made the most of his opportunities, he might come out on the better end of his exile. His initial band of fourteen followers had doubled in recent months. They were mostly vagabonds, lower class degenerates, and former loyalists with no place to go. The sort of hungry souls who needed strong leadership to supply motivation and a steady diet of results to keep their loyalty. Ammon delivered.

It was, by most people's standards, a reprehensible, undignified living. Even so, most kings started out this way. If his acquisitions happened to strike a blow at the fledgling Baldomar state, it made his little victories all the sweeter.

Yet, success was a fragile thing. One could not do what he did without risking provocation. Harassed travelers were nothing new and of little consequence. Vast quantities of stolen supplies were another matter.

Despite instructions to leave none alive, his subordinates were, at times, less than obedient. Smaller groups of travelers who put up little fight were robbed, beaten, and sent on their way. If such harried individuals made it to places with their own peace-keeping force – like Goldbur Gren – they might be inclined to point the proverbial finger in Ammon's direction. He'd rather that not happen at all, much less until he controlled a force strong and disciplined enough to withstand the retribution.

There might not be many Baldomar left in the world, but he'd heard enough to keep from dismissing them. It was rumored they'd been blessed by an elder dragon – a dead one, for whatever that was worth. At the battle of Nyassa, they'd been nearly unstoppable. People said they stood a head taller than the average man and could bend the forces of nature with a simple utterance.

Ammon wasn't sure what hope existed against a magic user in combat. If he was discovered before the opportune time, and the camp breached, it was over.

He'd tossed all night, plagued by nightmares about such a thing. It was two hours before sunup when he relinquished any hope of further rest. He propped himself on an elbow and listened.

It was quiet.

It ought to be.

Still, something in the air felt wrong.

Whether prompted by deep-seated survival instinct or the consequence of a restless night, he obeyed his uneasy stirrings. He dressed quickly in fine burgundy garments – his house's color – and knee-high riding boots. He never forgot the key for the chest beside his bed, which was strung along a thin gold chain with protective medallions he'd acquired from a soothsayer back home. This he tucked beneath his doublet, close to his chest. He donned the heavier gold chain over his jerkin. A man of his station had an image to maintain, even at this unholy hour. Lastly, he secured his sword to his side and tucked a dagger into his belt. It gave the appearance of preparedness, and truth told, he trusted no one but himself.

He stepped outside and breath from his nostrils clouded before him in the dim, early morning chill. In a stall nearby, his horse swished her tail while she tore up mouthfuls of grass. The glow of low-burning cook-fires outside wasn't near enough to guide Ammon throughout the camp with confidence. Annoyed, he returned to his dwelling for a lamp.

He took the main path running between the huts, barracks, and storehouses. His boots made a sticky sound in the damp, beaten earth. He listened hard, passing critical glances over the wooden structures.

All was still.

He stalked toward the wall to reassure his mind. The watchmen's campfire illuminated a wide space near the interior edge of the encampment. At a distance, Ammon observed the newest recruit abandon his place at the fireside to check something at the wall. The man called for his partner, and climbed atop the log for a better view of his comrade who'd apparently entered the trench in a drunken tumble.

An arrow thunked into the man's chest, fired from the darkness beyond. The man pitched forward over the ledge.

Ammon stopped short as the cold, heavy grip of mortal danger dropped through his body. He approached with caution, hand on his sword. Leaving the lamp by the fire, he chanced a peek over the wall. For his age, his eyesight was excellent, and he located the two watchmen as misshapen humps in the dark. There was a groan and wet wheeze from below. Then silence.

The hairs on the back of Ammon's arms prickled. His breathing ticked up. A mix of new, subtle sounds came to him at once from every side – the thrum of horse hooves in the direction of the gate, the rustle of urgent movements in a barrack nearby, and the muted tread of boots from within the shadows.

Ammon groped over his heart for the medallions tucked beneath his clothes, and his fingers brushed the key.

He turned from the wall and walked briskly toward the centermost storehouse. Finding the bell affixed to the eaves, he grabbed the rope pull and clanged it violently. "We are under attack!"

There was an instant, disorganized stirring within camp as men lurched from sound sleep and scrambled in the dark for boots and weapons. Ammon continued with purpose to his quarters. He never broke into a run, lest he incite panic or lead others to follow him. They were on their own.

He whisked inside, dropped to his knees beside the bed, and fished the key out from his doublet. Inside the chest were his choice valuables – a signet ring, the gold armband of his mother, a gilded flask embossed with his family's crest. A leather pouch held an ample stash of gold and platinum coins along with a few gems. He shoved these into his waiting satchel along with two days worth of dry foods. He threw his cloak over his shoulders, and swept from the dwelling.

In the short time he'd been inside, chaos had erupted in every corner. The sounds of men fighting for their lives filled the night. It sounded like fewer men –

fewer of his men – than he anticipated.

He kept moving.

Halfway to his horse's stall, the earth began to shake. Ammon's heart jumped into his throat. Along the main stretch, mounds of dirt, roots, and rocks burst from the ground with a thunderclap, making a choppy sea of the way of escape.

There was a battle cry in a language Ammon didn't understand. He caught a glimpse of an eerie blue glow as two men emerged from the shadows. One's sword was alight with unnatural fire. The other moved with the brutal efficiency of the northern wind.

Baldomar.

They weren't as massive in stature as Ammon was led to believe, but they were every bit the terror. They rushed at a group which tumbled out of the barracks and cut them down like a farmer threshing wheat. Two – then six – then eight – of his men in seconds.

Ammon's mouth hung open for a beat.

In the opposite direction, two men on horseback thundered through camp with swords, threading through uneven terrain with expertise.

Ammon pressed into a sprint, fairly confident he'd gone unnoticed, and snaked down the veins branching from the main path. Finding his horse jumpy and stressed, he took command of the beast and swung onto her back. With a click of his cheeks, he drove his heels into her flank. He ducked low and directed her as quickly and cautiously as possible out of the pen.

The gate wasn't too far.

Restraining his haste enough to thread along the less-seen spaces between buildings, Ammon made for the exit by a less-obvious route.

41

The soft drum of hooves drew Harek's attention from the man who'd just tried to lop off Finnion's head and now lay dead at Judge's feet. In the spaces behind the huts, a man on horseback was fast approaching. Not to fight, but with a clear desire to slip by unnoticed. He was older and better dressed.

The leader, if Harek had to guess, who hoped to escape the same fate as his men. It roused Harek's sense of injustice. *No, you don't.*

With the present group of enemies dispatched, Harek scanned for the next immediate threat. Ahead, four bandits converged on Billy and Cain, who were fighting back to back.

The jingle of horse tack drew closer. Behind a nearby building, the canter shifted into a gallop as the captain blew past Harek's position.

"Finnion!" Harek pointed. "Support Cain and Billy. I'm going after the captain."

Finnion obeyed without question.

With a word and the slightest tug of the reins, Judge turned from the raging battle. Luka locked his sight on the horseback leader, who'd just dashed into the clearing before the entry. Luka burst into an all-out run. Harek and Judge thundered after him.

✧

Ammon knew he'd been spotted as he made for the gate – not by his own, but by one of the horsemen. A glance over his shoulder confirmed. The man had given chase. Jumpy firelight caught the sword in his hand, already wet with blood.

Ammon turned his attention to the darkness ahead, and bent low over his steed. "Go! Go!"

It was too late to turn back. A gallop in present terrain in near darkness was reckless at best. Yet what choice did he have?

The resonant bay of a wardog sounded at Ammon's heels, and he cursed his luck. The unrelenting pursuit of the wardog was a thing of legend. His only hope was for the Baldomar to give up the chase in the dark and call off his beast.

Ammon urged his horse faster and pulled away from the dog, but the Baldomar rider seemed to come out of nowhere. He was upon him, nearly close enough to swing his blade and cut at the horse's flank.

"*Fyrir therr hondum!*"

At the words of the spell, something ran cold within Ammon. Panic closed in, driving him onward, heedless of direction. He kicked his beast without mercy. He wanted nothing more than to get away from the Baldomar. The distance between them grew, and the man's indistinct voice bellowed through the night.

Ammon's horse jerked her progression and tossed her head. Her ears went flat. With a wild scream, she reared.

Ammon was not prepared.

Thrown, he yelled as the ground rushed up to meet him, cutting the cry short as he slammed against the earth. The hard landing on his back knocked the wind from his chest. Pain shot through his entire body.

The panting of the wardog crescendoed. With a snarl and flash of teeth, the shaggy beast materialized on Ammon's right. It clamped its jaws around his leg.

Ammon tried to scream. It came out as a choked garble. Wincing through the pain, he groped at his belt for his sword.

✦

Harek saw the blade emerge from the sheath. His sense of urgency spiked. He drew up to the place where the captain fell and leapt from Judge's back.

Luka bit down harder and jerked his head, oblivious to the danger. The man managed an angry yelp. Still on his back, he bent at the waist and contorted himself into a better angle to strike. The sword arched in a graceless hacking motion.

Harek rushed forward, closing the distance. With two hands on the hilt, he swung his sword, cutting low and wide to intercept the man's blade before it lodged into Luka's neck and shoulders.

There was no clang of metal on metal.

The air thickened with the wet snick of sword cutting through bone and sinew as Harek cut off the man's hand at the wrist.

The captain's scream was delayed for just a beat, then cut off forever as Harek maneuvered his weapon and drove it into the man's chest.

Harek gave himself a moment, confirming that the man was truly dead, and turned to Luka. Luka released the leg and rammed his head affectionately under Harek's arm. He was unharmed.

Harek released a breath in the moment's relief. He scratched Luka's side, gave him a firm pat, and stood. "Good dog."

The captain's horse trotted closer to investigate. Close enough for Harek to reach out and touch her if he dared. She peered down her long nose at the dead captain and gave Harek a withering side eye and a snort.

She was a good horse in that she was steady, well-trained, and loyal. She knew nothing of good and evil. She deserved a better master.

Harek sighed. "I know," he said to her.

The distant clash and roar of the ongoing fight carried. He was too far from the edge of camp to identify specifics. From his position, he observed the chaotic dance of the struggle silhouetted against the glow of campfires and flashes of magic.

He wouldn't have given chase if he doubted his men in that moment. Still, the tides of a tight battle, such as the one taking place, could turn swiftly. All it took was one mistake, or one lucky maneuver.

Turning from the captain, Harek raced toward Judge. "Luka! Come."

He swung in the saddle, and directed Judge to race the short distance to the entry. His men needed him.

Harek spotted two bandits against the glow of a dropped torch. They dashed for the break in hopes of escaping the fray unscathed, much like their leader. Either unaware of the retribution rocketing toward them in the dark, or imagining they stood a chance of slipping away into the night.

They heard the pounding of hooves too late to adequately react, then Harek was upon them. With a cry, he wielded his blade with deadly effect, and kept moving.

He urged Judge onward toward the center of the camp where the bulk of all-out fighting had been taking place, relieved to find his men prevailing. They were scattered in ones and two, outnumbered but contending valiantly with the ten remaining combatants. He didn't see Grigory's horse, which concerned him.

Harek rode into the fray with a bark of direction for Luka, and tilted the odds more heavily in the Baldomars' favor, bringing swift resolution to the remaining skirmishes.

One bandit hiding in a doorway watched his comrades dispatched. One after the other. Desperate, the man abandoned hope, threw down his crossbow and dagger, and took two shaky steps into the open. He raised both hands to the heavens. "I surrender! Don't kill me! Look, I'm unarmed – don't kill me –"

His voice ratcheted up as Luka took notice and bounded toward him. Harek's voice boomed, cutting through the commotion, and brought him to a stop.

"Do not move," Harek ordered the man. He glanced over his surroundings. The dead littered the area in every direction. As far as he could tell, the surrendering man was the last one alive.

It was over.

He made a quick mental account of his men. He saw Grigory on foot, along with Cain, Billy, and Dorian. Oleksy leaned heavily on the nearest structure, which happened to be a wagon alongside a building. He was favoring one leg and appeared to be in great pain.

He turned his attention to Dorian, who stood nearest the surrendering bandit. "Bind the prisoner. We'll take him back to the Gren where he'll answer –"

A ragged yell interrupted Harek as Finnion emerged from the periphery. He rushed toward the last bandit, sword in hand. Intentions clear.

"Finnion –"

He ignored Harek.

Billy lurched into Finnion's path and threw his weight into knocking him off course. His shoulder crashed into Finnion, and slowed him.

Momentarily.

Finnion was undaunted. He gathered himself to push past and reach the bandit. Grigory and Cain swarmed, helping to hold him back until his battle fervor simmered.

"Stop fighting. It's over, brother!"

"He surrendered – you can't touch him."

If Finnion heard, he demonstrated no intent to listen. He roared and pushed harder, and Harek watched as three men slid backward against his advance.

Harek dismounted and joined in the effort. "Finnion! Stand down!"

It was like fighting against a mountain. As if Finnion possessed the strength of ten men. He writhed, and with a swing of his arm, Billy flew backward and landed hard on his back, narrowly missing a cookfire. This, more than anything, jarred him. The rage running thick in his veins paused long enough for him to gape at what he'd just done.

Harek grabbed him by the collar of his chestpiece, and yanked. "Hey! Come back to yourself. It's over."

Harek released him with a shove. Finnion shook himself. His eyes passed over the group, embarrassed and accusatory. He pushed past Grigory and offered Billy a hand up.

42

"He's lying," Finnion said in counsel with the other men, save Dorian. He'd been assigned guard duty over the prisoner.

"I know he's lying," Harek said.

"And we're gonna let him live?"

"He will be brought to the Gren, where he'll answer for what he's done."

"He'll lie to them too."

That was almost certain. Still, there were men at the Gren far better at skillfully pulling the truth from an initially reluctant weasel than Harek. Or anyone on his crew.

"He's done evil things," Finnion continued. "He doesn't deserve to live."

Harek agreed. He found it unlikely the man would escape the executioner's block. That justice wasn't Harek's to administer. Not at this point. They were no longer enemies in the heat of battle. There were rules. "He threw down his weapons and surrendered –"

"Doesn't make him less treacherous."

"We have orders," Harek said, ending the argument. "He remains under our close watch until he's brought to the Gren."

Scowling, Finnion glanced aside and shook his head.

Grigory sucked his teeth and sauntered toward a crate pulled from one of the storehouses. He lifted the lid with a creak and checked the contents. "Any extra fingers in here?"

A chorus of groans rippled throughout the group, even pulling a reluctant smirk from Finnion. Grigory moved on to a second crate. Investigating, he produced a bottle of hard liquor. He uncorked it with his teeth, plopped on the barrel nearest Oleksy, and offered him a drink.

Oleksy eyed it miserably and hesitated.

"For the pain," Grigory said, jerking his chin toward Oleksy's knee.

Oleksy consented with a defeated sigh. He took two enormous glugs, wiped his mouth with the back of his hand, and passed the bottle back to Grigory.

"What now?" Billy asked. Though midday, he appeared dead on his feet. It was late morning when he and Cain had returned after retrieving the unutilized horses who'd been tethered and waiting patiently nearby.

Harek blew a long, slow breath as he wrapped his head around what needed to happen next. The fight was over and the encampment won, but there was much to do. For a moment, the only sound was the grinding of Luka's teeth over bone as he savored a whole leg of lamb – his reward.

"Remove the dead," Harek said. "We'll use the wagons and save ourselves some effort. We'll take the rest of the day for rest."

"What about the plunder?"

"You mean our vast riches?" Cain said with a satisfied grin.

"Hear, hear!" Grigory raised his bottle.

The goods previously purchased by the Gren would be delivered to the Gren, down to the last nail. The extra was theirs to split fairly, with Harek getting a double share as the leader.

Apart from the personal stores of gold, loose gems, and jewelry discovered amongst the bandits' lodgings, the storehouses held goods, stacked floor to ceiling. One was for items which were immediately useful – food, medicine, oil, and clothing. The second was a stockpile of items which, at present, held little use, though might in time. Things like paper, ink, glass, tools, wheels, and ceramic. There were perfumes, spices, wine, and lace. There were even a few nice pieces of furniture.

Already, the Gren agreed to pay Harek and the others for their success.

Adding his share of the plunder to his earnings was more than enough to grant him the ability to return home with his head high. He could start a stable life with Wynne, doing work which pleased him.

In fact, he'd be the richest person at the Enclave.

"We'll make a proper inventory tomorrow," he said. "There's too much to carry ourselves. I'll write and request aid – able bodies and teams of oxen, enough to ferry these goods unmolested."

"Who'll carry the message?" Cain asked.

"Billy and Grigory," Harek said, avoiding Finnion's eye. He'd already given it thought. It may have been an opportunity to send Finnion home, like he wished. Still, Harek needed to ensure the message made it to the Gren. The safest option was to send those with command over their magic. Which meant Cain and Finnion stayed behind. Though he dared not admit it to himself, an unnamed caution provoked Harek to keep Finnion where he could keep his eye on him.

"What about Oleksy?" Billy asked. "Shouldn't he go?"

"I'm sure that'll be comfortable," Cain said, his voice thick with sarcasm.

"He'll get home sooner, so he can rest up." Billy winced and gestured to Oleksy. "That blighter kicked out your knee."

"I know," Olesksy said. "I was there."

"He can take my place," Billy said to Harek. "I'll go or stay. Whatever's best for the crew."

Billy meant well. It deepened Harek's appreciation for him. But Harek knew the answer already.

He jerked his chin toward Oleksy. "Which would be less painful – horseback now, or riding in a wagon with the rest of the plunder when help comes?"

"The latter."

"Billy, you're going with Grigory."

"When?"

"The sooner the better. If I can get letters written, tomorrow."

"I suppose we best be movin', then." Grigory slapped his legs and pushed up with a grunt. "Dead men ain't gonna haul themselves."

He passed the bottle to Oleksy, who took it without a word.

There was a collective sigh, though no one complained as they peeled away from the group. Finnion hesitated momentarily, as if torn between helping straight away, or sticking around to air a concern with Harek, one on one.

Oleksy didn't catch it. "Harek." He dropped his voice and cast Harek a pained expression. Wanting to maintain his dignity and recognizing the humility of his state. Upon realizing that Finnion wasn't on his way, he clamped his mouth.

Finnion's eyes jumped between them and his frown hardened. Harek patted him on the shoulder, and nodded for him to join the others. "I'll be with you in a bit."

Finnion said nothing. With a parting suspicious glance, he followed Cain, Grigory, and Billy.

Harek shelved the sinking feeling that he'd need to deal with unresolved issues later. He refocused on Oleksy and contended with a twist of grief. Harek was no healer, yet he understood that injuries like Oleksy's meant a lifelong limp, regardless of how it healed. Oleksy was a superb scout. One of the best. That future was gone. The options for his future livelihood had been cut down to near nothing. Like many of his kinsmen, he was illiterate, so he couldn't even help record the inventory when it came time. He imagined how demoralized Oleksy must feel, despite the victory.

Harek felt responsible.

He took Grigory's vacant seat beside him. "I wish I'd brought a healer with us. I'm sorry."

"Wouldn't matter."

He wasn't wrong. Taige Goodhill showed promise, but he couldn't be spared, and there wasn't a man alive to rival Sender's capabilities.

"Still," Harek said. "I'm gonna do everything in my power to help you get well." He already planned to include a letter for Sender, asking him to drop whatever he was doing in the Enclave to meet them in the Gren. He knew it'd take time for all parties to converge, and wasn't sure how much damage could be reversed by then. He was willing to pay Sender's expenses himself. "You have my word."

Oleksy said nothing. He nodded.

"In the meantime, what do you need?"

Oleksy scoffed in dismay. He dropped his eyes to the bottle. "I can't sit around, useless."

"Right now, resting it is the best thing –"

"I gotta do something. Give me something to do."

Harek watched him for a moment and understood. He cast his eyes beyond the group, up the main lane toward the once-campfire, where Dorian stood guard out of earshot. Nearby, the prisoner sat on a stump, ankles tied and hands bound in front of him, looking dour.

"Dorian could use another set of eyes. I'll find you a crossbow."

43

The door creaked open without announcement, followed by the familiar clop of Omri. He stomped the mud clods from his boots and allowed his voice to carry. "What smells good?"

"I'm cookin'," Wynne said from the greatroom where she'd arranged her ingredients on the end of the table, near the hearth.

"I'm helping!" Jai said brightly as Omri entered the room and appraised the scene.

"Yes, Jai is my helper. I told him I'd let him run around as a bear after. It was the only way I could get him to participate."

"I see."

"Why are you here? I thought you were eating with Lara's family tonight."

"I am. I'm looking for Pops. Had a question."

"What about?"

"Building my house. And other matters."

"Matters like what?"

"Don't be nosy."

Miffed, Wynne shot him a look. She lifted the cutting board and scraped the chopped leeks into the pot. "He and Mum stepped out. They'll be back in a bit."

Omri's gaze swept the end of the table. "Seems like a lot of food you're preparing."

"Kal turned a year older today. I wanted to make him a nice meal."

Omri's eyebrows jumped. He hummed in an attempt at masked neutrality, which Wynne saw through immediately and didn't appreciate. He watched her for a moment. "When did this happen?"

"When did *what* happen?"

"All this. I thought you didn't like him much. Call me curious."

"I never disliked Kal." She hesitated. "Much. He hasn't had a nice family meal in a long time."

"He eats meals with our family all the time."

"I meant for his day of birth."

Omri was quiet for a beat. "That's what he told you?"

A nudge of worry pressed against her. For a dreadful moment, for reasons she couldn't name, she feared she'd been duped. About what, she wasn't sure. She eyed her brother. *He knows something I don't know.*

"Yes." She dipped her chin, lowered her voice, and asked in earnest. "You think he's lying?"

"I didn't say that," Omri said, as though this notion just occurred to him. "I didn't realize you two talked so much."

"We don't talk an excessive amount."

"Yeah, but I worked with him for months. I don't know that. You do."

"It's because you're a man."

"What's that supposed to mean?"

"When's my day of birth?"

"Before the harvest festival."

"That's not specific."

"It's not a fair question. Mum always reminds us."

"Not fair? I'm your sister." She hoisted an eyebrow. "When's Lara's?"

Omri pulled his chin back in mock offense. Fighting a smirk, he wouldn't meet her eyes. "You're funny."

"I know when it is."

Omri hesitated. "When is it?"

"Before the harvest festival."

"Wynne."

She snickered.

"When you see Pops, tell him I want to talk to him about my house."

"You mean the Erlander house or the one you haven't built yet?"

"The one I'm building for me and Lara."

Wynne dipped the spoon in the pot and stirred. "How's that progressing?"

"I got most of the lumber. A plan. Nails. A pane of glass for the window."

"Fancy. Where'd you get that?"

"I sent for it. From Goldbur Gren."

Wynne's thoughts turned to Harek with a painful shift behind her ribs.

"I'm hoping to get the last of the material by the end of the week. Then, I only need the manpower. If I can manage all that, I'm hopin' to get it up in a few days. Then we can finally get hitched." He sounded uncharacteristically stressed. She wondered if Lara had been layering pressure upon him, like her parents.

"How's Lara been?"

Omri's smile took on a wistful quality which dismissed her concern. "An angel. We're just…" He rubbed the stress in his forehead and avoided Wynne's eyes. He opened his mouth, shut it, reconsidered, and tried again. "We're eager for our own home. As soon as possible. Back to all this." He wagged a finger at the pot, and waited for Wynne to react, or fill in the quiet.

She didn't.

"I thought it was Harek," he said.

Wynne contended with a pang of grief as a series of memories flicked across her mind. Harek, riding out with the rest to rebuild the city. Months without a word.

"It's a nice family dinner," she said. "That's all."

"That's all?"

Heat rose to her cheeks. She felt backed into a corner and forced to answer questions when she was still trying to figure out her own heart. "Look. I don't know what's going on with Harek. What I do know is Kal is here, and I want to do something nice for him. That's all."

44

Harek awoke to the sound of gurgling. Bleary eyed, he lifted his head and saw a boot. Not upright at the end of bedroll where it should be. Then a leg and an arm.

The wet choking sound continued, and the boot twitched.

Harek's fatigue vanished in an instant. He sat bolt upright at the same moment Luka roused himself to all fours. Cain stirred lethargically as life drained from a slit in his throat.

Harek grabbed his shirt and bent over him. "Cain!"

He met Harek's face. His mouth opened and closed like a fish trying and failing to gulp for what it needed to breathe. The panic in his eyes dimmed as the last flickers of life flowed out of him.

Whining, Luka pushed his head under Harek's arm. He wedged his body between Harek and Cain. Harek gritted his teeth, clamped his eyes shut, and released an involuntary groan. He dug his fingers into Luka's thick fur, drawing strength enough to focus on the immediate.

He cursed his heavy sleep and wondered at the stealth which allowed the murderer to enter without raising an alarm.

He should've listened to Finnion.

If the prisoner made it into Harek's shelter undetected, then what had become of Dorian and Oleksy, who were on guard? Or Finnion, who'd been resting until a watch-change?

Harek listened for movement outside his shelter, or someone still hiding within.

He was met with eerie silence.

He located his sword and pulled it from its scabbard without sound. On wool-socked feet, he stepped cautiously into the night air, with Luka at his heels and his sword held low in the ready position.

The camp was silent, save the crackle of the low-burning campfire twenty feet ahead. Beside the fire, two men lay motionless. Harek's eyes darted to the black spaces between the huts, beyond the penumbra of the firelight, searching for movement within the shadows. He approached on swift, quiet feet. Harek knew before he halved the distance to the fireside, there was no life left in either man.

Heavy amorphous dread took shape as Harek recognized Dorian, slumped forward onto his face. A dark glistening pool of blood collected beneath him.

The second man was the prisoner, tangled in a blanket on his bedroll, with hands still bound at the wrists before him. He'd suffered the same fate as Cain.

Oleksy's bedroll was empty.

A sudden cold shot through Harek as realization snapped into place.

At Luka's bark, Harek whirled around only to be knocked over the head. He hit the ground sprawling and lost his grip on his blade. Expanding pain in his skull clouded his focus and eyesight. The world buzzed in and out, leaving him semi-aware.

Luka snarled and latched onto Finnion's arm.

Finnion yelled and lashed out with his free hand. Luka yelped and released his bite. Harek's spotty vision came into focus as Luka flopped sideways, and Finnion swooped upon him. The wardog cried as Finnion beat him without mercy.

"Stop!" Harek pushed himself up, even as his head screamed at him. His ears rang and the world pitched. "My dog –"

Another blow, another yelp.

Without missing a beat, Finnion whirled around and lunged for Harek.

Hands grabbed at his clothes, face, and neck. It was like fighting chaos itself, and Harek was on his back. Finnion's face bent with exhilarated rage and madness. Harek managed to get an arm up, which kept him from being strangled.

A strange, gravelly voice issued from Finnion. *"Why are you holding back? Kill him!"*

Fresh terror gripped Harek by the heart.

A second voice came from Finnion's mouth, this one higher, hissing, and reedy. *"No, we need one alive!"*

"We'll find another." The gravelly voice again.

Finnion gritted his teeth. He half-moaned, half-screamed. Still pinning Harek, he freed one hand to drive the heel of his palm repeatedly into his forehead. "Stop! Stop! He's my friend. I can't – I won't–"

The gravelly voice took control of his mouth again. *"He is not your friend. We have no friends. He will kill you when the opportunity comes."*

"No – no –"

"He will tell what you've done – Murderer. Ha!"

Harek harnessed his courage in spite of the blind, paralyzing terror. "Finnion – if you can understand me at all – don't do this thing."

"Look at him beg. Selfish. Pathetic. Worm of a man. Kill him!"

The reedy voice took control. *"Don't kill him. Keep him."*

"He will use his magic and slip away."

"He must not slip away."

"He must not slip away."

"You know the words. I taught you the words."

"The words!"

"Do it."

What came next out of Finnion's mouth sounded like the tip of a nail scraped across glass. It was like torture on the ears. The sound of it made Harek feel weak and sick. Like he wanted to vomit. At once, his tongue glued itself to the roof of his mouth. He experienced a constriction in the inner parts of his throat. He couldn't make a sound.

Behind Finnion, Luka laid on his side. A faint whimper accompanied each shallow breath.

"I'm sorry. I have to," Finnion said. He pulled back his fist.

Harek felt a crack of pain in his skull. A sloshing sensation of the mind. Then his vision went dark.

45

"Your family's favored fishing spot, you say?" Kal threaded a grub onto the hook at the end of Jai's line, seated atop the tablerock jutting over the shallows. The Bekker flowed wide and shallow here. Irises and reeds flourished along the riverside, shaded by a droopy willow and shaggy elm. The sloping banks were steep enough to deter the faint of heart, the elderly, and mothers trailing young children from utilizing this stretch of the river for washing or play. With the hilly ridge behind, dense with blackberry and holly, the odds of enjoying an undisturbed afternoon were good.

Beside Kal, Jai kicked his legs dangling over the edge. "Yep. It's our best spot."

Wynne deposited the basket in the grass, but instead of joining the fellas, she picked her way along the water's edge for a few feet. The cluster of cattails caught her eye. She needed them.

Kal offered the baited line to Jai. "Throw that in and see if anything bites."

"What if nothing bites?" Jai said.

"Then we'll stick your legs in the water and see if you pick up a leech. They make good bait too."

Jai looked horrified.

Wynne snickered. "Be nice."

"I'm always nice," Kal said.

Wynne made a sound in the back of her throat. She returned her attention to her quarry. The cattails were not as close as they first appeared. She chewed on her lip, appraising the assortment of rocks suitable for stepping stones. She tip-toed into the marshy shallows without wetting her boots.

Kal's voice came from the boulder again. "Hold on, there. I thought we were here for fishing. I didn't realize this might involve a rescue."

She turned back with a playful arch of her eyebrow. "Rescue?"

"Not sayin' I won't dive into the Bekker to save your behind, but I'd rather not. The ice just melted. Don't slip."

"I appreciate the willing self-sacrifice, but it's less than two-feet deep here."

"Ah. So you're saying, no reward for my chivalry?"

She caught the roguish spark in his expression. Wynne wasn't sure she'd put *Kal* and *chivalry* in the same sentence. Still, color rose to her cheeks even as her eyes darted protectively toward Jai. "Mind yourself. Innocent ears."

Jai angled his chin, pleading. "Can I push her in?"

Kal threw his head back and laughed. "Innocent, indeed."

"It'd be good fun," Jai insisted. "Maybe she could catch a leech!"

Kal patted him on the shoulder. "No, my friend."

Jai sagged, disappointed.

Wynne pressed forward, grateful Kal couldn't see as she got her grin under control. She grabbed a low hanging willow branch for balance, stretched, and snagged the nearest stalk. With one hand, she snapped the lumpy brown pod off the end.

Jai's heavy sigh broke the quiet behind. "This is boring."

"You don't like fishing?" Kal asked.

"Not like this."

"How else would you catch the fishes? With your hands?"

"I'll show you!"

There was a pause. Then, "Whoa there! What're you doing, lad?"

At the alarm in Kal's voice, Wynne turned around to see Jai, all skinny and pink from the waist up, hopping on one foot as he attempted to free himself from a woolen sock. His sweater and boots lay discarded in the grass.

"Jairus Thar, stop that."

Jai planted both feet on the rock and faced Wynne. "I wanted to show how I can catch fish as a bear."

Wynne hesitated. She anticipated keeping him out of the water would be a challenge, bear shape or not. She thought he'd last longer than five minutes.

At least as a bear, he exhibited greater resistance to cold.

"Fine. But you go behind that boulder to change. No runnin' around in the nip."

Jai galloped for cover to complete his transformation. Wynne snapped two more cattails in quick succession and joined Kal.

"So what's this you've risked both our dignity for?" Kal asked. "I'm on tenterhooks."

"I need something to gift Lara for her bridal tea. What better than something dead useful?"

His mouth quirked up in the corner. "Naturally. What every bride wants."

"You're teasing me, now?"

"No," he said unconvincingly.

Wynne patted the air. "She'll get loads of pretty things from everyone else."

"Forgive me if I'm wrong, but isn't that the point?"

"We're Baldomar. We're practical people. A sachet full of rose petals – while lovely – doesn't keep the house warm or feed you." She picked one of the cattails open while cupping her palms to reveal the expanding white fluff inside. "Mixing this with melted pine resin makes an excellent fire starter."

Kal reached out and pinched the fluff in her hand, working it between his finger and thumb.

"You can wad it into balls, or clump it at the end of a stick for a torch. Or fill a hollowed-out branch along with a bit of cordage, for a candle," she said. "It burns longer than shavings or punkwood, so you can get a respectable fire going with less trouble."

"This would've been good to know on my way here." He pulled his hand back.

Jai emerged, a brown bear cub. He loped to the riverside and crashed into the shallows with both front paws thwacking the water. He was far enough that Wynne and Kal avoided the splash.

"His bear shape's grown." Wynne turned to Kal to discover that he wasn't watching Jai. He was watching her.

The rich chestnut brown of his eyes met hers, open and eager. He tucked a loose strand of hair behind her ear. His fingers brushed against her earring and a pleasant shiver ran down her spine.

Kal shook his head. "I don't know how anyone can take their eyes off you."

A smile found its place on her lips. Longing and restraint competed for dominance in her chest, making her flustered and less collected than she ought to be, given who she was. She broke eye contact for a beat, glancing toward the water. She had to keep an eye on her brother, didn't she? The simple gesture was enough to halt the effect of the desire thickening the air between them.

"Tell me," she said. "How many ladies have you used this charm on?"

Kal looked a little taken aback. "I'd like to think I'm a better man than I used to be. Consider it a special charm, just for you."

Wynne watched him, still drawn even as alarm bells clanged inside her. Was she supposed to swoon at this?

Her resistances awoke. She narrowed her eyes. "Why won't you answer the question?"

"Why does it matter?"

"Because I want to know." *Heavens forbid I desire a lay of the land.*

"Is this you tryin' to figure out how many women I've been with?"

"This is me trying to figure out whether you're faithful."

He turned up his palms. "Is there a number that would disqualify me?"

"Is there a number which would disqualify me?"

"Probably."

"Same answer," she said with emphasis.

"What is that figure for you?"

"I don't know."

"You don't know?" He turned toward the water, mildly annoyed.

Which was the wrong thing for him to do.

"No, Kal," she said, with new sharpness. "It's not something I've had to think about before. Upstanding folks around here take this sort of behavior seriously."

"What makes you think I don't?"

She stared hard at him. *Have you met you?*

Kal shook his head again. "Well, aren't we the most handsome pair. I've been with too many women, and no man is good enough for you. You know, I thought it might've been because I'm not a Baldomar. Turns out..." He laughed, but there was no humor in his eyes. "None of them are good enough for you either."

Wynne's scowl intensified as fresh fire entered her blood. "How dare you speak to me that way?"

"Someone oughta. Or am I not allowed to tell you the truth to your face?" He kept his voice down, but his frustration built, causing the words to tumble out in a controlled growl.

"Right. You care so much for speaking the truth. Must be why you won't say how many sweethearts you had before me – or is it because you can't remember?"

Jai chose that moment to waddle over, dripping wet in bear shape, with a fish in his teeth. He looked up at them, proud of his catch and happy as could be, totally oblivious to the argument.

Wynne clamped her lips shut and blew a controlled breath through her nostrils.

"Look at that," Kal said, shelving his hard feelings with effort to congratulate Jai.

Jai dropped the fish in the basket and missed. He didn't notice. He turned tail and galloped back to the water. Wynne popped from her seat to place the slimy creature in the basket properly, then resumed her spot beside Kal without speaking.

"You said, *sweethearts before me*," he said, emphasizing the last word.

"And?"

"Does that make us sweethearts?"

"I don't know what that makes us."

"You're mad at me now."

It was quiet for the length of a breath.

"I'd be good to you."

He spoke with conviction. She met his face, almost reluctantly. He watched her with eyes which were equally hard and open. He looked earnest.

"If I'm yours, then I'm yours. I'm not walking out."

She wanted to believe him. As she held his gaze, she was persuaded he believed himself. It softened her posture toward him, but it wasn't enough. How could she place faith in his character knowing so little? Yes, she'd see some of the man he'd become. Still, it was possible to imagine knowing someone, and be wrong. Sometimes promises were just words.

Jai returned, a fish still flapping in his jaws.

"That was fast," Kal said. "Well done."

Encouraged, Jai spit the fish into the basket and rambled back to the water. Kal watched, amused.

It prodded Wynne in the heart.

Her ire receded and she gave him a little nudge. A gesture. He seemed to accept it. The tension of lingering animosity between them relented.

They watched Jai stomp around for another minute until Wynne couldn't stand it. "I have another question."

Though the easy smile remained, Kal cast her a wary side eye, almost as if expecting a trap. "What is it?"

"Do you want children?"

A brief riffle of surprise passed over him. His smile slipped, as though she'd provoked some roving thought, pulling him somewhere distant. Kal cleared his throat, and turned his eyes toward the water, replacing whatever had passed over him with a mask she couldn't identify.

"Yeah," he said, in total sincerity but with a tone which invited no further questions.

They watched Jai chasing fish in companionable silence. His arm slid gently across her back and rested on her shoulder. She leaned into his side, even as the pangs of guilty conscience tormented her.

He wouldn't want you if he knew.

46

Harek came to, stiff, bruised, and immobile. It was dark. His skull throbbed, and his jaw ached from the gag forced into his mouth. His wrists rested in his lap, bound. He'd been positioned upright and tethered to a tree. The side of his face and the back of his neck stung, like he'd been dragged over the dirt.

Radiant heat of a nearby campfire warmed his right side. The flames flapped against the night air, casting jumpy shadows and illuminating the space nearby.

Harek didn't know where he was. It wasn't the encampment.

The too-familiar scent of burnt bodies made itself recognizable. Harek shut his eyes and offered a quick prayer. *No, please....*

He pushed against the rope lashed over his chest and his arms. There was no give.

Amid the foul stink in the air, he smelled something unfamiliar cooking. Before he finished a second visual sweep of his surroundings, Finnion appeared. He crouched at Harek's side with a bowl of food. His eyes were bloodshot and the dark circles beneath them had intensified. He rested the dish and reached for Harek's face.

Harek flinched. Finnion ignored his discomfort and proceeded to loosen the gag. "No magic," he said.

A warning.

Harek worked his jaw. It felt stiff.

"No talking. You have to eat." Finnion grabbed the dish. "You've been asleep for a day."

"Asleep?" Harek's voice sounded hoarse. "You knocked me unconscious. That's not *asleep*."

Finnion stabbed the spoon into the dish. "Stop talking."

"You murdered them," Harek said, half question, half accusation. Like he needed to hear that he was wrong. That this was all some nightmare. Finnion's grimace twisted.

It wasn't.

Something wrenched deep within Harek. "Those were our friends – our brothers –"

"Stop talking!" Finnion's voice became a roar.

Harek fell quiet.

Finnion drew several shaky breaths. He winced, scratched the space over his ear,s and gave his head a firm shake. "They said you have to eat – keep your strength."

"I don't want to eat. Let's just talk for a minute. Can you untie me?"

"No."

"Where are we right now?"

Finnion shook his head. He held the dish in one hand and the spoon in the other, prepared to feed him. When Harek hesitated a moment too long, his face tensed in anger. "Eat it!"

Afraid of what might happen if he didn't cooperate, Harek opened his mouth and allowed Finnion to provide a bite.

The flavor was strange. There'd been no attempt to season it, whatever it was.

Harek chanced a second glance toward the campfire in his peripheral. A spit had been constructed over the fire. It supported the carcass of a four-legged creature the same size as a wardog.

The same size as Harek's wardog.

Harek's stomach turned over as realization slid into place. Instantly, he spit the food. Stomach acid rose in his throat.

"No!" Finnion cried. "What are you doing?"

Harek gagged and coughed over Finnion's irate exclamations. He vomited again.

Finnion popped to his feet, bowl of food in hand. Broth sloshed over the edge as he paced forcefully. He drove the heel of his hand into the side of his head, gritted his teeth, and emitted an anguished groan.

His voice changed to the low, gravely one Harek heard before. "*Failure. Fool. You have to make him.*"

The second voice followed, reedy and weedling. "*I told you he wouldn't eat the dog.*"

Harek's blood felt like ice. Catching his breath, he watched Finnion stomp back and forth, arguing with himself in two voices which didn't belong to him.

"*Just kill him and be done with it.*"

"*No! This one. We need him strong. He has to eat.*"

Finnion groaned again. He banged the hand against his skull with each word. "No, no, no..."

"Finnion," Harek said. "Listen to me –"

"*Silence him!*" the gravelly voice roared.

Finnion stopped abruptly. He jabbed his index finger in Harek's direction. A string of nasty-sounding words spilled from his mouth. As before, Harek's tongue stuck fast. He couldn't speak. Couldn't protest. Couldn't cry out.

Finnion flung the food dish at the ground and stomped away into the shadows until Harek couldn't see him.

He could still hear him.

Anguished pleas were interspersed with altered voices arguing in the dark, indiscernible beyond the hiss and groan.

Harek turned his head toward the fire again. Toward Luka. Water rose to his eyes as the ache pressing against his chest intensified.

He leaned his head back against the tree, and lifted his eyes to the black.

A silent prayer rose in his heart even as hope leached out of him.

47

Wynne kissed her fingertips and touched Innora's pendant as she left her room, following the sound of her mother's and Catreeny's voices coming from the other side of the house.

"How long did it take?" Catreeny asked.

"Four days," Susi said, referencing the hullabaloo surrounding Omri's new cabin.

"Impressive."

"They didn't need to call upon Sender at all."

Catreeny released a bark of laughter. "There's a miracle. Ah! There she is."

Catreeny's frank, friendly face was a welcome sight as Wynne floated into the greatroom. Wynne brightened. "Good morning."

Catreeny resumed her conversation with Susi. Wynne floated to the kitchen to investigate the foods being prepared for tomorrow's bridal tea and scrounge some chow before her next watch began.

She leaned on the doorframe between the kitchen and greatroom, having acquired a square of brick. Catreeny grabbed a tray of rising sweet rolls and swept toward the front door. "I'm off. See you ladies tomorrow morn."

Wynne picked a raisin out of her brick and popped it in her mouth. Through the open kitchen window at her back, she could hear Jai hooting and hollering outside, narrating a little story to himself. "Where's Pops?"

"He's gone to see Sender."

"Is he unwell?"

"Not at all." Susi grew quiet for a moment. She cast a glance toward Wynne, reading her mood. "Did you know that Sender made quite a name for himself when he rode off to war?"

"He never talks about it."

"He's a humble man."

"I like that about him."

"Me too. He's honorable."

Wynne smiled in agreement. "He is."

"Glad you think so. He's coming to dinner."

Wynne froze. "By dinner…?"

"Yes."

"You want me to marry a middle aged widower?" Wynne cried.

"Sender Fife is a good man. He's well-liked –"

"Mum–"

"–he's clean and generous –"

"He's old enough that the two of you were *childhood friends.*"

"Age brings maturity and steadiness. He's well-able to provide for a family. What, with your midwifing, you'd make an excellent team." Susi's tone rose in pitch with the last sentence, as if she wanted to encourage enthusiasm for the idea and thought she might manage it, if she made a practical argument with enough excitement.

She can't be serious.

Wynne's lips parted, horrified as the potentials flashed across her mind. Sender Fife, with his rounded shoulders. The thinning hair. The double chin and belly. The thought of intimacy with him made her stomach turn.

Her mouth snapped shut. She gave her head a decisive shake. "No."

"Wynne–"

"Mum, please listen to me. I like Sender as a person. He's a talented healer. But you have told me enough stories about that man to eliminate him from consideration."

"I'm sorry you feel that way, but your father and I like him. We think he'd be a good fit for you."

"I'm not interested in marrying Sender Fife!"

"Well, Wynne, who are you interested in?" Susi said, her voice growing sharper. "We are doing the best we can to find someone suitable. No one is good enough. Not Garriden. Not Corbin. Harek has been silent for months. Kal remains a question mark. So, who then? Tell me."

Quiet fell.

The mention of Harek sent an unexpected pang in Wynne's chest. A sharp longing, complicated by his apparent rejection and her guilt of entertaining attraction to Kal despite her better judgment.

Wynne rubbed her hands over her face. "I wish you didn't plop this on me right before I had to go."

"Well, your father's asking today. We thought you'd like to know before it gets around the rest of the village."

✧

Wynne's watch included a good cry in the privacy of the lookout, as well as number of half-cooked schemes to wheedle out of the inevitable – from pledging herself to a life of celibacy and joining what remained of the Silver Shadow, to begging Queen Kalane to enchant her parents.

She plodded home in the afternoon, morose and defeated.

Elric looked up from his place at the table.

"When is it happening?" Wynne said instead of hello.

"Next week."

After the hubbub of the wedding settles.

Wynne said nothing. She trudged toward her room, feeling as though her life was about to end.

If they went through with this, it was only a matter of time.

48

As breakfast drew to a close, a knock resounded from the Thars' door.

"Early for Pia," Susi said with a note of irritation in her voice. Wynne knew that the past several weeks of preparations for the special day had tried Susi's patience more than she cared to admit. For all the efforts to forge a better relationship, she hadn't grown to like Pia one crumb more than she ever had. If Wynne had to speculate, she'd guess Susi liked Pia even less.

"It's her daughter's bridal tea. She's excited."

Susi dried her hands on her apron and moved toward the far end of the kitchen. She poked the dough on the counter to check the rise. "So am I. But guests aren't expected for hours. She'll be in the way."

"Are you goin' to answer or leave her outside?" Elric said even as he made his way toward the front of the house.

"It's probably Omri, hoping to steal a moment with his bride-to-be before the wedding," Wynne said from her position at the suds bucket.

"As if he hasn't had enough of that," Susi said under her breath with a stressed shake of the head. "If it's Omri, he's getting the boot. No men in the house once we begin." She scanned the area. "Where did Jairus go?" She hurried from the kitchen, and her footsteps receded down the hall.

Elric's voice carried from the door. "Sender, good mornin'."

An invisible noose tightened around Wynne's ribs. She fought the urge to bolt through the back door into the yard. She grew still and strained her ears.

"I don't mean to trouble you, Elric. I was hoping to speak with you. Outside."

The front door shut.

Wynne's breathing ticked upward. She bunched her eyes shut and braced her hands on the washtub. Water rushed to her eyes, and she tried to squeeze it back in. Not now. Not today. It was Lara's day, and Wynne needed to help. People would be here soon.

The one and only upside to an arrangement with Sender was that if childbirth went sideways, his skills as a healer could mean the difference between life and death. Maybe. She supposed it might be a little less humiliating – he'd already have seen it all.

She shuddered at the thought.

Susi returned, having located Jai and set him to work. Wynne continued to scrub the last of the dishes. Try as she might, she couldn't hear the discussion taking place outdoors with Jai's overzealous "helping" with the broom.

Elric reentered the house alone. He leaned against the kitchen doorframe and said nothing. His gaze searched Wynne for a moment. She couldn't read his expression, and it made the air in her lungs feel like it might burst.

"How's Sender?" Susi asked, distracted as she slid a tray over the coal box.

"There will be no dinner."

Wynne froze, uncertain whether she'd heard correctly.

Susi went completely still. "Husband, explain."

"Sender believes it would be in everyone's best interests if he not come."

It was quiet for the length of a breath.

Wynne wanted to punch the air in triumph. Her parents' demeanor bid her to restrain the impulse. "Did I do something wrong?" she asked.

"No," Elric said. "He's inclined to think there is somethin' between you and Kal."

Susi pulled her chin inward. "Kal?"

Elric raised a palm for her to let him continue. "Sender wishes to avoid gettin' in the middle, and he doesn't want to cast undue dishonor on one or both parties, if it comes to a no at the end of the meal."

Wynne wasn't sure what to feel. Gratitude? Anxiety over the questions to come?

"I'm not sure what to say." Susi sounded flustered. "This looks bad."

"I don't think so," Elric said. "It's not like word about their dinner spread through the village yet, unless you said somethin'."

"I haven't, but why didn't he discuss this with you when you asked yesterday?"

"He apologized for that. Says I caught him off-guard. He accepted, because it's the honorable thing. After sleepin' on it, he decided it best to back out."

Elric and Susi turned to Wynne, and she felt herself grow red in the face.

"What do you have to say?" Elric said.

Responses tangled in her mouth. The seconds spanned. She swallowed hard. "About what part, specifically?"

"Any of it."

"How about, regarding Kal?" Susi said.

"I'm not considering Kal." How could she consider anyone, when she knew what that eventually entailed?

"Oh, you're not?" Elric said. "Should we call Sender back and correct the misconception?"

"No," she said in a hurry.

Elric hummed. "Thought as much."

"What do you mean?"

"Daughter of mine, you realize I've been at the same table with you two. It's no secret he's fond of you."

Wynne felt herself flush at this. Ruefully, she wondered why a dinner with Kal hadn't been called yet. Not that she wanted that to happen, either.

Elric's bushy eyebrow twitched. He waved with a flick of his fingers, beckoning forth the bit Wynne wasn't saying.

"I was only thinking, I'm surprised you haven't called for a dinner with Kal already," she said honestly.

"We weren't sure how you feel about marryin' a non-Baldomar. Not sure how we feel, truth told. I got reservations."

"What reservations?" Wynne's concerns about the unknown awoke in the same way they had when speaking with Omri two weeks earlier. She hoped Elric could put words to the hesitancy lingering in her heart.

Elric considered his next words with care. "There's a great difference between knowin' a man for a few months, and observin' him over a span of years."

It was quiet for a beat. Jai began to gallop around the greatroom, using the broom as his steed.

Susi licked her lips. "How *do* you feel about marrying a non–"

"Can we talk about this another time?" Wynne asked.

"No, I think we should talk about this now."

The shrill, sing-song voice of Pia carried from the lane outside. A thrill shot through Wynne.

Susi's nostrils flared. She shut her eyes and forced out a breath. "Curse that woman's timing. We are not finished with this discussion."

49

"I'm so overwhelmed. People were far more generous than I expected," Lara said as she grabbed a basket overflowing with gifts from the cart. "Thank you for your help."

With a wink, Wynne came alongside her and hoisted a second basket onto her hip. "What are sisters for?"

Lara freed a hand and threw it around Wynne's shoulder, squeezing her in a half-hug. Her cheeks were rosy with the joy of the day, though she looked tired. Wynne thrived on the activity. Still, she understood it took a toll on some more than others.

Wynne followed her up the trail toward the new cabin, a small but stout L-shaped house with the bedroom at one end and the kitchen area in the crook. They rested their baskets on the table. Nearby, Pia straightened crocks on the counter. Lara's younger sisters fluffed an arrangement of flowers on the mantle. Wynne could see into the bedroom where Susi packed linens into a chest.

Wynne smiled over the little house, which looked warmer and inviting now that it had begun to fill with people and needful items for running a home. "You must be excited to move in here tomorrow. Omri did a fine job."

Lara's eyes creased into a smile, and she nodded.

Pia grabbed the edge of the counter and gave it a little tug, as if testing the give. "Yes, it's well-made, even if it is quaint."

Lara's expression tightened. "I think it's perfect."

Pia cast Lara a glance, as though she thought Lara was being unnecessarily silly. "I sure hope you think the same once the newlywed bliss wears off and it's crowded with children."

Fire entered Lara's eye, although she looked equally prepared to burst into tears. For a moment, Wynne wasn't sure which would win out. She'd always known Lara to be gracious and gentle, which Wynne attributed to the influence of Lara's aunt – it certainly didn't come from her parents. It was strange to see her riled.

Pia seemed to recognize that she'd struck a nerve. She patted the air. "I'm only saying, for your sake."

Lara took a controlled breath. "Excuse me."

Wynne watched her slip outside for another basket, trailed by her youngest sister. Wynne dropped her voice. "No one is making you live here, Pia."

"I beg your pardon?"

"Omri didn't build the house for you. He built it for her."

Pia pulled her chin inward. "I was only saying, it might feel cramped in due course."

"Something for *them* to work out, isn't it?"

Pia huffed. "Excuse me for wanting the best for my daughter."

"You think Omri doesn't?"

"Well, I have to wonder what it says that he didn't spare more expense to make it bigger, being an elder's son. He's certainly made her wait long enough."

"You realize, he's not an elder? He's done his utmost to make himself useful – in large part because he loves her." Wynne pointed toward the open doorway, indicating Lara outside.

Pia huffed again. "We don't?"

"Have you listened to yourself? You slighted my brother in front of her – and me – and you're acting like Lara's some infatuated dunder-head."

"How dare you talk to me that way!"

Susi stepped into the kitchen, wearing a look of concern. "Wynne–"

Wynne held up a hand and pressed ahead. "They're getting married tomorrow. Would it kill you to share in her joy for two days?"

"Wynne," Susi said, firmer than before. "That's enough."

"I'll say," Pia added.

Wynne clenched and unclenched her jaws. She felt warm, and she didn't trust her mouth if she kept around Pia.

"I'm going to go help Lara."

✧

As the sun dipped behind the western trees, Wynne drew a deep breath, enjoying the moment's reprieve. The cool spring breeze rustled the strands of her braid which had come loose during the hectic, and rather stressful, day. She paused before retreating indoors for the night as she surveyed the Thar land. She heard her name.

Her father appeared in the back door. With a flick of the hand, he beckoned her inside.

As one, Elric, Susi, Waylas, and Pia watched Wynne enter the crowded kitchen. Waylas stood with hands on his hips, miffed and indignant. Pia sniffed and practically turned up her nose. It took everything in Wynne's power to keep from rolling her eyes.

"What's going on, Pops?"

"We're tryin' to reach to the bottom of that," Elric said, even and steady. "Seems as though there was some sort of conflict –"

"I demand to know *exactly* why you found it appropriate to speak to my wife the way you did," Waylas cut in.

Wynne pulled her chin inward. She knew Waylas to be pushy, though usually innocuous. She'd never known him to act like a bully. Not to her. She'd taken the stories from Omri with a grain of salt – not that she mistrusted Omri, but it was better to let a person show who they were. They always did in time, if you paid attention. Another lesson from her parents.

She saw the bully now.

Heat rose to the surface of her skin. Even her blood felt hot. If he thought he could come into their house, interrupt her father, and intimidate her into submission, then he was woefully mistaken.

Squaring her shoulders, she took a step toward him, then caught herself. She glanced at Elric, drew a breath, then refocused on Waylas. "How much did Pia relay?"

He scoffed. "She told me enough."

Elric raised a palm to pat the air. "Let's simmer. I want to hear from Wynne regardin' what happened –"

"What more is there to hear?"

A wave of impatience passed behind Elric's eyes, but he mastered it. "It's been a mite of a week for everyone –"

"Now, Elric, I'll concede that we've all been feeling the strain. And I'm willing to excuse the impertinence." Waylas cast a patronizing glance at Wynne. "You're young. Lapses in grace are, unfortunately, to be expected. But I am, frankly, appalled."

"Does it appall you when someone belittles your daughter or soon-to-be son in law?" Wynne asked, voice steady.

Waylas grimaced and jabbed a finger at Wynne. "You owe my wife an apology."

At this, Susi's attempt to keep distaste out of her expression faltered. A new fierceness overcame her. She looked like she wanted to grab his finger and snap it off. "Mind yourself," she said, her voice a low warning.

This drew a dirty look from Pia.

Elric touched Susi on the shoulder. The silent, *I'll handle this.* Wynne knew him well enough to see he was equally displeased with Waylas. Still, he maintained a controlled calm which influenced her.

At least a little.

Wynne cleared her throat. Thought for a moment. Opened her mouth, reconsidered. Opened it again, and said, "No."

Silence fell.

She would've enjoyed the flabbergasted expressions if Elric hadn't tensed, as though preparing to swoop in and extinguish the flames she was actively fanning.

Waylas recovered first. "No?"

"Correct." She glanced at Pia. "Be offended if you like. I'm not sorry."

Waylas' voice ratcheted up, "How dare you—"

Elric spoke over him. "Wynne, you may go."

"Elric, you're just going to let her get away with this?"

"She's a grown woman. You asked for an apology. She said, no."

Waylas scoffed again. "Then make her!"

"I will manage my own house," Elric said, eyes hard. He took a step toward Waylas. "You have her answer. And mine."

Though far from satisfied, Waylas seemed to recognize his overstep. Unable to hold Elric's hard stare, he glanced at Pia, who huffed quietly and shook her head. Wynne noticed she wouldn't look at Susi.

Elric turned to Wynne. With a complicated look in his eye falling somewhere between *approval* and *let's not do this again*. "You may go."

50

Harek pressed against his bonds subtly, testing the give without alerting Finnion. If he could free himself, he could return to the camp. He had a vague idea where they were. The camp would be a better position to make a stand, in case Finnion followed. There was a possibility Oleksy was still alive. Harek didn't know. Finnion wouldn't say. He found it unlikely he'd catch up with Grigory and Billy on their way to the Gren at this point – they were moving in the opposite direction – but he could send a warning. He could signal a crow and persuade it to carry a message.

But it wasn't going to happen. No give.

"Don't move," Finnion said, as if he knew what Harek was thinking.

Harek said nothing, because he couldn't. Whatever spell Finnion had at his disposal, he'd used it daily to keep Harek silent. Which meant no incantation for the allur.

Rune magic was useful, but it had its limits. Despite the variety of magical expressions, a runebearer could only avail himself to the specific symbols he was born with. As a general rule, this required intent, knowing the runes and how they'd manifest when combined, then speaking the phrase.

But not always.

Working magic was like working a muscle. A person built strength and endurance through consistent training, until using abilities to their fullest became second-nature. Through practice and experience, verbalizing the incantation grew unnecessary. Activating the allur for a particular runeset became quick as thought.

Tethered securely to a large shrub, Harek watched Finnion stalk toward the crest of a rocky overhang jutting from the earth. Seeking a lay of the land. His back was turned.

Harek turned his attention to Judge.

Faithful Judge refused to leave Harek and had been captured as a result. He wouldn't allow Finnion to ride to him, and Finnion wouldn't risk Harek getting anywhere near him. Instead, he'd been treated as a pack animal.

Judge nibbled on the clover nearby. His reins hung loose, touching the earth. He wouldn't bolt.

He could, if he wanted to.

Or was instructed to.

Speaking with animals was an unusual quality. Not for elves. Any elf could do it if they took the time to learn. Harek could only do it because his runes gave him ability, and he'd taken time to practice.

A lot of time.

Harek wiggled his foot to get Judge's attention.

Judge continued to graze.

Come on. Look over here! Fyrir therr hondum.... The allur ran as a ceaseless stream through his mind. Harek scuffed his heel in the dirt, hoping the minor disturbance was enough to grab Judge's attention without raising suspicion.

Judge lifted his gaze, and Harek's heart leapt. He pressed into his magic. The runes on his knuckles bloomed from natural black to golden-orange.

Judge's ears swiveled forward, curious and attentive.

Harek didn't know whether it was possible to communicate with an animal through thought. Still, this was Judge. He had to have faith. If he wasn't tethered to a tree, he would've willed Judge to come to him. He could throw himself on his back, and they could gallop away. But horses couldn't pick knots. Not even Harek could pick Finnion's knots. He'd tried.

Judge, listen to me. Go back to the Gren. Find Aeryn. He had no idea whether Judge understood. None of it mattered if Aeryn wasn't there, or if Judge failed to reach the Gren, or if this wasn't working as Harek desperately hoped it was. *Tell her I'm alive and need help. Tell her Finnion cannot be trusted. Tell –*

"What are you doing?" Finnion's outraged voice interrupted Harek's stream of thought. He marched forward and stopped short when he saw the lighted runes across Harek's knuckles. He turned his attention to Judge. His face darkened.

Go! Judge, run!

Finnion shifted course. Judge blew out a snort. Ears flat, he took an uneasy sidestep from Finnion.

Judge, obey!

Finnion closed the distance, arm extended. Judge gave an angry whinny and pulled away as Finnion swiped for the reins and missed. He pivoted and aimed a kick at Finnion.

He missed, but it made Finnion back up a step, braced for more.

Judge tore up the earth as he fled across the moor.

"No!" Finnion screamed and ran after him.

51

The day of Omri and Lara's wedding arrived, bringing with it a hustle of last-minute preparations and foreboding, especially after the conflict with Waylas and Pia the previous evening.

To Wynne's relief, though Pia had been stiffer than usual, she and Waylas left Wynne alone. The ceremony was touching and picturesque, allowing Omri and Lara the freedom to enjoy their special day for what it was.

From the edge of the crowd, Wynne watched them dance joyously together. Musicians were in top form. Family and neighbors enjoyed one another's company as they feasted. Other pairings joined in the lively dancing. Everything felt fresh and intimate, full of mirth and fellowship.

Kal drew up alongside Wynne. He was dressed in his newer bark brown sweater which Wynne liked. His hair appeared neater than usual and he wore the same easy grin which made him easy to like. Wynne's heart lilted as he gave her a nudge hello. She acknowledged him with a little smile.

They stood side-by-side for a moment and watched the dance.

He angled himself closer to be heard over the music and surrounding conversations. "So, when are you getting hitched?"

He had a playful edge to his voice, which solicited a sarcastic side-eye from Wynne. She answered in kind. "When the right man comes along."

"What about me?"

"No," she said, not unkindly.

"Why not?" he asked, the good humor slipping.

A riffle of stress passed over Wynne. She turned more fully toward him. "I barely know you, Kal."

"Who's fault is that? I've been trying to get to know you." He was making an effort to keep his tone light, but he meant what he said.

Wynne fumbled for an adequate response. He waited.

The air between them grew still. Wynne felt herself grow warmer. Her thoughts, fuzzy. It didn't help that he looked particularly handsome. "I don't know what to say, Kal. What do you want me to say?"

He stepped in closer and ran his hand down the length of her arm. Tingles raced over her skin, making her heart beat faster. He angled his chin to better look her in the face and spoke so only the two of them could hear. "You don't gotta say anything."

Wynne caught the suggestion in his voice. For a flicker of a moment, the space between them seemed to energize. Her attention flicked to his lips, then back to the rich chestnut of his eyes. The temptation to close the space between them budded and strengthened.

His hand brushed her cheek, then came to rest gently on the back of her neck.

She placed both hands on his chest to stop him from leaning in fully. "Kal."

"I wanna be with you, Wynne," he said, more seriously, so close his forehead nearly touched hers.

"I know," she said, her voice softer. Part of her wanted to abandon all caution and let him. Yet, she foresaw it ending in one place. It was a place she couldn't go.

There was a pause as Kal waited for more, and she struggled to hold his gaze. She dropped her eyes, glancing down and away. "I don't know what I want."

It wasn't exactly true, but what was she supposed to say? She wasn't about to vomit her deepest thoughts. *I'm still not completely sure about you. Regardless, I'm not brave enough to be a mother, and you want children.*

Whether or not he sensed any of this, frustration entered his voice. "Is this about Harek?"

"No, it's not about Harek."

He pulled back a few inches. "Not Harek? Is it about someone else, then?"

She returned her full attention to him. "It's not about any man."

"Then what is it?"

"I don't know, exactly."

Another lie.

His expression told her, he didn't buy it.

"You know what I know?" he said. "There's a hundred things I could do to drive us further apart. But nothing I do brings us closer together." He placed his hands over hers, still pressed against his chest. The set of his mouth took a serious bend. The disheartened look in his eyes was like a knife twisted in her heart. "This. This is what you do. You keep me at arms length."

He gently removed her hands, turned from her, and walked away.

52

Kal set himself to take the next few days to work on his own house. He'd make a point to stop by Arlo and Fay's, but only to ensure the old couple had firewood readily accessible. He didn't have it in him to converse.

He was better off at the Enclave than elsewhere. In many respects. Yeah, life was hard, but life was hard everywhere. Better-paying opportunities existed elsewhere – the Gren even, from the sound of it – but he'd be starting from scratch wherever he went. At least here, he'd managed to etch out a place for himself. It was better than nothing. The people here were a different kind of good.

She was a different kind of good.

The daughter of an elder. A Baldomar amongst Baldomar.

Here he was. No runes. No paying job lined up this week. A master craftsman wasting away his talents, sitting in a one-room hut.

For all of his efforts to better himself and win her over, still alone.

The lonely ache in the back of his mind presented itself again. He wanted to know her. To love her. She was still everything he couldn't reach. What else was he supposed to do? He thought there'd been progress. Maybe he'd misread.

Maybe he misread everything, right from the start.

More discouraged than in recent memory, he stared into glowing coals as he chewed his bland porridge. He was tired of trading his art for potatoes and cheap meat to keep from starving. Tired of the mixed signals. Tired of the dodgy excuses which left him wondering.

Why do I keep doing this?

Knuckles rapped against the door. Grateful to be pulled from his misery, he set his breakfast aside, wiped his mouth, and unlatched the door.

Omri waited, hands in his pockets with an energetic smirk. "Morning."

"Shouldn't you be at home with your new wife?" Kal said.

"A man's gotta work. Besides, I owe you a favor. What needs doing?"

✧

Streaky gray clouds drifted across the sky. Late spring in Noemar was Kal's favorite time of year. Sure, he relished the chill like any respectable Northerner – he'd never gotten used to the heat and humidity of Hollis – but the mild swing was always welcome after an endless bitter winter trapped indoors.

He tried to remind himself of this as he bent over his shovel while he and Omri worked the ground into a neat little rectangle for Kal's would-be garden. Truthfully, Kal hated the idea of farming. He hated the prospect of starvation more. A number of goodwilled neighbors had offered seeds and cuttings in recent months. Kal was starting to get embarrassed over his excuse that he lacked a place to plant them. A person could get by here without growing their own food, but not well, and most folks grew at least a few items. If he was here, it seemed like the thing to do.

His shovel sliced into the dirt and stopped abruptly with a sharp clank. He stifled a sigh.

"Another rock?" Omri said.

"Yup." He set about digging it out.

"Not much for farming, eh?"

Kal snorted. "How could you tell?"

"Late spring. Nothin' planted yet."

Kal tried not not to feel chafed. "No time."

"No shame meant," Omri said.

Kal said nothing. The earth loosened its grip. He levered the shovel and pried the rock from the ground. It was the size of a bread loaf.

He moved it to the growing pile beside his house. There were enough rocks to give him ideas. He didn't work with stone much, but how hard could it be to make a short barrier encircling the fire pit in the middle of his floor? It could be a decent surface for resting a cooking pot – far better than the dirt beside the coals – and safer than leaving the pit exposed where he risked kicking embers by accident. He'd done that already and nearly set fire to the mat he acquired.

He turned back to the garden plot with dismay. He released a slow breath.

"You alright?" Omri asked.

"You know what it is?" Kal said. "Just occurred to me now."

"What?"

"I don't like the uncertainty."

"Of farming?"

"Yeah."

"You sow, you reap."

"Ideally. But there's no promise."

Omri shrugged.

"Look. I'm a craftsman. I know if I pour my sweat into a work, there will be a result. Good or bad, it's guaranteed. It's in my hands. This?" With a sweep of the arm, he indicated the plot and let it fall to his side. "I could do everything right, and it still fails. Pests. Disease. No rain. Bad seeds. Reasons entirely out of my control. I don't like that."

Omri rested his hoe upright and placed both hands over the butt end of the tool. He made a thoughtful survey of their progress.

Kal returned to the area he'd been working with a shake of the head. "Don't know why I should be surprised. That sums up my life."

He laughed, but couldn't keep the edge out of it entirely. He jammed the shovel back into the earth with force.

He struck another rock.

"You gotta be joking!"

Omri laughed.

Kal jabbed at the dirt in search of the outer edge of the rock. "Gods, how big is this blighter?"

Omri swapped hoe for spade and joined him. When they finally unearthed it, they discovered it was the width of the average man, and over a foot thick. It took both of them to haul it to the rock pile. They paused to catch their breath. Kal assessed the effort, and some of his former bitterness ebbed. It was difficult to imagine neighbors so willing to help anywhere else. He supposed he ought to be grateful.

Kal used the back of his arm to wipe the sweat beading his forehead. "I appreciate the help."

"O'course." Omri brushed the grit from his hands. "So. About Wynne."

Kal tensed inwardly but kept it off his face and out of his voice. He wondered if Omri'd noticed that they barely spoke at the wedding two days earlier. "What about her?"

"You need to tell her the truth."

Kal said nothing.

"Regarding your past – why you left Hollis. Or anything else you're not telling her."

Kal's face tightened.

Omri's stance changed. "Look. I never said anything before because, frankly, I didn't think you had a chance with her."

Kal heard the implication there. *It's different now. I think you do.*

"I saw you two at the wedding. She deserves to know."

✧

They didn't talk about Wynne at all after that. They finished the plot before midday. Omri returned home to his lady. Kal retreated indoors by himself. He didn't remove his cap, coat, or boots. He didn't sit. He surveyed the loney space while his mind roved.

She deserves to know.

The words had weeded into his head. They were a stone in his shoe which could not remain unaddressed.

Maybe some people could self-expose and find grace. Maybe that was true for Omri and Lara. Or maybe Omri's rationale was diluted by newlywed idealism. He hadn't even heard the worst of it.

She deserves to know.

Omri seemed to think that Kal had a chance with Wynne. It was possible he knew something Kal didn't. It had given Kal hope.

And an enormous problem.

Kal's thoughts flicked over his life's transgressions. If Wynne harbored uncertainty now, baring his history was probably enough to drive her away completely.

Her words came back to him, too. *I barely know you.*

He tightened his jaw and released a slow breath. Necessity settled down upon him, like a heavy rock on his chest.

It felt stuffy inside. He needed to clear his head.

Then he'd find her.

If she didn't want him after she'd tasted the truth, then so be it. At least she'd have a real reason.

53

Wynne leaned onto the windowsill of the lookout tower. In the branches six feet away, a mated pair of mountain sparrows tended their brood. The mother bird nestled her fat body over the scrawny babies.

"How do you do it?" she asked. But she didn't possess magic to communicate with the bird. She didn't have Harek to translate.

She didn't have Harek at all.

He was off in the new Baldomar city, helping build it from the ground up, with special responsibilities and esteem. She was here, in the lookout blind. Alone.

Talking to a bird.

When she considered all the reasons for his prolonged silence, she had to concede that perhaps Tess was right – Wynne hadn't hitched her cart to that horse, and some other lady did.

Swallowing this felt like pain. She didn't understand why she'd feel jealous of some potential imaginary woman, when he was never truly hers to begin with. Her sweetest friend though he'd been, he never acted when he had the opportunity. Not properly. She wished he had, but the times weren't right. The snag in her heart felt like it might never go away.

For all his faults, she never guessed where she stood with Kal. He wanted her enough to act on it. Though he remained a mystery in some respects, he wasn't the same man she tackled in the woods months ago. It certainly seemed like time and hard work had shaped him into someone respectable. Or distilled the good already there.

Seeing him walk away hurt worse than she expected. It felt like watching her future recede in the distance. It kicked up the pang of loss and rejection she'd been contending with for months.

At this point, it felt like she was doing it to herself.

The image had lodged in her mind and been with her for the last two days, making her feel like a wretch. In the time they'd known each other, they suffered no shortage of conflict. She'd hardly been faultless, but more often than not, he'd taken the first step to reconcile.

Now?

It felt like it was on her to remedy the situation, if there was any hope to be had.

She wanted to.

It was within her control.

Yet she knew what it required.

The way she saw it, honesty over her deep-seated feelings about motherhood would be decisive. Either he'd find the truth distasteful and that was it. Or, he'd want her anyway. One extreme or the other.

She couldn't envision a middle-ground.

Wynne trekked toward the village after her watch. Nervous energy hummed in her bones, making it hard to think straight. She told herself not to raise hopes or to brace for the sting of rejection. Attempting this felt like walking a razor's edge, and she managed to fail at both.

Then she heard him.

Kal crunched along the trails near the edge of the wood where folks sometimes took their horses for a trot. She drew to a stop and glimpsed him through the trees as he approached a bend, hands deep in his pockets and thoughts far away.

He hadn't noticed her.

A wiggle of panic squirmed inside of her. *You could slip into the woods. He'd never know you were here.*

She forced her breathing under control. In through the nose, out through her lips.

Just double back, and just let him go.

He continued to move along the trail, oblivious to her presence. Getting closer.

No one has to know you're a coward.

Wynne wrung her fingers.

If you do this, there's no going back. It's out there. Is that really what you want?

Kal appeared unobscured twenty feet away. Still watching his feet.

Is he really who you want?

"Kal?"

He looked up and stopped suddenly.

"What are you doing?" She couldn't tell if he was pleased to see her.

"Taking a walk. What are you doing?"

"Coming in from my watch."

He nodded and said nothing.

Wynne licked her lips.

Last chance.

The thought of him walking away returned with a wrenching sensation. *That's what you get to look forward to if you don't do this now.*

Something within her hardened. Despite her dread, a stronger sense of defiance – or maybe it was that famed Erlander knack for confrontation – reared inside her. She might not be brave enough to be a mother, but she was no coward. She was Wynne Thar. She still had to live with herself.

"There's something I need to tell you." Before she could overthink, she took a few tentative steps toward him. "You said I've kept you at arm's length. You're right. You deserve the truth."

Wary but open, Kal shuffled a step nearer. "Alright."

"First, you need to understand something about my clan. You've probably noticed already. We're a family-centered people. Most folks marry young, then start a family. Usually, a big one. Usually right away." Wynne moved toward him as she spoke. "That's a beautiful thing –"

"You want a big family?"

She stopped and turn her empty palms toward him. "I don't know if I can be a mother at all."

This seemed to surprise him, though he didn't shut himself off. "You can't have children?"

"No, I mean childbirth terrifies me."

"...You deliver babies."

"I know. It hasn't helped. The thought of being in that position myself? Exposed, in pain, then – if something went terribly wrong, – not knowing what's going to happen to my child – "

The words rushed out and picked up speed. Her gestures grew increasingly animated, as she moved forward again.

"My whole life, I've wanted to grow up and be a wife and mum. I'm not brave enough for all of that. I can't exactly go around saying so. I'm a Baldomar – building strong families is what we do." She took a breath, forcing herself to slow down, and met his face. "You asked why I'm not hitched yet. The reason I turned down Corbin months ago. That's why."

Kal watched her for a long moment. His posture toward her relaxed somewhat. He stepped closer until they were only a few feet apart. "This fear. Do you think it's something you'll ever get over?"

"I hope so," she said, realizing the truth in those words, even if she wasn't optimistic about the odds.

Kal took a thoughtful breath. "I don't know if it makes a difference, but I'm willing to wait for children. And I think you'd be a wonderful mother."

She didn't realize how badly she needed to hear that. Her throat thickened painfully. She fought back a rush of tears and bobbed her head. She offered a small smile.

Kal tried to smile back, but he looked uneasy, and Wynne wondered if she'd misunderstood his reaction.

"There's something I need to tell you, too."

His confession poured out of him like water – the unintentional adultery in Gallendahi, the friend who caught wind of danger before it befell him, and how he was forced to flee.

Wynne felt cold and a little sick as she listened. Part of her wasn't surprised. He was thirty years old, never married, and hailed from a culture lacking the same ethic as the Baldomar about this sort of behavior.

The other part of her was appalled.

Even so, she recognized that he'd chosen to lay out the ugliness of his past because she was worth the truth to him. That said something, and it tugged on her heart in a way she didn't expect.

"When we met, you asked if I was some sorta criminal. I said no," Kal said. "I don't know what it's like here, but adultery is a crime most places. So I guess that was a lie."

"Thank you for telling me," she said when it seemed to come to an end.

His lips compressed into a tight line, and she realized he wasn't finished. "I fathered a child once."

Wynne stared at him for a stunned moment. "You have a child?"

Kal shook his head. He broke eye contact and ran the back of his hand beneath his nose in a vain attempt to mask the rush of emotion which swept behind his eyes. He loosened his throat with a cough.

"What happened?" she asked, gentle.

"Around three years ago, I got word of some matters which needed settling back home, in the village. You remember, after my apprenticeship, I found work wherever I could. Jobs might last weeks or months, then it'd be off to the next place. I was focused on becoming a master of my craft, and I did."

"Right."

"Between this, and traveling all over, family wasn't something I could devote myself to. My father walked out when I was two, and we never saw him again. I got no memory of him. He might as well've left us for dead. I promised myself, I'd never do what he did." Kal's voice strengthened as he spoke. "Which meant I had to be careful. No family. Try not to get involved. And I kept that promise."

"So what happened three years ago?"

"My mum left the house to her brother, and he died. I needed to go back and see about that. While there, I reunited with an old friend. Isolde. She got pregnant."

"How long were you together?"

"Only a few months."

"Did she lose the baby?"

Kal released a bitter bark of laughter. "She said it was gonna upend her life. She was worried the folks she was livin' with would kick her out. Said she had no money, she couldn't do it – all manner of excuses. I told her I'd stay. I could set up shop in town. I'd never earn what I was before, but I was willing to swallow that. I wouldn't leave my kid wondering why his father don't love him enough to stay. She wouldn't listen. She knew my work had me traveling all over before. She thought I'd grow to resent them, leave, then she'd be doing it alone. I never gave her reason to disbelieve me, but truth told, we really didn't know each other that well. She got some..." He searched for the right word as his mouth twisted in a grimace. "...some sort of poison, to hide what we'd done before anyone found out. I begged her not to take it. That was our babe – my child, as much as hers. She said she'd made up her mind, and I couldn't stop her. So I left for Hollis, and I didn't look back."

Quiet settled between them. Kal swallowed hard, looking miserable. The water pooling in his eyes spilled over.

"That was the lowest point of my life. I couldn't protect my kid from his own mother. It destroyed me."

Wynne's throat tightened. She closed the gap between them, slipped her arms around his waist, and rested her head against his chest. She held tight.

He gently enclosed her in his arms, laid his cheek atop her head, and hugged her back.

54

Summer in Noemar was a pleasant time. Gardens bloomed. Milder weather and more hours of daylight brought no shortage of work. With grain harvests well under way, the whole village was busy, cutting, threshing, and winnowing.

But folks took a break when the courier came to town.

Neighbors, relatives, and friends swarmed, all eager for word from the Gren. Wynne picked out the happy, hopeful faces of the Goodhills, the Haranaes, Sender, Catreeny and Ben, and Micha Jaeger amongst the throng. She recognized Simone by her sheet of hair along the edge of the crowd with Tawna and Tawna's mother. Simone's gaze met Wynne in chilly acknowledgement before she angled her body away.

Wynne rolled her eyes and sidled up to Tess, who chatted with Fiona nearby. She was glad to see Fiona out and about with her daughter. The baby was secured to the front of Fiona's body in a complicated wrap, gnawing on her chubby rune-covered fingers. Drool streamed down her chin.

"You ladies expecting a parcel?" Wynne said, indicating the courier's cart.

"Nah, I just like the buzz," Tess said.

"On that topic," Fiona said. "I hear Lara and Omri are expecting."

Wynne beamed and bobbed her head.

A baby's belly laugh drew their attention to Fiona's daughter and a round of smiles from everyone within earshot. Fiona gave Wynne a nudge. "You next, eh?"

Wynne's voice tightened involuntarily. "Pardon?"

"Don't be coy." She winked. "It's well known. That Kal has made himself rather eligible. Word is, he's got his sight set."

Wynne said nothing while her face turned crimson.

Simone pulled a noise of disgust from the back of her throat. She glanced over her shoulder and her eyes made a second brief sweep of Wynne before turning toward Tawna to continue whatever hushed conversation they'd been having.

Fiona shook her head and dropped her voice to address Wynne. "They're jealous. Don't let 'em eat at ya."

Wynne wasn't sure what to say to that. She understood there was an element of envy fermenting in the hearts of the Enclave women. The coolness and whispers which divided her from certain young women in the village weren't new. They were there before Kal. Back then, she attributed it to her status. She was the daughter of an elder. The sister to the rune leaders. Lovely in appearance and well-off. Realistically, she could have anyone she wanted.

Over the past year, the chilliness of the unattached Baldomar women had taken a new, definite shape. Non-Baldomar though he was, Kal was the desired one, and he desired Wynne.

Mercifully, an opening formed in the swarm surrounding the cart.

"Excuse me," she said, slipping into the gap like an eel. She angled her chin upward to better see Paul straddling bundles in the back of the wagon, sorting through packages and letters, matching bundles with recipients. "Anything for the Thars?"

"Not this time, I'm afraid," he said before his focus jumped beyond her. "Oy! Willem..."

Wynne contended with the tug against her good mood, and it put her out of sorts.

"Why you look deflated?" Tess asked when she'd threaded her way back. Fiona had moved on.

Wynne opened her mouth, spotted Micha, and reconsidered.

Tess subtly followed Wynne's line of sight. Sensing a potentially sensitive topic, she adjusted Asmund on her hip and nodded toward the main road. "Walk and talk?"

Wynne bobbed her head in the affirmative and led them away from the throng.

"Still nothin' from Harek?" Tess said when it was just the two of them.

"No. I feel stupid."

"I heard there were supply issues."

Wynne glanced over her shoulder at the happy faces of her neighbors, clutching letters and other effects affectionately sent from the Gren. There was Paul, standing in the wagon bed, cheerfully dispensing bundles like a benevolent gift-giver. "Right."

"You still waitin' on him?"

Wynne tipped her head skyward with a little groan.

"Let me put it to you this way. Wot if he came back tomorrow and said, *Wynne, I'm ready – be my wife!*"

"I'd say he had some questions to answer."

Tess made a conceding dip of the head. "Wot about Kal?"

"What about him?"

"You tell me. You were awfully quiet back there. Fiona's not wrong. Everybody knows."

Wynne said nothing. She was aware of village whisperings that the pair of them were an item. She wasn't sure she'd characterize it that way.

"Wait – we still like Kal?"

Wynne chewed on her lip and shot Tess a look.

"Okay, that's wot I thought. And where might you be goin' then with that basket? I distinctly remember your home is that way." Tess nodded over her shoulder.

Wynne felt her cheeks grow red. "To see Kal."

"Oh-ho-ho."

"I'm inviting him to dinner. And you can get that look off your face. It's a normal supper."

He'd been at the Thar house at least once a week – at her invitation, not Omri's. She was astounded Elric hadn't posed the question yet, though she knew it was a conversation her parents were having amongst themselves.

"Do I need to supervise this social call?"

"Tess."

"Wot? You know how people talk."

"I appreciate you looking out for my reputation, but I don't think a two minute conversation at his fence is enough to besmirch my character."

✧

Tufts of greens marched in neat rows across the garden plot beside Kal's house. The walls had recently received a fresh coating of daub. From the lane, Wynne glimpsed a partial view of the completed addition. It was the size of a bedroom. A good workspace, he'd told her, or storage for his growing accumulation of tools until he built a shed – his next major project after he finished some indoor improvements. She wanted to see it up close but knew better than to indulge her curiosity.

She leaned on the fence near the road and listened to his whistling coming from the rear of the property for a moment. Her voice took a sing-song tenor. "Oh, Kalomir..."

The whistling stopped. He swished through the grass around the side of his house. He broke into a grin. "You can't be here right now."

She arched an eyebrow. "Why not?"

"I'm working on something, and you can't see it. Not yet."

"What is it?"

"A present for your family."

She perked up. "Tell me. Please?"

"Nice try. You can bat those pretty eyes someplace else." He paused, and reconsidered. "Actually, don't."

She snickered.

He came to the fence, leaned against it from the yard-side, and allowed his arms to brush against hers, like they'd done a dozen times before today. He gestured to the small covered basket in her hands. "What is this?"

"Also a present." She passed it to him.

He peeked inside. "You grew these?"

"I did."

"What are they? I've never seen a white berry like this."

"It's a snowberry."

"In summer?"

"You should always be careful of white berries if you're foraging. Nine times out of ten, they're poison."

He gave the basket a little shake. "I'm not about to find out that I've done something wrong, am I?"

Wynne lifted her chin, plucked a berry from the basket, and popped it into her mouth. *Proof – not poison.*

"Oh, swell. Now we're both gonna die."

"You gotta lot of sass, sir."

He gave her a knowing up-down. "You're one to talk." He dug his fingers into the basket. "What've you been up to this morning?"

"Garden work."

He glanced back at her with a fresh smile. "Yeah?"

They talked for two minutes – or ten, or twenty – when Wynne remembered what she'd come to ask. "Do you want to come for supper? Omri and Lara are coming."

"Always." He jerked his thumb toward his house. "Though I oughta get back to work if that's so. I'm hoping to finish today."

"You're teasing me."

"I would never," he said with mock innocence.

Wynne made a noise in the back of her throat. He made no move to leave, but instead brushed a knuckle against her arm. In sheer enjoyment of one another, they shared a quiet, lingering smile.

Wynne broke the quiet with, "Please tell me."

He laughed and leaned a little closer. "Persuade me?"

"I already gave you berries," she said, whispering her reply.

"Which may or may not melt me from the inside."

"Name your price."

He shrugged. "Tempt me."

Enjoying the game, Wynne tipped her eyes skyward as she thought. "...The satisfaction of..."

"Ha! No. You'll see with everyone else." He gave her a playful backhand wave. "Go on now."

"Are you shooing me?"

"Yes, I am."

She pulled away from the fence and gave him a coy look and a wink.

✧

Wynne returned home, buzzing on the wind and distracted from her prior disappointment – enough to dispel the sting she'd been wrestling with because of Harek.

I reckon he won't make it back in time.

Wynne wondered – not for the first time – if that would be such a bad thing.

She and Kal had walked away from their confessions with the sort of fondness which only came from knowing and being known. A mutual grace sprang up between them, allowing for natural attraction, affection, and real friendship to bloom into something Wynne didn't want to run from.

Her ruminations vanished when the Thar house came into view. Micha stood in the open doorway, speaking with Susi.

"There she is," Susi said when she noticed Wynne.

Micha followed her gaze to the footpath, looking anxious and uncomfortable. Wynne's stomach rolled over.

"Is everything alright?" Wynne asked.

"Wynne, I wanted to ask something of you," Micha said.

Wynne tried to quell her sudden, uneasy rush. She braced for the question, *I thought it was you and Harek, and now it seems like it's you and Kal – what's going on?*

Calm down, she told herself. *You've done nothing to compromise yourself. You got nothing to feel guilty over.*

"Ask away," Wynne said.

"Leland and I are concerned," Micha said. "We haven't heard from Harek. I understand there were supply issues, and he's busy. Or maybe he's out of sorts about something – you know how he can get. Still. It's been months and months without a word. Would you mind writing to Aeryn or Josef before Paul leaves for the Gren again? I understand they're sometimes in the city and sometimes not, but if anyone could get an answer, I'm sure they could. I don't even need him to write back – I just want to know that he's well."

Wynne's last letter came to mind. *Out of sorts, indeed.* She took no comfort in the fact that his silence extended to more than just her. Concerns about herself ebbed, replaced by a pricker of compassion for Micha and Leland. That, and frustration with Harek that he'd make his parents worry.

Wynne touched Micha gently on the arm. "Of course I'll help."

·

55

"Who's there?" Wynne's voice cut through the dead of night, the eerie darkness of the wood, and the less-eerie tromp of Harek's boots. He raised his lamp higher and turned toward the sound of her voice. He craned his neck toward the yellow glow in the openings of the lookout hutch. It was probably a single lighted oil lamp, but it stood out as a beacon against the surrounding dark forest. How had he missed it?

Wynne's knot of hair wobbled as her shadowy head and shoulders thrust out the window.

"Wynne? It's me – Harek."

"Heavens, you scared me half to death!"

"Sorry. I didn't mean to."

"No, it's okay. Is everything alright?" she asked, relief replaced by concern.

"Yeah. Everything's fine."

"...What are you doing?"

"I'm coming to visit you."

"Oh! I thought you were leaving."

It had taken him a good deal of courage to work up the nerve to come out here. Now doubts unfurled, goaded by the embarrassment of overshooting the tree. He was imposing. Assuming too much. This was Wynne Thar – one of the bravest women Harek knew. She wasn't afraid of the woods after dark. She liked people, but she could handle being alone. She didn't need him. Why would she want him here?

He covered it with a laugh. "Well...that's why you're the scout, and not me. Can I come up?"

"Yes," she said in a hurry. "I'm glad you're here. Hold on."

He could hear the enjoyment in her voice without seeing her face, and it halted his inner spiral. She disappeared from the lighted window and Harek tried to keep the riot bounding around his chest under control.

She's glad I'm here.

A moment later, shadow obscured the hole in the floor and the rope ladder unfurled from on high.

Harek breached the hole, and Wynne's delighted face made his efforts worth it, tenfold.

"You've never visited me at the hutch before," she said. "To what do I owe this little visit?"

"You said it was your first overnight watch alone. I thought you might like the company. At least for a little while."

Her expression led him to believe that his assumption was dead on. Her eyes softened. "That's sweet of you."

"Will this get you in trouble?"

"Rakel's not here to yell at me about it, and I'm not gonna tell. Do your parents know you're here?"

"Well, no."

"You rebel," she said deadpan, which pulled a smirk from him.

"How's it been?"

Her smile took a pained quality. "There's not much to do except keep eyes and ears open. I brought material to make rope, but I can only do that for so long before my fingers get numb. So I switched to feather sticks."

He followed her gaze to the heap in the corner, where a tangle of cordage rested beside a vast quantity of curly wood shavings. There had to be at least twenty feather sticks there.

"What's in your bag?" she asked.

"I brought food and a game."

Wynne perked up. "Is it the bean game?"

Harek must've been there for two hours before they found themselves shoulder to shoulder at the window, watching the herd of pikdeer mosey by, little more than shadowy lumps picking their way across the forest floor. His focus drifted to her pretty face, lighted dimly by the moonlight filtering through the trees. She really was gorgeous. She caught him looking and gave him a playful nudge with her arm. They returned their attention to the stars.

Harek watched those same stars now through the tangle of dead branches overhead.

Finnion no longer conversed with him. Any communication came in the form of orders. *Eat. Go. Sleep now.* The isolation borne from this felt profoundly demoralizing.

So it had been for weeks. They'd fallen into a high-stakes rhythm, largely driven by Finnion's increased paranoia. He talked with himself more. Usually not in front of Harek. His voice would change, then it was like listening to a far-off conversation between three people. Often an argument, or reviewing the steps of a plan.

Harek paid attention. Even so, he remained unsure where they were going, or what might happen when they got there. They'd meandered south in a manner which made him inclined to believe that there wasn't a plan. At times, they hid for days before resuming the drift further and further from Noemar.

Which didn't bode well.

There was nothing for Finnion to do with him. After the murders he'd committed, there was nowhere he could go where justice didn't await.

There was nothing Harek could do beyond cooperate in the hopes that it would preserve his life until the opportunity for freedom presented itself.

So far, it hadn't.

He had no idea whether Judge made it back to the Gren. Whether he'd delivered the message to Aeryn, or one of the other elves in the city. Whether help was coming. Whether Oleksy was alive.

Whether Wynne was worried about him.

He spent every waking moment unable to speak and under constant watch, at the mercy of Finnion's inhuman strength and deteriorating sanity.

He glanced toward the campfire, to the dark form of his once-friend. After the chittering and hissing in some awful gibberish, Finnion finally quieted down. He laid on his side, eyes shut. If he was asleep, it was a light sleep. Harek didn't count on it to last. Harek's sleep was a far cry from restful, and Finnion never slept as long as he did.

Harek leaned his back against the tree.

Half-dead branches extended overhead like crooked fingers against the blue-black of the night. An ache lodged in his chest as the stars winked. He wondered if this would be the last time he'd see them.

56

"Want to come inside?" Kal asked.

Wynne hesitated from her usual spot at the fence. "I don't know if that's a good idea."

"Why?"

"Because we're alone."

His smile took a roguish quality. "You afraid temptation might overtake you?"

"You're a funny one."

"So you've said." He tapped her lightly on the arm and jerked his head toward the house. "I want to show you what I've been working on. It'll only take a minute."

He looked and sounded so sincere. Wynne cast her eyes up the empty road, and relented.

She followed him up the trodden path to the open door and ducked in after him. With a sweep of the arm and a proud grin, he watched her reaction.

"Kal..." she said with admiration as she took in the cozy, furnished home.

He nodded toward the central fire. "This was a pit before. I built up the stones around it. Safer, and better for cooking. I stocked the loft up there and fixed the ladder." He pointed at the small table pushed against the wall. "I'm working on chairs next. I also made this..."

Beside the table, a set of shelves held tools, dishes, and clothes. He stepped around her swiftly, as though he'd forgotten something important which needed attending, and grabbed an item from the shelf. It fit into his palm. He promptly shoved it beneath the pile of towels. "Don't look there."

Wynne hoisted an eyebrow. "Why? What was that?"

"A gift for you, but not until tomorrow. Don't ask questions."

A smile crawled onto her lips. Tomorrow marked her day of birth, and Lara and Omri wanted to host them for supper.

"Watch this." He drew her attention to the side-room. He ducked into the shadowy space. Out of sight, a second door scraped open, and daylight flooded in.

"Makes for a nice breeze," he said, pleased as he reentered the main space. "I haven't decided what the room is for yet. Animals maybe, until I get a proper barn out back? Though I'd have to make a half-door, so they don't come into the rest of the house. I want to get a proper floor built up. I got these rugs in the meantime."

"I like them. They look warm."

"The bearskin cost a good bit, but it'll be worth it, come winter."

"That's a big bed," she said with a nod to the curtained four-poster on the opposite side of the room.

"I figured we'd want the space."

She shot him a startled glance.

"You heard me," he said.

"That's brazen, even for you."

"Pardon me for assuming I'll be sharing a bed with my wife."

Wynne flushed. "Your wife, eh?"

"Yeah. We'll see what your pops says once I finish all this."

Despite her best efforts, a grin crawled onto her face. He seemed to relish it. "You like it?"

"I do," she said sincerely.

He stepped closer. "It's not a palace. But I want you to have a nice place to live. Can you see yourself living here?"

Her eyes passed over the home but were irresistibly pulled back to his. He ran his hand affectionately down her arm, making it difficult to think straight. As she gazed up at the rich chestnut brown, her heartbeat quickened.

"I can," she said.

Instantly, something roiled inside her chest. *I can?*

In that moment, Wynne realized several things at once.

First, she could see herself here. Happy. Loved.

Second, a small part of her had been holding onto hope for Harek. Hope that he'd return and somehow set things right. She didn't know what that looked like, but she couldn't shake it and never had.

She didn't understand. Kal was here. Harek wasn't. Kal wanted her. Harek wanted to put her off for later. Or never. She ought to be thrilled with the man before her.

She ought to be certain.

Yet the ordeal with Harek had snarled her heart into a rat's nest of the opposite.

A future with Kal meant letting go of Harek for good. Still, it felt wrong to move on without a conversation to mark the finality of whatever had been between them.

She dropped her eyes and cleared her throat, buying time and granting herself a little space before Kal got any ideas. She flashed him a regretful smile as she moved toward the open door. "I'm gonna leave now, before you get yourself in trouble."

He followed and leaned onto the doorframe. "Is trouble a possibility?"

A voice at the road drew Wynne's attention over her shoulder. Pia was on a walk with her younger daughters, Tawna, and Tawna's mother. Wynne drew a cool glance from Tawna, who said something to her mother. The eyes of both older women jumped toward Wynne and Kal, idling in his doorway.

She hardened herself against the bud of anxiety about that and returned her attention to Kal's handsome face. "I'll see you tomorrow."

✧

"How'd you know Skeggis was the right one?" Wynne asked Tess a short while later. She had a block of time before her watch and needed an ear to help untangle her thoughts.

Tess shrugged. "He's the one I wanted. Then I got him. I guess that makes him the right one."

"Okay..." Wynne reconsidered her phrasing. "Do you think there's a *right person* in a grander sense?"

"Wot? Like destiny?"

"Yeah. Like, you were always meant to be with someone particular."

"Don't know about that." Tess cut her eyes in confusion. "Who are we talkin' 'bout right now?"

"How'd you know you weren't settling?"

"Is this 'bout Kal?"

Wynne said nothing, but her expression said it all.

"I thought we liked Kal."

"I do. But he's also not a Baldomar." *He's not Harek.* "He's older and worldly. Most of his life, his ways haven't been our ways."

Tess' face tightened. "I should smack you."

Affronted, Wynne pulled her chin inward.

"Wot are you? Princess of the Enclave?" Tess shook her head. "Gods. Is anyone good enough? First it was Harek. I know – he wasn't ready to be a husband. Now, Kal. Is he perfect? No, he's a human bean. But he's a good man. Part of that is 'cause of you. You been a good influence on him. Wot more do you want?"

Skeggis reentered the house, signaling the end of girl-talk. Wynne pulled her cup to herself, chastened.

"Pop!" Asmund abandoned his blocks, rose unsteadily, and toddled in his chunky one-year-old way to meet him at the door. "Pop, Pop, Pop."

"Little man." He lifted the boy, holding him with one arm.

Asmund planted a clumsy kiss on his father's cheek with an exaggerated, "Mwah."

Tess' eyes creased into a smile at the show of affection. Skeggis clopped across the room, grabbed a loaf of crusty bread from the counter, and plopped into the chair beside Tess. He ripped a hunk with his teeth and his eyes passed between Tess and Wynne, oblivious to having interrupted a conversation of any kind.

"You tell her?" he asked around a mouthful of food.

"Not yet. I was waitin' for you."

"Tell me what?" Wynne asked, fearing they were about to announce that they were leaving the Enclave sooner rather than later. She wasn't sure she could handle this today.

Tess turned her gap-toothed grin on Wynne. "We're havin' another baby."

Wynne's inner spiral halted. Her focus jumped between them, and she matched Tess' joy with her own. "That's wonderful news!"

"For serious." Tess patted her belly. "This is just the start of it. We're gonna repopulate the village."

Skeggis cast her a suggestive grin. "You know it."

Wynne choked on her tea and rested her cup. "I'll take that as my cue to go."

Tess pointed a finger at her. "You're midwifin' for this one."

"Of course I'll be there – "

"No, you're misunderstandin' me. No Catreeny. I love her, but I swear to you, I will kick her. I won't miss this time."

Wynne hesitated. "I believe you."

"And you better think about what I said. 'Specially if you want this." She gestured to indicate her family and her home.

57

It was still light enough to make out the path and the shape of one another as Kal walked Wynne home after supper. His eyes passed over her profile to the gift he'd given her – a polished wooden comb with flowers, leaves, and berries carved along the spine. It pleased him that she adored it and immediately tucked it in her hair.

They cleared the stretch of road before Arlo and Fay's house and he gave her a nudge. "Would it be outrageous if I took your hand?"

Wynne hesitated, but he heard the smile behind her voice before he saw it. "No."

"Oh. Nevermind, then."

She tipped her head back and laughed. She'd done that a lot this evening. Without waiting for permission, he took her hand. A first.

It felt good.

Wynne's focus landed on their clasped hands and lingered, as if she was weighing something important. She squeezed gently. Her shoulders relaxed, and her shining eyes met his, open and sincere. In that breath, he felt as if he could see them forty years in the future. Shrunken and wrinkled, still at one another's side.

They heard the tavern before they rounded a bend and saw it. Yellow light spilled from the two high windows at the front of the building. Though muffled by the building's walls and accompanied by normal, indiscernible tavern jabber, a rollocking medley of fiddle, drum, and vocals emanated from the building.

Wynne drew them to a stop in the lane and listened for a moment.

"That's new." She sounded surprised. "It's actually well played."

They listened for a long moment. Kal liked a good reel as much as anyone. It was the sort of enjoyable lively number which made a body want to tap along.

"You know what we've never done?" she asked.

A number of bold suggestions presented themselves to Kal. It had been a pleasant evening, and he wanted to avoid sticking his foot in it.

"Tell me," he said instead of any half-serious offerings.

She turned her face toward him, half lit by the tavern's yellow glow. "Dance."

The corner of his mouth hiked up. "You want to?"

"In there?"

"Here."

The song inside came to an end with cheers. The musicians immediately picked up the next. Where the first had been jaunty, this was a little slower. No less energy, but flowing. Inviting. An obvious show of what the musicians were capable of.

Wynne watched Kal for a long moment. Her smile built.

With eyes fixed tenderly on each other, he adjusted their handhold and turned fully toward her, resting his hand against the small of her back. She allowed him to hold her and lead. The music lilted. Neither spoke.

Wynne stepped in closer and rested her head against his chest. Deep affection flooded him. Kal shut his eyes as they swayed, cherishing the closeness.

The moment.

Her.

The tavern door banged open. Brighter light spilled into the night. The crooning instruments, squawks of conversation, and clank of dishes spiked. Two men stumbled outside. One veered quickly left, beyond the beams of light. The second noticed Kal and Wynne holding each other, rocking in the lane.

"Oh-ho-ho..." He made a suggestive grunt, then belched.

Kal shooed him with a back-handed wave, but it was too late. Wynne pulled back, equally annoyed at the interruption.

In the shadow, the first man bent double and vomited.

✧

Kal tried to let it go. It wasn't the first moment between them which had been cut short, and probably wouldn't be the last. At least it wasn't his doing this time.

The Jai-sized bear carving he'd gifted the Thars stood in the front yard like a monument or guardian. In the gathering dark, it forced Kal to look twice.

Wynne laughed. "I know. I constantly mistake it for a real bear at night, too."

He held the gate for her and they slowed as they drew up to the door.

"Thank you for celebrating with me tonight," she said, turning to face him before she went inside.

Kal brushed his fingers against her soft cheek before letting his hand drop, for both their sakes. As much as he liked touching her, it was not going to make going home without her any easier. Especially after that dance. "You're worth celebrating."

"You're a good man." Her voice was soft. Earnest. He read something in her expression he hadn't quite encountered before. It both thrilled and sobered him.

"You're a good woman."

Wynne hesitated, then moved forward an inch.

Kal's reservations gave way. He stepped in, pressed his lips against hers, and lost himself.

Another first.

She pulled back, but not away. Her cheeks were flushed.

"I want to do this every day for the rest of my life," he said, holding her close. "I love you."

She stared at him for the length of a breath. "I love you, too."

She stole a second, briefer kiss, gave his hand a squeeze, and left him wishing for more.

✧

Wynne shut the door and gave herself a moment as the flutters bounding around her chest settled into something more solid.

"Wynne?" Susi's voice came from the greatroom, accompanied by the slow creak of the rocking chairs and the distinct slurp of her father drinking tea before bed.

"I'm home." Wynne shrugged off her coat and hung it on its peg as the evening danced across her thoughts. Laughing around Omri and Lara's table. Hand holding. Dancing. Declarations of love. She'd never kissed anyone before. Not like that. She finally understood why people liked it so much.

She tried to give herself another moment, allowing her cheeks to resume their natural color. She focused, working up her courage. With a steadying breath, she squared her shoulders and entered the room to face her parents.

"How was your time?" Susi glanced up and cocked an eyebrow. "You're wearing a look. What's funny?"

"Nothing." Wynne wrung her fingers and bit her lip as she drew closer. "Pops? What do you think about Kal?"

Susi's fingers stilled over her knitting.

Elric picked a tea leaf out of his cup. "He's diligent in his work and gets on well with others."

When Elric lifted his gaze, his expression slid to one of apprehension. The tell-tale, *Is this going where I think it's going?*

"What do you think about calling for a dinner with him?" Wynne said.

Susi's spine went poker straight. Her eyes jumped from Wynne to Elric with excitement.

Elric spoke carefully. "By dinner...?"

Wynne took a breath. "Yes. That kind of dinner."

58

Harek wasn't sure how long it'd been. Not anymore. Not precisely. The chill in the air betrayed the death of summer. Wynne's day of birth would be around this time. It would be the second he'd missed since leaving for the Gren. She'd be eighteen this year.

Homesickness lodged against his chest. His thoughts tracked back in time to the Harvest Festival when she first held his hand. He was twelve years old.

The imagination of young men was sometimes given to ludacris audacity where girls were concerned. This usually took the form of interpreting stronger interest than what matched reality, or believing there was a chance when none existed. Harek's awareness of this propensity came, first, from being a male himself, and second, from watching Eoin, along with their two older sisters who were happy to set the poor guy straight.

Harek was a hopeful guy, but he harbored no delusions about Wynne. They'd always been friendly, but Wynne was an elder's daughter. That was that.

He'd noticed her skipping along the periphery of the hall. She was the sort of lively girl who'd take to muddy fields for a wild game of tag wearing a dress. She might be mucking a stall or clomping through the half-melted slush on her way to the market, but by golly, she was going to look pretty while she did.

She drew up to a knot of other girls her age. Harek knew they were her sometimes-friends, though less and less as time progressed. He didn't know the reasons. The dynamic between girls was far more complicated than necessary. In the crowded hall, raucous with celebration, he heard little more than the garbled chirp of their exchange. Still, he caught the looks on the girls' faces which betrayed a measure of disdain. Like Wynne had interrupted their circle. Not outright mean, but enough to let her know she was being punished in the cool, distant manner girls sometimes used against each other.

Wynne stiffened, squared her shoulders, and raised her chin. She flounced away from them with a forced dignity to hide the hurt feelings or keep her temper in check. It could've been either. She made it a quarter of the way around the hall when she spotted Harek. Her demeanor changed instantly.

"Harek!" Mean girls forgotten, she rushed forward with a genuine smile in her eyes and her face full of question. As much as Harek liked this, it made him nervous. She grabbed his hand and tugged gently as she shifted course toward the center of the hall.

Harek's heart skipped. *She's touching me.* The happy thought rang in his mind like a resounding bell. Immediately taken over by the feckless confidence which befell his male kinsmen, he found himself standing taller, smiling reflexively, and allowing himself to be led.

"Come dance with me," she said.

"Dance?"

His spark of confidence died, reborn as a jolt of panic. His knees locked up. It took Wynne another step to realize she wasn't trailing a willing participant.

She looked askance at him. "Yes. Dance. You know." She gave a little goofy wiggle to demonstrate.

"I don't really dance..."

"Bosh."

"No, really."

"You could." She thought for a moment. "Please?"

"Don't you bat your eyes at me, Wynne Thar."

Her eyes fell to their still-clasped hands. "Then why are you still holding my hand?"

Harek's cheeks burned, but he didn't dare let her go. "Well...alright. One dance."

She beamed and tugged him along without further ado.

Harek didn't like recalling the specifics of that dance. There was a good bit of awkward shifting back and forth. He wasn't sure what to do with his hands. It was enough to prompt him to take refuge in the back courtyard, far away from such festivities, to avoid embarrassing himself. Enough to make him realize he needed some help if he ever worked up the nerve to dance again.

Finnion appeared in Harek's peripheral, which brought an immediate end to Harek's reminiscing. He crouched with a dish of food in one hand – the leftover meat from a pikdeer snared the day before. He rested the bowl in the dirt and laid his knife across his knees.

The same knife that killed their friends.

The same knife used to carve up Luka.

Finnion saw Harek looking at it. He gave a single slow shake of the head.

Harek dipped his chin once in understanding. He offered his wrists.

Finnion untied them, but left the rest of him bound. He uttered the string of coarse, unintelligible words Harek heard whenever meal time came. Harek's tongue and throat loosened, and he found that he could speak again.

Finnion passed the dish to Harek without a word. He settled to watch Harek eat, knife within arms reach.

Harek took a bite and chewed.

Finnion waited, alert but with an unfocused quality which gave the impression he wasn't in full command of himself. He looked ragged. Since taking Harek captive, he'd made no effort to rid the mats from his hair. He smelled awful. Harek was no better.

Unlike Harek, Finnion was growing increasingly gaunt. His eyes possessed a sunken quality which emphasized the skeletal structure of his face. His hands and arms had taken a sinewy appearance.

They never ate together. Harek rarely saw him eat at all.

Harek swallowed the flavorless meat. "Where's yours?"

"No talking," Finnion said in his own voice. "You know the rule."

"You don't look well. Did you eat?"

Finnion's muscles tensed. He shook his head, a single violent snap, and the shrill, reedy voice burst from his mouth. "*Make him quiet!*"

The gravelly voice followed. *"He disobeys. Cut his tongue out."*

"No! He will bleed to death. We need him whole. We need him strong."

Harek's blood chilled. Marshaling his courage, he looked Finnion full in the face. Whatever light once existed behind Finnion's eyes was gone – not extinguished, but suppressed.

Harek spoke, addressing the voice. "Why do you need me strong?"

Finnion turned his head toward Harek. A wide grin crawled across his face. The laugh started slow in the weedling tone, and built.

Harek shoved aside the creeping sensation and hardened himself. "I'm talking to you!"

Abruptly, Finnion grabbed his knife and stood. The blade hand hung loosely at his side. His expression and voice returned to normal.

"Eat up," he said without feeling and turned away.

59

Kal approached and laid a hand on Wynne's back. She grinned up at him, and he leaned down to kiss her cheek. Wynne blushed as he climbed onto the bench at her side. She caught a tightlipped little smile from Lara across the table.

"I hope I'm not interrupting," he said as he settled himself.

"No, no," Lara said. "I was just about to go find...to get...Catreeny. Excuse me." She abandoned them with a subtle wink at Wynne, and slipped into the crowd which filled the meeting hall for the Harvest Festival.

Kal leaned closer to be heard over the music and dancing nearby. "Your father invited me to a special dinner four days from now."

Wynne's eyes brightened. "He asked?"

"Did you put him up to it?" He gave her a look. "Be honest."

"And if I did?"

"Then I approve. I didn't realize one kiss could have that effect. I would've done it sooner."

"Behave yourself." She gave him a playful nudge. His hand slipped around her waist and he kissed her cheek again. She would've enjoyed it more if not for the look she drew from Ned Goodhill's wife. A small wave of embarrassment rushed over her.

It's just a little affection. It's fine.

"Tell me how a wedding goes around here," Kal said.

"You've been to Omri's."

"As a guest."

"Usually the ceremony is held here. The community comes together to show their support and share in the happiness."

"From what I hear, an engagement can be rather brief."

Wynne hummed in the affirmative. "Could be days or weeks. Some folks officiate the wedding the same night as a dinner."

"You don't say."

"They can't be bothered to wait."

"How do you feel about that?"

Wynne studied his face and bit her lip, keenly aware of the warmth and pressure of his body close beside hers. "I see the appeal."

A pleasant, loaded silence settled between them. A brazen idea entered her mind. She rose. "Follow me."

Surprise and intrigue entered his expression. "Where?"

Feeling mature and little rebellious, Wynne swiped a candle in a jar from one of the tables and led the way swiftly and unobtrusively to the back rooms situated in a wing running between the open space of the meeting hall and the courtyard out back. The corridor was empty, with folks enjoying the music and feasting inside, or socializing outdoors. She chose an unlocked closet at random. Kal glanced over his shoulder. Finding the way clear, he drew closer and followed her in.

It was cramped. Boards leaned against one wall, with casks and crates stacked at various heights. She rested the candle atop the nearest barrel.

She threw her arms around his neck and kissed him without reserve.

Kal's hands traveled to the front of her dress where he picked at the tie over her heart. She hummed in the negative and rested her fingers over his to stop him.

"No?" he said.

"No."

"Okay."

"It's four days."

"It feels like four years."

"I know." She pressed her lips against his again.

✧

The latch on the door clattered. Wynne's heart jumped out of her body. She pulled away from Kal as light flooded the room. The noise of the feasting and merriment grew precipitously louder as the door flew open.

"Oh, heavens!" Pia's shrill voice sent a second jolt through Wynne.

Kal removed his hand from her leg, grabbed her by the waist, and shifted her off his knee so she was sitting beside him. It was a tight fit atop the square crate. He leaned forward, clasping his hands before him, and shot a scathing look toward the door. "What is it?"

"Wynne, what do you think you're doing?" Pia demanded. "This is not the place!"

"Thank you for that," Kal said. "You can leave now."

Pia huffed. Her eyelids fluttered with indignation, then she left them with the door hanging open.

Wynne pushed the wisps of hair away from her forehead, catching her breath. The music from the hall took a pause as one song came to an end and the next began.

Simone appeared in the open doorway. She didn't look at all surprised to find Kal and Wynne here.

"Back hall again? Must be your favorite place." Simone shook her head in mock disapproval. She turned her attention to Wynne. "Well, you know where to look for him if he ever goes missin'." The corner of her mouth hiked up. "Probably won't be alone."

The mean glint in her eye intensified.

Wynne gritted her teeth. Her cheeks burned. Before she could respond, Simone departed with a swish of red hair.

Wynne turned to Kal. "What was she talking about?"

Kal rubbed his hand over his hair. He wouldn't quite meet her eyes.

A new uneasiness settled down upon her.

"Kal," she said, firmer.

He hesitated. Resigned, he assumed the expression of someone who'd tasted something bad. "She and I kissed in the back hall at the tavern –"

Wynne's brow bent. "When?"

"A long time ago. Before you and I."

"When?"

"A few weeks after I got here. I was working on the boarding house. It was the day it got finished, actually. You and I argued."

His showy log-chopping returned to Wynne and lit a fire inside her. "Did you suggest to her that she come by to see you work that day?"

"No," he said, sounding affronted. "I didn't say a word to her. She showed up at the tavern."

"Then threw herself at you?"

"Pretty much."

"Pretty much? Cut the vaguery, Kal."

Kal turned up his palms. "What is it you want to know?"

"Tell me what happened."

He released a controlled sigh which made Wynne think his reluctance was equal parts the desire to spare her feelings and save himself the discomfort. "She sat beside me at the bar. Introduced herself. Asked if I wanted to go somewhere. I took her to the back hall and kissed her."

"Is that all you did?"

"Yes."

"Then what?"

"Then I put a stop to it and went back to the boarding house."

"Alone?"

"Yes, alone." His face tightened and the first marks of frustration entered his voice. "Let me remind you, Wynne, you wanted nothing to do with me at the time."

"Is that supposed to make me feel better? This is the first I'm hearing of

338

this – and from Simone, no less. Not you. It makes me look and feel like an utter fool."

"I'm sorry. You're right. I should've told you sooner."

"If there's anything else I ought to know, you need to tell me now."

"I'm not hiding from you, Wynne," he said. "I haven't gone back to the tavern, or spoken more than two words to her since."

"Well, you certainly left a lasting impression." Wynne jabbed toward the open doorway. "Apparently we both have an enemy now, no thanks to you."

"No thanks to me? What about you?" he said, his voice sharper. "Yes, I did what I did, but I didn't know at the time how much she hated you. What did you do to her?"

"I didn't do anything!"

"You must've done something. When she approached me that night, she said, *Wait until Wynne hears about this. Don't worry, she can't please a man like I can.*"

Wynne's stomach flopped.

"Isn't it obvious she wanted to get at you?"

Wynne knew about having enemies. All Baldomar did. This was different. It was personal. She always thought she was above petty venom and social strife. That she couldn't really be touched.

She was wrong.

Kal's voice, still firm and direct, interrupted her jumping, flustered thoughts. "Funny, you never never asked why I left."

"Why did you –?"

"Because of you."

Her mouth tightened into an angry frown.

"I knew then that I wanted to be with you. I wanted to be a man worthy of your respect, so I got out of there. I've never been unfaithful to you, Wynne."

Disheartened, Wynne's forehead sank into her hand. She was quiet for a long moment. "How are we ever supposed to work?"

"What is that supposed to mean?"

"Look at us." She lifted her head from her hands. "Arguing. Always arguing about something."

"And?"

"I don't like it."

"Yeah, I don't like it either. I'd rather be enjoying your lips right now." He grabbed her hand and some of the hardness in his voice and expression broke. "I still care about you. I still love you. An argument certainly don't change that I want to be with you. Does it change it for you?"

Wynne felt chastened, but touched. She softened her posture and her voice. "...No."

"I love you," he said, calmer and earnest.

"I love you too."

They shared a tender look for a beat and he moved in for a kiss. She stopped him with a finger to his lips. "That does not mean this continues. It means we survive to kiss another day."

Kal grunted, which pulled a smirk from Wynne.

"We need to get back out there."

60

The rumor mill went to work immediately. Wynne caught the glances and whispers. It was one matter to be the object of gossip, but this was new territory. Part of her wanted to crawl under a rock in shame. She did her utmost to harden herself against the sting.

It shouldn't matter. She hadn't lost her dignity. *Let them be jealous.*

She stayed close to Kal for the rest of the evening, lest Simone acquire any lofty ideas about what she'd accomplished. Though news spread of their upcoming dinner, it was difficult to feel as happy as she ought.

When they replenished their plates at the food tables, Wynne turned her attention to the hall. She located Elric in some sort of serious conversation with Lugh, which might've been anything. She caught the loaded expressions from young women who'd been staring a moment earlier and only just turned away to whisper to their friends. She spotted Pia conversing with Fay.

Kal read her discomfort as he passed her a pint. "What's wrong?"

"People know."

"About what?"

"Our activity in the back room."

"And?"

"I have a bad feeling my folks are going to hear about it before the night's over."

Kal thought for a beat. "Will it impact the dinner?"

"I don't think so. Still, they're not going to be pleased."

"What do you want to do?"

"Leave."

"We can't leave. It makes us look guilty."

We are guilty. Wynne searched his face. "What do you think we should do?"

"Stay and enjoy the rest of the night. If it comes up, we'll deal with it," he said. "What's the worst thing anyone can say? *Two people about to marry were kissin' in the back room?* I guarantee you, most folks here did a whole lot more than that in their day."

If that's what he thought, he still had a lot to learn about Baldomar customs. "Don't know about that."

Micha swept past them. She wouldn't even look at Wynne. It sent a stab of guilt – a different kind of guilt – through her.

Kal stepped in closer and looked her straight in the eye with affection. "Stop worrying."

✧

"Heavens, Wynne. What were you thinking?" Susi said when the family returned to the Thar house late that evening.

"It was only a kiss," Wynne said as diplomatically as possible.

"They said his hands were all over you." Elric kept his volume down for sleeping Jai's sake, which made his voice more of a low, forceful rumble. "My gods, Wynne. It was the middle of the festival. Have you no restraint?"

Something stronger than embarrassment washed over Wynne in the face of Elric's disappointment.

"Your father is an elder," Susi said. "He could officiate after the dinner, if you really couldn't wait until a big wedding."

Wynne didn't appreciate insulations about her lack of self-control. She squared her shoulders and dug in. "So we're not allowed to kiss until we're married? Tell me, which married folks in the whole Enclave haven't done the same thing before their wedding?"

"You are missing the point, Wynne."

"Am I?"

Susi shook her head. "First Omri, now you..."

"What do you mean, first Omri, now me?"

"We're not discussing that."

"You disapprove of who we want to marry that much?"

"Enough," Elric said.

Thick, heavy tension settled like a smothering blanket over the room. Elric appeared to grow in size. Wynne could only wonder what he was thinking, but he seemed to be getting increasingly upset with each passing moment.

"Fine," Wynne said, regaining her calm and mustering some dignity. She hated this. She wanted to move toward peace so she could go to bed. "Perhaps the meeting hall wasn't the wisest choice – "

"The place is not the issue," Elric said. "Kal not your husband. Not yet. A half-dozen folks made comments to your mother and I about your unbecomin' behavior tonight. I'm embarrassed of you."

The words stung, and Wynne fought against a rush of tears. Cheeks burning, she stuck out her chin. "He's going to be my husband."

Elric said nothing and shook his head, which was worse.

"Wynne, have you considered how you're going to feel when you go out and face the village after you've shamed yourself this way?" Susi said. "We taught you better than this *for a reason*. We don't want that for you."

"For me? You sure it's not about you and your reputation?" she said.

"Wynne."

"Tell me I'm wrong."

"Do not speak to your mother that way –"

Wynne opened her mouth to argue but Elric cut her off again. "That is my wife."

Wynne shut her mouth.

Elric gestured toward the hall. "You're actin' like a fool. I've had enough of you for tonight. Go."

Wynne clenched and unclenched her hands. Furious. Hurt. Humiliated. Too proud to accept any truth in her parents' words.

In four days, it wouldn't matter. She and Kal could skip the large ceremony if they wanted, then she wouldn't be Elric's problem. She'd be Kal's wife. What was the worst anyone could say then? The whole messy ordeal would blow over.

She gathered herself to go to her room. She made a concerted effort to carry herself with dignity rather than indulge her injured pride and flounce away like a petulant child. "To answer your question, Mother, I suppose I'll get a good idea when I'm out on the rounds tomorrow."

✧

Wynne lied awake far longer than she liked. Apart from the argument with her parents and the indignity of being the object of gossip, a bud of jealousy had bloomed within her over Kal and Simone. She hated it.

Kal was right – Wynne wanted nothing to do with him at the time, which undercut her right to feel betrayed. He'd also walked away from temptation for Wynne – before they were a pair. She didn't take that lightly.

It still bothered her deeply, leaving her with a disquieted aggravation she struggled to shake. Back then, she suspected he'd move on quickly if she didn't give him what he wanted. She felt like she'd been proven right. What might happen the next time they got into a serious argument?

She reminded herself that Kal was a better man now than he was. She mostly believed it.

Simone was another matter. She'd probably seen them slip away, then directed Pia to the back hall with the intent of exposing them and ensuring everyone heard about it.

It was the parting remark which dug under Wynne's skin like a thorn.

She reasoned that Simone hadn't told anyone about the tavern. Wynne would've heard about it by now. Simone might want to stir up trouble for Kal, but there was no way for Simone to share the story without making herself look like a jilted hussy. It would accomplish nothing except to mutually damage their reputations.

Her remarks certainly exposed her to Wynne, but that was a worthwhile gamble. They carried the reward of driving a potential wedge between Wynne and Kal. Simone also knew Wynne wouldn't smear her throughout the village. If she succeeded in sabotaging Wynne and Kal, Wynne could never state the real reason without making herself look like a naive fool. *You fell for the chancer who almost bedded another woman.*

It was a masterful vengeance, made more impactful by the step toward marriage they were about to undertake.

Wynne wondered how long Simone had been looking for an opportunity to shame her or punish Kal. They were far from friends these days, though it still felt like a betrayal. It left Wynne longing for satisfaction, and feeling completely impotent. She could imagine Tess pulling Simone outside by her hair and giving her something to cry about if Simone dared to come after Skeggis. But Wynne wasn't Tess, and Kal wasn't Skeggis, and in Wynne's position, there was little she could do beyond continuing toward a happy future with Kal, defiantly proving Simone wrong. *Your plan failed, you conniving hussy.*

Wynne wondered how long she'd need to keep looking over her shoulder for Simone, or someone like her. She could imagine Simone getting drunk and flapping her lips at the wedding feast just to mar their day.

She'd always imagined a grand wedding celebration, surrounded by friends, family, and the support of the whole community. In light of everything tonight, perhaps it was best to accept they weren't going to have a big ceremony.

That was fine. The party wasn't the point anyway.

Four more days, she told herself as she finally drifted off. *Four more days.*

61

A vicious wind tore across the landscape, unhindered by trees or hilly banks. It forced the tall grasses to ripple and lie prone. It bit into Harek's chapped skin. His eyes watered. The sky was a colorless drab. He hadn't seen a bird in days, much less any living thing apart from Finnion. It made him uneasy. It seemed unnatural. The Heartlands were reputedly rich with fertile soil and large, roaming game – the designated neutral hunting ground for dragons, any time of year. He hadn't seen any dragons overhead either.

In the distance, a mound rose on the horizon like a slumbering giant beneath its covers, interrupting the otherwise desolate expanse.

Harek knew before he glanced over his shoulder to confirm. Finnion plodded behind him – always behind him – a shell of a man. The gray pallor of his skin contrasted with the dark circles beneath his eyes. He looked exhausted. He'd been observing the distant hill in his bloodshot, unfocused manner until Harek's glance drew his attention. He tensed and gripped his knife tighter, as though he expected his bound prisoner to attempt something rash. His sunken features hardened. With a jerk of his chin, he indicated onward, toward the mound. "Keep moving."

It took hours to reach. As they drew closer, thorns and thistles replaced scrubby dull green or smooth golden of long grass awaiting the warmth of spring. Eventually, even this turned brown and black with decay.

A dark opening was cut into the hillside, bordered by masonry which indicated deliberate construction. Harek couldn't see inside. Finnion squatted nearby and produced a torch. He spent a few moments lighting it.

The dark maw pulled Harek's eye. He found it difficult to look away. He half expected a monster to crawl out of the shadow the moment he did. The wind howled, making him imagine whispers from within the opening.

There were practical reasons for seeking shelter in weather like this. Survival, for one. But Harek didn't want to go inside. It wasn't even his distaste for close quarters with Finnion. A different kind of darkness hung about this place which made the hair on the back of his arms prickle. Paranoia perhaps, but after what he'd seen and heard from Finnion, he was beyond dismissing the worst possibilities.

The torch blazed to life.

Finnion stood and planted himself beside the stonework. Light in one hand, knife in the other. "Go in."

Again, he made Harek walk ahead of him.

As Harek stepped inside, an oppressive darkness seemed to swallow him. It was heavy. Consuming. Devoid of hope.

His eyes struggled to adjust as he shuffled forward. He struggled to breathe. A silent wordless prayer rose in his chest.

Then, he felt the full weight of the dark lessen. It was still there, allowed to press against him. But not to crush him. It was restrained. He had no explanation, yet he knew it as sure as he knew his right from his left. A spark of encouragement settled against his heart.

The dirty floor sloped downward. Torchlight at Harek's back cast jumpy shadows over the passage. Eventually depictions adorned the surrounding surfaces.

Horrific depictions.

Monsters covered the walls and ceiling. They were shaped like men, though disproportionately muscular. Curved horns protruded from their skulls. Their mouths gaped in a silent roar, full of jagged teeth like glass shards. Their eyes were solid black.

The mural melded from portraits to a scene. In it, a progression of humans, elves, and orcs lined up to serve the vile creatures.

Further on, another scene. Men, women, and children were chained together while servants marched them toward an altar. There, a masked figure stood with a knife raised over a man. Droplets of blood ran down a stone slab into the earth, where the same evil-looking monsters danced, mouths open to relish the blood of the innocent.

In the next scene, one hellish creature from the abyss was drawn up into the body of the man on the altar. He arose, body restored and visibly stronger than the victims behind. His eyes were solid black.

The corridor opened up into a vast space. Harek's feet stalled as the torchlight behind revealed a descending set of steps. Finnion drew up close. He uttered a horrid string of indecipherable words. At once, sconces throughout the chamber ignited.

Harek took in the room with a press of dread. There were only three steps down, which circled the entire area. Carved stone pillars supported the high ceiling and were staggered throughout the space. An altar rose in the center of the open lower floor. Black smears stained the stone.

This was the end.

Finnion grabbed Harek by the arm and directed him forward. Harek's knees locked, and he braced to resist. He knew refusal to cooperate might earn him a knife between his shoulder blades. He'd rather meet the knife here, at the top of the stairs, than on that altar.

There were things worse than death.

Finnion's inhuman strength was an afterthought. He tightened his grip and half-pushed, half-dragged Harek down the steps. Harek lost his footing, and tumbled, taking Finnion with him.

The next moments were a chaotic, crushing tangle of arms, elbows, and knees. Harek fought, bound though he was, to escape Finnion's grasp.

Don't do this thing!

He tried to cry out.

He made no sound.

Finnion struggled to his feet. With a roar, he grabbed Harek by the shirt and hauled him upright. Harek tried to pull away, and failed. Finnion thrust him toward the altar. Harek stumbled forward, and hit the stone slab with his upper torso. He twisted around, not wanting his back turned.

Then Finnion was upon him, trying to wrestle him onto the altar with one hand. In the other, he held the knife.

He raised his blade, and brought it down hard.

62

Elric and Susi were quiet over breakfast. Neither were cold or spoke harshly to Wynne. It was like they felt no need to punish her with another diatribe. Like they knew she'd experience enough punishment socially.

It was difficult to tell whether the loaded glances she received from her neighbors were imbibed with real judgment, or imagined. Catreeny said nothing, which was either a miracle or indicative that Wynne was in her own head. She went about her work, grateful for the distraction.

One of the boarding houses was home to a new set of refugees, mostly from the Austerholt area. Wynne was more than a little curious to see what the people of Kal's homeland were like. Most of them hadn't attended the festival and were ignorant of the gossip.

A reprieve.

Wynne found three women in good spirits around a small cookfire. The eldest appeared a decade beyond middle-age. The other two were in their twenties. Of these, the younger was pregnant and busy scrubbing rags in a bucket. The other played with her dark-haired young son who'd made it his purpose to investigate the drips of water splashing over the side of the flume running by. The boy pressed his hand into the mud, squished it around, and then waddled toward his mother to show her. She made a silly face, and he broke into a belly laugh that brought smiles to Wynne and the other women.

"G'mornin', dearie," the oldest woman said as Wynne approached with a basket of bread and clean socks. "Wot can I help yeh with?"

Wynne introduced herself. She indicated the basket on her hip. "I've got bread, and I've got socks."

"Well, we got mouths, and we got feet," the older lady said with a laugh. "Many thanks. I'm Helena." She gestured toward the pregnant woman. "My daughter, Blaike. That's Isolde."

The woman with the little boy flashed a palm and her striking blue eyes creased into a smile.

Wynne crouched to wave at the boy. "Who's this little guy?"

"My son, Kalomir." Isolde scooped him into a hug, heedless of his muddy fingers. He squirmed as she planted a kiss on his chubby cheek.

Wynne's smile slipped. She cocked her head. "What did you say?"

"His name is Kalomir."

"Is that a common name where you're from?"

"No. It was his father's name. Why do you ask?"

Wynne's stomach clenched. It felt like all the energy leached from her body, through the soles of her feet, into the earth.

Isolde...from Austerholt. Oh gods.

Her eyes went unfocused on the grass as she tried to orient herself and regain her bearing.

Coincidence. Don't jump to conclusions.

Wynne glanced at the little boy and saw Kal in the dark hair and the chestnut-brown eyes which tipped upward in the corner when he grinned. She met Isolde's face again and realized there was an unanswered question still hanging between them. She forced a polite smile. "Excuse me."

✧

Wynne found Susi at the cart conversing with Catreeny, Verelle, and Pia. Jairus and Pia's youngest daughter dashed through the grass nearby in a game of chase. As Wynne hurried toward the cart, she noticed the stiffening in Pia's posture. She looked down her long nose at Wynne in the same chilly, distant demeanor she'd reserved for Wynne all day. As though she thought she might catch shame by association if she wasn't careful to demonstrate disapproval.

Wynne tried to avoid eye contact with her and resisted the impulse for a rude gesture. She angled her body away from the others to address Susi discreetly. "Mum. I need to go. I can't finish."

Concern swept over Susi. "What's wrong?"

Wynne dropped her voice further. "I feel like I'm going to be sick."

True enough.

Susi studied her, brows knit. "Should we call for Sender?"

"No. It won't help," Wynne said in a hurry. "I just need to go."

✧

Wynne rocked back and forth on her feet as she waited for Kal to answer his door. He smiled when he saw her, which made doubts unfurl in her mind. *It couldn't be. You're overreacting. He wouldn't lie to you. Why would you even bring this up?*

"Can I come in?" she said.

A nudge of concern entered his expression. "What's wrong?"

Wringing her hands, Wynne stepped through the low door, into the dimly lit space which was to be their home. It was cozier and more comfortable than the last time she saw it. She didn't have the wherewithal to fully appreciate his improvements. She turned to face him as he shut the door.

"Isolde – that was the woman's name?"

Kal processed the question for a beat before Wynne identified the tug of remembrance behind the eyes. "Yes." He watched her carefully, with equal desire to figure out where this was coming from and avoid another telling about the woman who ruined his life. "Why? You seem upset."

"She's here. She has a little boy named Kalomir, named for his father. He's two or three years old."

Kal looked like he'd been smacked. "What?"

"He looks just like you."

Kal's breathing ticked up and his eyes went unfocused. He rubbed the back of his neck as he collected his thoughts. "Are you sure?"

"What do you mean, am I sure? Do you think I'd make this up?"

Dumbstruck, he pushed the hair away from his forehead. He said nothing.

Wynne searched his face for deceit, fearing the worst. "Kal, did you leave your family?"

"No! How can you ask that? I know what that's like – I'd never do that to my child."

"Then how do you explain this?"

Kal said nothing.

Wynne stayed rooted to spot as he moved with purpose across the room. "Where are you going?"

Halfway to the door, he stopped and turned back to her. "To get to the bottom of this. Wait here. Please."

63

Wynne waited forty five minutes while every torturous possibility ran through her head. She believed Kal when he said he didn't abandon his son. At least, she believed that he believed that. Given his history, perhaps it was more probable than she wanted to admit.

She felt blindsided. Foolish. What else had she ignored, swept up by him and her own feelings?

At this point, telling herself it was a coincidence felt like a stretch. He'd had a lover named Isolde. She called the boy a son of Kalomir. The timing and the age of the child fit Kal's story of what transpired.

Any one of those might be a coincidence, by itself. Together, not so much.

Someone wasn't telling the truth.

She blew out a shaky breath.

She decided the best case scenario was *misunderstanding*. Maybe Wynne saw a resemblance that wasn't there.

Or maybe Isolde claimed her boy was a son of Kalomir because she had to pick someone. She might've been guessing. The father could be anyone.

It was still problematic. It was easy to imagine all the reasons why she might stick to her story, whether she believed it or not. Especially considering who Kal was now or what she thought he had to offer. If she went around falsely claiming her child was Kal's son, it would besmirch his reputation, his standing, and his opportunities in the community. And by association, Wynne's.

They were just about to marry. This was how they started their life together – with another woman trying to elbow her way back into Kal's life? With humiliation and more indignity to live down?

This sort of thing didn't happen around here.

Wynne paced as her line of thinking turned inward.

She could've picked anyone. She chose the man open to accusation given his less-than-noble past.

Because he was willing to bear with her, despite her fears.

Because Harek wasn't interested anymore.

Because she loved him.

She gazed over the home he'd made for them to share. She could picture herself here into the future. Working and laughing. Eating together. Loving each other. Growing old. Maybe even raising a child.

All of it dangled by a thread.

✧

Wynne flew to the door when Kal returned. She searched his face. "What happened?"

He met her eyes briefly. "Sit with me."

We should sit for this usually wasn't a good sign, but she managed to temporarily suspend her conclusions. Cold dread hummed around inside her as she followed him to the bed. They sank to the edge and he took her hand. Somber, he nodded.

It felt like the foundation of the earth pitched. "Are you sure?"

"I got little doubt."

The world seemed to spin around her. She drew a deep, steadying breath.

"She said she never took it – the poison. She was going to, but had a change of heart after I left."

"You believe her? After what she did to you?"

"I've seen the boy, Wynne."

"Is there any chance she's mistaken? She got pregnant by someone else?" It made her feel like a reprobate, wishing for this, but it had to be said.

"I asked." He shook his head.

It was quiet for a long moment. The happy future she imagined slipped through her fingers like sand.

Kal rubbed his face. "I feel like a wretch. My son hasn't known me. I'm just like my father."

"You're not." She gripped his hand tighter.

"I didn't know."

"I believe you. But now you do."

He nodded.

"Kal," she said softly. "I can't marry you."

He stiffened, looking wounded and stunned. "You don't want me anymore?"

"That's not it – "

"Look. I know that this isn't what you bargained for, but it don't change how I feel about you." Kal angled toward her and took both her hands in his. "I want to spend the rest of my life with you. We'll get through this. We'll figure it out. I'm willing –"

"You have a child with this woman." Wynne's voice was firmer. "By Baldomar standards, you're already married to her."

"That's not how it works."

"That's how it works here." Tears rushed to her eyes and her throat thickened painfully. She pressed ahead, feeling like she was being shorn in two. "You need to bring Isolde into your home. Forgive her. Raise your son together."

"Wynne –"

"You owe it to her." Though forceful, she was unable to keep the choked quality out of her voice. "Be there for your family."

Kal stared at her. For once, at a loss for words.

Wynne took her hands back. She swiped the liquid pooling at the corner of her eye and stood abruptly. "I'll talk to my father about calling off the dinner."

With a touch, Kal stopped her before she traveled to the door. "Wait. Can we take a breath?" He stood to better face her.

It hurt to look at him. It took everything she had to keep herself together in that moment. "I can't stay."

"I love you."

She tried to keep the tears in and failed. Forcing a weak smile, she reached out to touch his cheek. "You need to love your son."

✦

Wynne didn't remember the walk home.

It felt like she was standing outside herself, passing through a dream as a ghost. She drifted to her bedroom, collapsed atop her bed, and cried until she fell asleep.

64

Wynne wasn't at home when Kal came by the next day to explain matters to Elric. Despite what she told Kal about talking to her father, she hadn't done it. Unable to face her family with the news, she'd remained in bed the rest of the day and slipped out the next morning before sunup, well before the house was awake. The loneliness of the woods did nothing to nurse the cavernous ache threatening to consume her. The events turned over in her thoughts repeatedly, as if searching for some way to remedy the situation.

Only a remedy didn't exist. Kal had another family. There was no going back. That was that.

Partway through her watch, she started to worry about her parents continuing to act under the assumption of normalcy. She could imagine Susi making a plan for how to decorate the table or what foods she and Elric would offer for the dinner that wouldn't happen. She could visualize Elric mentioning the event to an inquisitive neighbor in the course of casual conversation.

A deep anxious regret settled inside her. She spent the rest of her watch agonizing over how to broach the subject with her parents and set them straight. How they'd react was anyone's guess.

When Wynne returned home in the afternoon, all she wanted was to crawl back in bed and wait for it to stop hurting.

Instead, Elric met her at the door.

One look, and she knew that he knew. It took everything in her power to keep from crumbling, utterly humbled before him.

He strode forward with no hesitation and crushed her in a fatherly hug.

She remembered clinging to Elric in tears as a little girl. The instances were many and varied, but the one which rushed to the forefront was the aftermath of learning what happened to the family she'd been born to. How those same strong arms held her and comforted her. How he reassured her that she was always wanted. That she'd always be his daughter.

When Elric spoke, his voice was a low, gentle rumble over the top of her head. "Daughter of mine, I'm sorry."

She scrunched her face to pinched back the wave of emotion. She swallowed the lump rising in her throat. "He came by?"

"He did."

Wynne said nothing for a beat. "Are you upset with me?"

"No."

"Was he upset with me?"

"No. He asked me to tell you he's sorry."

Wynne said nothing.

"I don't know how much you want me to say on the matter, but I don't want it comin' as a shock when you see," Elric said. "He says he's goin' to try to do right by the woman and his son. Says you encouraged him to."

Wynne said nothing.

"I'm proud of you for that."

She threw herself at her father's chest a second time and held tight.

✧

The day that would've been the dinner came and went. Wynne traded a watch with Roran, who was all too happy to give up his overnight, no catch. At the time, she'd convinced herself that a night of solitude in the woods would be preferable to sitting at home, being reminded of what wasn't happening.

She'd been wrong.

She wondered how long it would take for Kal to get over his feelings for her so he could fully love his family. She supposed it would be better for him the quicker he did. She tried to keep her mind from straying to what they might be doing right now.

She wondered if they'd be happy.

She shed enough tears in the lookout blind to know she'd have a throbbing headache and bloodshot eyes come morning. She didn't care. The thread holding her world together had unraveled on her. She thought she'd seen matters for what they were, and she'd been wrong. The future she'd envisioned. The good man who loved her. Even her idea of who he was. It was gone. She wasn't sure what to call it besides some form of grief.

Eventually the tears stopped. Her thoughts turned, as they always did, to Harek. For all his flaws, he'd never fooled around with another woman or started a family he didn't know about. Wynne dried her eyes on her scarf with a derisive snort. *That's my standard now?*

Her mind sloshed over the stack of letters in her room, to the man he'd grown into, and the gradual slide that brought the quiet.

The heaviness of regret threatened to floor her.

Her sweet friend.

She missed him with an ache too deep for words.

65

A small cart trundled behind Isolde's stout, undersized donkey, holding her belongings. An iron pot. Blankets. A few articles of clothing. A lamp. They turned up the worn path to Kal's door without speaking.

There'd been a discussion. Several discussions. About the customs surrounding marriage and family here. About his activities of late. About hers.

Their son.

How Kal intended to care for them.

She took convincing, which discouraged and frustrated him more than he anticipated, and he had anticipated quite a bit. Even now, as she followed with their son on her hip, a tentative caution hung around her. It made the whole situation feel businesslike. Contractual. Like their arrangement – their little family – was bound up in duty more than love.

Kal supposed *duty* was one form love took, and he ought not to confuse *love* with *affection*. In any case, it was the form he was choosing – moment by moment – to lean into, in the faith that feelings of family bondedness would come later. It was all he had to give. It still felt like part of him had been ripped away, leaving a raw, gaping wound.

He hadn't seen or spoken to Wynne since that day. She was avoiding him. He couldn't blame her for that. Still, he wasn't sure whether this made things better or worse. He missed her. It felt surreal to be headed home with anyone else.

He glanced over his shoulder at Isolde – his wife now, apparently – and the boy. She'd let her pretty hair grow. It now fell to her waist. She offered him a small smile which made it difficult to remain dour. At her best, she was a sweet woman with a goofy sense of humor. It showed in the kid. During their conversations over the past week, he'd been continually reminded of it. As long as he did nothing stupid to prove her doubts correct, they'd probably get along fine.

"Stop the cart here," Kal said. "Leave the bags. I'll get them in a minute."

"I can help," she said.

"No, come see your house." It stung something behind his ribs to speak those words to anyone besides Wynne. He shifted the thoughts of her out of his mind with effort. Dwelling upon her wasn't going to make this easier.

He opened the door and gestured for Isolde and the boy to enter before him.

The tour was brief. He pointed as he spoke. "Food storage in the loft. Fire pit. I've been keeping my tool in the side room. There's space for yours, too and probably the donkey. Do you still spin flax?"

"I can, but I had to leave my equipment behind."

She hadn't elaborated on the details behind their decision to leave the village as abruptly as they had. Still, he'd heard enough to generate a deep appreciation that she'd protected their son. That tug returned to him, complicated by the guilt that he hadn't been there to help.

"We'll get you a spinning wheel. Whatever you need. You can keep it there, if you want." He shifted a few steps further inside and rapped his knuckles on the small, square table he'd built. "Don't got much of a kitchen, but here's shelves and a washbasin."

Isolde deposited the boy on the ground. He clung to her leg. When Kal offered him a smile, he hid his face in her skirt.

Kal refocused on Isolde. "I'm sorry, I've only got two chairs. I'll make a third."

"You don't need to apologize, Kalomir."

She always did use his full name. He'd forgotten how much he liked that.

He gestured to the four-poster and let his hand fall back to his side.

"There's the bed I made."

She looked twice.

"You made that?" She sounded impressed.

He dipped his chin. "It's warm with the curtains and wool blankets. Big enough to share. Or I can make a separate one for myself, if you prefer."

She said nothing. She stepped closer to investigate and touched the carved detailing of the post. The boy followed, grabbing the edge of her skirt. Upon noticing the soft heap of blankets, he released her. He threw himself at the side of the bed, bounced against it, and did it again.

"It's big," he said. "An' soft."

Another body-slam bounce.

Kal smirked. He ruffled his hair and lightened his tone. "I'm gonna make you a bed too."

The boy's eyes brightened. "A big un'?"

"One just the right size for you."

"What 'bout when I'm big?"

"Then I'll make you a bigger one."

"You're big. Big and stwong." Without warning, the kid threw himself at Kal's legs, wrapped his chubby arms around his knees, and hugged tight. "I wanna be big like you."

Kal's eyes crinkled into a smile. He was surprised by the tightness in the back of his throat. He bent, scooped the kid up, and hugged him back.

66

You can't avoid going out forever. You're going to have to see people. Wynne had been telling herself this for days, as if it would help prepare her to face the community. She'd been a recluse over the last week, so she could only speculate at the whisperings she knew were taking place.

Word had spread about her and Kal in the back room at the Harvest Festival. No surprise there. In hindsight, the ordeal framed her unfavorably, especially now that she wasn't going to marry him. While she didn't exactly carry the stigma of a jilted woman, everyone knew that Kal and Wynne had parted ways, and he'd gone straight into the arms of another woman.

Raisins. Wool. Salt.

Wynne set her shoulders, repeating her list to herself as she moved from market stall to stall under the critical eye of her neighbors. No one said anything overt, yet too many remained too distant to shrug off as simply the odd individual stuck in an unfriendly mood that day.

As she paid for a packet of raisins from Hanna, she caught the derisive murmuring of Hanna's elderly aunt coming from behind the stall, where she evidently thought Wynne couldn't hear her. "...Daughter of an elder, too good for our Baldomar men, and this is who she picks? Serves her right."

Hanna cast an uneasy glance over her shoulder and offered an apologetic look to Wynne. Another buyer sidled up, requiring attention. Hanna seemed relieved and jumped at the opportunity to help.

Wynne felt her cheeks grow hot, but she kept the ripple of pain from her expression. She shoved her purchase into her market basket, and snatched up her gloves. She could feel the other buyer's condemning gaze sweep over her. She raised her chin level with the ground and moved on with as much dignity as she could muster.

Vinegar. Beeswax. Tallow.

This last item drove her to the Jaegers, which she dreaded most of all. As she approached their lot, she recognized Paul the courier on the front porch. Micha dropped to her knees, sobbing. Leland clutched a letter, but he wasn't reading it. He was red in the face with restrained grief.

Wynne slowed and watched at a distance, feeling as though she'd been kicked in the chest by a horse. Paul offered condolences, turned away with a heavy face, and plodded toward the road. Noticing Wynne idling in the lane, something like sympathy or regret passed over him.

"Paul," she said when he drew up, fearing she already knew. "What's happened?"

✧

Wynne rushed home to find Jai playing in the yard, romping after the sheep in his bear form. She blew past the bear carving from Kal and burst into the house.

"Mum!" she cried. She dropped the market basket on the floor and rounded the corner to find Susi knitting furiously in her rocking chair. "Mum! Harek's dead."

Susi looked up from her stitches abruptly. "What?"

"He led a group to stop bandits targeting the supply train to the Gren – that's why he hasn't written. He's been away for months. He sent two men back to the Gren for more help – apparently they were successful – but when they came back to the place..." Her breath caught as a sob tried to escape. "They searched and found bloody clothes– and burned bodies."

Somberness swept over Susi. "That is very sad. I'm so sorry, Wynne." Her shoulders dipped and she took a breath as though steeling herself. "Why don't you come here so we can talk?"

There was a seriousness in her tone which prompted new concern with Wynne. "...About this?"

"About you."

Wynne hadn't been expecting that. She sank on the edge of the bench nearest Susi's rocking chair.

Susi took a breath and pressed ahead. "There are rumors going around. Specifically, that your story regarding your behavior during the festival was not true."

"Not true, how?"

"That you were caught in the act of..." Susi seemed embarrassed. "That you were caught in the act."

Wynne's expression bent in outrage as she caught her meaning. Her mind jumped to Pia, and she wondered whether she or someone else was responsible. "That's a lie."

"In addition to that, there's gossip that you've been sleeping with Kal for some time now, and that you're carrying his child."

"It's not true, Mother!"

"You've been seen leaving his house, alone."

Wynne started to refuse, then caught herself.

"Tell me you didn't, Wynne."

Wynne cringed inwardly. "I went inside once."

"When?"

"When I found out about Isolde."

"You told me you were sick."

Wynne said nothing. She remembered more. "Also, I stepped inside briefly – a few weeks ago."

"That's more than once, Wynne."

"He only wanted to show me what he was working on, then I left. Nothing happened."

Susi's forehead sank into her hand.

"Mother, I've never done anything apart from kiss him. Ever."

Susi was quiet for a long moment. When she lifted her head, there was a new fierceness about her. She set her knitting aside. "I believe you. I need to find your father right now."

Susi whisked from the room, leaving Wynne feeling brushed off during her time of distress. "You're leaving me?"

Susi reentered a moment later, wrapping a scarf around her neck. "Stay here. Keep watch over Jairus. I'm going to get to the bottom of this."

Wynne was tired of this direction. Still, the years had engendered a trust in Susi which Wynne could rely upon. She knew the look in her mother's eye. She'd seen it before. It was best not to ask questions or interfere at this time.

Left alone in the house, Wynne's thoughts jumped around, agonizing, as a new revelation dawned on her. *That's why I've been getting so many looks. Not because of how things ended with Kal – they think I've been foolin' around with him and got knocked up!*

A feral desire for confrontation rose within her, which Susi probably foresaw, hence the orders to stay put. It made Wynne want to scream, or punch a hole in the wall, or drop to her knees and weep.

She brought her hands to her head as the truth slammed into her and seeped in.

Everyone has probably heard this. My reputation is shot to pot. I'm used goods. No one's ever gonna want me.

Not even Harek.

Not that it mattered anymore. Harek was gone.

67

Lara met Wynne and Omri at the door, anxious. "Did you tell her?"

Wynne refrained from the obvious, but annoying, *Tell me what?* She was already miffed at Omri for summoning her to his house, which involved a walk through the village. It was bad enough trying to keep herself from unraveling at the memorium for Harek and the others two days earlier. Moreover, given her grief over Harek, the upheaval in her relationship with Kal, and the circulating rumors made all the stronger because they'd been interwoven with bits of truth, she didn't want to show her face in public. She'd much prefer to crawl under a rock and die. A stroll through town undermined that.

Yet, in the short time since her life upended, sides had been drawn. Tess stuck to Wynne like a burr. She made it a point to tell-off anyone she overheard repeating lies, even before confirming the truth with Wynne. *I didn't need you tell me,* she had explained. *I know you, Wynne. You'd never do somethin' like that.* She'd nearly came to blows with Bera in the market. While Wynne didn't want Tess to get herself in trouble, her loyalty meant more than Wynne could express.

Omri and Lara had done much the same, with less threat of violence. So when he showed up at the house and told her, *We need to talk,* she really couldn't refuse.

He and Lara passed a silent conversation, like Wynne witnessed in her parents countless times. Omri jerked his head toward the table and chairs. "You might want to sit."

Wynne remained standing. At this point, she doubted any news could stagger her into a chair if she wasn't already seated. She already knew this was related to the rumors. She didn't want to keep talking about it. The fact that she found herself unable to stop thinking about it was bad enough. Yet, some sick part of her needed to know how much worse it had gotten.

"Just tell me what's going on," she said.

"I'm so sorry, Wynne." Lara took a step forward. "This is our fault."

"Why would it be your fault?" Wynne asked, braced for a stupid response like, *We encouraged your relationship with Kal, and look how that turned out.*

"Because Lara got pregnant before the wedding," Omri said.

Wynne had not been expecting that.

Quiet fell. Her focus jumped between them. She felt less stunned than she would've expected. "You never said anything."

"Of course not."

"When did you find out?"

"Before the house was up. Before I'd finished gathering materials, actually."

Which made Lara further along than Wynne anticipated. She simply assumed that Lara began to show earlier than most because she was thin, which sometimes made pregnancy more obvious, sooner.

"Did Mum and Pops know?"

Omri dipped his chin. "Pops loaned me the funds for the remaining supplies to get the house up quick. I've been paying him back, bit by bit. We'll be square come spring harvest."

"My parents knew too," Lara said. "That's why all this vicious gossip has come upon you."

Heat rose to the surface of Wynne's skin. Her thoughts turned to Pia. "Explain that."

"My Mum...discovered, you with Kal –"

"We weren't – "

"I know." Lara patted the air. "I believe you, Wynne. Susi brought the less-wholesome story to our attention the other day. She asked if it came from my mother."

"I'm surprised she didn't ask Pia directly."

"I think she hoped to avoid the conflict before she knew for sure. They're already at odds," Lara said. "I was so worried about your mum's suspicions, that night I couldn't sleep at all. Omri and I went to my parents' house the next day, and I asked them directly. My mum confirmed. She said she *suggested the natural conclusions*. When I asked her why she'd do such an awful thing, my father grew upset. Then my mother tried to frame it like she did it for me, and I ought to be grateful."

"What does that mean?" Wynne asked.

"A load of crap," Omri said. "That's what."

Lara ran a hand over her pregnant belly. "She claimed folks were starting to suspect, and the rumors about you took the focus elsewhere to protect me."

Wynne clenched and unclenched her jaw. She didn't buy it. Not after their conflict on the day of the bridal tea. Pia had been especially stiff toward her for months.

This was revenge.

"For all I know, she was in her own head," Lara said, struggling to make sense of the excuse she wasn't convinced by either. "I don't know that anyone ever suggested a thing. They hadn't to me – not even Catreeny, and she's as subtle as an ox. What is clear is that, from the moment my folks found out about the baby, they were more concerned about the public face. Almost immediately, they started to hint how they could use this to their advantage, to advance the family."

Lara's chin trembled once. She set her face like stone and lifted her head with dignity. "I told them off."

Omri ran his hand across her shoulders. Proud of her, and recognizing how the rift with her parents hurt deeply.

"I think, at this point, they've given me up as a lost cause. The silly wayward under the sway of Omri Thar."

"I'm sure the parting words I had for them didn't help." Omri's face tightened. "It makes me upset how they belittle you. They treat you like you got no head."

"What did you say?" Wynne asked.

"What I just told you – and some stronger words."

"It needed to be said," Lara said. "I've felt that way for a long time."

"I know."

"Wynne, I feel like I've done nothing but give them fodder to hurt you, and Elric and Susi. Your family has been nothing but good to me. I'm so sorry." Lara looked from Wynne to Omri and matching tears spilled down her cheeks.

Wynne sighed. She stepped up to fold Lara in a hug. "You're my family too. All three of you."

It was as good as it would ever get.

68

Months slipped by in a gray haze. Deep winter brought shorter days, heaps of snow, and bitter cold. The mild winters of years prior became a distant dream. Few folks ventured outside if they could help it. In the past, the limited social opportunities of winter were met with efforts to stay connected – the Ice Throw and feast which followed, the Craftsmen's Guild for the men, Susi's Craft Club for the ladies.

But the fabric of the community had changed. So had its needs. Participation was less than in previous years. In some ways, it felt like a sort-of death.

There had been too much of that.

Wynne was a Thar – she had responsibilities, whether or not she preferred to hunker inside where she didn't have to rub shoulders with anyone. She dug her mittened hands deeper into her pockets and tucked her chin as she crunched over the packed snow alongside Elric.

"Never thought I'd be goin' to a memorium for a cow," Elric said.

Wynne snorted. "Poor Peig."

"Ripe time for all this."

Wynne concurred. If she had her way, she'd be at home, nursing her melancholy with strong tea and her cat. Not facing the neighbors who questioned her moral fiber amongst themselves, or treated the turmoils of her life like some kind of tragic entertainment. The only consolation was that she couldn't imagine many folks willing to come out in this weather, even if it was their own grandmother who died. "What is he going to do with her? Eat her?"

"That would be the smart thing," Elric said.

"But?"

"It's Lugh."

"He can't bury her. The ground is frozen solid."

"He wanted to lay her to rest in the tombs."

"You can't be serious."

"I wish I was."

"I take it you told him no."

"Adamantly. He was none too happy with that."

"Wynne Thar!" Elric and Wynne stopped short and turned to see Ben Hodd, bundled to the nose, jogging after them in an uneven lope. The surrounding frost made his voice sound thin. He was out of breath when he reached them. "Catreeny needs you to come right now."

"Come where?" Wynne asked, noting the stress in his face which stretched beyond exposure to freezing cold. "What's wrong?"

"It's Omri and Lara," Ben said. "She fell and had a great pain. I don't know much. Catreeny went to their house straight away and sent me to find you. Omri's gone for Sender."

✦

Wynne rapped against the hardwood and announced herself. Catreeny's voice beckoned through the door. She didn't look as Wynne bundled inside. Tools, tinctures, herbs, and other implements were arrayed across the table where Catreeny stood. A quick sweep of the home revealed no Omri or Sender.

Lara stood in the bedroom doorway, one hand braced against the frame. She looked pale, distressed, and sweaty. She held a bundle of wet, bloody towels against her body. When she saw Wynne, she burst into tears. "I fell."

Wynne swooped to her side, depositing her bag on the kitchen chair as she went. "I know. It's gonna be okay."

"It hurts."

"Did you break your waters?" Wynne asked Lara with a glance at Catreeny.

"Yes," they answered at the same time.

"Have birth pains begun?"

Lara shook her head no.

Catreeny said nothing.

Wynne tried to quell the stirrings of fear rising in her. She drew a steadying breath, and took charge of Lara, keeping her tone compassionate and businesslike. "Let's get some water for you to drink and make you as comfortable as we can."

Lara allowed Wynne to lead her toward the bedroom until they heard boots kick against the side of the house. Her brows pitched toward the center and she grabbed Wynne's arm. "I don't want Omri to see me like this!"

"He's your husband, and he loves you," Wynne said. "He can handle this."

Lara looked only marginally comforted. She bent to snatch a soiled towel from the floor. "But, Sender." She grimaced. "I'm embarrassed."

"Lara, Sender does not want to compromise your dignity in any way. He's an exceptional healer. He only wants you to be well." Wynne wasn't sure what inner well she drew from at that moment. She spoke with such conviction – such confidence in her co-laborer's character – she wholly believed herself. Not because of self-deceptive denial, but because it was true. New focus and peace came over her like they hadn't before. She took the towels from Lara's hands. "You have nothing to feel ashamed –"

"Lara?" Omri rushed into the house with a blast of chilly air.

"Where's Sender?" Catreeny said, noting the absence of the healer.

"He won't wake up!" Omri said. "Apparently, there was a huge issue last night at the tavern, and then some kid had a problem this morning. He's exhausted himself."

Catreeny swore under her breath. "That man. Well, we'll just have to do this without him."

✧

"Right now, the babe is still moving around," Catreeny said as she worked over the herbs. "That don't mean nothin'."

"No movement would be worse," Wynne said, bringing a glass of water to the table.

"Aye." The rasp of mortar and pestle filled the kitchen area as Catreeny ground the herbs to a pulp. She glanced up at the young couple with more compassion than she usually expressed while she worked. "I'm sorry, but I don't mean to be givin' you false hope. Babe can't live in the womb for long once the waters break, and Lara's losing a lot of blood."

On the opposite side of the table Omri gripped Lara's hand so tight his knuckles turned white. Lara spoke in a steady voice. "This mixture...?"

"Horse nettle, brackenbark, and red clover."

"This is supposed to move things along?"

"That's the idea." Catreeny scooped the pulp into a cup of water and stirred it with a metal spoon. "Lara, drink all of this."

She took the cup with shaky fingers and began to chug.

"What does that mean?" Omri said. "The idea?"

"Sometimes it works, sometimes it don't. It depends on the person."

"I don't like your uncertainty."

"Neither do I. But it's our best hope."

"What if it doesn't work?"

"Then there's a good chance one or both don't live."

A pit dropped through Wynne. *Births could be risky.*

Omri took a few shallow breaths. "That's not gonna happen."

Lara passed the empty cup back. "Catreeny, Wynne, if this doesn't work –"

Omri abandoned the tableside and rushed for his coat hanging by the door.

"Where are you going?" Lara said.

"I'm going for Sender."

"You said –"

"I know what I said." He bent double to tug one boot onto his foot, then the other. "I don't care if I gotta bang on his door til it comes off the hinges and drag him here by his ankles –"

"Won't happen," Catreeny said. "That man sleeps like the dead when he's spent."

"I have to do something!" Omri cried. He straightened up, fighting a surge of fear unlike anything Wynne had ever seen in him. "My wife could die. Our baby could die."

"Better you be here, then. Not wasting time."

It was quiet for half a beat. He turned, snatched his coat from the peg, and thrust his arm into the sleeve. Wynne didn't try to stop him.

Lara returned her attention to Catreeny and Wynne. "If this doesn't work, and it's between me and the baby – pick the baby."

Catreeny said nothing.

"I mean it," Lara said. "Do everything to save this child. Promise me. I know what that might entail. If you have to do it before I've passed..." She couldn't finish the sentence.

Omri halted and turned back with his hand on the door latch. "Lara, don't talk like that. I'm coming back with Sender –"

Lara's expression turned fierce. Her voice, resolute. "Omri, I love you, but I will not sacrifice this child's life for my own. We've talked about this. If I have to die for this baby to live, then I need you to be okay with it."

"You're not going to die." He didn't look convinced. "Just...hang on."

He swept from the house, snapping the door shut behind him.

✧

Omri didn't come back with Sender. Catreeny had been right. *Sometimes it works, sometimes it don't.*

The house was quiet. In the kitchen area, Catreeny packed her tools into her case without speaking. In the bedroom, Omri sat in a chair beside the bed, looking like a shell of a man. He cradled a tiny bundle in his arms.

"I have water," Wynne said from the doorway in a hushed tone.

Pulled from his haze, Omri gave a weary nod toward the little chest of drawers at his right. *Put it there.*

Wynne rested the cup. She offered a faint flickering smile. Encouragement, she hoped.

He didn't return it.

She caught herself before leaning against the chest. She was a mess. She watched the baby for a moment. He had the same slightly-squashed appearance of all newborn and a thick head of curls. He was awake, watching Omri.

"Do you know what you'll call him?" Wynne asked.

"She wanted to name him Tobin."

"Tobin Thar," Wynne said, trying it out.

Omri was quiet for the length of a breath. Then, "What now?"

"Let him rest."

"I'm afraid I'll break him."

"He's a Thar. He has strong parents. I think he'll be alright."

Omri's eyes drifted from his son to Lara's still form in the bed. Blankets covered all but her face. Her eyes were shut. She looked peaceful. It was hard for Wynne not to feel awed. She'd always known Lara to be gentle, if not meek. Today, she'd witnessed a side to her which she'd only caught glimpses of before.

"I know you're proud of her," Wynne said. "I am too."

"I keep thinking about what she said."

"Which part?"

"*If it's between me or the baby, pick the baby.* She didn't hesitate. It was never a question for her. It's like she wasn't even afraid."

Wynne said nothing for a beat. Lara's decisive willingness to give up her life for her son had staggered and humbled Wynne as well, illuminating murky corners of her heart.

"She was afraid," Wynne said.

Omri turned his attention back to Wynne, brows dipped as though Wynne had slighted his wife.

"Lara was scared. Her love for your son was greater," Wynne said. "That's what love does to a person. It makes you brave. It makes you able to run at an army, or fight a dragon, or bring another person into the world."

Wynne paused as the words resonated within her, bringing things into alignment which had been shrouded before. "Love makes you willing to give up yourself for another. Fear will make you hold back the good you ought to do, if you give way to it. Lara didn't."

Omri thought for a long moment. "You remember how Pops used to say, *We were made to do brave things?*"

Wynne's mouth twitched in the corner. She nodded. "He's right. We were made to love and do brave things – hard things – even when we're scared. Sometimes in spite of it. Like Lara. She should be honored."

Omri offered a small, weary smile. He gazed down at his son. The baby grasped his finger in his tiny, rune-covered grip.

Wynne watched them and felt like she was observing a different person – not her mischievous playmate of childhood. Omri had changed. Grown up. Marriage didn't do it to him, though that was the start.

The baby squirmed in his bundle and made a fussy noise.

In the bed, Lara stirred. She lifted her head and blinked at her family. She propped herself.

Omri glanced tenderly at her. "That was a short rest."

"He's hungry." She extended both hands. Omri leaned forward, depositing Tobin in her waiting arms and a kiss on her forehead.

Wynne gave him a nudge when he resettled himself in the chair. *Give her the water.*

"Wynne, can you get Catreeny?" Lara asked.

"Nursing help?"

"Yes."

Catreeny's blunt voice came from the open doorway. "I'm here. Finish that water, first."

The little bedroom was getting crowded. Wynne sidestepped to trade places with Catreeny and provide the family space to bond. She felt peace. She was pleased and satisfied that she'd done her part. Grateful the herbs worked and everyone was well. Lara cooed over her baby, and it filled Wynne with a happy ache.

I could do this.

For the first time since fear had gotten its claws in her, Wynne possessed faith that the same ferocious bravery was hers for the taking. That she had the power to look her terror in the eye when her time came.

But it won't.

The thought came swift, sober. The previous lilt within her chest crumpled. Wynne's gaze swept over the little family with affection and sorrow. She couldn't foresee a future where any of this was possible for her.

69

When Wynne was four years old, she fell into the Bekker. She and Omri were supposed to stay in the yard, not play on the bridge. Skeggis and Peder showed up, and the boys proceeded to horse around.

She wanted to be included in the game. The boys weren't interested in playing with any girls. She distinctly recalled her flash of anger with Omri. He had no qualms playing the same game with her when it was just them. So she pushed him.

Not to be outdone, he pushed her back.

Over the edge she went.

She couldn't swim.

She remembered the panic of falling. The water closing over her head. Feeling like the river was trying to swallow her.

Thrashing. Choking. Helpless.

Strong arms grabbed her around the middle and hauled her up, keeping her head above the surface until they reached the bank.

Rakel was nineteen at the time. Dripping wet and madder than a drenched cat, she crouched beside Wynne and fixed her with a stern, icy-blue gaze. "Can you breathe?"

Wynne coughed and bobbed her head. She was crying. Omri was there hugging her neck, begging forgiveness.

"Then get up." With a single flick of the fingers, Rakel waved for Wynne to follow. "C'mon. Omri, you too."

Omri lifted a tear-streaked face. "Where are we going?"

"To your parents."

Wynne remembered holding Omri's hand as they trailed behind Rakel through the village. Dripping, shivering, and anticipating the correction to come. Rakel demonstrated no sympathy as she returned them to Elric. But she'd saved Wynne's life, and in a way, Omri's. Wynne never forgot it.

In many respects, Rakel was a far cry from feminine. She was, at times, ruthless. Today, she was a vision. Wynne had never seen her so at peace. The kohl usually smudged around her eyes was gone. She looked fresh-faced, like a normal lady. Beautiful, even. Her gown was simple linen with crimson detailing down the sleeves. She wore a crown of spice-colored flowers.

Sender walked her down the center partition of the meeting hall. To Wynne's astonishment, Rakel kissed him on the cheek before joining Corbin at the altar where Nialls waited to officiate their marriage. Face to face, Corbin teared up as he looked upon Rakel with affection.

That could've been you.

The thought flitted across Wynne's mind as she sat in the benches with her parents and Jairus. The meeting hall was packed to capacity with villagers who'd come to celebrate. Wynne never thought she'd see the day when Rakel married – much less someone as agreeable as Corbin. Even now, it was difficult to believe. Rakel was seven years older than Corbin. Hyper-vigilant. Sharp-tongued. Illiterate.

And Corbin chose her.

Wynne reminded herself she hadn't wanted Corbin when she had the opportunity. She earnestly wanted to share in their happiness, like everyone else. They'd enjoy the pleasure of lifelong companionship, the fulfillment which came from raising children, and the satisfaction of partnering together in meaningful work. They'd have the honor of being respected in the village.

They were going to have a beautiful life.

That could've been you.

✧

Immediately following the ceremony, capable hands arranged benches, set up tables, and rolled out the keg. Someone produced a fiddle, another a drum, and heaping dishes of food found their way into the hall for the wedding feast. In the hubbub after the initial toasts and round of feasting, Wynne lulled at her table as she sipped a pint and scanned the crowded room. People had made their way to the center floor for dancing. It was hard to imagine anyone selecting her as a partner.

She supposed she ought to get used to it.

During the ceremony, she'd been seated closer to the front. She hadn't noticed Kal before. She noticed him now. He was well-dressed and so was Isolde. She wrinkled her nose and laughed at something he said, which pleased him. He touched her on the shoulder and introduced her to Omri and Lara. The women gushed over each other's little ones. Lara passed Tobin to Omri and extended both hands to hold Kal's son. Isolde handed him over with an obvious word of thanks. She and Kal moved toward the dancing.

His eyes met Wynne's. Something behind her ribs clenched.

Just as quickly, he returned his focus to Isolde, as if seeing Wynne afforded no more than a passing thought. Isolde moved into position. He took one of her hands and laid the other on the small of her back. He spoke to her, grinning down at her with the same air once reserved for Wynne.

If he glanced her way again, she didn't see.

"Where are you goin'?" Tess said, stepping in her path as she bundled towards the double door.

Wynne avoided eye contact and tried to step around her. "I need some air."

Tess grabbed her arm to stop her and got a better look at her face. Wynne fought back the flush of water to her eyes. *Please don't ask...*

"If my parents ask, tell them I went home."

"Wot's the matter?"

Wynne shook her head and continued on her way.

Only the reminders that I'm going to be alone the rest of my life. And it's my own fault.

✧

Under most circumstances – scouts being the exception – entering the woods alone was not only ill-advised, but off-limits. Wynne didn't care. Everywhere else was too full of the reminders of how she'd made a mess of her life.

Still, the woods were far from empty. Scouts patrolled. Huntsmen might enter in groups, in search of boar. Newcomers could pass through on their way into town. Even after the elders placed a ban on tent-living, there were a few who took to the woods and continued to do so anyway. Despite efforts to get rid of them, the Baldomar couldn't enforce the rule in the same way they could in town, where everything was visible and there was the pressure of the whole village. So there they remained.

Wynne knew how to avoid them all.

She roamed until she was confident she'd found a spot where no one would disturb her. She'd brought along a water skin, a small amount of food, and a few other supplies. She knew how to make a fire. What plants to avoid. How to use a length of cord and blanket to make a shelter.

She thought about contacting Aeryn and Josef. She could stay with them in Goldbur Gren for a while and give herself the space not to be dogged by shame wherever she went. Maybe she could stay there forever. Start over.

She knew it was tantamount to running from her problems, though she wasn't sure it was a bad thing. If Kal wasn't rumored to be leaving for the Gren with his wife and son next year, she might've seriously considered it. At this point, she didn't want to see or think about him. He couldn't leave soon enough.

There existed another reason to eliminate the Gren as a possible escape. The city was a perpetual reminder of the man who never returned.

The good man she could've had, if she'd been patient and humble. She longed for him with an ache too deep for words.

It felt unfair. She'd bearing her lot, allowing time and perspective to waft away the airs which put a swagger in her step and an edge in her voice. Now, when she finally had faith to face her fears, to wait for the right one to be ready, and release the pride she'd so-foolishly clung to, there was no hope to be realized.

There was nothing to look forward to.

✧

It took two days for Wynne to decide she'd had enough of hermit-living. She was hungry. Her head throbbed. She knew her eyes were bloodshot and puffy from the tears shed during her stint of isolation. The yearning for human interaction beckoned her to quit moping.

To lick her wounds, buck up, and go home.

The trek into town from the southern wood felt impossibly drawn out and cruelly short. She followed the river, past the tannery. At a distance, it looked like more activity than usual was taking place in and around the village, which was confirmed when the walk home brought her past Josef's old cabin. There was a cart parked on the grass, along with a familiar gelding.

Judge?

The door stood open. Folks milled around the front of the house, unloading and bringing goods inside or to the little shed out back. Her spirits rose in hopes that Josef and Aeryn had returned for a visit. Yet, there was a notable absence of the Haranae family and a large concentration of Jaegers. She heard Skeggis' voice somewhere out of sight.

Tess waddled up the lane from the opposite direction with Asmund on her hip. She was just about to turn up the footpath to the cabin when she noticed Wynne. She changed course to meet her. "Where have you been? You disappeared halfway through the weddin' – no one's heard hide nor hair from you for two days."

"Are Josef and Aeryn here?" Wynne asked.

"No. Harek is."

70 ,

Staggered, Wynne stared back at Tess, wondering if she'd heard correctly, and hoping against hope that she had. "Harek?"

"I ain't seen him yet. I just got here," Tess said. "Word is, he bought Josef's house."

Wynne's spine went rigid. Her throat tightened as a thrill shot through her. "He's alive?"

A familiar, fair-haired man exited the cabin. The mop of thick, wavy hair had been shorn. His once-patchy beard appeared thicker and even. A scar claiming part of an eyebrow didn't detract from his appearance, but complimented it. He stood half a head taller, broader in the shoulders, and more muscular than before.

Tess swore under her breath. "He's...grown."

Wynne gripped Tess' arm to steady herself. She pressed the back of her free hand to her mouth. Her heart swelled with an ache so deep she wasn't sure whether she'd dissolve into sobs or a fit of laughter. It took everything in her power not to rush forward and fling her arms around him, old resentments forgotten in the simple joy of seeing him alive.

Tess snapped her attention toward Wynne. She dropped her voice to a hiss. "You got leaves in your hair. And a twig. Wot is this?" She picked at the strand over Wynne's shoulder.

"Another twig."

"Wot have you been doing? Roughin' it in the forest for days on end?"

"Yes."

"Well, straighten up. Or go home and wash yourself. He's – oh, gods, he's looked this way. He sees you."

He did. He didn't look happy.

Harek spared a brief word with his family at the cart. They followed his gaze to the road.

To Wynne.

An anxious, otherwise unreadable slide came over them. Micha and Leland nodded to Harek. Adults began to usher the children toward the house. Harek waited until they neared the door to make his way toward the road.

Tess nipped Wynne on the sleeve. She cast Wynne a look. *Good luck.*

"Harek! You're back." Tess hiked up the kid on her hip and made her way toward the house, intercepting him before he reached Wynne. She flung out an arm.

Harek shelved whatever strong feeling he'd been carrying a moment earlier and obliged with an awkward half-hug. "Good to see you, Tess."

"I'll let you…"

"Yeah," he said. "Your husband's in there."

"Oh, I heard him," she said even as she moved toward the cabin, leaving Harek behind.

His eyes returned to Wynne, and his expression turned stony. Without wasting another moment, he marched toward her. "We need to talk, you and I."

No hello. No pleasantries whatsoever.

"Alright," she said, feeling like she was in trouble.

"Want to tell me what you've been doing?" At the note of accusation in the question, Wynne knew instantly. *He's heard about Kal.*

She resented the uneasy tightness in her gut. "Harek –"

"I came here ready to become husband and wife. Come to find out, you've been entertaining a relationship with another man."

The urge to justify herself rose within her like fire. He'd been gone – silent for almost a year. They weren't pledged – they could've been, but weren't. He had no right.

Harek continued. "I'm home for less than an hour, and I hear about how you've been sleeping with him, and you're carrying his child."

Her jaw dropped in outrage. "I never did anything of the sort. How can you think that of me?"

"So you weren't caught in the act at the festival?"

"No!"

"So his hands weren't all over you when they found you two in the back room?"

Wynne clamped her eyes shut and rubbed her temples. "Harek..."

"You're not denying it."

"Would you stop?"

"How do you think that feels? First, I'm not good enough for you. But the guy with another family? That's who you pick. The one who – from the sounds of it – will bed anything that moves –"

"That's not what he's like."

Harek's eyebrows jumped. "You defend him, now?"

Wynne stifled a growl. "I didn't start considering Kal until I stopped hearing from you."

"I don't buy it. People say there's been something between you two for months. That he's been sniffing around you since he showed up last year. Funny, you never mentioned that."

Wynne said nothing.

"No answer?"

"Mind yourself, Harek. How dare you come at me like this."

"First I'm too meek, and now I'm too aggressive? Nothing makes you happy, does it?"

Do not let him see you cry.

It was too late. Angry tears smarted her eyes. She swiped the water away, sniffed, and glanced aside. She didn't even want to look at him.

She couldn't look at him.

She hated being spoken to this way. Especially by Harek, who'd never raised his voice at her before. It made her want to push back. Hard.

"You held that back," Harek said. "You held a lot back."

"And you held back from me, so I guess we're even."

"What does that mean?"

"It means you have no one to blame but yourself." She puffed herself up and stepped toward him. "It could've been me and you a long time ago. If you wanted to be with me, then maybe you should've acted on it."

"I asked you to marry me!"

"You were drunk!"

"I went to the Gren – for you. I busted my hide to make something of myself – for you."

"I never asked you to leave! You didn't have to leave."

"But I wasn't good enough for you here. I wasn't ready. Remember saying that?"

Wynne bristled and said nothing.

"You have no idea what I've been through. And all that time, I never stopped thinking about you," he said.

Of course he hadn't.

"How does that hit you? Or do you feel nothing about that?"

Something complicated wrenched within her chest. Wynne slapped the tears leaking from her eyes.

"Gods. I can't even look at you without seeing you and him –" Harek cut himself off in angry silence. He swatted the air and stormed away.

"Don't you walk away from me!" she shouted.

He turned, his face a deep scowl, and marched back toward her. "I never wanted to."

As he closed the gap, she saw the pain and longing wrapped up in the curve of his brow, the set of mouth. With no hesitation, he took her face in his calloused hands and pressed his lips against hers.

Wynne shut her eyes and melted, wrath and wounded feelings temporarily forgotten.

Harek pulled away. Nose to nose, he held her gaze for a beat, allowing her to see the storm behind his eyes. Close and intimate. He dropped his hands to his side and stepped back.

"Now, I don't know what to want."

71

"Mum, I need to confess."

Susi's gaze jumped to Wynne in the doorway, and she hesitated over the basket of linens. Wynne caught the subtle dip in the line of her mouth and the set of her shoulders, as if bracing. Then it was gone. She set aside her folding, sat on the edge of the bed, and patted the spot beside her. "Tell me, my girl."

Wynne moved stiffly across the room, wringing her fingers, and sank onto the edge of the bed. She drew a deep breath and cast aside the last vestiges of her pride. "I should've talked to you long before. I've made a mess of everything."

It was like the breaching of a dam. Something inside of Wynne cracked. She leaned forward, elbows on knees, hands covering her face. "I'm going to be alone the rest of my life, and it's my own fault. I know I shouldn't feel sorry for myself, but I can't bear it."

Susi was quiet for a long moment as she tried to interpret what she could from Wynne's distress. When Wynne struggled to produce more words, Susi filled in the silence. "Is this about your reunion with Harek?"

"You heard?"

"It was rather public, dear."

Wynne said nothing.

"I'm sorry it wasn't the joyful reunion you would've hoped for."

Wynne said nothing.

"I know you've been having a difficult time these past months." Susi's voice was gentle but steady. "What happened with Kal's family could not have been predicted. Frankly, your father and I bear some blame for allowing any serious consideration –"

"Mum, please stop. I picked him. I did what I did. I've been paying the price ever since. Which is nothing less than what I deserve."

"You're being far too hard on yourself."

Wynne shook her head in dismay. "Tell that to Pia, and the rest of the village who think I'm some kind of wayward hussy."

Susi took a patient breath. "I won't lie to you. What happened was bad. But we still love you," Susi said earnestly. "Your parents still think well of you."

"You shouldn't. Thars are brave and fair. I'm not. I've thought too highly of myself for too long, and I'm a coward. I have nothing to be proud of."

Susi cocked her head. "A coward?"

"Because I'm too scared to have children. Or, I have been. I've felt this way for a long time." Her voice ratcheted up as she spoke. "You have to be brave to give birth. I'm not brave!"

"Wynne. Being brave doesn't mean you're not scared."

Wynne shook her head adamantly. "Mum, you don't understand. I was convinced childbirth would kill me. I wanted no part of it. So where did that leave me? I still want to be loved. Yet, what self-respecting man doesn't want to be a father? For a while, it didn't matter. I wanted Harek, but he wasn't ready. The longer I could put off having to address the issue, the better."

"Oh, Wynne." Susi's face softened. "I wish you would've told me this sooner."

"I know. I should've just been honest with you."

"We could've helped you."

"There was nothing you could've done."

"We would've handled the whole dinner-situation differently."

Wynne said nothing.

Susi thought for a long moment. Then, "Have you ever wondered why you don't have more siblings?"

"You said it was because you were satisfied with the three of us."

"I am," Susi said. "Very much. Also, I didn't want more. It was nothing against children. They're wonderful. It was me."

"What do you mean?"

"The idea of many children to care for felt completely overwhelming. It felt like accepting the inevitability of being stretched thin in every imaginable way." Susi turned up her palms. "I could not fathom how I could be pulled in twelve different directions and also provide each of my children the attention and care I believe I ought to. I know there are those who do it, and they manage it well. The Jaegers come to mind. But I didn't think I could handle it. Your father disagreed." A smile pulled at the corner of her mouth. "He had more confidence in me than I had in myself. It was a point of serious conversation between us during the early years of our marriage."

"I didn't know."

Susi gave Wynne a look. "I know the prevailing attitudes about family in our clan – it hasn't changed one lick since my day. It's good for our stability as a people. I also understand that the pressure is immense. I was concerned to share my true feelings on the matter with your father, but I did the eve before our dinner. I still had to live with myself and my choices, just as you do. Guess what happened?"

"He didn't reject you."

"No, he didn't."

"That's different. He's Pops."

"I'm telling you this because when you love someone, you strive to work these things out together. You bear with one another." A softer smile warmed Susi's face. "There's so much grace to be had."

Wynne dropped her eyes, and she picked at a pill on the blanket. "Kal knew. He was willing to wait for kids while I sorted myself." She snorted in derision. "I did. At least, I think so. I'm still scared, but I saw what happened with Lara and Omri. She was brave. Her love for the baby was greater than her fear. I thought, if she could do it, so could I. Now it doesn't matter."

"What do you mean?"

"I mean, who else would want me? After what happened with Kal, I'm tainted. I severed off all possible options when my reputation *was* intact, and now it's too late. Tess said it would blow over, but the damage is done. Kal has someone else. And the one I wanted most never..." Wynne's throat tightened painfully, choking off the words. "If I meant enough to Harek, he would've done something about it sooner. Right?"

Susi struggled for a response.

Wynne cupped her face in her hands and felt her mothers arm across her shoulders as sobs wracked her body.

"I waited and hoped for him. I don't know why I wasn't enough."

Wynne leaned into her mother's side until the tears stopped coming.

"I wish things had worked out differently," she said as she regained her composure.

Susi squeezed Wynne's shoulder tighter. "I know, my girl."

"I think I could've been happy with Kal. But he wasn't Harek." Wynne clamped her eyes closed to pin back a wave of emotion. She was ready to stop crying. "I've missed him so much. I've hurt him so badly, and I can't take it back. He hates me."

"I don't think he hates you at all."

"Oh?" she said, almost as a challenge.

"Let me ask. Do you hate him?"

Wynne said nothing.

"I'm not asking if he's hurt your feelings, or whether you feel justified feeling upset with him. Do you hate him, or do you love him?"

72

Wynne shuffled across the kitchen, still groggy after the late watch and too-short stint of shuteye. Outside, the hooting and hollering from Jairus, which prevented her from further rest, continued. She located the bowl of cold porridge left on the counter for her. She turned over the mixture, thick and sticky by now, and wrinkled her nose. It was better than nothing. At least she hadn't needed to make it. She cast her gaze around the kitchen in hopes of locating a similarly cold cup of tea to wash it down. Tea never seemed to be in short supply, but today, there was none. A trivial matter, but it pricked against her mood.

Gretta frisked around Wynne's ankles, vocal and hopeful for a morsel.

"Stop nagging me," Wynne said with a gentle nudge of her foot.

The cat ignored Wynne's attempt at shooing and continued the irritating petition.

Jairus' ruckus crescendoed as he barrelled toward the back door, followed by Susi. The door banged open, and he clattered into the kitchen. The startled cat froze behind Wynne's legs for a beat before seizing her opportunity for the open door, and darted outside.

"Wynne! Guess what," Jai said.

"Your ruckus has awakened the dead?"

"Pops is takin' me fishin' for eels."

Wynne hesitated with her spoon halfway to her mouth. She hadn't been fishing with Elric in ages. "When are you going?"

"Later."

"After midday," Susi clarified as she heaved a bucket of milk from the goats onto the counter. "After chores."

"Am I invited?" Wynne asked.

"No, only men," Jai said with an air of importance.

Wynne cocked an eyebrow at him. "Your trousers are on backwards."

Susi frowned down at him to see for herself. "Heavens, they are. Jairus, go fix them. Wynne, I'm going to need you this afternoon. And I wanted to speak with you about something."

Susi gave Jai a nudge. He darted out of the room, feet thundering across the house.

"Where's Pops?" Wynne asked, noting the absence of a bald head bobbing around the back of the property.

"He's got business to attend to," Susi said. "Including speaking with Harek."

Wynne's features dipped into a frown. She stabbed her spoon into her breakfast. She said nothing for a beat, but curiosity quickly got the better of her. "What about?"

"He's asking him to dinner."

Wynne looked up from her porridge abruptly. "What?"

"I said, he's asking –"

"Why?" she cried.

"Because I know how you feel about him, and I think he feels the same way."

Wynne set aside her bowl and brought both hands to her temples. Her eyes went unfocused on the floor.

"He's shown himself capable, honorable, and prepared for –"

"Oh gods, Mum. I gotta – I gotta go."

If she was going to salvage any shred of dignity, she needed to nip this in the bud.

✧

Wynne marched up the front walk toward the cabin which had been built by Josef, stewarded by Omri, and now apparently belonged to Harek. Judge nibbled grass in the yard. At her approach, his ears swiveled toward her. Harek wouldn't leave him unattended. Which meant he was home.

She knocked on the door and waited, trying to prevent her emotions from running away with her clarity.

Her parents were only trying to help, but the situation was volatile enough without a dinner invitation thrown in. What did they expect? A miracle to occur? It didn't matter what she felt for him – he didn't want her. This invitation would only end in more humiliation and pain. After her conversation with Susi the day before, how could they do this to her? Had her mother been paying attention at all? She tried not to linger on the sense of betrayal pressing against her – she could deal with that later.

She waited.

A strange mix of jitters, dread, and shame mingled inside of her. How could she want to see him and hate the prospect at the same time?

What if he opened the door, saw it was her, and slammed it without a word? She clenched her hands into fists. She had half a mind to wedge her toe in the door and give him a piece of her mind.

She stood there for a long time. No answer.

Which she took as further evidence that he didn't want to see her. It wasn't as if he couldn't hear the knock. It had been purposeful. The house might've been a comfortable size, but it was still a one-room cabin.

If circumstances were different, she would've taken the hint and left him alone. This was not the sort of matter she could simply let go.

She reached out to knock again when the door opened. Her breath caught. She noticed lines in Harek's face which hadn't existed before. There was a hardness which echoed maturity.

Harek kept one hand on the latch out of sight. His expression was stoic.

Cautious.

Curious.

It wasn't as if she expected a warm welcome. Still, she found it more discouraging than she anticipated.

"Hello," she said, more gruffly than intended.

Harek said nothing for a long moment and slipped his hands into his pockets, which she supposed was better than *What do you want?* Finally, "What brings you by?"

His words came out direct and neutral, and not at all the sort of tone to set her on her heels. Which made this a little less unpleasant.

She cleared her throat. "I don't mean to bother you, and I realize I'm asking a favor which you might not want to do, and I don't fault you for that. But I've been informed that my father plans to come talk to you." Wynne licked her lips. She suddenly felt warm in the face. "To ask you to come to dinner. As in, *the* dinner. Decline."

Harek watched her carefully for a long moment, his expression displeased but otherwise unreadable. "Why?"

"Because you're just going to say no at the end of the night. After..." Her thoughts jumped to their confrontation in his front yard with a surge of pain and indignity. "After what happened. You're mad at me, and I'm..."

She glanced aside, and took a breath to collect her thoughts which were growing increasingly fuzzy here before him. *Don't get worked up...*

"Do I seem mad?" he asked, pulling her attention back.

She cast him a wary appraisal. Truth was, he didn't.

Guarded, yes.

Not angry. Not like he was.

All at once, the sharpness within her relented. She saw past the injury of their argument to the man who'd once been her sweetest friend. It came flooding back and threatened to make her weak in the knees.

You came here to do something. Now do it. Whatever it takes.

Wynne maintained steady eye contact with effort. She forced herself to accept the humility of her position, to put herself at his mercy, and make it plain.

"What's happened is difficult enough to bear. This will only hurt and embarrass me further," Wynne said. "If you ever cared one lick for me, then please don't do that to me."

"Have you thought about what that does to me?" Harek said. "What happens when people find out I was invited and refused to come?"

She hadn't. "People won't find out –"

Harek leveled a knowing look. "People will find out. It's not only my honor at stake. There's also the respect for your father."

Wynne tensed. She could sense herself getting worked up as his counter-arguments landed and her hopes of escaping this unscathed drew thin. She cleared her throat and pushed out a cleansing breath, trying to buy time so she could think straight. She opened her mouth to argue, still not sure what was going to come out.

He spoke over her.

"And before you say anything else, I already accepted the invitation."

She wasn't prepared for that. "You did what?"

"Your father already asked me. He left a half-hour ago. I told him I'll be there tomorrow night. I'm not going back on my word."

There was a whisper of defiance in his voice. No anger. No spite. *I'm coming, and that's that.*

73

When Harek entered the Thar's home, he was by most appearances the picture of reserved masculinity. He'd trimmed and conditioned his beard with oil, and the scent of cedar and cloves hung around him. He wore a dark wool sweater, free of hay bits and tufts of fur. He'd cleaned the mud from his boots. He carried himself with respect. The too-shy butcher's boy had been refined.

Long familiarity allowed Wynne to read the nerves buzzing beneath the surface. His movements were stiffer than normal. His cheeks, a little flushed. He struggled to look at Wynne more than a brief second at a time as the Thars greeted him by the door and welcomed him into their home.

A formality.

She knew how this was going to end. He was here out of respect for Elric. Nothing more.

She couldn't stop thinking about what a fraud she was standing there, dressed in white. The new gown was gorgeous. Susi had insisted on it. Apart from the purest gold, it was the color most symbolic of cleanliness, truth, and honor. Wynne should've felt like a queen. Instead, she felt like an imposter.

Elric extended an inviting arm toward the table. Harek paused before following him. He finally looked Wynne full in the face. His smile softened and warmed. "You look beautiful."

She would never forget the look in eye and knew, right then, it was going to break her heart when he said no at the end of the night.

Pleasantries, she told herself, as if it would help.

Susi had arranged flowers and candles down the center of the table, along with a single pitcher of mead, a platter for roasted root vegetables, a basket of herbed bread, a tray of baked pears, and a goose. Wynne wouldn't go so far as to say it was over the top. Still, it was nicer than what her parents put together for the dinner with Corbin. Elric positioned himself in his usual place at the head of the table, with Susi on his right. Harek took the place at his left. Wynne chose the seat beside her mother, which placed her as far from Harek and her father as possible.

She didn't mind this. There had been a fantastic row the evening before. Tears were shed. *How could you do this to me?* Elric listened, empathetic but unmoved. He spoke little. There'd be no secret signal with the napkin. The dinner would continue. End of discussion.

She was still displeased with him for initiating this night of humiliation on her behalf. As if she hadn't done a fine job of that herself. The only thing she could do was participate and try not to make it worse.

Elric prayed a blessing over the evening, and polite remarks were exchanged as cups were filled. Wynne kept her lips clamped.

She felt distracted. Her thoughts kept flitting to the confrontation in Harek's yard, to his adamance the day before at his door, to the look in his eye after he kissed her.

"The food looks and smells delicious," Harek said the first servings were apportioned. "Thank you for hosting me this evening. This is far more than I deserve."

"You honor us by bein' here, son. We're glad to have you at our table." Elric picked up his utensil. He stopped himself before he tucked in. His eyes passed between Wynne and Harek. He thought for a moment, as though he had something to say and wanted to make sure it came out right.

It set Wynne on edge.

"I want to be clear," Elric said. "I am well aware that the reason for which we've gathered is, by no means, the only question heavy on the minds of us all." His mustache twitched. "With the exception of Jairus, perhaps."

At Harek's side, Jai looked up from the bread he was busy stuffing into his gob.

Wynne's eyes grew rounder, uncertain whether to feel relieved or sick. The argument yesterday ought to have prepared her. At the time, Elric made assurances regarding a *clearing of the air*. She didn't know what that entailed, but it sounded uncomfortable, and she'd been unable to think of anything else since.

Elric continued. "Much has transpired since you left. It would be a neglect of my duty as a man if I allowed certain matters to remain untouched. Let there be no matter too sensitive to be brought into the open." He let his gaze pass between Wynne and Harek again. "None."

Harek said nothing.

Wynne said nothing.

Elric dove his spoon into his dish. "That said, we're mighty glad to have you back, safe and whole."

"Thank you sir," Harek said.

"So. What happened?"

"Sir?"

"I presided over your memorium six months ago. Tell us where you've been. How it went at the Gren."

Harek took a breath, collected his thoughts, and began at the beginning.

He reiterated much of what Wynne already knew from his letters. The clean up efforts. Laboring with stone. The training grounds. Hearing the retelling from his own lips stirred Wynne's pride in him and made her feel unfathomably distant.

When Harek shared how he'd been tasked with addressing the supply train issues, Elric spoke again. "That's quite the honor."

A new sobriety stole over Harek. "I wish it went better."

Elric hummed. "We were all deeply sorry to hear about your men. I understand you were successful against the bandits, but truth told, no one's quite sure what happened."

Harek said nothing for a long moment. Then, "We were successful in taking the bandits' camp. There were thirty-five or so, led by a man named Magnus Ammon. We gathered that he was formerly a baron in Wolfwind who likely fled with the regime change after the Empire fell. He'd been collecting a following of mostly other outcasts. They amassed wealth by targeting travelers and caravans. We left one survivor. We intended to bring him back to the Gren as a prisoner. The goods and others supplies, some of which were intended for the Gren originally, was not something we could feasibly transport ourselves. There were seven of us, too few wagons available, and one of my men had been injured." He glanced at Wynne. "You remember Oleksy."

She did. He'd been numbered among the fallen.

"I sent Grigory Hodd and Billy with instructions to the Gren. Which left Oleksy, Cain, Finnion, Dorian, the prisoner, and myself at the camp." Harek's mouth turned grim and his eyes dropped to the tabletop. "Finnion murdered them."

Complete silence fell.

"He also killed my dog, Luka. And he took me as a prisoner."

"I thought Finnion was your friend?" Wynne said, stunned.

A complicated sadness passed behind Harek's eyes. "He was."

"How long were you captive?" Susi said, gentle and earnest.

"Months."

A sudden, guilty sinking feeling stole over Wynne as the reasons for his long silence became plain.

It wasn't neglect.

Not boredom with her.

Or hard feelings.

Or rejection.

She felt like a wretch and a reprobate for doubting him.

"At first, he hid us among the moors in Noemar," Harek said. "Then he led us into the Heartlands."

"What was in the Heartlands?" Susi asked.

Harek considered his next words carefully. "There was a temple mound, deep underground. An evil place, for evil purposes. There, it became clear that he'd kept me alive to offer me as a sacrifice of some sort."

The table fell silent again. A cold shiver rolled over Wynne's spine.

Jai looked from person to person. "What's a sacrifice?"

Elric patted the air. "We'll talk about that another time." Then, to Harek, "How'd you come to be free?"

Harek glanced at Jai, as though he'd said too much and regretted it. "I apologize."

"It's alright, son. Continue."

"I tried to stop him. In the struggle, he lost his balance. He struck his head against the stone steps when he fell. He died instantly."

Susi placed a hand over her heart. "I'm so sorry, dear."

Harek nodded graciously. "It took me weeks to return to the Gren. When I finally reached it, they welcomed me as a hero." There was no bravado in his voice. Just a statement of fact, with a hint of humility betraying that he didn't necessarily share their opinion. "It was like I'd come back from the dead. I found my gelding, Judge. Also Billy and Grigory. I learned they'd come back to the camp with many hands to transport and protect the plunder, and found it devoid of a living soul. They found remains and personal effects, and I was presumed among the dead. They thought we were killed by other bandits belonging to the group, who hadn't been at camp when we took it. They didn't know what happened with Finnion."

Elric hummed. "You told them?"

Harek nodded. "That was a difficult conversation. He'd been like a brother to them as well, but they were owed the truth, and I bear some of the blame for what happened."

"You couldn't have predicted how he chose to be, son."

"But I chose him," Harek said. "On the way, there were indications that he wasn't well. He asked to be sent back. I said no."

"I'm sure you had good reason."

"Leadership took the stance that I made the best decision I could with the information I had. Truth is, without Finnion, we couldn't have taken the camp without great loss, if we could've taken it at all. They were pleased with our efforts and credited me with the overall success. Despite what happened," Harek said. "They asked me to put together another team. Something more permanent, based in the city."

Elric leaned back in his seat, visibly impressed and at a loss for words.

"Does that mean you'll be returning to the Gren?" Susi asked.

"I turned them down."

It was quiet for a beat.

"The Enclave is home. I wanted to come back." His eyes traveled with uncertainty to Wynne, and rested there. He cleared his throat with a little cough. "I'd earned enough money to buy a home, if not build one. So I spoke with Josef. Well, here I am."

"What do you think you'll do here, now that you're back?" Elric said.

"I did just buy a house. I'd like to live in it for awhile," he said with a laugh. "Eventually, I'd like to build my own outside the village. One of stone."

"Stone?"

"Yes, sir. I like it as a building material. I worked with stone quite a bit in the Gren."

He calls me Stonebreaker.

"Costly."

"Yes, sir."

"Why outside the village?"

"The space. I want enough room for a family of my own, and to raise and train horses as a viable living."

"I remember you wanted to work with horses," Wynne said, her voice small. She was happy for him.

"I plan to start as soon as I can."

Elric seemed surprised at this. "Another costly endeavor."

"When I returned to the Gren, I was afforded a sizable cut of the riches acquired in the taking of the bandits' camp. I've come home with a sum which makes all this a possibility," Harek said. "Although, I'd rather it not be known around town. I haven't even told my parents about the wealth I came into."

"Of course," Elric said. "It doesn't leave this table."

"Thank you, sir."

"I respect your discretion. Wise. You oughta be proud of your accomplishments servin' the Gren."

"Sir, the reward was an unexpected boon. It was important to me that I not return empty handed. I needed to show myself a worthy man, capable of leading a family, and able to hold my head up in the community."

"Son," Elric said, suddenly serious. "You don't got a thing to prove. Never did. It was already well-known you were a man worthy of respect. After your efforts in Nyassa, there's no Baldomar man who would've spoken an ill word."

Touched and encouraged, Harek dipped his chin. "Thank you."

Though it tweaked Wynne's heart, it put her on her back foot. Elric's description did not match the Harek she knew prior to his leaving for the Gren. How much did she know, really? She didn't inhabit the same circles as the warbanders, or even the other men, and she'd never bothered to speak frankly with her father about this matter.

Her memory skipped backward to the homecoming feast. Harek's camaraderie with the other men took on new significance. With a humbling pang, she wondered what else she'd failed to fully recognize or appreciate.

"Even so," Harek continued, "at the time, I wasn't marriage-ready. "

"Says who?"

Harek hesitated and his eyes darted to Wynne.

"We had nowhere to live," Wynne said.

Elric turned up his palm and gestured to his house. "Nowhere?"

"I mean a home of our own. That's supposed to happen first."

"An ideal scenario, daughter. Nowadays, half the Enclave doesn't have a home of their own. A house isn't what makes a family."

Wynne stared at her father, and her face grew warmer. The way he spoke, it was almost as if he would've approved a marriage with Harek the very week he returned from Nyassa.

"Consider the raid. Many homes were burned or destroyed," Elric said. "Many people were displaced, but that didn't make them less of a family."

"Of course, but they had a place to live to start with."

"Most enjoyed that privilege, yes. But, as was the case for our people of old – and seems to be true for many now – havin' your own home remains a privilege. It was never required to establish a marriage," he said, conversational and reasoned. "It's true that not havin' your own walls is humblin' and brings its own challenges. But it doesn't make a family's love any less legitimate."

Elric's words cut to Wynne's heart. Her eyes drifted to Harek.

You don't got a thing to prove. Never did.

The conversation lulled as Wynne bore this unsettling revelation. Duly chastened, she drew into herself. Not only was she blind in her expectations for starting a life with Harek, but she'd been wrong in her estimation of him. They weren't unequally yoked – not when he came back from Nyassa.

But they were now.

He truly surpassed her.

She was entitled. Picky. Too impatient to appreciate the good man – the worthy man – he was.

She may not have asked him to leave for the Gren, but he certainly went because of her.

To prove himself. For her.

He suffered unimaginable tribulation. Because of her.

Now, here he was, having turned down a respectable position to return to her, and he came home to a nightmare.

Rumors.

Disgrace.

Her temper.

Their confrontation in his yard returned to her.

She could barely stand it.

When she lifted her eyes from her lap, she noticed the uneasy expression in Harek.

Elric noticed too. "Seems like you have a mind to say somethin'."

"I have a question, sir."

"Go ahead with it."

"I would like to know what happened between Wynne and Kalomir. The truth. Not the town gossip."

Wynne drew a shaky breath. Suddenly cold, she parted her lips, prepared to divulge all. But Elric dipped his chin once and looked Harek in the eye as he spoke. "There was some affection between the two, but he never lay with her. I had asked him to come for the dinner. The two of them got ahead of themselves. I'm quite certain she's aware of her folly. The dinner never occurred."

No mitigating or excuses. Just the truth in a manner which satisfied the question and covered Wynne.

She ought to be grateful for his handling of the question.

She was.

Yet, as he spoke, Wynne's ears started to buzz. The thrum of her heartbeat pulsed in her head. Her eyes smarted.

What are we even doing here?

She tried to swallow the lump in her throat, but it grew painful. She buried her face in her hands, unable to hold back the avalanche of guilt. It overtook her with a rush, and built.

"Wynne?"

Susi's voice through the haze.

Wynne lifted her tear streaked face and took in the alarmed expressions around the table, compounding her shame. She couldn't look at Harek. She didn't even deserve to be at the table with him.

And she couldn't do this anymore.

Abruptly, she pushed away from the seat and rose. Outrageous and disrespectful toward everyone gathered, especially her father, but it didn't stop her.

"Wynne–"

She threw her napkin in her empty place. "This dinner is a waste of time," she said, her voice hoarse and sharp as she turned on Elric. "We all know nothing is going to come of it. Harek is clearly a man of good reputation and accomplishment and now a man of great means. He deserves a woman beyond reproach. That's not me." She spared the briefest glance in his direction as she made her escape. "That'll never be me."

74

"Wynne, come back."

Susi's plea, followed by the steady rumble of Elric bidding his wife to remain at the table with their guest, receded behind Wynne as she whisked into the shadowy hall. She shut herself in her room, startling the cat as she plopped onto the edge of her bed and wept.

She couldn't decipher the conversation which continued after her departure. She didn't need to. Elric would find some way to tactfully bring the dinner to a close. They'd see Harek to the door and wish him well. Probably apologize for Wynne's behavior – another embarrassment she'd brought upon them all. Then he'd be gone.

He'd be gone forever.

He'd have fulfilled his obligation and he'd leave knowing the truth. That's what he wanted.

That's what she wanted.

As she finished her cry, she kept her ears pricked for Harek's tread leaving. Instead, she heard rapid, muted thunking against the front door. Another male voice joined the hum on the other end of the house, deep, frantic.

Recognizable.

Wynne shushed Gretta, who'd taken to aggressively purring while she kneaded the bedspread. There was an indistinguishable word from Susi, followed by her mother's quick, familiar steps drawing close. Susi opened Wynne's door without knocking. "Pull yourself together."

"What's happening?"

"Where's your midwifery uniform?"

Wynne was on her feet in an instant. She rushed into the passage, following the heightened voice of Skeggis. Thoughts of Lara and Fiona entered her mind unbidden, quickened her stride, and sharpened her focus.

She found Skeggis standing in the greatroom, windswept and with a nervous look in his eye. He braced both hands against his temples. Elric and Harek stood closeby, each wearing a look of concern as they attempted to calm him. Jai watched from the bench, helping himself to the bread basket.

"Skeggis?"

"Wynne!" He pulled his hands away from the sides of his head, causing his hair to stand out like a wildman. He broke away from Elric and Harek and surged toward her.

Wynne raised her hands in an *easy* gesture. "Tell me what's happened."

"It's Tess – baby's coming!"

Wynne took a breath and felt herself shift further from the despair she'd been nursing. "Okay. It's gonna be alright. I'll get Catreeny. We'll be over as fast –"

"No!" he cried. "No Catreeny."

"Skeggis –"

"Tess won't have her. The baby is coming now." His voice tightened in panic. "There's blood. There's so much blood. I don't know what to do!"

Fear pressed against Wynne's heart, but she drew another deep breath. A well-practiced directness swept over her. "Where is Tess now?"

"Home."

"Alone?"

Skeggis bobbed his head.

"Here's what I want you to do. Go back to her, but keep your boots on in case you need to go for Sender. I'll change and grab my things. I'll be right behind you."

"Okay."

"Go now."

Skeggis turned on his heels without another word and tore from the house.

"I can help," Harek said before the door swung shut. Wynne hesitated before darting to her room, and he stepped forward. Then, more definitely, "I'm coming too."

"You don't have to walk me," Wynne said. "It's okay."

"If history serves, Skeggis doesn't handle this well."

Wynne couldn't argue with that. She offered a simple, "Okay," then rushed down the hall.

✧

Wynne and Harek left the house, shoulder to shoulder at a brisk pace. He pulled ahead to reach the gate first, and opened it for her.

"Thank you," she said, struggling to meet his eye as she swept through it.

They walked in silence up the twilight-lit lane, her midwifery bag in one hand, and the creaky, unlit lantern in the other. Half of her mind wanted to review every bit of training she'd ever received from Catreeny. She'd never performed a delivery without her, and she dreaded the possibility of a mistake.

The other half couldn't stop agonizing over Harek's presence at her side. She felt awkward and exposed after the way she'd left her parents' table. Upon stealing a glance, she found him none too ruffled.

He caught her looking. "Can I hold your lantern?"

"I can carry it."

"Yes, I know you can. But if you carry it, then I can't hold your hand."

She cast him a perturbed side eye. He wasn't mocking her. Still, after that disaster of a dinner, he couldn't be serious.

"Can I hold your hand, please?" he said, open and sincere.

Warily, Wynne passed the lantern into his outside hand. Without hesitation, he took her empty one in his. It felt warm and strong against hers. He gave her a gentle squeeze, then adjusted his handhold to entwine their fingers.

Wynne contended with a sudden tweak in the back of her throat. She watched their clasped hands for a beat, unsure what to make of it or whether it marked a last gesture of affection before they parted ways for good. It felt almost cruel, if that was the case.

Regardless, she wanted to enjoy it as long as she could.

Harek gazed up at the spattering of stars against the clear, dark sky and released a slow breath. "Out in the wilderness with Finnion, I didn't know where we were going, or what he was planning. I didn't know if I'd live through the night. I'd watch the stars as long as I could and pray. I'd think about how I had to live, so I could get back to you."

Wynne's heart wrenched within her. "I'm sorry about your friends."

"I don't really want to talk about them right now."

"Okay."

He quieted, like something weighed heavily against his mind. She tried to brace for whatever came next, be it another question about Kal, or an explanation of whatever-this-was between them now. She told herself he'd speak when he was ready. She ought to be mature enough to be willing to wait while he worked over whatever hung thick and unresolved between them. It made her feel like ants crawled around in her bones.

He was slow.

"I'm sorry," she finally said, unable to bear it any longer.

He glanced at her in question.

"For everything. The dinner...and before that..." Wynne trailed off with a flush. "I disgraced you. After all you endured, you came home to a tempest. I was so mean to you. You deserve better."

Another gentle squeeze from him. "I forgive you."

They rounded the bend. A night breeze rustled the long branches of the willow they used to climb when they were kids.

"I know I made you wait," Harek said with regret in his voice. "It wasn't because I didn't want to be with you. It was never that."

"It was my fault."

"No, it wasn't."

"Harek, please. My expectations weren't even sound." She looked up into his face. "For too long, I thought too much of myself. I'm sorry for that too."

Harek said nothing for a long moment. "Well, I'm sorry too."

The house belonging to Skeggis and Tess appeared over the hill. Puffs of white smoke trailed from the chimney. Light seeped through the gauzy linens covering the front window. Wynne's mind turned more fully to labor ahead. She lifted a silent prayer for Tess.

"You know, I'm willing to wait for children," Harek said. "I don't want you to worry about that."

Startled, she cast him another wary glance. Her confession to Susi returned to her with vivid detail. She felt suddenly betrayed by her mother. "What exactly did you talk about when I left the room?"

The corner of his mouth hiked up as they drew to the edge of Tess and Skeggis' plot. The same teasing enjoyment she'd shared with him in years past – the play which made her temporarily shelve her stronger feelings.

"Harek –"

The door flew open with Skeggis silhouetted against the warm glow within. "Hurry!"

75

Wynne scanned the small house for Asmund, and didn't see him.

"Boy's with Brinja." Tess waddled into the room, holding the side of her rounded belly. She cringed in discomfort.

Wynne placed a hand on her shoulder and steered her toward the bedroom. It was less of a separate room, structurally. The only thing which separated it from the rest of the house were the sheets tacked to the ceiling which hung like curtains for a modicum of privacy. "Let's get you comfortable."

Tess barked a sarcastic laugh.

"As much as we can, I mean."

"Skeggis, why don't I keep you company out here?" Harek said, gesturing to the main area of the house.

Skeggis, who'd been following Wynne and Tess in an awkward shuffle, needed no convincing. He bobbed his head and switched course immediately. He took to pacing between the hearth and the table.

"Wynne, is there anything we can fetch to help?" Harek asked.

Wynne rested her bag on a chair in the corner and took a quick stock of the bedroom. "A dish of clean water. And extra rags, if there's any."

"Of course," Harek said. "Skeggis, you get the – oh!"

Wynne glanced over her shoulder. Skeggis' skin had taken a gray cast. He fluttered his eyes and swayed.

Harek swooped in, grabbed his arm, and directed him to a chair before he passed out. "Deep breaths, brother. She's not dying."

Skeggis breathed a shaky acknowledgement. Harek offered Wynne a reassuring smile and waved her back toward Tess.

She mouthed the words, "Thank you."

"Sorry 'bout the timin' of all this," Tess said, keeping her voice down as Wynne adjusted the curtains for decency sake. "My babes really know when to join the party, eh?"

"It's alright." Wynne cast her gaze around for evidence of excessive bleeding. If it indicated a problem beyond Wynne's ability to help, they needed to call for Sender without further delay. She found two damp towels beside the bed. No more blood than usual. She sighed and a measure of relief broke over her. *Oh, Skeggis…*

"How'd it go…?" Tess cut herself off. Gritting her teeth, she groaned through another wave of birth pains. "Woo. They're gettin' stronger."

"How far apart?"

"Comin' quicker." Tess nodded toward the sheet. "So? And make it quick before another one comes."

Wynne chewed her lip. She wasn't sure how to answer, and it felt like it would take too long to explain given the circumstance.

"Wynne?" Harek's voice on the other side of the curtain saved her from a clumsy explanation. Wynne poked her upper half through the curtain to retrieve the armload of rags and bowl of clean water. Meeting her eyes, Harek dropped his voice as she took the dish from him. "You're gonna do great. Let me know if there's anything else."

Wynne's smile reached her eyes. "You don't have to stay the whole time, if you don't want to. This could take awhile."

"No, it won't!" Tess' voice carried forcefully through the house. "We're gonna get this babe out fast. Asmund took near two hours to push out. I'm not doin' that again."

Wynne said nothing. It didn't work that way, but arguing the point with a woman in labor, especially if that woman was Tess, was the height of folly.

She did it in ten minutes.

"A boy!" Wynne cried as she took the baby in her hands.

On the other side of the curtain, Harek whooped. A chair knocked over as someone popped to their feet. She could hear Harek clapping Skeggis on the back.

The baby's tiny rune-covered fists punched the air as he began to cry. A surge of victory and maternal care rushed over Wynne as she passed the child to Tess.

"A son." Skeggis sounded dumbfounded, but she could hear the smile in his voice. A breath made a forceful escape. "I have another son."

✧

It was some time before Wynne and Harek left together. She was exhausted in mind and body, filthy despite balling up her smock, and riding a gentle tide of mirth despite the earlier part of the evening.

"You did well," Harek said with sincere admiration in his voice.

"Thank you for your help," she said.

"We made a good team."

Wynne said nothing.

"Did you hear what they're going to name him?" Harek said.

"No."

"Skeggis says they're going to name him Peder."

Her memories tracked backward, to Skeggis brother, fallen in battle. She shared a sad smile with Harek and nodded. "Peder is a good name."

They walked in a comfortable quiet and Wynne's thoughts passed over the events of the last few hours. They turned to the new baby. Downy fuzz covered the top of his head and his fingers were tiny. Tess asked if Wynne and Harek each wanted to hold him. Wynne had cradled the child, truly sharing the joy of his parents, and able to forget the pang that such a wonder would never be hers.

Able to forget herself entirely.

Harek had watched her holding the baby with a look she couldn't read. He took the little bundle in his arms with great care. When he lifted his gaze to meet hers, eyes soft and bright with joy, her heart felt full.

He could've been the father of my children. The thought entered Wynne's mind unbidden and with jarring sobriety. And like that, the tide of mirth ebbed.

Harek slowed. He raised the lantern to better observe the little house they were passing. It was Rakel's place – the one she built with minimal help, and lived in until marrying Corbin. It stood empty. Rumor was, she was considering offering it as a base for the newly formed town watch.

"Do you remember that round of *bang and bolt* when we chose Rakel's house?"

It returned to Wynne with a rush. Slipping out after dark to meet the others. The shushing and shoving as ten less-than-sneaky teenagers crept toward the door and jockeyed for position. The chorus of rapid, simultaneous fists against hardwood, interrupted as the door swung inward. The screams as they scattered like roaches in the light.

"Oh, I remember," she said. "It's like she was waiting for us."

"She knew we were coming. For sure."

"Who's bright idea was it to choose her house?"

"Your brother was involved. He tried to frame it like an interesting challenge."

"That sounds like Omri."

"Do you remember what she did?"

Wynne groaned with empathy. "Why'd she choose you?"

"No idea. There were ten of us to pick from. I wasn't even the slowest, or easiest to catch." He made a single chopping motion in the air. "She set her sights and locked on."

"You ate dirt," she said, not unkindly.

"She knocked the wind out of me," he said with laughter in his voice. "Then she towered over me, yelling at me to go home."

"She yelled at us too."

"Yeah – from afar, while you all ducked behind trees."

Wynne was laughing in earnest. "Don't be mad. Rakel is scary enough when she's happy."

"I'm not," he said. "Though, I didn't hear the end of it for months. Still not sure I've lived it down."

"Come on, now." She gave him a nudge. "We had fun together."

"We did."

Tess' words came back to her. *You can keep havin' fun together when you're married.*

"Shame the dinner turned out the way it did." In her fatigue, the words slipped from Wynne's mouth before she had the chance to restrain them. Heat rushed to her cheeks.

Harek shrugged, none too bothered. "I had an aim going in."

Wynne tried not to feel the painful tug in her chest and failed. "I know. Respect my father. Keep your honor."

"Well, yes. But, I wanted some answers. And to try to make things right, if we could."

Wynne glanced up at him, too nervous to ask the thing she really wanted to know. *Do you think we have?*

He didn't seem to hate her. That was something. In some ways, it felt like she had her friend back. Still, she knew better than to expect it to last. It wouldn't be the same – how could it?

"I'm sorry it ended the way it did," she said.

"I think it ended fine."

Wynne said nothing.

"You know, when Rakel tackled me in her yard...that's kind of how it felt when I proposed to you two years ago."

"That's how it felt?"

"Yeah." Harek drew to a stop. "Wynne?"

"Yes?"

"Will you be my wife?"

She stared at him, startled.

He seemed to enjoy this and his mouth quirked up, deepening the crease in his face. He meant what he said.

He still wants me?

He still wants me.

Euphoric and out-of-sorts, Wynne wasn't sure whether to laugh or cry. She dropped her gaze, and blinked as she tried to gather her thoughts. "Well, we – I guess we gotta see what my father says."

"I already talked to him."

"You – when? The dinner..."

"...continued after you left the room," he said. "Your father offered me your hand. I accepted, on the condition that you also want mine. Do you want it?"

She looked up at him, lips parted. The ache in her chest intensified, and slid into something pleasant. A smile overcame her and built. Her eyes softened with affection and she tipped her head back and laughed. "I am covered in blood, and exhausted. You know how to pick your proposals, good sir."

He stepped in, chin angled to better look her in the face. "I have spent too much time *not* married to you. Why don't you just say yes and let me kiss you already?"

Dear Josef,

    It's difficult to believe that it's been nearly five years since I've last seen you and Aeryn. Your academy keeps you far too busy. I'm proud of you for learning to read and write, and I've enjoyed exchanging letters, but it seems the need for that draws to a close.

    I'm excited to share that Harek and I are beginning a new adventure. We're moving to the Gren.

    The decision to leave the Enclave feels bittersweet, but it's time. We've been discussing it for years, laying plans, and now Patrik is old enough for travel. With the demand for well-trained horses in the Gren, the time is right. Besides, Aeryn tells me that Tess and Skeggis have made it their personal mission to repopulate the Baldomar clan, so the Gren will need a midwife at the ready.

    Harek says that choosing a plot for our home and our horse farm will be easier once we are there. He tells me that constructing a house of stone could take a year. Billy and his wife have graciously allowed us to stay with them until we make arrangements.

    Harek and I sold the house to his sister, so the cabin remains in the family. Omri and Lara will welcome their fourth baby any day now. After that, Harek, the boys, and I will be headed your way. We're bringing a caravan of animals and supplies. I would not be surprised if our dragonish neighbor hitches a ride during the last leg. She remains quite open about who her favorites are (I can't decide whether I envy you for this), and I doubt she'lll be able to resist the opportunity to visit with you and Aeryn.

    On that topic, Kalane has been busy blessing the abundance of newborn children recently – with flaming red hair like her own when she takes her human form. (Wait until you see my Arthur.) I'm curious whether she has spread this "blessing" to babies being born in the Gren too. I think we may need to talk to her about it. It's raising some questions, especially amongst those who have no red-hair in the family.

My sons cannot wait to meet their cousins, and I can't wait to meet your girls in person too!

Affectionately, your sister,

Wynne Jaeger

Author's Note

Thank you for reading *Princess of the Enclave*. If you enjoyed this story, please consider leaving a review. It really helps.

If you'd like to learn what happened with Josef, Aeryn, and Queen Kalane, be sure to pick up *The Silversaar Legacy* trilogy.

When Things Are Set Right
Book 1

On Your Hands
Book 2

Freely Given
Book 3

If you're curious about what happens to Goldbur Gren, watch for more to come from Jordan St. James.

Visit HouseofQLLC.com and follow us on Instagram and X
@HouseofQLLC

About the Author

Jordan St. James is the pen-name for co-authors Gustavo and Jordan Quintana, a husband and wife duo based in Knoxville, Tennessee, USA. Their novels include *When Things Are Set Right: The Silversaar Legacy Book 1,* which won the Bookfest 2023 Silver Award in fantasy, and its follow-up, *On Your Hands.* The last book in the trilogy, *Freely Given* is expected for release in late 2025.

Princess of the Enclave marks Jordan's first solo novel.

When not writing stories, you can find Jordan and Gustavo spending time with friends and family, playing tabletop role-playing games, and enjoying the wonderful outdoors and the creatures in it.

Made in the USA
Columbia, SC
03 June 2025

58737722R00255